Angela Thirkell

Angela Thirkell, granddaughter of Edward Burne-Jones, was born in London in 1890. At the age of twenty-eight she moved to Melbourne, Australia where she became involved in broadcasting and was a frequent contributor to the British periodicals. Mrs. Thirkell did not begin writing novels until her return to Britain in 1930; then, for the rest of her life, she produced a new book almost every year. Her stylish prose and deft portrayal of the human comedy in the imaginary county of Barsetshire have amused readers for decades. She died in 1961, just before her seventy-first birthday.

"Mrs Thirkell writes with an asperity and wit and gracious clowning that are all her own. *Love Among the Ruins* is a delightful novel."
—*New York Herald Tribune Weekly*

"[Angela Thirkell's] observation remains acute. Her talent for easy, light characterization does not seem to be flagging."
— *Times* [London] *Literary Supplement*

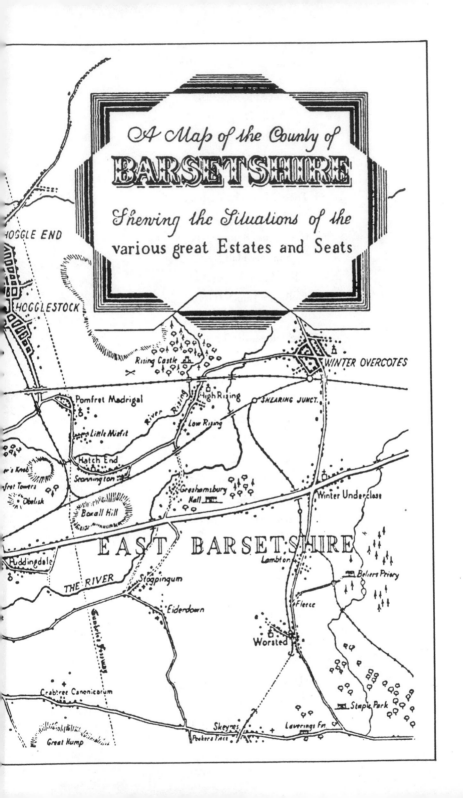

LOVE AMONG THE RUINS

A Novel by

Angela Thirkell

MOYER BELL

Wakefield, Rhode Island & London

Published by Moyer Bell
This Edition 1997

Copyright © 1947 by Angela Thirkell
Published by arrangement with Hamish Hamilton, Ltd.

**LIBRARY OF CONGRESS
CATALOGING-IN-PUBLICATION DATA**

Thirkell, Angela Mackail, 1890–1961.
  Love among the ruins : a novel / by
Angela Thirkell. — 1st ed.
    p. cm.
  ISBN 1-55921-204-7
  I. Title.
  PR6039.H43L68   1997
  823'.912—dc21   97-6463
                                      CIP

Cover illustration: *Faustine* by Maxwell Armfield
Chapter illustrations from *Kilims: Masterpieces from Turkey* by
Yarri Petsopoulos

Printed in the United States of America
Distributed in North America by Publishers Group West, P.O. Box 8843,
Emeryville CA 94662, 800-788-3123 (in California 510-658-3453).

LOVE AMONG
THE RUINS

CHAPTER I

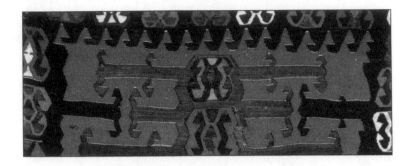

Beliers Priory, as all East Barsetshire knows, is a very large and unmitigatedly hideous house, the property of Sir Harry Waring. During the war it had been a military hospital while Sir Harry and Lady Waring retired to the servants' wing, finding themselves there far more warm and comfortable than they could ever be in the main house. So when the blight of peace descended upon Barsetshire they decided to stay where they were and to hand over the unwieldy mansion, which just fell short in the county's estimation of being a seat, to their niece Leslie and her husband, Philip Winter, who wished to start a preparatory school for little boys.

To this end they had waited till Leslie's brother, Lieutenant Cecil Waring, R.N., was on leave, and summoned him for a weekend, an invitation which the gallant lieutenant accepted with great reluctance. Not that he disliked his uncle and aunt, but as his professional life was spent at sea he naturally counted every moment of leave wasted that was not spent at a very uncomfortable angle in a small sailboat, or cooking sausages and coffee on an oil stove with waves bursting over it. Still, he was his uncle's heir, and a Nelson-like sense of duty made him feel that he must go and see what the old man wanted, so he left the friends with whom he was spending his leave at Bosham and drove at a mostly illegal speed across country to Beliers. Here his uncle and aunt received him with the affection that always embarrassed him because, as he said to his sister Leslie Winter, it stood to reason that if your only son had been killed in 1918 you couldn't really feel as loving as all that to a nephew who was standing in a dead man's shoes; to which his sister Leslie merely replied not to be so silly.

Leslie, who had lived for some time during the war with her uncle and aunt and was very fond of them, knew that they still preferred to discuss matters of business with the leisurely calm of a past age and in any case would look upon such discussion during dinner as quite out of the question. So, aided by her husband, who had recently been demobilized, she managed to keep the conversation on such general subjects as whether old Jasper the gamekeeper, son of a professional witch well known by all to have spent a good deal of her life in the shape of a black hare, would allow himself to be pensioned and whether it was a good moment to sell the near-Lawrence of Sir Harry's grandfather.

A fellow at the Club, Sir Harry said, had told him now was the time to sell. And when Sir Harry said the Club, he did not mean The Club, nor Boodle's, nor the Athenæum, for to Barsetshire these two words denote the County Club in Barchester. Most of its members have a club in London, but that is merely a suburban affair compared with the County Club. Who the fellow was, said Sir Harry, he couldn't at the moment remember. It wasn't Belton and it certainly wasn't Pomfret and it couldn't have been Stoke.

Lieutenant Waring asked why it couldn't have been Lord Stoke; not that he cared in the least, but if Uncle Harry wanted to talk like that he was ready to help him.

"Pictures aren't in Stoke's line," said Sir Harry. "Tumuli and Vikings' bones and that kind of thing, but not pictures. You remember the dreadful daubs he has over at Rising Castle, my dear," he added, turning to his wife. "He used to buy a couple regularly every year at the Royal Academy. Sort of pictures you see in a dentist's waiting-room," which remark led to a discussion on Waiting-Room Art, Lady Waring saying that her mother's dentist had nothing but Highland Cattle with steam coming out of their noses, while Leslie upheld the merits of a picture, indissolubly connected in her mind with having her front teeth straightened, of the Lady of Shalott looking like Ophelia's mentally defective sister in a kind of mediæval punt. Philip Winter said he used to squint on purpose so that his mother would take him to an oculist who had a picture of a little boy asleep between the front paws of a large dog of nondescript breed and sphinxlike appearance. Lieutenant Waring was about to expatiate on a picture of a little girl in a poke bonnet and crinoline called Blue Eye Beauty, with which simulacrum he had been violently in love while waiting to have a tooth stopped in Portsmouth while he was a midshipman, when Sir Harry cut across the conversation and said it had all come back to him.

His nephew and niece and niece's husband dutifully stopped talking and his wife sympathetically asked him to explain.

"It *was* Stoke," said Sir Harry. "And the reason I remember it is because Adams was lunching at our table and he was telling us about a picture he had bought, one of these newfangled pictures by some fellow with a foreign name."

Lady Waring expressed interest, but her thoughts below the surface were running on different lines. This was how times had changed. Ten years ago, perhaps five years ago, Sam Adams of the Hogglestock Rolling Mills would not have belonged to the Club, would not have met Sir Harry and Lord Stoke at lunch, and most certainly would not have been buying pictures by people with foreign names. Now, in the whirligig of time and the fortunes of war and the misfortunes of peace, Sam Adams, M.P., was a figure that counted, elected to the County Club, liked and respected by the hundreds of workers he employed, liked and respected by the best of the City and the Close, and not particularly popular with the Party Committee in Barchester. For though he had stood for Parliament as a Labour candidate, he had announced from the beginning of the campaign his

intention to vote as he thought fit and in so doing had scandal-
ized many of his supporters.

"That's right," said Sir Harry, encouraging himself as it were.
"Adams was telling us about this foreign artist, I'd never heard
the fellow's name, and Stoke said now was the time to sell
anything you wanted to sell. He said he had sold that picture of
three cardinals eating lobsters to some man in St. James's for
more than he gave for it."

Lieutenant Waring said he adored pictures with cardinals in
them, especially if they were eating, and he was willing to bet
that the man who bought it would sell it at a profit at once.

At this point Lady Waring took her niece Leslie away to the
drawing-room so that the men could get on with their job,
which was to discuss whether Lieutenant Waring as his uncle's
heir would be agreeable to the Winters' plan of turning the
Priory into a prep school.

"But you know they won't talk about it, Aunt Harriet," said
Leslie Winter. "Anyone can get Uncle Harry to the point, but
twenty men can't make him stick to it."

"I know exactly what they are talking about," said Lady
Waring thoughtfully.

"So do I," said Leslie. "The war."

"And the last war—or first war or whatever you please to call
it," said Lady Waring, rather unfairly laying the responsibility
on Leslie, for no one has yet invented an accurate method of
distinguishing between the two World Wars, or Wars to End
War, and the more wars we have the more difficult it will be to
know which is which, "and other wars."

And then she was quiet. She did not sigh, for she was not
demonstrative, but her thoughts went back as they still often did
to the war that now seems to us so small, in which her only child
had been killed long ago. Leslie knew what was in her aunt's
mind and knew that her aunt did not wish to obtrude her quiet
undying grief, so she said perhaps it would be simpler if she and
Aunt Harriet had a talk before the men came in.

So the two ladies discussed very fully the possibilities and probabilities of Sir Harry agreeing to the school and Leslie's brother joining his assent to Sir Harry's, and Leslie produced suggestions and figures, for she was a very capable woman and had considered the affair seriously with her husband. And by the time the men came in, the whole plan was settled by the ladies and nothing wanting but the mere formality of the men's opinion being asked.

Conversation was then on general topics. The near-Lawrence was examined and hopefully appraised, the prospects of some shooting were discussed, various plans made for the benefit of the tenants, and an allusion made to the difficulty of getting a good man for the kitchen garden whose produce the Warings sold quite advantageously to a large firm called Amalgamated Vedge. But of the proposed school nothing was said and the ladies let the subject rest. As bedtime approached, Philip Winter began to show signs of restiveness, for the temper that went with his flaming hair was not altogether extinct, though subdued now by him to good purposes.

"By the way, sir," he said to Sir Harry, though what way he would have been hard put to it to say, "about the Priory. I hope you don't mind my bringing up the question, but Cecil and I have had a talk about it and I'd be very glad to know if you feel like discussing it."

Sir Harry, a soldier and a man of great physical courage, gave a lifelike representation of a horse putting its ears back and showing the whites of its eyes and digging its forefeet firmly into the ground.

"Yes, yes, Winter," he said. "A splendid idea. Let's talk about it some time. Tomorrow perhaps. Your aunt will be wanting to go to bed and, by Jove, I'm ready for bed myself and I expect you are."

He looked round for support and was dashed by receiving none.

"I'm sorry to press you, sir," said Philip Winter. "But it really matters a good deal to Leslie and myself. If you could spare half an hour, sir—"

"Right!" said Sir Harry, seeing a chance of escape. "Tomorrow morning let us say. No; that won't do. I'm on the Bench tomorrow morning. Well, say tomorrow afternoon; late afternoon because I have to go to Winter Overcotes earlier. Then we'll have a good talk. Good night, Leslie."

"No, Uncle Harry," said Leslie firmly. "Cecil has given up his leave to come here and talk about the school and you promised to consider it."

Sir Harry said, rather weakly, that Rome was not built in a day, to which his nephew Cecil very sensibly answered that even the old Romans had to make a beginning somewhere and if Romulus and Remus had gone to bed instead of getting down to work, Rome wouldn't have even begun to get built.

"Now, look here, Uncle Harry," said Lieutenant Waring. "Leslie and Philip want to have a school. Well, that's all right by me if it's all right by you, sir. Of course, I love the place and all that and I'd always try to do my duty here, sir, but I'm not likely to be at home for years to come. That is unless this Government scrap the navy as they always do after a war. If only Beliers were on the coast—but it isn't, you see, and you can't sail on the Dipping Ponds. If you want to know what I think, Uncle Harry, I say a school would be a jolly good thing. And that's really about all. So that's settled, sir, if you agree."

It is very probable that Sir Harry did agree, for he was very fond of his nephew and his niece and the alternative to a school might be a sanatorium, or a lunatic asylum, or, even worse, a branch of a Government department. But to be asked to make a decision was almost more than he could bear. His wife recognized the symptoms and came to his assistance.

"I have been talking it over with Leslie," she said, "and the whole plan seems to me very reasonable. Cecil approves and I think we shall all be happier to have some young life here. What do you feel, my dear?"

Never had a woman appealed to Sir Harry in vain.

"Just as you say, my dear," he replied. "If you approve, I approve. Have a talk with Leslie and Philip and Cecil and thrash it all out. So that's all settled. Good night."

He went quietly out of the room. Leslie and her brother began to laugh.

"It reminds me," said Lady Waring, "of the time during the war when that very nice Major Merton and his wife were billeted on us. He and Harry spent a whole evening together and were too shy or too silly to discuss terms, so Lydia and I had to do it and of course we arranged everything in a few moments. Now I am going to bed. Tomorrow we will have a talk after breakfast and then, Cecil, you can get back to Bosham by lunchtime. Good night."

"A fine, sensible, upstanding woman, my Aunt Harriet," said Lieutenant Waring when the door had closed. "I'll catch the tide nicely about two o'clock tomorrow. And if you want me to break the entail or anything, Leslie, a letter to the Admiralty will always find me. I'm off to bed too."

Leslie and her husband, very happy and a little overawed by the fulfilment of their hopes, sat for half an hour or so talking of the future, with a thousand hopes and plans. Next morning Sir Harry was caught and cornered and agreed to all the suggestions that the Winters and Lieutenant Waring put forward. He then said that he was a very old man and would not trouble anyone much longer, mounted his horse, and rode off to visit old Jasper the gamekeeper, after which he was out until half past five and came home in very good spirits.

"A capital idea to make the Priory into a school for little boys," he said to his wife. "I wonder it never occurred to any of you before. It's the obvious thing to do."

"Your ideas are always good, my dear," said his wife, pouring out a belated tea for him. Something in her voice may have struck him, for he looked at her with a faint inquiry, but as she went on pouring out tea he laid the thought to rest.

*   *   *

This scene from domestic life had taken place about two years previously and Beliers Priory was already a flourishing prep school in a small way. As the Priory had been a military hospital during the war it had central heating and very adequate plumbing and was altogether far more comfortable than it had been since the days of Sir Harry's grandfather, who had fourteen indoor and twelve outdoor servants, let alone the hangers-on and odd-jobbers. One cannot say whether the change was an improvement. It depends on what you like. When there are no servants, you are grateful for central heating and perpetual hot water and fixed basins. But some of us are still unregenerate enough to think wistfully of bedrooms with a fire crackling when you went up to dress for dinner and the same fire being relaid and lighted by a print-dressed housemaid when she drew the curtains in the morning; of capacious washing-stands with a large jug and basin and a small jug and basin (whose use was always a matter of conjecture) and below its frilled chintz front a china slop-pail and a large foot-bath; of a hip-bath before the fire, with thick bath towels warming beside it, for no lady would have used the one bathroom which was tacitly appropriated by the hunting men; of roaring fires in hall and dining-room and living-rooms, with footmen replenishing the huge baskets of wood and the massive coal-scuttles; of valets and ladies' maids waiting till their masters and mistresses chose to go to bed; of weekend luggage which would now seem rather too much for an expedition to the Far East; of roast partridge and boiled pheasant; of church on Sunday morning with a positively irreligious display of hats and toilettes and the regulation visit to the stables or the conservatories afterwards; of a life now dead and appearing to the younger generation, if any of them were interested in it, the baseless fabric of a vision.

Luckily for Philip and Leslie Winter they were young enough and intelligent enough to take the new world as it came and to bury their nostalgia. To be busy is one of the best cures for regrets, and very busy they had been. An efficient matron had been found through the matron at Southbridge School. The question of a cook had been more difficult and Leslie Winter had begun to consider seriously whether she would have to do the cooking herself, when Providence took the whole matter out of her hands by directing her (for even Providence uses today's jargon, we suppose) to have a baby.

"Oh dear," said Leslie to the vicar's wife, Octavia Needham, youngest daughter of the Dean of Barchester, "it is all very nice and of course I am enchanted, but now I will *have* to find a cook."

"Of course you will," said Octavia. "You don't want a fallen one, do you? I could do you quite a nice one if you don't mind two children. I don't think she knows who either of the fathers are, but she is a really devoted mother."

Leslie, who never ceased to marvel at Octavia Needham's competent and practical view of life, said rather doubtfully that it would be very nice to have a good cook, but mightn't it be a bad example for the boys, to which the vicar's wife, whose imagination was practically non-existent, said boys of prep-school age wouldn't be in the least affected, and that as they would be growing up in a world where Ishmael would see no difference between himself and Isaac, it might be quite a formative influence. Which mixture of Biblical allusion and current jargon so confused Leslie that she said they would go and see her Aunt Harriet.

Accordingly they went through to what used to be the servants' wing of the Priory, where Sir Harry and Lady Waring lived. In the drawing-room they found Lady Waring sitting at her tea-table in talk with a plump, pretty, middle-aged woman.

"Hullo, Selina," said Leslie. "You remember Selina, Octavia, old Nannie Allen's daughter who married Sergeant Hopkins who was a hospital orderly here. How is Hopkins, Selina?"

"Very well, thank you, Miss Leslie," said Selina. "You know old Mrs. Hopkins died, poor old lady. Hopkins was quite upset and so was I, miss. She just passed away in her sleep quite

peaceful and I said to Hopkins I hoped it would be given to me
to go the same way when my time came," and Selina's lovely
dark eyes filled with effortless tears, which did not ravage her
face in the least.

Octavia Needham said whatever is suitable for a vicar's wife to
say under these circumstances, and if she said it with more brisk
efficiency than deep sympathy, even a vicar's wife must be
allowed some armour and protection against her unprotected
position as helper and sympathizer in general. And as her
husband had lost an arm in North Africa during the war, she
found her official veneer of manner an additional shield for him
when parish matters pressed too hard. But she had a truly kind
heart, even if she preferred to give her kindness rather to the
ninety-nine black sheep of this horrible new world than to the
one sheep that stays quietly at home and does its job.

Leslie Winter then inquired after the greengrocery business
that Sergeant Hopkins carried on in Barchester.

"That is exactly what Selina came to see me about," said Lady
Waring. "Hopkins finds the difficulty of collecting and deliver-
ing getting worse and worse and he is thinking of selling the
business to Amalgamated Vedge."

There was silence. To hear of yet another private enterprise
being sucked into the insatiable and unfeeling maw of a big
company made the tea-party quiet and sad. Probably it was
inevitable, but that didn't make things any better.

"So Hopkins says we'll go to Chaldicotes and he'll go in with
his brother who has a dairy farm," said Selina. "I dare say it's all
right, my lady, but I can't see Hopkins with cows. It's the green
stuff his heart is in. You should see the vegetables we get off our
allotment, my lady. You never saw nicer stuff."

And in proof of the niceness of the stuff Selina shed several
diamond tears.

Lady Waring, Leslie Winter, and Octavia Needham were
each in her own way extremely intelligent and practical women.

The same thought struck them almost simultaneously. Their eyes met.

"I should like to speak to your husband, Selina," said Lady Waring. "He must not do anything without consulting Sir Harry. Will you tell him to come over and see us as soon as he can and not to do anything about selling the business till Sir Harry has spoken to him?"

"Hopkins is in the kitchen, my lady," said Selina. "Him and me came over to see mother, so we all came up to see cook, and then your ladyship was kind enough to send for me, so I left mother and Hopkins in the kitchen."

Lady Waring, who rather enjoyed the patriarchal hospitality exercised by her kitchen, a hospitality that, we must add, was often its own reward in the shape of odd presents of home-grown food, or odd jobs done after a cup of tea, told Selina to go and tell her husband to come up to the drawing-room. And even as Selina shut the door behind her, the conspirators' tongues were loosened.

Octavia was the first to speak, as indeed she usually was, having an exalted though quite impersonal idea of the status of the parson's wife. Not that she would ever have thrust herself before Lady Waring or interrupted her, for she was well bred, but being one of those lucky women whose belief in themselves is secure, she felt it was the general good of the community that she should make her influence felt.

"It seems," said Octavia, fixing Lady Waring with the eye that controlled Women's Institutes, "as if it were Meant."

"I suppose you mean, my dear," said Lady Waring, somehow infusing a tone of kind though condescending majesty into her words, "that Hopkins might do for the kitchen garden."

Octavia admitted the soft impeachment.

"It might be possible," said Lady Waring, "but where could they live? Our man lived with his old mother and there isn't a cottage to be had anywhere."

"But, Aunt Harriet," said Leslie, suddenly rushing in ahead of

Octavia, "perhaps Selina would cook for the school. Then she and Hopkins could sleep here. There are those rooms at the back that the hospital turned into a flat for the matron, with a kitchen and a bathroom."

Lady Waring, though struck by the idea, cautiously said that it required thought. But before her younger friends could begin to chafe at this reasonable suggestion, or in Octavia's case to argue about it, a knock at the door heralded the return of Selina with her mother and husband.

"Well, Nannie, how are you?" said Lady Waring. "Good afternoon, Hopkins. I am sorry to hear that you are thinking of leaving these parts."

"Hopkins is a fool, my lady," said Nannie Allen, her black jet bonnet trembling with just indignation. "To take Selina over to Chaldicotes. I never heard such a thing in my life. He'd do better to mind his own business, my lady. I don't want Selina away among the foreigners in West Barsetshire. I'm used to having Selina come over twice a week and see me, my lady, and I don't intend to be left alone at my time of life. Why, if Selina was at Chaldicotes the Lord might see fit to take me any day, and then who would look after my lodgers?"

For Nannie Allen since her retirement on pension from the Warings had taken specially selected lodgers, preferably from among the children or grandchildren of her ex-babies, and her rooms were in constant demand.

"I'm sure I don't want to neglect mother, my lady," said Selina, her bright eyes raining tears, "but if Hopkins says it's Chaldicotes, I'll have to go, like it says in the Bible about cleaving."

"If you read your Bible properly, Selina," said Nannie severely, "you'd see what it says about honouring your father, not that you ever knew him nor that it would have done you any good if you had, and your mother. I won't hear of you going to Chaldicotes, and I've told Hopkins as much and I'll tell him again."

The unfortunate Hopkins, too shy to open his mouth, sat red-faced and wretched while this conversation was going on, twisting his cap in his hands, as he had once twisted Sir Harry's muffler when discipline forbade him to take his cap off his head.

"Well, Hopkins," said Lady Waring. "What do you think about it?"

The ex-sergeant was understood to say that he'd done his best, he had, but no man could do more than a man could do, and these big firms they fair knocked the heart out of a man. What, he said, was the good of building up a nice little business in green stuff when the big fellows could undersell you everywhere? It would have been better for all concerned, he added, if he had stopped one in the war, at which remark his wife's effortless tears flowed afresh.

"You know Crammer has left us," said Lady Waring. "His father wanted him back to help on the farm. Sir Harry doesn't know what will happen to the kitchen garden."

"I've nothing against Crammer," said Hopkins slowly. "His early peas were always a treat and his strawberries. But there's one thing he didn't understand, my lady, and that's celery. Sometimes when I was at the hospital here, I'd go and look at his celery trench and I could have cried. Cruel it was."

"Well, you had better wait and see Sir Harry when he comes in," said Lady Waring.

"And say thank-you to her ladyship," said his formidable mother-in-law sharply. "And now, Selina, we'll have no more nonsense about Chaldicotes. There's plenty you can do to help me with my lodgers. Anyone'd think you were ungrateful."

"Oh dear, no, mother," said Selina. "I'm ever so grateful to her ladyship. I was only thinking I'll miss my little kitchen," to which Mrs. Allen replied that there were plenty of other kitchens in the world.

Leslie then said that she thought she heard Uncle Harry coming in, so Hopkins had better go to the study and consult him and she would take Selina over to the school, which she did from dormitories to offices. Here, in a large well-lighted kitchen, for the basement was only a couple of steps below ground level, they found the little boys' high teas being cooked by a pleasant-faced elderly woman in a white apron.

"Cook, this is Mrs. Hopkins who used to be my aunt's maid," said Leslie. "This is Mrs. Trotter, Selina. She came as a temporary, but she has to go on to another job now and I really don't know what we shall do without her. The boys do enjoy her cooking so much."

"Well, it's a pleasure to cook for young gentlemen," said the cook. "I was at the Deanery for twenty years, Mrs. Hopkins, and that was a family it was a pleasure to cook for, with all the young ladies and gentlemen and their children coming and going. But I'm past that now and I only take temporaries. I've a nice little house of my own in Barchester."

Selina expressed deep admiration of the sausage rolls that were keeping warm on a hot-plate and she and the cook fell into professional talk, while Leslie listened and wondered whether the fish would rise to the bait. Then she took Selina away and showed her the little flat with bathroom and kitchen where the cook lived, and so they walked back along the passage to the Warings' quarters. When they were in the little hall, Selina stopped and began to cry.

"Cheer up," said Leslie, entirely unmoved by Selina's peculiar habits.

"It's not that, miss," said Selina, who as an old retainer stuck to Leslie's spinster status. "I was just thinking what lovely teas Cook was sending up for those dear little boys. If there's one thing I like, miss, it's seeing young gentlemen eat, and mother is just the same."

"Well, I'm needing a cook for the school," said Leslie.

"You're joking, miss," said Selina reproachfully.

"Indeed I'm not," said Leslie. "Cook is going at the end of the month and I can't hear of another, and I'm expecting a baby in the spring or I'd take on the cooking myself."

"Indeed you mustn't do no such thing, miss," said Selina. "I'll come and cook for you myself, miss. I'd sooner do that than go to Chaldicotes. Hopkins is a good husband, but his sisters I can't abide. They haven't got no appetite, miss, they just peck at their food, and that's what I can't get used to. Flying in the face of Providence I call it."

"It might be an idea," said Leslie. "We'll see what your husband has to say and your mother. Of course I'd love to have you here, and the little flat would be very handy for you and your husband." And without waiting for an answer she went into the sitting-room where Lady Waring and Octavia were having a delightful conversation with Nannie Allen about Marigold, the village problem girl, who used to be general help to Nannie.

"The films, that's all she's fit for," said Nannie darkly. "Airs and graces and nylon stockings. It all comes of those Americans we had at the camp. Though I must say for them they were more sinned against than sinning. The way that Marigold used to make up to them! 'Marigold,' I used to say to her, 'you'll wake up one fine morning with a black baby,' but you might as well have talked to Mr. Attlee if that's his name."

Then Sir Harry and a sheepish Hopkins came in from the study and Sir Harry announced that he had given Hopkins a good talking to and told him he had better take over the Priory kitchen garden as soon as possible.

"I believe Adams has an interest in Amalgamated Vedge," said Sir Harry. "Or if he hasn't, he'll know somebody that has, and we'll see that you get a fair deal, Hopkins."

"Then," said Leslie in a matter-of-fact way, though inside she was trembling with excitement, "Hopkins and Selina can move into our flat and Selina will cook for the boys."

Whether Mr. and Mrs. Hopkins had any doubts as to the high-handed ordering of their affairs we cannot say. We think not, for they had grown up in a world where the gentry were expected to be Universal Providers and mostly provided well. In any case it was soon too late for them to make any protest, for Sir

Harry set to work, and by Michaelmas the couple were installed at the Priory School. Leslie sank back with a sigh of relief to devote herself to the expected baby, and Nannie Allen was able to exercise beneficent domestic tyranny more than ever.

As any of our readers who were at the Deanery dinner-party in the dreadful cold summer of 1946 will know, Leslie's baby was a boy and everyone was doing very nicely. At the time when our story begins, for up to now we have only been going over the ground, partly for the sake of our readers but even more to clarify our mind such as it is about what had been happening at Beliers in the last few years, the baby was a year old and a nursery had become so much part of the routine of life that Leslie and Philip could not believe that there had been a babyless period in their lives. A nurse had been found by Mrs. Brandon through the head of the Nursery School that she had harboured during the war. Nurse was a pleasant, stout woman, not too young but not very old, and Master Noel Winter seemed to think very well of her, announcing the same by a series of melodious but unintelligible remarks.

"The little villain," said Nurse Gale, whose affection took the form of calling the baby by any opprobrious epithet that came into her head. "He's a little villain, he is. Tell Galey you're a villain, you little horror. Isn't he a villain, Mrs. Winter?"

Leslie, who had determined to take Nurse Gale as she found her, and after many inward struggles had succeeded, agreed that baby was a villain and then Nurse Gale said some people had been in the garden long enough and wanted their tea, and Master Noel was carried away, laughing very heartily at a joke of his own invention which was too recondite for any grown-up to understand.

Philip and Leslie were enjoying the sun in their little bit of private garden, waiting for a few friends to look in. The whole of England was also beginning to put out its horns cautiously and come out of its shell as the sun, whose face except as a pale uninteresting heatless disk was almost forgotten, began to show symptoms of life. In the distance the first batch of boys arriving for the summer term was visible and audible, though in a distinctly agreeable way.

Among the Winters' nearest neighbours were Mr. Birkett, the lately retired headmaster of Southbridge School, and his wife. Under Mr. Birkett Philip had before the war been classics master, and under Mr. Birkett he had begun to control his temper and be the happier for it.

"When I think," said Philip, "what a boorish and odious young man I was then, I can't think why Birkett didn't kick me out. I was all full of imbecile love for the Russians, about whom I really knew nothing at all except a bit of their alphabet, which I must say is a very silly one, and I must have been an infernal nuisance."

"Perhaps," said his wife, "they will learn to use the proper alphabet in time. After all, the Germans are getting into the way of it."

Philip said that was true. On the other hand, he said, he didn't think Goethe or Heine felt quite the same in roman type. There was something about the gothic type that was inextricably mixed up with their words. Leslie agreed, adding however that all the Russian books she had read were so awfully dull, whether in French or German or English, that perhaps they might as well stay in their own alphabet.

"The one advantage I can see of having a language and an alphabet that nobody understands," said Philip, "is that it makes you a good linguist. I mean if nobody knows your language, you have to learn theirs. Like the Russians and the Dutch and all the Swedes I have met, though I must say so dull that they made me squint. I expect a high level of State education makes people like that, and doubtless the English will be as dull as ditch-water in another fifty years."

Leslie said stoutly that Barsetshire would never be dull,

however State-educated it became, and then the Birketts arrived
and were asked to give an opinion on the subject.

"If you ask me," said Mr. Birkett, sitting down in a deck chair
and at once getting up again because one side was in the wrong
notch, "education is not in such a bad way."

"Do you mean you *like* all this State education?" said Leslie.

Mr. Birkett said not at all. What he meant was that he had
noticed among the real Barset people a growing ability to slough
such education as they had, a sign of the times that appeared to
him distinctly favourable.

"I know what you mean, Henry," said his wife. "We have got
a kitchen maid," she continued, turning to Leslie, "don't ask me
how, as it is all so mixed up with Mrs. Phipps, who goes out by
the day and produced a delightful girl called Lily-Annie with an
illegitimate little girl whom, I must say, she looks after splendidly. Lily-Annie had a touch of bronchitis last winter and I
kept her in bed and went up to see if she would like some books
and she said she couldn't read."

"But that's surely impossible," said Philip.

"So one would think," said Mrs. Birkett calmly. "And when I
asked her if she hadn't learnt at school, she said she did learn to
read but she didn't seem to take no interest in it and had
forgotten."

There was a short but reverent silence.

"Thank God for Barsetshire," said Philip. "And for all the
people who know what they don't want, which is much more
difficult than knowing what you do want. With an illiterate
peasantry we might begin to get somewhere."

And if, said Mrs. Birkett, there were no higher education for
women it would help.

"It makes me sick to hear the expression 'higher education,'"
said Mr. Birkett violently. "Mrs. Phipps who goes out by the day
is far better educated than that crop-haired she-devil that nearly
ruined the prep-school Latin by one term's ignorant teaching.
Thank heaven we got rid of her and she went off to one of those

sham organizations that are called by their initials, only no one knows what the initials stand for."

"It was the P.E.U.G.I.," said Mrs. Birkett. "Pan-European Union for General Interference. But I believe she had a row with the secretary, Geoffrey Harvey, and he sacked her."

"Banks. That was her name," said Mr. Birkett. "I don't like Geoffrey Harvey, but I'm glad he sacked her. What mischief is she up to now, I wonder."

No one knew. Mrs. Birkett said she was probably living with her friend that she lived with. They mostly did, she added, which cryptic remark appeared clear enough to her listeners, who laughed and smiling put the question by.

"By the way, sir," said Philip to his old headmaster, "I have a young man coming to see me this afternoon and I would be grateful if you could cast a professional eye on him. I need another master now."

Mr. Birkett looked with friendly amusement and indeed some pride at his old classics master. To have risen from pre-war territorial to full colonel, to have married a suitable wife and produced a creditable baby, to have got a prep school on such a footing that more masters were needed, the whole within the compass of the war and the subsequent so-called peace; these things made Mr. Birkett swell with vicarious pride.

"With pleasure, Philip," he said. "But you are just as competent as I am. Or perhaps you would rather ask Everard."

For though Mr. Birkett had been on the whole glad to retire from Southbridge School and though he had great admiration for and confidence in his successor, Everard Carter, formerly his senior housemaster, he could not help occasional pangs of envy for Everard's life, and the form these pangs took was to denigrate his own abilities with a modesty that deceived nobody.

"Don't be silly, Henry," said his wife. "Who is the young man, Philip?"

"Name of Belton," said Philip. "Twenty-fivish, good war record, one year at Oxford before the war. The usual thing."

"Crippled?" Mr. Birkett asked.

Philip said not so far as he knew. Not that it mattered, said Mr. Birkett, thinking how well Robin Dale, who had lost a foot at Anzio, was doing at Southbridge. And then he asked if the young man was married or engaged.

"I never thought of asking," said Philip. "I rather hope he isn't engaged."

"It all depends," said Mr. Birkett. "Some of them take it in their stride. Some don't. You didn't."

In spite of being an old married man with a baby Philip went red with confusion, thinking of the summer term when he had been engaged to the Birketts' lovely, addle-pated elder daughter Rose and what havoc that state of bliss had wrought in him.

"You may well blush," said Mr. Birkett, eying him sternly. "If I hadn't had my eye on you as Lorimer's successor I'd have sacked you at once and put Rose in a convent. The most troublesome term I've ever had."

"Did you really think I could carry on Lorimer's work?" said Philip. "I thought it was only because he died and you wanted someone in a hurry and I happened to be there. If I had known I'd have been frightened out of my wits."

"Young man," said Mr. Birkett, "you may be a headmaster but you still have a great deal to learn. When you have been running this little school of yours for a dozen years or so, you may just begin to understand what I mean. You have to have eyes in the back of your head and a head full of water-tight compartments, and you have to live for the day and also live ahead for the next two or three years. When you have been at this game as long as I have you will begin to know exactly what every member of your staff is capable of. And by that time you will be an old man and have to retire."

"Excuse my asking," said Philip, "but did you always know that Colin Keith wouldn't do for schoolmastering?" For Colin Keith, now a very rising junior at the bar, had spent a term at Southbridge School before the war.

"I did," said Mr. Birkett. "He wanted a job just to show his father that he could get one, but his heart wasn't in it, though he did quite well."

"As a matter of fact, Henry," said his wife, "you told me at the time that his neck was too thin. I remember your saying that no master was up to his work till he took a fifteen-inch collar."

And as she said these words a young man came up the drive on a bicycle, saw the party on the lawn, dismounted, leaned his bicycle against a tree, and came across the grass towards them.

"That is my new master on approval," said Philip, getting up. "Come and be introduced, Belton."

The newcomer was a well-built young man with a cheerful open countenance and the indescribable but unmistakable look of one with whom the world has hitherto gone well. Most often this look is blurred and changed as life goes on, but sometimes a man can carry it through life, though to do so must also mean that good luck leaves him unspoiled and it is a rare gift. The company were looking at him rather more intently than is usual in polite society. He showed no embarrassment under their gaze, being apparently entirely unselfconscious. But even had he been slightly embarrassed, he could never have guessed that everyone present was putting a mental yard measure round his neck.

Tea was then brought out by Marigold, the village problem girl, whose mothlike desire to be a film star had been temporarily sublimated into the excitement of helping at Miss Leslie's school, for by this name the Priory was generally known at Lambton, the nearest village and railway station. How this was managed we do not wish to inquire. The Labour Exchange, which controlled the part of Barsetshire served by the Winter Overcotes & Shearing railway, was run on feudal lines and if Miss Leslie needed a pair of hands at her school it stood to reason that Marigold (mostly known to her elders as that Marigold) would be better employed there than getting herself into trouble at a factory. This fine Sherwood Forest attitude had so far been justified that Marigold had up to the present behaved quite well and had even condescended when on duty to wear a pink plastic apron, which was quite hideous and smelt horrid; which indeed describes most things made of plastics whatever they are. While in her early teens Marigold had had the advantage of working for Nannie Allen and under that martinet had been so drilled in the kind of behaviour the gentry like that she gave Leslie very little trouble.

Marigold put the tea-things in front of Leslie in a hearty way, had a good stare at the newcomer, and went back to the kitchen to tell Selina she thought the new master was a lovely man with a nice little moustache like Hash Gobbett at the Barchester Odeon in *Stiff Upper Lip;* to which Selina made no answer at all and went on with her preparations for the boys' tea.

"I do hope I'm not late," said Mr. Belton. "The trains are quite impossible between us and here and I did mean to come by three buses, but I had forgotten the times are different in double summer time, so I missed the first one and came on my bike."

Mr. Birkett said, rather pedantically, that he believed we were never to have double summer time again. He could only hope, he said, that this would please somebody.

"It does seem a shame, sir," said Mr. Belton. "I was up in Scotland last summer at my brother-in-law's place and you can't think how jolly it was having that extra time. We used to go up to the mountains behind Aberdeathly and see the sunset and just a bit of the sea away in the west. There was some good rough shooting too."

Though this description of what was evidently heaven was of a very sketchy nature, such was Mr. Belton's enthusiasm and so pleasant his confidence in his hearers that they all felt deeply nostalgic for Scotland, which most of them had never visited.

"Did you say Aberdeathly?" said Mr. Birkett.

"Yes, sir," said Mr. Belton. "My sister married Chris Hornby and she lives up there a good deal. She's got two awfully nice children, a girl and a boy."

"I was on a committee with Hornby during the war," said Mr. Birkett. "Are you Freddy Belton?"

"No, sir, that's my elder brother," said Mr. Belton. "He's a naval man, a captain now. I'm Charles."

"But of course we have heard all about you from Mrs. Carton," said Mrs. Birkett.

Mr. Belton looked puzzled for a moment.

"Oh, I know," he said. "I can't help thinking of her as Miss Sparling, because she was the headmistress of that girls' school that took my father's place at Harefield. She had some rum girls there. There was one girl called Heather Adams, like a great sulky spotted pudding, and I got into awful trouble for not dancing with her. Her father's terrifically rich now. If I hadn't put my foot in it I might have married her and gone into her father's works. She fell into our lake that winter and my brother got her out, but he didn't marry her either. It's a pity, because the old man is pretty hard up and we need an heiress or two."

There was an agreeable frankness about this confession that made all his hearers laugh and it was generally felt that the newcomer had made good his footing and would be accepted by the neighbourhood. Presently Philip took his guest away for a private talk and Leslie and the Birketts sat lazily in the sun, comparing notes about the horrors of last winter.

"I sometimes hope I shall die before next winter," said Mr. Birkett thoughtfully. "Log fires are all very well and we had plenty of wood at the Dower House, but mostly we couldn't get anyone to cut it up. If it hadn't been for a couple of the Deans' boys on leave, the twins that are sailors, we should have had to stay in bed. They came over with a two-handed saw and made a very neat job of it. We were able to have a fire in the little study every day and dried the logs for the next day's fire at the same time. Of course we had to shut up all the other rooms. Luckily we have gas fires in the bedrooms, but when the pressure was reduced that wasn't much help. Still, with stone hot-water bottles and all our overcoats on the beds we managed to keep fairly warm."

"We had just enough coke to keep the boys from freezing," said Leslie, "and we mostly lived ourselves in the study, just as you did. Luckily Nurse has no conscience at all, so the nursery had an electric fire and an oil stove in the night nursery and sometimes a coal fire in the grate, which luckily we hadn't had taken out."

"Our pipes were the worst trouble," said Mrs. Birkett. "For ten days we had to remember to empty the cistern every night and see that the daily woman didn't light the kitchen boiler till it was full again. And every night an oil lamp in that downstairs cloakroom till the oil ran out and then we just defied the Government and ran an electric fire off the light. It was a piece of sheer luck that we had one that ran off a light, as all the others ran on power."

Mr. Birkett said he did not intend any criticism, but why should one run things off a light and on power.

"I don't know," said his wife. "I simply said what came into my head. And when I think what I wore in bed, words fail me."

"It wasn't only bed here," said Leslie. "It was always. In that awful fortnight I wore the same underclothes, two sets of everything and the thickest I had, day and night without stopping. It was the only way to keep warm."

Having made this proud boast she felt slightly ashamed, but the Birketts' admiration for her heroic deed was so outspoken that she felt quite conceited.

"Never mind," said Mr. Birkett. "It will be much, much worse next winter. Not only will there be less fuel, but we shall be even less fit to face the winter in our progressively undernourished condition. We shall mostly become cripples, our minds and bodies will no longer correlate, we shall gradually become purblind, and what with cold, hunger, and the intense boredom of this life many of us will become decidedly queer and all our tempers will be on the border line. And I hope," he added venomously, "that They will be pleased."

"There is only one thing I hope," said Leslie, "and that is that the King and Queen will be allowed to be warm." At which words everyone nearly cried with loyalty.

"I wouldn't put it past Them to cut off all the gas and electricity from wherever their Majesties are, just for spite," said Mr. Birkett angrily. "And I hope that all Their wives will get moth in their mink coats. Who's that?"

A small car came rapidly up the drive. A good-looking young woman in Red Cross uniform got out of it and came across the grass.

"I've come to collect those books of Philip's for the Hospital Libraries," she said to Leslie. "Hullo, Mrs. Birkett, how are you and Mr. Birkett?"

Leslie said that Philip was in the house interviewing a prospective master and offered her guest fresh tea.

"Don't bother," said the Red Cross visitor, who was Susan Dean, sister of the twins who had cut up Mr. Birkett's wood. "I'll have some dregs if there are any. Who is your new man?"

Leslie said his name was Belton and his people lived at Harefield.

"Oh, I know," said Susan Dean. "Lady Pomfret knows them. They are proper county, not intruders like us. The twins know one of them that's a captain in the navy."

Leslie said this was the younger brother who had been a soldier, and then Philip and his candidate returned. The Birketts, though burning with professional curiosity about the result of Philip's interview, did not like to ask before an outsider; but Philip very kindly put an end to the suspense by introducing Mr. Belton to Miss Dean as the latest member of their staff.

"You're Charles, aren't you?" said Susan. "My brothers know your brother Freddy. You must come over to tennis one Sunday if Philip will let you loose."

"I'd love to," said Charles Belton. "I say, what are you? I

thought the Red Cross was over now. I mean now there isn't a war."

Susan good-humouredly said that the Red Cross had got into the habit of supplying hospitals with books and couldn't stop, and she was the Depot Librarian for Barchester, which caused Charles to look at her with great respect. She then said she would go and fetch the books Philip was giving to the Red Cross, and Charles offered to help her.

"So that's all right," said Mr. Birkett as soon as the couple were out of earshot. "What did you make of him, Philip?"

"As much as you made of your assistant masters when you first interviewed them, sir," said Philip. "I like him. He appears to like little boys. He has a decided turn for mathematics, and if he can manage a bit of Latin as well, we shall do. I'm not sure if he is cut out for schoolmastering, but he is keen about it and he happens to be a gentleman. I also turned the conversation to collars," said Philip, smiling, "though it took some ingenuity. He takes a fifteen-inch collar but rather likes a fifteen-and-a-half-inch in the summer."

"He'll do," said Mr. Birkett. "Good God, Amy, look down the drive!"

His wife, thus apostrophized, showed no concern, for she was well used to her husband's ways. Up the drive were coming a middle-aged couple, recognized at once by everyone as Mr. and Mrs. Tebben from Worsted. With Mr. Tebben, a quiet scholarly man lately retired from the Civil Service, Mr. Birkett had much in common, but unfortunately it was next to impossible to get Mr. Tebben without his highly educated and very well-meaning wife.

"News, news," cried Mrs. Tebben, waving her hand gaily as she came across the grass. "Simon Dansk has come home again from cruising with his buccaneers."

If Charles Belton had been there he might have been excused for thinking the visitor demented, but Leslie and the Birketts were used to Mrs. Tebben's methods and Leslie at once deduced that Richard Tebben, their only and adored son, had come home for a holiday from wherever he happened to be. So she congratulated the Tebbens warmly.

"It was quite unexpected," said Mrs. Tebben. "No; no tea, thank you. We had a gypsy tea with a thermos on the common. And then I said to Gilbert why not go and tell our delightful news to the Winters. Yes, Richard is now in one of Mr. Adams's many ventures, in Stockholm. His experience with Mr. Dean's firm was of great value to him and he has forged ahead. Gilbert and I were planning a little jaunt to Stockholm if we could afford it, or rather if the Government could afford it, as they seem to be so very badly off when it comes to letting one use one's own money to do any travelling, when suddenly a telegram from Richard! He arrives tomorrow and I have been very busy preparing things for him. So difficult to give the dear boy the kind of food he has been used to in Sweden, but I found a tin of peanut butter, gift of one of Gilbert's American friends, the vice-president of the Harvard branch of the Snorri Society, so I managed to get a few plain biscuits on our last points and shall spread the peanut butter on them. And with some of my turnip wine, just a drop left from a bottle that blew up, we shall cry Skal!"

Her husband, who wore the meek but determined look of one who was determined not to cry Skal, nor anything else, took a chair next to Mr. Birkett and fell into talk with him about Lord Stoke's recent find in the Stokey Hole, a large natural cavern opening onto the bank of the Rising, of what his lordship claimed to be a Viking's armour in an advanced state of rust and decomposition.

"It is very difficult to contradict Stoke," said Mr. Tebben in his precise tired voice, "because he bellows you down and in any case he can't hear what you say. But as far as my limited knowledge extends," said Mr. Tebben with false modesty, for he was perhaps the foremost authority on Norse remains in England, "the metal in question is not earlier than the Great

Exhibition and was probably dumped in the Stokey Hole when Stoke's father made his alterations to the Castle and cleared out a lot of junk of the romantic period. It was difficult enough to deal with Stoke when I was in the Civil Service, but at least I could plead pressure of work. Now I have retired he sends a brougham or a dog-cart over for me on the slightest pretext and it is really very difficult to refuse. However," Mr. Tebben added, in a studiously neutral voice, "he does not include Winifred in his invitations, and his lunches are very good."

And if a quiet scholarly retired Civil Servant could be said to wink, that action was adumbrated by Mr. Tebben.

Susan Dean and Charles Belton now rejoined the party, carrying a large laundry basket full of books.

"A new face!" exclaimed Mrs. Tebben dramatically. "Not our dear Susan, but the young man."

Mrs. Birkett, trying hard to keep out of her voice the slight chill that Mrs. Tebben's remarks were apt to produce, said it was Charles Belton from Harefield, Philip's new assistant master, late of the Royal Artillery.

"I must talk to him!" said Mrs. Tebben. "He is sure to have met Richard somewhere. It is a wonderful comradeship between these young men and gives one high hopes."

Leslie nearly said hopes of what, but restrained herself in time and introduced Charles to Mr. and Mrs. Tebben.

"Oh, how do you do? I'm awfully sorry I can't shake hands," said Charles, showing how very dirty they were. "I don't know what it is about books but they simply throw out dirt like a cuttle-fish."

Leslie was about to say that the reason these particular books were dirty was that they had been waiting in an empty room for the Red Cross for several weeks and it was nobody's business to dust them, but Mrs. Tebben, scenting what she called a good argument, leapt into the fray.

"Dirt, my dear!" she exclaimed. "In me you see the world's authority on dirt! My life, my *whole* life, is spent in fighting dirt!

As for Gilbert's study! One of those old-fashioned bookcases with leather frills along the tops of the shelves that literally disintegrate under your eyes. And our little furnace in the basement which is supposed to provide hot water but fills the house with blacks. Look at my hands!"

She spread out her hands on her lap, turned them upside down for inspection, and waited for comment. She had not overstated her case, for a more dirt-ingrained pair of hands even the years of peace had not beheld; every line ingrained with black, her nails obviously resistant to the fiercest cleaning. Mr. Tebben, used as he was to his wife's well-meant complaints, guiltless as he was of the condition of her hands, suddenly felt for his wife a sense of guilty pity; which feeling was quite unnecessary, for it was not his fault that the coke furnace spewed out dirt, and as a matter of fact he usually cleaned it out and lighted it himself because one never knew if the daily woman was coming or not. But at times the memory of Miss Winifred Ross wearing a blue muslin dress with white spots on the Norwegian cruise where they first had met came surging into his mind, and he felt (quite unnecessarily) that he had ruined her career by marrying her. In which he was entirely wrong, for without marriage she would have been another of the many women with degrees who don't know what to do with them, and, whether she knew it or not, was far happier as she was.

The question of dirty hands is a depressing one. Every lady present looked at her own hands and wished they were somewhere else. At this moment Selina came out of the house with a large tray.

"I'm sure you'll excuse me, Miss Leslie," she said, putting the tray on the grass and beginning to collect the tea-things, "but I had to send Marigold down to the village on her bike to collect those eggs for the broody, so I thought I'd get on with the washing-up."

Leslie thanked Selina, who collected the rest of the tea-things and went away.

"Did you notice Selina's hands?" she said, addressing no one in particular. "She works harder than any of us and scrubs and peels potatoes and washes vegetables and scours saucepans. It doesn't seem fair."

The same thought had struck the other ladies present, for Selina's hands, though workmanlike, were softer and whiter than the hands of most so-called ladies.

"It must be something to do with the amount of fat you have inside you," said Susan. "It's no good putting on lotions and things. I simply hate my hands every time I look at them."

There was silence, for no woman likes to have rough dirty hands with dull nails, yet it is the fate of most of us. As Susan Dean truly said, lotions and things are very little good, and polish on abraded nails is disheartening. Sometimes one tries to feel proud of working hands, but the delusion does not last and one could cry over the ruins. Part of the price one pays for the privilege of being alive in this almost hopeless world. Silence fell upon the party, for the women recognized the truth of Susan's words and the men felt guilty without knowing why.

A distraction was offered by Marigold, who came up the drive on her bicycle, dismounted, and came across the lawn. She was a nice-looking girl though no beauty, but had very cleverly acquired an air of film-stardom which deeply impressed her contemporaries, especially those of the male sex. Her whole being was modelled on Glamora Tudor, the famous movie star, and as she had the obliging kind of hair that stays wherever it is put and a neutral (or shall we say sallow) skin on which she was able to perform cosmetic fantasies, she made a quite startling effect on people who saw her for the first time.

Conscious of a gentleman she hadn't seen before, she was overtaken by a fit of that self-consciousness which can only express itself in giggles and writhings of the body, and appeared unable to speak.

"What is it, Marigold?" said Leslie.

"Oh, please, Miss Leslie," said Marigold, who had adopted

Selina's name for her mistress, "I was in at the post office and Mrs. Hamp was talking to Palmyra Phipps on the Worsted telephone exchange and she passed the remark young Mr. Tebben had just phoned up from London and she said she'd seen Mr. and Mrs. Tebben go up to the Priory and to let you know, please."

"Richard!" exclaimed Mrs. Tebben. "And we are not there to greet him, Gilbert. Quick, quick!"

She rose, picked up her raffia bag containing the thermos and the remains of the gypsy tea, and proposed to go home with no more ado.

"But we don't even know where Richard is, my dear," said Mr. Tebben, who had not got up. "If he only rang up from London just now he can't be at Worsted and he couldn't get down till late in any case."

"But I must be *there*," said Mrs. Tebben. "Come, Gilbert. Good-bye, Mrs. Winter, and thank you for a delightful afternoon. Good-bye, everyone. I must hurry back and see what we have in the way of left-overs for supper. Richard will be hungry."

To this Mr. Tebben replied that he understood the Swedes were very well fed and Richard had probably brought over food with him, but his wife preferred to think of a prodigal son with nothing to eat but husks and insisted on getting back to look for the peanut butter as she was not sure whether she had left it in the larder or under one of the drawing-room cushions. Her husband rose with resignation and after distracted farewells from Mrs. Tebben the couple went away. Marigold, who had been an enthralled spectator of the scene, now transferred her attention to Charles Belton, suddenly realized she had no business on the lawn, gave a final wriggle in which she appeared to be doing her best to burst out of all her clothes, and fled towards the house.

"Marigold," Leslie called after her. "Don't forget the eggs!"

Checked in mid-flight, Marigold returned and wheeled her bicycle with the eggs in the carrier away towards the kitchen regions.

"I'm sorry about Marigold, but you'll have to get used to her," said Leslie to Charles Belton. "She's quite a nice girl, but movie-struck like so many of them. Did Philip show you the room you will have?"

"No, I didn't," said Philip. "That is the headmaster's wife's job. When would you like to come, Belton?"

Charles said the sooner the better, because he wanted to start work. So a date was arranged and Charles said good-bye.

"Don't forget you are coming over to tennis while you are here," said Susan Dean. "And my sister Jessica is usually here at the week-ends. She'll amuse you."

Charles thanked her though obviously without much comprehension of what she said, and she went away in her little car with the books for the Red Cross Libraries.

"I suppose you've seen Jessica?" said Philip.

Charles said he didn't think so. He had never met any of the Deans till he met that Miss Dean. Then his expression altered.

"You don't mean Jessica Dean?" he said incredulously.

"Well, that's her name," said Philip.

"Not *the* Jessica Dean?" said Charles. "But of course I know her. I mean I've seen her in Aubrey Clover's plays. They came out and gave some jolly good shows for us when I was in India. I never knew she lived down here. By Jove!"

Mrs. Birkett suggested that if he was looking for heiresses, Jessica Dean must be doing pretty well and could probably support a husband in luxury, if not comfort.

Charles said he didn't really mean he wanted to marry money; a statement that all his hearers felt to be very true. But he said if he did marry an heiress he could give his father and mother a bit of fun.

"I'd like you to know my mother, Mrs. Birkett," he said earnestly. "She's not bad. I mean she almost understands things."

Mrs. Birkett expressed great enthusiasm for mothers who almost understood, adding that she had never understood her own children very well, though she had done her best by them, but perhaps that was because they were girls.

"Mrs. Birkett might add," said Philip Winter, looking affectionately at Ma Birky, as Southbridge School used to call her, "that she understood four hundred boys or so extraordinarily well over a number of years, not to speak of a lot of masters, including myself when I was far, far nastier than I am now."

Charles said seriously that he didn't think Mr. Winter could have been nastier, at which Mrs. Birkett laughed and lured him on to talk about himself. Leslie had observed the scene with interest. Her chief wish, apart from a great many other chief wishes, was to be a proper headmaster's wife, and she had already realized that the job was not easy and needed as much concentrated effort as the war jobs that she had done so well. She knew that never could she come within a mile of Philip's gift for little boys, but she had secretly determined to learn everything she could and to that end had made a special study of Mrs. Birkett.

It had not escaped her notice that Charles had at once confided in Mrs. Birkett, though she was quite middle-aged and not particularly good-looking. It would be a long time, she thought, before Charles or any young master would confide in her, although she was very intelligent and on the whole kind. There was something in Philip that made people work for him. Perhaps the army had helped. The younger men would probably bring their troubles to her husband, but she did not think they would bring them to her. She did not exactly envy Mrs. Birkett, for she liked her too much, but she wished she could ever be as much help to Philip as Mrs. Birkett had been to Mr. Birkett, and determined to ask her some day how one became a good headmaster's wife.

"Well, thank you most awfully, Mrs. Birkett," said Charles, though for what he did not quite know, except that she had made him feel safe and comfortable. "Perhaps you and Mr. Birkett could come to Harefield some time. Mother would love

to see you and we've got quite a nice church and we've got a kind
of pavilion thing called the Garden House. I mean it's all falling
to bits but it must have been rather jolly once in the eighteenth
century and I believe it's quite a good one and it was in *Country
Life*."

He stopped, wondering whether his description of the charming, deserted melancholy relic of English rococo had conveyed
anything at all to that nice Mrs. Birkett, or if she would just think
he was a ghastly bore. But to his surprise and gratitude the nice
Mrs. Birkett said she and her husband had a little petrol in hand
and would love to come over during the summer.

"Well, good-bye, Mrs. Winter," said Charles, finally tearing
himself away from Mrs. Birkett. "It'll be awfully nice to be here
and I'll do my best. Good-bye, sir, and thanks most awfully. My
father and mother will be as bucked as anything that I've got a
job."

Philip and Leslie shook hands and wished him the best of
luck. Charles got onto his bicycle and rode away and the
schoolmasters and their wives were left alone.

"Well, sir?" said Philip to Mr. Birkett, falling into the old
mode of addressing his headmaster.

"I'm not quite sure," said Mr. Birkett, "whether you mean will
Charles Belton do well or have you done well."

He looked piercingly at his late classics master over his
spectacles.

"As far as one ever knows what one is thinking," said Philip,
who was used to Mr. Birkett's ways, "I was wondering if I had
behaved like a proper headmaster. As for Belton I don't see why
he shouldn't do quite well. He fell for Ma Birkett at once."

"I agree with you about young Belton," said Mr. Birkett. "He
may not stick to schoolmastering, in fact I am pretty sure he
won't; but he won't let you down and he ought to get on well
with your boys. Of course he fell in love with Amy. They all do."

He spoke lightly, but Philip knew, though possibly Leslie
didn't, how deep was his pride in the wife who had stood by him

from the days when he was headmaster of Southbridge Junior School, through the war and the difficulties of receiving an evacuated school, through the lean and the increasingly leaner years of peace, through the vagaries of their beautiful but very troublesome daughter Rose, through the reactions that inevitably followed his retirement. And so, Philip thought, had Leslie stood by him from the day when they had unromantically plighted their troth at Winter Overcotes Junction with the ring that had once bound Philip to the silly lovely Rose Birkett, and when even as they spoke their love the train had carried Philip back to the war and an unknown destination. And he had no doubt that she would continue to stand by him.

But all these thoughts passed through his mind so swiftly that he answered Mr. Birkett almost without a pause, thanking him for backing his judgment of young Belton. Then the Birketts went away.

It was Leslie's custom to drop in and visit her uncle and aunt almost every day, between tea and supper, for dinner was too dignified a name for the evening meal. Accordingly she went round to the Priory back yard and in by the kitchen passage. Upstairs she found Sir Harry reading the evening paper and Lady Waring at her desk, engaged in correspondence about her endless committees and good works. As Sir Harry did not like to be disturbed while reading his paper, Leslie put a kiss on top of his head and sat down by her aunt, who, like most very busy people, could always spare some time. Lady Waring inquired after Master Noel and asked how young Belton had got on.

"Nicely, thank you," said Leslie. "Philip engaged him and he is to start at once. I didn't remember that I had told you he was coming."

"No more you had," said her aunt. "But I was at the Women's Institute meeting at Nutfield and I saw Mrs. Belton, who told me her younger son was hoping to get a job at the Priory School. She is an extraordinarily nice woman. Her elder son is at the

Admiralty at present, so she hopes he will come to her for week-ends. We must ask them over to lunch one Sunday."

"Cecil knows Captain Belton," said Leslie, her voice warming as it always did when she spoke of her brother. "He likes him very much."

"Neither of Mrs. Belton's sons is married," said Lady Waring thoughtfully. "One somehow expects everyone to get married now the war is over, but there seem to be more bachelors than ever. Both the Beltons, Cecil, young Tebben, the Dean twins, and I am sure there are several more."

"It's funny," said Leslie, "but I can't think of enough girls for all the men we know, though one would expect it to be the other way round. Except Susan Dean I can't think of anyone at the moment in this part of the world."

Lady Waring, who though a discreet woman was not above a quiet gossip with Leslie, whom she knew to be safe, said she had been under the impression that Susan was fond of Mrs. Brandon's son, who had married that pretty widow that Harry liked so much. Leslie, a little more up-to-date than her aunt, said she didn't think it had been serious, but that she believed Lydia Merton's brother, Colin Keith, had been at the Deans' a good deal. Both ladies agreed that it was high time Susan got married or she would settle down into one of the well-bred spinsters that inform the English countryside and become a little more authoritative and efficient with each passing year.

"If only there were a few more people like Philip," said Leslie, who had had the good fortune to marry her only love and had been quietly and deeply happy ever since.

"George would have been nearly fifty now," said Lady Waring, who rarely mentioned her only son. "I sometimes wonder whom he would have married. He was in love with Dr. Crawley's eldest girl before he went abroad, but she was only fifteen and we didn't think seriously about it. It would have been pleasant to have grandchildren."

So rarely did Lady Waring speak of her old grief that Leslie was at a loss what to say. They had been speaking in low voices because Sir Harry hated conversation while he was reading his paper, though increasing deafness made things easier now, and it seemed to Leslie that they were playing on muted strings. Her aunt, though ceaselessly kind, had never been given to confidences and at this moment Leslie felt that she had been received into a kind of inner circle. She would have liked to say something helpful, but what help was there for an elderly woman who would have loved to have grandchildren? All she could do was to offer what she had and ask her aunt if she would come and see little Noel being put to bed.

"It is very kind of you, my dear," said Lady Waring, laying her hand for a moment on Leslie's, "but not this evening. How is Selina?"

Sir Harry, having read the paper from beginning to end, threw it on the floor and said he didn't know what we were coming to. The strings were no longer muted. What was that about Selina, he said. Why hadn't Selina come up to see them?

"It's always rather busy in the kitchen at the beginning of term, Uncle Harry," said Leslie, "but she will come as soon as the boys' teas are washed up. She always comes over on Sunday evening to see cook."

"Best day's work I ever did when I got Selina and that husband of hers to come here," said Sir Harry. "Hopkins is first-rate with the vegetables. If I hadn't thought of having them here, where would we all have been?"

Lady Waring and Leslie, avoiding each other's eyes, said with one voice: "Where indeed." And then Leslie went back to the school.

CHAPTER 2

A fter this Sunday every snail went back into its own shell so to speak. The Winters were busy with the first weeks of term and Charles Belton was finding his feet. Mr. Birkett was working against time on his edition of the Analects of Procrastinator, his wife was away visiting her daughter Rose Fairweather and the new grandchild. The Warings were ceaselessly occupied with their county work. Mr. and Mrs. Tebben at Worsted were enjoying the society of their son Richard, whom time had slightly mellowed, though his ears stuck out as much as ever.

Since the days before the war the social centres had shifted all over England. Pomfret Towers, once a rallying-place for the county, was being run on a skeleton staff, the family living in the nursery wing, the big room shut and dust-sheeted, except the dining-room, which was kept as a kind of board or committee room for local activities, for the Pomfrets took their duties seriously. Lord Pomfret, never in robust health, attending the House of Lords as much as possible in addition to his county work, had caused his wife a good deal of anxiety during the bitter winter, but with the warmer weather she was able to relax her vigilance and let her anxiety rest for the moment. At Staple Park, which had during the war been let to an evacuated school, now returned to London, Lord and Lady Bond were also living in part of the servants' wing, but Lord Bond never regretted it, for the change had enabled him to give notice to his butler, under whose tyranny he had suffered too long. His heir, the Honourable C. W. Bond, whose initials covered the shame of being called Cedric Weyland, was living with his wife and family at the White Cottage next to Laverings, where Mr. Middleton the architect and his wife, owing to that mysterious law of Providence which watches over people with no children and enough money, still lived in a good deal of comfort, for the county round Skeynes was still feudal and women could be got to cook and scrub. Over at Rushwater Martin Leslie and his wife were farming as hard as they could, aided by Martin's stout and competent cousin Emmy Graham. And so from one end of the county to the other, people were marooned, first by the amount of hard work they were doing and then by the long and hideous winter of everyone's discontent, which had made roads impassable for weeks at a time and caused an amount of inconvenience and actual suffering that must have amused an all-merciful Providence very much; unless we incline to the more charitable view that Providence's mind was elsewhere.

Over at Harefield Mr. and Mrs. Belton were living in the village at Arcot House. During the war their big house had been let to the Hosiers' Girls' Foundation School, and so successful had the experiment been that the Governors of the school had decided to build on part of Mr. Belton's property, a piece of land of no great farming value along the Southbridge Road. Pending the building of the new school they had renewed the lease of Harefield Park, and as They were determined not to allow anything useful to be done for education beyond shoving the school-leaving age up to a point that made it impossible for any school to accommodate its pupils, it seemed probable that the Hosiers' Girls, under their excellent new headmistress, Miss Holly, might still be at Harefield Park long after Mr. and Mrs. Belton were dead.

Not long after the very mild events related in the last chapter Charles Belton, being off duty on a Sunday, came over to

Harefield to see his parents, determined to answer any questions they were ill-advised enough to ask as kindly as possible, though we all know how difficult this is for both sides. After further consideration of trains and buses, Charles came to the conclusion that a bicycle was his quickest and best mode of transport. Deeply did he pine for the piping times of war when one could get a lift from any lorry or commandeer someone else's motor bicycle, but these glories were past and he was a civilian and very lucky to have a job with nice employers, so he pumped up his tires and left the Priory School, unaware of Marigold's admiring looks from the stable-yard, where she had no business to be.

"Mr. Belton's a lovely man," said Marigold to Selina. "He's just like Hash Gobbett in *Where Next*. He got lovely pyjamas with a blue stripe. I saw them when I was helping Doris make the beds."

To which Selina, busy with her saucepans, said that was quite enough and Mrs. Winter would be ever so upset if she heard Marigold talk like that and to peel those potatoes for her.

Though no one quite liked to tempt Providence by mentioning it, the summer appeared to have made up its mind to behave. As warm day succeeded warm day England held its breath, waiting for the inevitable rebuff. Ill-conditioned ungrateful people began to complain of feeling too warm. Rumours of drought were spread abroad. But to most of the underfed shivering people of England the gift of sun was accepted with a touching gratitude. So easy, one would think, for the sun to shine; but apparently the sun was not of that opinion. Others again held that They were responsible for the past winter, and the present warmth was a direct challenge to Them by any beneficent powers that had survived Their bullying and regimenting.

To a healthy young man like Charles Belton the dozen miles or so to Harefield were of very little account, and he reached his home a little before half past twelve. The house was empty so he left his bicycle in the hall and walked up the High Street towards the church. Morning service was just over and the congregation were exchanging news under the lime avenue in the churchyard.

"Hallo, mother," said Charles, singling his mother out from a small crowd.

Mrs. Belton looked round, smiled, and gave Charles a kiss, clinging to him for a second, or less than a second, for she never disgraced him in public. Deep in her heart she knew she would never really recover from the quick leave-taking in the hall of Arcot House when Charles disappeared into the war and no news came. Charles had come safely through the war, had at last been demobilized, and now had a promising job. There was really nothing to worry about. But Mrs. Belton knew, quite fatally, as thousands of mothers all over England knew, that she would never recover from what might have been a final parting. So deep was the wound that no one would ever see it, but if she lived to be a hundred and knew Charles's children and his children's children, the deep scar would remain. Never glad confident morning again. This Charles would never know. No one would know it. But this mark would be found as deeply on her heart and on the hearts of all the other women as ever Calais was on Queen Mary's. Never again could she be free from apprehension, however well things were going. Never till her life ended would she cease to feel the sick pain. As for what might happen afterwards, she was too tired to care.

"Darling, how nice," said Mrs. Belton. "Elsa and Chris are here and Freddy. Elsa brought us a couple of ducks and some salmon from Aberdeathly. How is the school?"

Charles, who knew quite well that his mother was not interested in the school except in so far as he was a master there, said it was going nicely and was there any sherry in the house as if not he would take Chris and Freddy to the Nabob on the way back. Then Charles's sister Elsa joined them with her husband, Admiral Hornby, followed by Charles's elder brother, Captain Belton, R.N., and there was a good deal of loud cheerful talk.

"Where's father?" said Charles suddenly.

"Churchwardening with Mr. Oriel," said Mrs. Belton, and in

a few moments the vicar came down the lime walk in talk with Mr. Belton and made Charles so welcome that he felt like a prodigal son. The question of a drink at the Nabob was raised, but Captain Belton, who knew that his parents' pride was secretly hurt when their family went to drink at the inn, urged the party homewards.

"I say, Freddy, I hope there *is* some sherry at home," said Charles to his elder brother as they walked down the High Street with its fine red brick houses on the south side, its cheerful little shops opposite.

"As a matter of fact there is," said Captain Belton. "I have a feeling that father doesn't much like the family going to the Nabob. After all, he was the big house and they would never have dreamt of letting a guest pay for a drink as long as they lived there. I don't believe mother has ever been inside the Nabob, though she likes Wheeler, who is a useful man on local things. Personally I'd as soon go to the Nabob as not, one picks up a lot of useful information there, but I only go when the parents don't officially know about it."

Charles said he saw what Freddy meant and it was jolly decent of him, but as he was only a younger son he thought it would be all right for him to go to the Nabob from time to time. Gavelkind, or Borough English, or something of that sort, he added. His elder brother laughed and they joined the rest of the family party and went into Arcot House.

After lunch Charles was caught by Wheeler, now general utility and formerly his nurse, and put through a searching questionnaire about the Priory School, what the boys were like, what the masters were like, what the food was like, and whether Charles was remembering to change his socks often enough. All these questions Charles answered very good-humouredly and volunteered the statement that Mrs. Winter was awfully nice.

"That's the headmaster's wife, isn't it?" said Wheeler.

Charles said it was and, scenting in Wheeler's comment a subtle disapproval, added that she was really most awfully nice.

"That's as may be," said Wheeler, "and if we are to believe what we hear, headmasters' wives aren't no different from the rest of us."

It was now clear to Charles that his ex-nurse was insanely jealous of Mrs. Winter, as indeed she had been of the matrons at Charles's prep and public schools and all the masters' wives, regarding them as ravening wolves whose special mission in life was to hurt her nursling. While he was in the army her jealous fears had had a rest, except for dark suspicions of girl drivers and all A.T.S. personnel, but now it was abundantly clear to her that her Charles, her last and best-loved nursery charge, was going to fall a prey to a headmaster's designing wife.

"There's a film I saw at the Barchester Odeon, Master Charles," she said. "*Young Woodley* was the name. A nasty sort of film and I wouldn't have stayed only I wanted to see the newsreel with Mr. Churchill afterwards. It just showed what schoolmasters' wives are like."

"But that was a boy who fell in love with the headmaster's wife," said Charles, "not a master. You couldn't imagine anyone falling in love with Mrs. Winter. She's just most awfully nice," to which Wheeler made reply that that was the way things started and not to blame her if he found himself in trouble and he'd better bring back his socks to be darned as she knew the girls there wouldn't darn them properly.

"I shouldn't think Marigold would," said Charles. "She doesn't look like it. But Mrs. Hopkins sewed a button on my shirt splendidly."

These were rash statements for which Charles was immediately called to account by his old nurse. His description of Marigold was received with a blank disapproving face, pursed-up lips, and a stony silence, but when he began to describe Selina, Wheeler perceptibly thawed.

"Who did you say Mrs. Hopkins's mother was?" she asked.

Charles said Mrs. Allen. Mrs. Winter, he added, always spoke of her as Nannie Allen.

"Now that will be Nannie Allen that was Nannie to poor Master George Waring that was killed," said Wheeler, calling up her reserves of county nursery knowledge. "And then she was Nannie to Lady Emily Leslie's David and in a lot of good nurseries. Her daughter will be all right, Master Charles. I remember Nannie Allen quite well. I dare say I'll be coming over by the bus to see her one of these days and bring you a cake or something. You tell her it's Sarah Wheeler. She'll remember my cousin Bill Wheeler. He's the only sweep that understands the Pomfret Towers chimneys, and he was walking out with Nannie Allen's daughter, but Nannie Allen put a stop to it. I hope Selina did better for herself, I'm sure. Bill is still a bachelor and he's got plenty of money put away."

As this social register showed no signs of coming to an end, Charles gave his old nurse a violent hug and went back to the drawing-room, where his sister Elsa was showing her parents some snapshots of her two children and explaining, after the way of parents, that they weren't a bit like and Catriona was really much prettier and little Freddy had two teeth, only you couldn't see them.

Mr. Belton then expressed a desire to walk round the place, his usual Sunday afternoon employment, and invited his wife and family to accompany him. No one particularly wanted to go, but there was no really adequate reason for refusing, the afternoon was pleasantly warm, so they all went up the long garden, through the door in the wall, and so along the lane and across the fields towards their old home, whose rather gaunt Palladian front, connected by an arcade with a pavilion on each side, dominated the village of Harefield.

During the past five or six years (for the Hosiers' Girls' Foundation School had not taken Harefield House till the war had been going on for some time) Mr. Belton had made this walk several hundred times. In the beginning he had done so because he felt it would be cowardly not to, because if his home was no longer his it behoved him to show he did not mind. Then having sufficiently proved to himself and his neighbours that he was not afraid of grasping nettles, he continued to walk that way because it had become a habit. And by the time peace was getting into the third year of its increasingly uncomfortable progress, he found positive pleasure, which he would sooner have died than admit, in following the slanting path across the fields, entering the garden by the little iron gate, and so arriving at the West Pavilion. And if the truth is to be told, he had come to take much pleasure in talking with Miss Sparling, who was then the headmistress; and now that Miss Sparling, or Dr. Sparling as she had become, had retired and married their old friend Mr. Carton, he had transferred his patronage to the present headmistress, Miss Holly. Miss Holly accepted his visits with her usual calm and often found it very convenient to be on friendly terms with her landlord, especially in matters like taking an extra piece of land for tennis courts and the right of way that ran across the back drive.

"There were still some deer here when my father was a boy," said Mr. Belton as they breasted the garden slope.

His three children looked at one another. A few years earlier one at least of them would have had the giggles or turned sulky, for ever since they could remember their father he had made this remark at this particular point in this particular walk. But all three were by now so absorbed in their own lives, lived outside the Harefield sphere, that they merely felt a tolerant boredom and Elsa good-naturedly, though with a faint touch of humouring an idiot, said how nice it must have been. Her elder brother looked quickly at her, and then at his father, for as he grew older it was more and more borne in upon him that his father was no fool. But Mr. Belton appeared to take the remark in good part, so Captain Belton said nothing.

The whole party had now arrived at the West Pavilion, where the headmistress had her private apartments, but Ellen Humble, granddaughter of William Humble the cowman and private body servant to Miss Holly, after recovering her wits, which the sight of so many Beltons had caused to be more scattered than ever, said she was ever so sorry but Miss Holly had gone away till Sunday night and she knew Miss Holly would be ever so sorry.

Elsa asked after Ellen Humble's aunt, Miss Faithful Humble, who kept the little stationer's shop and the lending library.

"Oh, Auntie's all right, Miss Elsa," said Ellen Humble. "Her leg's swollen up again quite dreadful but she's got a lovely new medicine Dr. Perry gave her. She'll be ever so pleased you asked after her, Miss Elsa, oh dear, Mrs. Hornby I mean, miss."

And Ellen Humble went red in the face and kicked her own ankles. But Elsa said she liked being Miss Elsa and Ellen Humble must come down to Arcot House and see the new photographs of her babies.

"Oh, I'd love to, miss, I mean madam," said Ellen Humble. "My Aunt Sarah, she's got a new baby. He's called Poyntz."

"Dear me!" said Mr. Belton, interested in this Durbervilleish outbreak of an old name. "Why was that?"

"Aunt Sarah didn't rightly know who the gentleman was," said Ellen Humble, "because she only met him at a dance, but it was the last week of the rations when he was born and she'd no points left because she'd spent them all on golden syrup and a tin of pork sausages, so when Dr. Perry said the baby was a boy she said she'd call him Points. We did laugh."

By the time this artless tale had drawn to its conclusion the gentry, though well used to village morals, which have not been altered by the war and the peace so much as one might think, being in their nature eternal, felt that Ellen Humble's Aunt Sarah had really overstepped the limits. But knowing well that Sarah was incapable of remorse or shame, being a very good-natured girl whose only fault was that she could never say no, they congratulated Ellen Humble on her new nephew, left messages for Miss Holly, and turned away.

"That's the second, isn't it?" said Charles Belton. "I remember she had one baby just before I went abroad."

His mother said, rather abstractedly, that it was the third, and no one, not even Sarah herself, seemed to know who the fathers were, or to worry about it. Captain Belton said he didn't really mind about illegitimate children, except in so far as it distressed Mr. Oriel, but what did frighten him was the growing power of matriarchy in England. It was obvious, he added, that unmarried mothers had quite overcrowded public opinion and would soon control the whole manpower of England. Especially, said Elsa, as the middle classes continued to think poorly of illegitimate children and on the whole didn't have them. Mrs. Belton looked anxious. It was not that she was shocked, for she had always lived among the people of Barsetshire and considered that their old and tried qualities outweighed any number of children of shame; not to speak of the fact that these young women of the Brave New World looked after the children of shame very competently and even affectionately. But she was old enough to feel that such subjects were not quite suited for discussion between herself and her children, although she did not for one moment consider her daughter and her two sons ignorant of the world and the way things are going.

Captain Belton, who was quietly fond of his mother, and had told her once a sadness in his own life that only one other person knew, realized that she was not comfortable and suggested a visit to the solicitor Mr. Updike and his wife, who would love to hear about Charles's new job. So they walked past their old home, down the drive, and into the High Street again, where cats were lazily basking inside shop windows, the hot Sabbath sun pouring comfortably on them through the glass, and so to Clive's Corner, where they found the Updikes in their garden.

And when we say the Updikes, we mean not only Mr. and Mrs. Updike, but their four children, which was a rare event.

"May we all come and call on you?" said Mrs. Belton.

Mrs. Updike, a tall fair thin woman who looked ridiculously young for the mother of so many large grown-up children, was darning an old pillow-slip before it went to the laundry, for, as we all know, it is not much use waiting to darn linen till it comes back, for the laundry sees to it that there shall be nothing left to darn.

With an exclamation of pleasure she got up, dropped her sewing, nearly tripped over a cricket bat that was lying at her feet, and greeted the Beltons enthusiastically.

"I hoped I would see you in church this morning," she said, "but I set the alarm clock wrong, so I went to early communion instead, because if you are up early it seems such waste not to do something useful. But Phil and the children went to the eleven-o'clock service and they told me Charles was back, didn't you, chicks?"

The chicks smiled in a friendly way but said nothing, for what with a silent father and a mother whose gentle flow of talk never ceased, they found it simpler not to talk, though none the less devoted to their parents and each other. It was generally believed in Harefield that the eldest boy, who was now a fullblown solicitor in a well-known Barchester firm after rising to the rank of colonel during the war, the elder girl, who after doing excellent work in the W.A.A.F.'s was now running a large domestic-science school, the younger girl, who had won a research scholarship at Cambridge, and the younger boy, who was about to do his military service with such a bag of scholarships and exhibitions as would see him through Oxford six times over, sometimes conversed together when alone. But this no one could say with certainty, because they were all extremely fond of their mother and when in Harefield were never to be seen except in her company. The two younger Updikes silently took possession of Charles and dragged him away to see some puppies in the old stables.

"I knew you would be glad to know that Charles has a job," said Mrs. Belton to Mr. Updike. "The Priory School sounds very nice and I hope to go over and see it some day, only getting about is so difficult now."

Mr. Updike said he had always taken a special interest in

Charles since he had the pleasure of making his will for him before he went abroad.

"I hope you don't mind talking about wills," he added, seeing Mrs. Belton look a little agitated. "They upset some people."

Mrs. Belton smiled and said she didn't mind wills a bit, in fact she had practically been brought up on them as her old Aunt Mary had made a fresh and always very unfair and unreasonable will at least once a year through a long and quarrelsome life. What she did not tell Mr. Updike was that the mention of Charles's will had reminded her of the day on which he signed the will and had left her for an unknown destination, and even as she thought of it her heart bled afresh for the loss of her youngest child, though that child was well and happy within a few yards of her.

"Don't forget," said Mr. Updike kindly to Charles, for he took a personal interest in all old clients and the children of old clients and was by now quite ready to take an interest in their grand-children, "that marriage invalidates a will, Charles."

"But I'm not married," said Charles, alarmed lest marriage should suddenly have come upon him unawares.

"Younger than you are happy fathers made," said Mr. Updike, "though I'm not sure if it is a good thing for all these young men to have wives and families before they have jobs. Still, that's the humour of it."

Charles, whose knowledge of the Bard was confined to such plays as he had rather unwillingly attended when a schoolboy and later in the army, where a certain number of officers and men were obliged to do fatigue when touring companies de-scended upon them in Africa and the East or even Cardiff, thought he didn't quite understand Mr. Updike but supposed it was all right. He knew a man, he said, who married an awfully pretty girl and he was twenty-three and the girl was twenty-one and they had two babies and lived in two rooms in Chelsea.

"But couldn't their parents do something for them?" said

Mrs. Belton, in whose experience parents, however badly off, always managed to do something for one.

Charles said that Joe, that was the name of the man, hadn't got any parents, only a grandmother, and he had spent all his year's income and his gratuity on the honeymoon and hadn't got a job. He thought Vivien, that was the name of the girl, had a family, but she had quarrelled with them and went on the stage.

It all sounded very peculiar to Mrs. Belton and not at all comfortable, which shows how sheltered her life had been and how little she really knew of the difficulties of the Brave New World that the young had partly forced upon them and partly were making for themselves. Though Lucy Thorne's family were of as good blood as any in Barsetshire and looked upon the Beltons with faint contempt for having made their money in trade, or in other words being the sixth generation from the Nabob, some people had said that she did well for herself when she married young Belton, bringing a very small dowry with her. Now the Belton fortunes had also shrunk, but although Thornes and Beltons were conscious of being badly off, they continued to lead something of their old life. If their houses were too large they lived in a corner of them like the Warings or the Bonds, or let the big house and moved into a smaller one as the Beltons had done. But there was always a house of dignity for them, there was always enough money, if carefully handled, for the present and a little to put away for the next generation, and though Mrs. Belton's world was tottering, she did not stand, as many of the new generation were standing, on the edge of a gulf. Of the life that the Joes and the Viviens were leading, the descent of decent young people into real squalor, the terrible nostalgie de la boue to which so many of them fell a prey, of all this she was entirely ignorant. Life in the country and in country towns had become hard, often very hard, but not yet sordid. Life in the towns was apt to run downhill only too easily, and the untaught young, schooled to hard work during the war but untrained in the art of gracious living and making the best of a little money, were slipping into a Slough of Despond. They were not unhappy in the Slough, though occasionally they had immortal longings in them, but they were not doing any particular good and she wondered what the future of their children would be. And on this topic she might have wondered indefinitely, for everyone's future is impenetrable darkness and most plans are thwarted, had not Charles indignantly disclaimed any idea of getting married. Even if he did want to get married, he said, he didn't see any girls. They were either married already, or they were doing jobs and doing them as well as a man, and Charles was Thorne enough to feel that his woman should be in a state of contented subjection.

"But there are *hundreds* of girls," said Mrs. Updike, who was at the moment nearly as upside down as the Quangle Wangle when he had to sit with his head in his slipper, having dropped the darning-needle on the grass and trying to find it without laying down her work.

Her elder son stooped, picked the needle up from the grass on the side where his mother was not looking, and restored it to her.

"Oh, thank you, my pet," said Mrs. Updike, rethreading her needle with concentration. "I mean there seem to be girls *everywhere.*"

The elder Updike girl said there were certainly millions of girls in London and in the towns, but there didn't seem to be many in Harefield.

Everyone thought, and it was but too true. Apart from the Hosiers' Girls' Foundation School, which wasn't Harefield, and a number of girls from the cottages, the two young Updikes appeared to be the only girls available. And very nice competent girls they were and will both make suitable marriages in time as Updikes always do; but they will probably marry in London or Cambridge where their work lies, for they in their turn find that there are no young men in Harefield. Dr. Perry's boys are all established in London in hospitals or Harley Street, everyone else is middle-aged or old.

"I wonder," said Mrs. Belton, "if the little country towns are going to die."

Her words were like a knell and made everyone uncomfortable. It sounded too probable. Too true a prophecy. The little groups of civilized people here and there were becoming marooned. Their girls were working too hard to think of marriage, their sons sought other brides. There was Francis Brandon, Mrs. Brandon's son at Stories. For many years he had been allotted in the minds of the county to one or another nice local girl. What had happened? He had married a newcomer, a widow. An enchanting widow it is true and she was making a charming wife and getting on like a house on fire with her mother-in-law, but she was not Barsetshire. There was Colin Keith, Mrs. Noel Merton's brother. He also had been allotted to one girl after another by the older people. Everyone had thought he would marry Susan Dean, but the thought did not appear to have occurred to the two people concerned. There was Oliver Marling, who appeared to be a born bachelor. All great waste, thought the ladies of Barsetshire. And there were all the delightful hard-working, well-born, and well-bred girls: Lucy Marling, absorbed in local work; Emmy Graham ferociously breeding cattle in Rushwater; Susan Dean doing the Red Cross work as well as a man; Clarissa Graham, who ought to be coming out and being presented, was going to college in the autumn. Everywhere the young men and the girls, on very friendly terms, but seeming under the surface to be in different camps. It was not the world that Mrs. Belton had been brought up in and she did not like it. Her elder son ought to marry. Charles ought to marry. Would either of them take the trouble? Or would they, even worse, slide into marriage with an outsider?

"I know," said Mrs. Belton, speaking very firmly, suddenly voicing her thoughts, "I know I shall like *all* my daughters-in-law, but I can't promise to like their families."

To which her elder son, who was very fond of his mother and had shared with her and only one other living soul the reason why his heart was unmoved by charmers, said she must not be rash, and she might find that she adored her son's in-laws but didn't like their wives.

"I shall adore *everybody*," said Mrs. Updike, her pretty, fine-drawn face flushing with enthusiasm. "Especially my grandchildren. It will be heavenly."

In proof of which she gave the darning-needle a very vigorous shove and then uttered a slight scream. A red patch appeared on the pillow-slip and rapidly spread.

"Oh dear," said Mrs. Updike. "I have pricked my finger again. Run upstairs my pet," she said turning to her elder daughter, "and get the sticking-plaster."

She let her sewing fall on the grass and applied herself to sucking her own blood like an amiable vampire. The elder Miss Updike shortly came back with a bowl of water, some cotton wool, a box of sticking-plaster, and a roll of bandage. While Mrs. Updike was dabbing her finger and much enjoying the elegant marbling that blood makes in water, a car was heard at the side gate and Dr. Perry came up the garden.

"At it again!" said Dr. Perry sardonically. "If I sent you a bill for every time I found your wife in trouble, Updike, I'd be a rich man."

"So would I," Mr. Updike retorted with some spirit, "if I sent you in a bill every time you bring me a letter to the B.M.A. that needs toning down. That's enough washing, Betty. I'll tie you up properly."

Mrs. Updike, holding out her thin, work-worn hand, said it was quite extraordinary how much blood came out of a small prick, and she had always had a thing about that needle which had pricked her before. Mrs. Belton meanwhile had picked up the pillow-slip and began to fold it. It was for some reason not easy to fold. She took the needle out, put it carefully into Mrs. Updike's needlebook, and shook the pillow-slip.

"Do you know what you have done?" she said to Mrs. Updike. "You have darned both sides together. The pillow can't get in."

At this bad news Mrs. Updike laughed her very young, carefree laugh and said she had an absolute thing about that pillow-slip, which was the one that always got its buttons torn off at the laundry. Then Dr. Perry began to talk about his three sons, Jim the brilliant young surgeon, Gus one of the leading authorities on skin diseases, and Bob already well known to Harley Street. The first two were already married to doctors' daughters who had brought money with them and had nice children. Dr. Robert Perry was not yet married, but his engagement to the daughter of the well-known consultant, Sir Featherly Hargreaves, had just been announced and no one had the faintest doubt that he would do extremely well and be a Knight and a Royal Physician before many years were gone.

His friends congratulated him warmly and Mrs. Belton felt that this very nice family were all marrying young and well. Of course the Perrys were not county, though the family had been physicians to the county for several generations and had a kind of squatters' right. Perhaps one had not to be county for one's children to marry properly now. Perhaps there was a kind of curse on those who still walked in the old ways and held by their own faith. Then she put these thoughts away from her as ungrateful, for was not Elsa at least well and happily married. But her Charles, through whose innocent fault her heart would never again be at peace; her Freddy, whose heart had lost its love and remained faithful to a ghost; what was there for them? Then she blamed herself for being morbid and talked to the elder Updike children, and when Charles came back from seeing the puppies she said they must go home as people were coming to tea and Charles had to get back to Beliers.

"Good-bye, Charles, and don't forget to come to me about a fresh will when you get married," said Mr. Updike.

Mrs. Updike bade them all an affectionate farewell, only marred by the bandage coming off and the finger beginning to bleed again; the young Updikes in the fewest possible words expressed their pleasure at the visit and then the Belton family went back to Arcot House.

It was a warm afternoon and Mrs. Belton would have liked to have tea in the garden, where there was a cedar most suitable for having tea under, but her faithful maid and ex-nurse Wheeler was adamant on this subject. If the gentry wanted tea in the garden they must do it properly. When she was in the nursery, said Wheeler, tea in the garden *was* tea in the garden. The footmen brought out the tables with their lace tablecloths and disposed cakes and bread and butter in thin curly rolls upon them; the butler bore the silver tray with its silver kettle, teapot, sugar-basin, sugar-tongs, milk-jug, cream-jug, long silver trumpet for extinguishing the flame, and other suitable accessories. But tea out of doors without menservants was, in Wheeler's opinion, entirely against etiquette, so tea was laid in the drawing-room and the sun warmed the windows that looked south over the garden.

The first guests were Lady Graham and her second daughter, Clarissa, whose unexpected passion for engineering draughtsmanship had caused her to work furiously at mathematics and carry off a very good scholarship. Like most of the women of her family she had happily missed the awkward flapper age and was as elegant and self-possessed as a very young lady can be without being a conspicuous prig. Much to the amusement of Admiral Hornby and Captain Belton, she greeted them with the tempered affability that the wife of the First Lord of the Admiralty might show to a midshipman, an attitude that roused Elsa Hornby's resentment. Charles, not very perceptive of these undercurrents, accepted her as Clarissa Graham, whom he had known since she was a little girl, and was entirely unimpressed by her worldy wisdom, so they got on excellently.

"How nice your Charles looks," said Lady Graham to Mrs. Belton. "He is a master at Eton, isn't he?"

Mrs. Belton said not exactly; he was an assistant master at the Priory School.

"Of *course*," said Lady Graham, who obviously could not imagine any son of any of her friends being a master at any school but Eton. "The school the Warings' nephew has, or is it their niece? Is it for backward boys?"

"No, Agnes," said Mrs. Belton firmly, "it is *not* a school for backward boys. It is just a prep school and the boys are mostly from naval families."

"Like your nice Freddy and Elsa's delightful husband," said Lady Graham. "It all sounds perfectly delightful and you must come to Little Misfit and tell mamma about it. She is so fond of Robin Dale, who is such a friend of Martin's, partly because they both lost legs or feet in Italy, poor darlings," said Lady Graham, an expression of incredibly sweet sadness on her still lovely face. "Darling Charles, tell me all about your boys."

"Well, there really isn't much to tell," said Charles, basely deserting Clarissa for her mother. But Clarissa was used to this and, being wise in her generation, she had also noticed that even her enchanting mother was a little neglected when her grandmother Lady Emily Leslie was in the room, and had determined that in good time she would so outshine her own daughter and her granddaughters.

"Are they nice people, your schoolmaster and schoolmistress?" said Lady Graham. "Mamma will want to know *everything* about them and I must bring her over to see the school if this warm weather goes on and her neuritis is better."

Charles said the Winters were very nice and so were the boys and he was awfully lucky to have such a nice job. But he wasn't thinking very much about what he was saying, because he had suddenly fallen in love with Lady Graham and was walking in rose-pink clouds and golden light. Most men, young and old, who knew Agnes Graham had fallen in love with her at one time or another, which passion left her entirely unmoved, partly because she was so very fond of her husband, General Sir Robert Graham, K.C.B., partly, as her brother David Leslie had often remarked, because she was too divinely silly to notice anything.

But Charles had been a soldier and knew that duty must come before love, and time was getting on.

"I say, Lady Graham, I am most awfully sorry," he said, "but I have to be back at the Priory by seven. It was so awfully nice to see you and I was awfully glad to see Clarissa again and I am awfully sorry Lady Emily has neuritis and it would be really most awfully good of you to come over and see the school and the Winters would be awfully pleased."

To which impassioned appeal Lady Graham made no particular answer, but looking at him with doves' eyes murmured something kind in her soft cooing voice, which Clarissa looked on with a kind of sardonic friendliness. Charles then kissed his mother and sister, bade a general good-bye, and went off on his bicycle. And so deeply had Lady Graham taken possession of his heart and senses that he missed the turning at Worsted and went quite a mile and a half out of his way, only just getting to the Priory in time.

Mrs. Belton did not like to lose Charles, but he had his work and that was that, so she continued to talk with Lady Graham while Clarissa practised charm on Mr. Belton until her mother took her away.

"Nice girl that girl of Agnes Graham's," said Mr. Belton.

Elsa said she thought Clarissa was rather spoilt.

"That's only because she didn't worship your husband," said Admiral Hornby. "It's time you realized, my girl, that to young women of Clarissa's age I am an old fogey."

Captain Belton said he supposed he was an old fogey too.

His sister told him not to be silly and said it was high time he got married. Not, she added, that she wished him to marry Clarissa, who was a bit of a minx, but if he could find a nice girl who was even half as nice as Christopher was, he had better marry her at once. By which inane remark her husband was suddenly touched, for his rather farouche Elsa was still a little untamed and only by chance did she sometimes betray how deeply she adored him.

"Well, find me a girl half as nice as Christopher and I'll consider it," said Captain Belton, and his mother, quietly listening, wondered if he meant what he said, whether his heart was beginning to live again.

"Lucy!" said Mr. Belton. "I've just remembered a confoundedly awkward thing."

"Yes, Fred," said his wife calmly. "Do tell us."

Mr. Belton embarked upon a long, angry, and rather rambling statement, the upshot of which was that the Conservative Association were having what they called a rally next month and, with hideous disregard of county interest, had chosen to have it at Staple Park on the 29th of July.

To his family this did not appear unreasonable. Lord Bond was a staunch supporter of the Conservative Party, and there was nothing wrong with the 29th. If, said Captain Belton, it had been the 29th of February it might make one think, because then it would be leap year, which it wasn't. But the 29th of July was quite normal.

"It's no joking matter, Freddy," said Mr. Belton ominously. "The Barsetshire Pig-Breeders have had that date fixed for a year past."

Admiral Hornby said they might alter it. Or Lord Bond might alter the date of the Conservative Rally.

Mr. Belton nearly told his distinguished son-in-law not to be a fool, but controlling himself, though rather red in the face, he said that Bond had a good dairy herd and some good bulls, but about pigs he knew nothing at all. If, said Mr. Belton, the Conservatives were against pig-breeding, let them come out into the open. Even Lord Stoke, whose dairy herd was as good as anyone's, understood pigs. Stoke, he said, would as soon spend half an hour on a Sunday after morning service leaning over a sty and scratching a pig's back with his stick, as any man in England. It was all an infernal muddle.

It was then that Captain Belton showed the stuff of which the British Navy is made.

"Where are the Pig-Breeders having their show, sir?" he said to his father.

Mr. Belton said angrily that it wasn't fixed. It was to have been on the Duke's estate, but there was a nasty swine-fever scare in West Barsetshire and they didn't want to risk having to cancel the meeting.

"Well, sir," said Captain Belton, "it seems to me that the Pig-Breeders might do worse than ask Lord Bond if they can have their show at Staple Park, and kill two birds with one stone."

As a father Mr. Belton naturally felt obliged to pick holes in his suggestion. It was unheard of, he said, to combine a Conservative Rally with a Pig-Breeders' meeting. The gutter press, he said, thereby meaning all newspapers, would make political capital out of it and throw mud. Captain Belton did not press his point, for he really did not very much care which meetings took place where, but he noticed with kindly amusements that his father was gradually talking himself round and was in a fair way to take up the suggestion with enthusiasm. Mr. Belton then went off to visit the old cow-man, a piece of Sunday ritual. The naval gentlemen talked shop and Mrs. Belton and Elsa talked about the children and how much they were looking forward to their grandparents' visit to Aberdeathly in September; though this was not strictly true, for the young Hornbys had little or no recollection of their grandparents, owing to their tender age.

After supper Mr. Belton retired to the so-called library, which was really a kind of makeshift estate room, and was heard by the family bellowing impatiently into the telephone. Presently he came back to the drawing-room, sat down in his favourite chair, and ostentatiously opened the Sunday paper, which it was his habit to ignore until the evening. His family went on talking about nothing in particular.

"Well," said Mr. Belton, secretly mortified by their apparent indifference, "nothing in the paper as usual. We don't seem to have any luck in the by-elections."

"Never mind, father," said his daughter Elsa. "Wait till the municipal elections in the autumn."

Mr. Belton said he would probably be dead then, but finding that this statement roused no interest, he brought out his trump card.

"I suppose you wondered what I was telephoning about?" he said, looking round with the pride of a dog who lovingly lays a half-dead rat at his master's feet.

Elsa said under her breath that they weren't. Her husband, not approving rudeness to parents, even under the breath, said to Mr. Belton that they would very much like to know.

"Well, Freddy," said Mr. Belton, "old heads do sometimes grow on young shoulders and your idea wasn't a bad one. I have been speaking to Bond and Stoke—it's a funny thing Stoke's deafness is much less trying on the telephone—and Fielding and they are quite ready to discuss it."

Admiral Hornby asked who Fielding was.

"Chancellor of the diocese, Sir Robert Fielding," said Mr. Belton, impatient with anyone so ignorant. "His wife is a charming woman. He stood for the Conservative interest at the General Election and was beaten by Adams of Hogglestock. He is political and Stoke is pigs and Bond is a bit of both, and they all think a combined Conservative Rally and pig show would be a splendid thing for the county."

Mr. Belton's family were loud in their applause and even managed tactfully to convey the impression that it was Mr. Belton's own plan. And indeed Mr. Belton by now almost came to think that it was, but he generously allowed some credit to his elder son for having as it were helped to extract the idea from his father's mind.

Captain Belton lingered behind the others to talk to his mother, for the presence of so much family had made conversation general. The evening light, untrue though one knew it to be, was very lovely, giving to garden, trees, and distant park the nostalgic artificiality of a beautiful stage scene.

"Isn't Clarissa a charming girl?" said Mrs. Belton.

"The answer, my dear mamma," said Captain Belton, "is Yes and No. Regarded as a dainty rogue in porcelain crossed with a sweet girl graduate in her golden hair, she is a perfect work of art. But, to use the word which the lower orders now use to an extent that practically puts it out of court for us, a little too sophisticated. She may go to college and be a learned pig, but she must obviously marry a guardsman. And in any case, to set your mind at rest, I am much too old for her."

Mrs. Belton said she was very sorry, because she had thought Freddy liked her.

"I did, darling mamma," said Captain Belton. "I was captivated. But that doesn't make one want to marry people."

Mrs. Belton said, with slight hauteur, that she had not said anything about marrying people.

"Never mind, mamma dear," said her son. "I understand you perfectly well and you understand me. How well Elsa is looking! If I were Christopher I'd beat her occasionally."

His mother said it all came of girls having had responsible jobs during the war. In her younger days, she said, they had married almost straight out of the schoolroom and perhaps it was a good thing that the girls like Elsa had seen the world before they married.

"My good mamma," said Captain Belton, "you may have married young, but you have held more responsible jobs than anyone I know ever since I can remember. Being in an office like Elsa means nothing. You run about with blinkers on and get puffed up. Short of being Prime Minister I know nobody who has taken more responsibilities in every way than you. Harefield and a family and all your county work. Elsa doesn't know what experience means."

Mrs. Belton said Freddy was exaggerating, but all the same her heart warmed to his praise. She then tried to be fair to everyone by pointing out Elsa's devotion to her husband and children, the way she had tackled the big place in Scotland and was also helping Christopher to stand for Parliament if and when there was a General Election.

"I admit it all," said Captain Belton, "and I'm very fond of Elsa and she and Christopher obviously suit each other down to the ground. But until further notice I consider you a much more useful and important person and that's that."

No mother is entirely unsusceptible to flattery from a son, and if she thinks the flattery is partly true, why all the better, and she let the subject of Clarissa drop. But inside herself she continued to think that eighteen and thirty-eight were really very suitable ages and determined to see more of Agnes Graham.

"Quite a strange event," said Mrs. Tebben at supper to her husband and her son Richard. "I was coming back on my bicycle from the Manor House, where I had been having tea with Louise, and just at the crossroads I nearly ran into that nice young master we met today. He was lost and I had to put him right for the Priory."

"Anyone might lose their way at the crossroads," said Richard, "unless they happened to know where they were. It's all the fault of that signpost that says Worsted ¾ mile on one arm and Worsted 1½ mile on the other."

"But they are both correct," said Mr. Tebben. "As a matter of curiosity I have paced them and one takes exactly twice as long as the other."

Richard, who had been pushing some food about rather unkindly with his fork, asked what it was.

"Just one of our little peace-time makeshifts," said Mrs. Tebben gaily. "A bit of Spam left over from a tin sent by that kind American friend of your father's with some of last night's macaroni cheese and a few nasturtium pods. Oh, and the end of a bottle of Worcester sauce that I found on the top shelf of the larder. I think Mrs. Phipps must have hidden it. She can only come two days a week now, Richard, because she is looking after Doris's children while Doris goes to work four days a week at the aeroplane factory. You know Doris married Bert Margett who was head porter at Worsted. He is station-master now since Mr. Patten retired."

"In Sweden," said Richard, "married women with children wouldn't be going to work."

If his parents felt, as they had had every occasion to feel during the last few days, that they never wished to hear how things were ordered in Sweden again, they were afraid to say so.

"But Doris likes it," said Mrs. Tebben. "She was a railway porter at Winter Overcotes all through the war and when she got married she missed the company. She is a very good wife and mother, and Mrs. Phipps looks after the children splendidly."

Richard said possibly that was so, but it was a pity the day-nursery system had not been introduced into England. In Stockholm, he said, the day nurseries were models of efficiency and the children were growing up civically minded.

"But, my dear boy," said his mother, embarking joyfully upon what she hoped would be an interesting and stimulating discussion, "that is all very well for a town. Worsted is the country and the conditions are so different. You must go and see Mrs. Phipps. The cottage is so clean and the children so well and happy."

"Anders Krogsbrog, a remarkably intelligent exponent of civic economics," said Richard, "has written an extremely interesting paper on the Parent-right and State-right and their influence on children. It is in Swedish, so you wouldn't understand it."

"Yes, I would," said his father without heat.

"I thought it was Icelandic, father," said Richard, surprised. For Mr. Tebben was, as we know, perhaps the leading authority in England on the Icelandic Sagas and a corresponding member of societies for Icelandic study wherever such societies exist.

"So it is," said Mr. Tebben. "It is also the Scandinavian languages in general. During the last war, Richard, which you cannot remember as you were barely born then, I was in the censor's department dealing with Scandinavian affairs. My spoken languages are, of course, very rusty now, but I find no difficulty in reading. I should like to see the pamphlets you mention."

To say that Richard was flabbergasted is to put it mildly. All through his rather ungracious life he had despised his parents, though they might with equal rights have despised him for wasting his time and their hard-earned money at Oxford and taking a poor third. But parents are incorrigible forgivers and also moral cowards, so no one had ever told Richard how badly he had behaved and he had continued to despise them. Chance had brought him to the notice of Mr. Dean, father of Susan Dean. Mr. Dean had given him a job on the business side of his engineering firm, in which he had done well, and he had later been taken into the business of Mr. Adams, the great Hogglestock ironmaster. Here he had also done well and was now, as we have already heard, second in command of the Stockholm agency. He had never so far as his parents knew, though this we must admit does not count for much, been in love, and Mrs. Tebben took every opportunity of annoying her son in a well-meaning way by calling his attention to various young ladies of a suitable age.

"You would like Krogsbrog, father," said Richard, finally giving up the struggle with his mother's made-dish and laying his knife and fork down with an unnecessarily disgusted air.

"An egg!" exclaimed Mrs. Tebben. "Not that the hens are laying at the moment, but Louise Palmer gave me half a dozen and one is slightly cracked and needs using. I can whisk it up with a little marge and some of my dried herbs into a French omelet in a moment."

"Oh, don't fuss, mother," said Richard. "I'm dining with the Deans tomorrow and I'll get heaps to eat there."

"That," said Mr. Tebben, adjusting his pince-nez and looking at his son, "is not the way to speak to your mother, Richard."

If a jelly-fish had suddenly grown legs and walked Richard could not have been more surprised. All through his hobblede-

hoyhood he had unmercifully browbeaten and bullied his parents, who were too gentlemanly to hit back; a foolish position we
admit, but how many parents can lay their hand on their heart
and say that they have not weakly given in to their children?
Their daughter Margaret was as sweet and loving as Richard
was difficult, but Margaret had married Susan Dean's eldest
brother, Laurence, years ago and lived much abroad. Then
Richard had also gone abroad, first to the Argentine for Mr.
Dean, then to Sweden for Mr. Adams. And while he was away
his father had noticed how much more easy home life had
become.

"When Richard next comes home, Winifred," he had said to
his wife while Richard was in Sweden, "I think it is my duty to
make him understand that I will not be treated like an elderly
half-wit, nor will I tolerate his manner to you."

To which Mrs. Tebben, whose feelings towards her son were
a mixture of idolatry and fear and pride, had replied that Richard
was very sensitive.

"So am I," said Mr. Tebben. "And so are you, my dear, if it
comes to that."

And he went for a long walk by himself and came to the
conclusion that he had been weak with Richard far too long. It
was partly, he knew, to avoid friction with his wife, partly
because of the natural cowardice that many parents feel when
confronted with the next generation, and partly, he must own,
laziness. For what with his work as a Civil Servant and his
private work on Icelandic and Scandinavian subjects, he had
been so busy that he shrank from domestic scenes. Also he was
in London for most of the week and so avoided them. But now
he had retired he saw no reason why his pleasure in the company
of a son of whom he was fond should be so ruined by that son's
uppishness. So he made a secret resolve to take Richard up very
sharply when he next needed it.

"I'm sorry, father," said Richard, who was then so much

surprised by his own apology that he could find nothing else to say.

"That is right, Richard," said his father, "and I hope we shall not have to mention the subject again. I have read Krogsbrog's book on the legal aspect of the Laxdaela and Njal Stories and found it very interesting, though of course his views are limited by his politico-economic views. We had some correspondence about it, but you were in the Argentine then."

"In Swedish, father?" said Richard.

"It was easier," said Mr. Tebben, permitting himself a tight-lipped smile of effortless superiority. "Krogsbrog's English though fluent is so colloquial as to be almost incomprehensible. So like educated foreigners. What is he like; personally I mean?"

"Oh, I hardly know him, father," said Richard. "He's an awfully big person and very rich. He owns an iron-ore deposit that we are negotiating about. I've met his daughter Petrea. She is frightfully keen on social work and child welfare."

Mrs. Tebben, whose eyes were almost moist at this conversation in which both her men were doing her such credit, said Petrea didn't sound like a Swedish name. It sounded more Eastern.

"I expect," said her husband very kindly, "you are thinking of the rock city of Petra, my dear. Probably Richard's friend is called after Petrea who put the clothes-peg on her nose one night to try to improve its shape."

"I say, father, you do know a lot!" said Richard, an ingenuous expression of admiration that flattered Mr. Tebben more than all the tributes of learned societies. "There's a statue of Fredrika Bremer in Stockholm; I saw it. Petrea loves her books."

At this point it appeared that the millennium had set in, but an ill-advised reference by Mrs. Tebben to some jam tarts that had just a tiny bit of mould on them but she had wiped it off and just warmed them through in the oven caused Richard's brow to darken ominously. His father watched him but made no comment and Richard added, though without quite the ring of conviction that might have been wished, that he expected the tarts wouldn't kill anybody and probably the mould was only penicillin. The rest of supper passed uneventfully and Mrs. Tebben's struggling Martha-like heart was made happier than it had been for a long time. Richard went out to the Woolsack about nine o'clock to see if he would meet any old friends, and Mrs. Tebben praised her husband for his courage and tact in a way he was not at all accustomed to.

"Do you think Richard is in love with Miss Krogsbrog?" she asked.

Mr. Tebben said he hadn't the faintest idea, but if Richard was to get married he ought to do something about it as he was thirty-three or thirty-four, he never could remember the children's ages, and apparently doing very well at his job.

"Do you remember the summer Richard got his third in Greats, Gilbert?" said Mrs. Tebben. "It was the year Louise Palmer had the performance of *Hippolytus* in the barn and Margaret got engaged to Laurence Dean, and when Jessica fell off the donkey and Richard saved her life."

"So he did," said Mr. Tebben, "and laid the foundation of a prosperous business career with Dean's firm."

"We all thought," said Mrs. Tebben, "that he might be thinking of Susan Dean. He called his little car after her."

"I never thought anything about it," said Mr. Tebben. "Who were the thinkers?"

"Oh, everybody," said Mrs. Tebben vaguely. "Louise Palmer and Lady Bond and the Deans' nurse and Mrs. Phipps and quite a lot of people."

"All I can say is that no one said anything to me about it," said Mr. Tebben, "and if they had I shouldn't have taken any notice. And I don't suppose he is in love with Petrea Krogsbrog either."

Mrs. Tebben sighed. Her husband, who was feeling particularly well disposed to his wife since he had asserted his supremacy in the house, asked very kindly what it was.

"Nothing, Gilbert," said Mrs. Tebben. "At least I was thinking how many young men are unmarried and it seems rather a waste. Richard and that nice Charles Belton we met today and Colin Keith and Oliver Marling and several others whose names escape me."

"Not like us, are they, my dear?" said Mr. Tebben. "I can still see the blue muslin dress you wore the day we visited Christiania, which I shall *not* call Oslo. I fell in love with you on the spot and I don't think we wasted much time."

"You looked so nice in your grey flannels," said Mrs. Tebben, "and I wondered if mother would like you."

"I think life was easier and better then," said Mr. Tebben. "Well, Richard must look after himself. He is a good boy but he is taking a long time to ripen."

"You have been very patient, Gilbert," said Mrs. Tebben. "And Richard is partly my fault. I did spoil him rather. Oh, Gilbert, a knotty point. I think the red speckled hen, the one we call Pandora, has really stopped laying and Louise Palmer is going to let me have some ten-day-old chicks to rear, so shall we kill Pandora?"

Mr. Tebben said that the hens were his wife's province and he supposed what she meant was *who* was to kill the hen and whoever it was it wouldn't be himself.

"But, Gilbert, it is quite easy to wring their necks if you know how," said Mrs. Tebben.

"And I have been told by Lucy Marling, that rather terrifying Amazon," said Mr. Tebben, "that to slit their throats with a sharp knife is as easy as jumping off a table. I have no wish to do either, nor will I wring anyone's neck."

"Than," said Mrs. Tebben resignedly, "I suppose it means bribing old Phipps as usual. Ah, well."

When Charles got back to the Priory he just had time to wash his hands before the early supper which was the rule on Sundays and indeed on most other days because Selina liked to spend the evening with her husband, and Marigold wanted to meet one of her many swains, though talking to Selina over their tea she said she was properly browned off with the boys. All the nice boys she said were going into the air force or the army or something and didn't take a bit of interest like.

"There's Geoff Coxon," said Marigold. "He's a lovely boy, Mrs. Hopkins, but he's eighteen and going into the navy and he can't talk about nothing else. Him and me and some boy friends and their lady friends we was all going to the Barchester Odeon on Friday night to see Glamora Tudor in *She Kissed and Told* and when we got there the ninepennies were full up and one of the boys said he'd just had a birthday and he'd treat us to the one and six-pennies and Geoff said the picture wasn't worth it and he'd like to see the film about Nelson at the Propeelium, and I said did we come to Barchester to see Glamora Tudor or not, and Geoff was quite nasty."

Unmoved by this tragedy, Selina told Marigold to finish her tea because there was the young gentlemen's supper to get.

"Funny name for a cinema," said Marigold reflectively. "But it's there all right. Look, Mrs. Hopkins."

She pointed with a dirty finger tipped with a repulsive purple-red nail to a copy of the *Barchester Advertiser* that Selina had laid on the kitchen table to save dirtying it. Selina followed the raddled finger and saw the words "Propylæum Cinema: *The Lass that Loved a Sailor* (U)."

"And a U-film too!" said Marigold. "So I'm not going with Geoff Coxon, Mrs. Hopkins."

Selina remarked mildly that Geoff Coxon's father was going to take Geoff into his garage when he was out of the army and there was no need for Marigold to cut off her nose to spite her own face and to hurry up with her tea.

"Ow," said Marigold, whose seat faced the kitchen window, "there's Mr. Belton putting his bike away," to which Selina made no answer at all and determined to ask her mother to speak to Marigold, for Nannie Allen could be relied upon to deal faithfully with the young and Marigold had a wholesome awe of her, contracted in the days when she was sent by her mother to help Nannie after school hours.

Charles Belton had by now joined his headmaster and wife in the study, where were also a senior and a junior master, though neither was much older than Charles, the rest of the staff being out for the evening. During supper Charles was posted in any important events that had occurred while he was at Harefield. Addison had been stung by a wasp and was a good deal swollen but enjoying the fuss. Pickering had fallen off his bicycle and abraded his knees, but luckily it was knickerbockers not trousers, so it didn't matter. But the crowning exploit was young Dean, who had had the extraordinary luck of nose-bleeding in church and had to be taken out by the vicar's wife and given first aid in the churchyard.

"I can't tell you what a blessing it is to have Octavia at the vicarage," said Leslie Winter. "She is very competent. If we had the Black Death at Lambton she would know exactly the right things to do and the right forms to fill up. And everyone likes Tommy so much and I am sure he will be a bishop."

The junior master asked if one could be a bishop with only one arm. To this no one could give an answer, but there was a general impression that once an ordained clergyman, no physical defect could stop one's progress. The senior master said he believed that in some churches certain physical defects were a bar to priesthood, but as he either did not know or did not like to say what those defects were, the discussion perished for lack of nourishment.

"You don't know the Needhams, do you?" said Leslie to Charles Belton. "I must ask them to dinner one evening. She is Dr. Crawley's younger daughter."

Charles said that the Crawleys were old friends of his people and he thought his sister had been at the Barchester High School with Octavia Crawley, and then the talk went back to school topics again, varied by talk of the war, for all the masters present had seen service in one form or another.

The senior master said that the one good thing to be said for schoolmastering was that you always came across fellows who had been somewhere where you had been, or knew some fellows that you had known. Not but what, said the junior master, it could be a bit awkward sometimes. For instance, before he came to the Priory he had applied for a job at a school in Norfolk and found that he would be senior to his own ex-commanding officer which would have been very awkward; but luckily they wanted someone who could do games and ever since he had crashed in a fog somewhere in Kent his right wrist had been a bit wonky.

"By the way," said Charles, "I got a bit mixed up at the Worsted crossroads, because all the signposts say Worsted, like all roads leading to Rome, and I completely lost my bearings. It was awfully stupid of me, but I suppose I wasn't thinking where I was going, and that Mrs. Tebben who was here yesterday came along on her bicycle and very kindly put me right. She said she was sure I must have met her son somewhere, but I couldn't make out whether she meant in the war or on the Worsted road."

Philip said that was very characteristic of Mrs. Tebben.

"While you were helping Susan with the books yesterday," he added, "Mrs. Tebben did say that she wondered if you and her son Richard, who was a conceited young man before the war whatever he may be now, had come across each other."

Charles said he didn't remember meeting anyone named Tebben.

"And she said that the wonderful comradeship between young men who had been in the army made her hopeful for the future," Philip added, to which his three assistant masters with one voice said: "Oh Lord!"

Charles looked so anxious that Philip had to reassure him that he was not likely to see much of Richard Tebben, who was only at Worsted on holiday, his present job being in Sweden.

"Unless of course you meet him at the Deans," said Leslie. "I believe he was rather in love with that nice Susan Dean before the war."

For some reason which we will not attempt to explain, Charles for the moment felt that Richard Tebben's society was going to give him no pleasure at all.

"Is young Dean who had the nose-bleeding any relation of the Deans you were talking about, sir?" he asked his headmaster.

"Grandson," said Philip. "Son of Laurence Dean, who married Margaret Tebben. Nephew of Susan Dean, whom you met here. He is as clever as the rest of his family. I should not be in the least surprised if he made his nose bleed deliberately."

The senior master said he had once made himself sick to avoid going to the dancing class, but he didn't know if one could make one's nose bleed.

The rest of the evening was uneventful and everyone went to bed early because of Monday next day.

CHAPTER 3

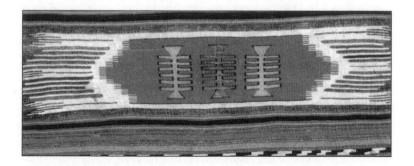

On Monday morning Miss Susan Dean, Depot Librarian of the St. John and Red Cross Hospital Libraries, did a good deal of telephoning from her office. The dinner-party to which Richard Tebben had been invited for Monday evening was getting out of hand. It had begun as a family party of Mr. and Mrs. Dean, their daughter Susan, and Richard. Then the vicar of Lambton and his wife had been asked. Then Lucy Marling had rung up from Marling Hall to say she wanted to talk to Susan about a Red Cross Fête at Marling and could she come to dinner? Then Susan's sister Jessica, whose theatre did not open on Mondays, said she would spend Monday night with them and so they were two men short. Not that anyone took much notice of even numbers now, especially with double summer time and dining at what was really teatime, but Mrs. Dean, who liked her parties to be rather over- than under-manned, suddenly decided at breakfast that it was absolutely essential to have two more men.

Mrs. Dean was one of those women for whom other people toil. She was not selfish, but somehow she always managed like Mother Carey to sit quite still and by some subtle influence cause things to be done. So when Mrs. Dean was mildly exercised at breakfast about her dinner-party, her daughter Susan said she would find some men and her mother wasn't to bother.

"Only *not* Sir Edmund Pridham," said Mrs. Dean, "because

he doesn't like parties if Mrs. Brandon isn't there." Which showed in Mrs. Dean more perception than most of her friends gave her credit for.

As Susan drove into Barchester in her little car, she ran over the names of eligible gentlemen in her mind and found her task less easy than she had expected. Francis Brandon, being now a married man, was useless. Colin Keith was in London. There was Canon Joram, the ex-Bishop of Mngangaland, but he didn't quite seem to fit. Various very young men who might have done as stopgaps were doing their naval, military, or air service. The names of several more impossibles flashed before her and she felt annoyed. Surely there were as many men as there ever had been. In her particular circle the war had spared nearly all her friends. It was all most annoying. Then she thought of Charles Belton, whom she had met at the Priory School, and as soon as she got to the office she rang him up, forgetting that he would by now be in school. So she had to leave a message for him to ring her up at lunchtime and think again. There seemed to be nothing for it but to ask Lucy's brother Oliver. He was very nice and had good manners and probably her mother would like him. So she rang up Lucy Marling, who undertook to bring her brother at half past seven, dead or alive. Susan then complained to Lucy about the difficulty of getting enough men to satisfy her mother's appetite for even numbers.

"I'll tell you what," said Lucy Marling. "Ask Freddy Belton, Charles's elder brother. I know he's on leave at the moment because I saw him at Cousin Emily's on Saturday."

Susan said she really couldn't ask a man she didn't know at less than a day's notice, to which Lucy said rot. But Susan was adamant, said good-bye to Lucy, and thought of men. But no more men came into her head, and her morning's work was now on the table, so she decided to hope for Charles and stop worrying, which turned out to be a reasonable decision, for at half past twelve Charles rang up and said he would love to come and his headmaster had been awfully nice about it.

The Depot Librarian then had lunch at the Red Cross canteen and got through a good deal of work with her calm efficiency till between three and four, when cups of tea began to appear and a general relaxation took place. While Susan was drinking her tea the telephone rang. Her secretary answered it.

"A Captain Belton wants to know if he can see you," said her secretary.

Susan, who had a vague impression that Charles Belton had left the army with the rank of captain, in which she was perfectly correct, wondered why a schoolmaster should be loose in Barchester at four o'clock on a Monday afternoon and asked the doorkeeper to send Captain Belton up. In a few seconds the door was opened and in came a stranger. He was about Charles's height but less broadly built. His eyes were deep set and very blue, and Susan had a quick impression that he must be very like his mother, whoever she was.

"Miss Dean?" said the stranger.

"I am Miss Dean," said Susan. "I am so sorry. I thought they said you were Captain Belton."

"As far as I know, I am," said the stranger.

"But I met Captain Belton at Beliers on Saturday," said Susan.

The stranger laughed.

"On the contrary, it is I who am sorry," he said. "Charles and I are both captains, but I'm Royal Navy. I am Freddy. I do hope it doesn't matter."

Perhaps Susan had been a little flattered by the impression that Charles Belton had sought her out at the Red Cross; at any rate she coloured slightly and her secretary thought Miss Dean was looking quite her best and it must be that the warm weather suited her. Susan pulled herself together and asked Captain Belton what she could do for him. The secretary brought forward a chair and he sat down.

"Will you want me, Miss Dean?" said the secretary, who was

a very nice girl and cherished a romantic admiration for the Depot Librarian.

"I don't think so," said Susan, "but you might get on those letters for me to sign and I'll ring if I need you. And now, Captain Belton, how can we help you?"

"First of all," said Captain Belton, "I want to thank you. I was in the *Barsetshire* during part of the war, and the county, as you know, adopted us and we got a lot of books through the Barchester Red Cross. Of course a formal expression of our gratitude was made, but I was talking about it to my mother, and she said I ought to call at the office and tell you myself how grateful we were, and I was in Barchester today, so I thought I'd look in. That's really all and I do hope it isn't a nuisance."

As Captain Belton spoke, his blue eyes became even bluer with enthusiasm and Susan was visited by a passing thought that Charles might be better looking but Captain Belton was more interesting. Why she could not quite say. Perhaps a combination of his very pleasant manner with an impression that he didn't care who she was except as the Red Cross Depot Librarian. Having delivered himself of his thanks, he sat at ease and Susan observed that his hair and complexion were a good deal darker than his younger brother's.

"That is very nice of you, Captain Belton," she said, "and I wish our County President could hear you. I will just see if she is in the office."

She pressed the buzzer and her secretary appeared.

"Will you see if Lady Pomfret is in the office," said Susan, "and say that Captain Belton who is here would like to tell her how our work was appreciated on the *Barsetshire*."

"In," Captain Belton corrected her; or at least conveyed the correction to the secretary without appearing to criticize Miss Dean.

"My mother has met you at Red Cross meetings," said Captain Belton as the secretary left the room. "She said you wouldn't remember her because she was only an audience, but she remembers you very well."

It was difficult to make quite the right response to this, and Susan wondered if Captain Belton realized that the Deans were not county. Not but what the county liked the Deans, who had won their position partly owing to their relationship to Mr. Palmer at Worsted, but mostly because of their niceness and their willing help in all county enterprises, and would probably be allowed to slide into the county ranks in the present generation. The secretary then opened the door and stood aside to let Lady Pomfret come in.

"What luck that I was kept in the office," she said, shaking hands warmly with Captain Belton. "I didn't know you were at home, Freddy. How are Lucy and Cousin Fred?"

"Quite bobbish," said Captain Belton, "and Elsa is down with Chris for a week, and Charles has gone and turned himself into a schoolmaster at Beliers. How are Gillie and the children?"

"I had a bad winter with Gillie," said the countess sitting down and crossing her elegant legs. "I thought he would have pleurisy and pneumonia again and again, and he *will* go up and sit in the Lords. But since this warm spell he has really been much better. You must come to the Towers for a night and tell him about the *Barsetshire*. The children would love to see you too. And what are you doing, Freddy? Going to get married?"

Captain Belton said he was having a spell at the Admiralty and that was how he happened to be at home for a long weekend and he was going up to town that night.

"Well, let us know as soon as you are down again," said the countess, and she kissed Captain Belton and went away.

The Depot Librarian, who had been rather ostentatiously busied with papers during the brief encounter, stood up as her chief left the office.

"Good old Sally," said Captain Belton. "It's a dog's life being in her shoes, but she adores Gillie and that's that. Thank you very much, Miss Dean. And I hope you will let my mother come and see you some time when she is in Barchester, which isn't very often now. She is always grateful to anyone who has been kind to Charles and me. And she is extraordinarily nice," he added.

He then shook hands rather painfully, made a gesture as of a kind of friendly, unofficial salute, and went away. Susan pressed the buzzer and the secretary came back with a sheaf of letters for signing.

"Wasn't it lucky that Lady Pomfret hadn't gone?" said the secretary, standing by the window and looking out at the High Street.

"I didn't know she was a relation of Captain Belton's," said Susan, signing her letters in her neat writing.

"It's really Lord Pomfret," said the secretary. "Mrs. Belton was a Thorne and old Lady Pomfret was a Thorne of another branch. Lord Pomfret is a nephew of old Lord Pomfret of course, not of Lady Pomfret, so it isn't a real cousinship, but they treat it as one."

"How on earth do you know all these things?" said Susan, blotting her last signature.

"Oh, I don't know," said the secretary. "One just does. Mother had an old aunt over at Allington when she was a girl, Aunt Lily Dale, and she was great on families and used to snap mother's head off if she didn't know who was whose relation, especially in East Barsetshire. She had some kind of dislike to the de Courcys, mother never knew why, and wouldn't talk about them, but otherwise she was a walking *Who's Who*. Is there any more to do, Miss Dean?"

Susan thanked her secretary and said she could go. Then she put her papers away, got into her little car, and drove towards Winter Overcotes, reflecting on the events of the afternoon, and especially her secretary's information about the Beltons and Pomfrets. She had never particularly thought about her secretary's background. She was a nice girl, a lady in every good sense, quick and reliable at her work, daughter of a parson somewhere over Chaldicotes way; one of the numberless good, efficient girls who make no particular mark and often don't get married. Yet Miss Susan Dean, unusually intelligent, rising high in the Red Cross, with health and quite enough good looks and with money behind her, suddenly felt an outcast beside Miss Grantly, the parson's daughter, who knew at once why Captain Belton was connected with Lady Pomfret and how. At the Winter Overcotes level crossing traffic was held up and Susan found herself next to Sir Edmund Pridham, who still drove himself about all over the county in a very dangerous fifteen-year-old car. Sir Edmund touched his shabby old hat to her and asked her through the window of his car how her mother was.

"Very well thank you," said Susan. "Oh, Sir Edmund, you know everything about the county. Who is a clergyman called Grantly, somewhere near Chaldicotes? His daughter is in the Red Cross office and is very nice."

Sir Edmund said that would be one of old Major Grantly's sons, a grandson of the Grantly who was Archdeacon of Plumstead in the sixties or thereabouts, and a cousin of the Hartletops. The level crossing gates then began their slow relentless opening, all the cars and buses and bicycles roared and jiggled and hooted and rang their bells. The traffic surged across the railway line and Susan drove home and put her car away. She then went to find her mother, who was sitting in an angle of the house in the sun alternately doing a little embroidery and going to sleep.

"Well, darling?" said Mrs. Dean, looking up with a smile.

"It's all right, mother," said Susan. "Charles Belton is coming and Oliver is coming with Lucy, so we'll be five of each."

"Thank you, darling," said Mrs. Dean. And then she appeared to go to sleep again, so Susan went up to her room, got out of her uniform, had a bath, and put on a summer dress suitable for a friendly dinner-party. And while she dressed she reflected at length upon the importance of knowing who people were. There was her secretary, of whom she had never thought except in office hours, turning out to be a cousin of a marquis and knowing all about everybody without having to learn it. Susan felt her own ignorance very deeply and determined if necessary to read right through Burke's *Peerage* and his *Landed Gentry* and make a serious effort to understand what those little things like circles and black diamonds meant. But even so she would never, she feared, be within hailing distance of those happy few who knew it all by nursery and schoolroom talk without having to learn it. In which she was right to a certain extent, but tended to value the knowledge of interrelationships rather too highly, for the most spiteful and boring outsiders, like that dreadful Mr. Holt the professional parasite, now unregrettably dead, knew all these things and were not any the better for them. It was time for someone to tell Susan that her family inheritance of good looks, good sense, and plenty of brains was in a fair way to be itself a tradition, or the beginning of a tradition. But no one knew what was going on inside her mind, so no one was likely to tell her.

Her sister Jessica then came into her room with her hair done in a new way.

"Hullo, darling," said Jessica. "I've come to you to have oil poured into my wounds. I've just been in to see mother and she said I looked like an Aubrey Beardsley. Too, too unkind."

"I expect she meant it to be nice," said Susan. "After all, Aubrey Beardsley was quite fashionable when mother was young, wasn't he?" said Susan, who laboured under the delusion, common to most of us, that anything between Queen Victoria's coronation and the 1914 war happened during our mother's lifetime.

"I don't know," said Jessica. "Anyway I'm like an Aubrey Clover, which is more to the point. Who is coming to dinner?"

Susan ran through the list of guests.

"And do remember," she said, only thinking of Jessica as her younger sister, not as the star of the Cockspur Theatre, "that Richard Tebben saved your life when you fell off the donkey."

"I couldn't forget if I tried," said Jessica. "Nursie used to tell me about it till I never wanted to hear Richard's name again. What is he like now? I have a vague remembrance of something large."

"I don't know," said Susan. "Father took him into the firm and he went to the Argentine and then after the war he went into some other engineering works. I've not seen him for ages, but Mrs. Tebben rang mother up and she felt she really must make an exertion because of you and the bull, so she asked Richard to dinner."

"How sweet of mamma," said Jessica, mockingly but not unkindly. "I notice that she didn't ask his parents. Was Richard in love with mamma?"

Susan said she didn't suppose he was, but it was all long before the war and did Jessica think she looked all right.

"Much righter than I do," said Jessica, eying her new coiffure in Susan's glass with some disfavour. "But Gaston says I must wear it this way for at least a month and then all his old customers and a lot of new ones will rush to have a hair-do like mine. Gaston is such a pet and I couldn't say no. Come on, darling, and watch mamma greet her demon lover."

If anyone else had talked as Jessica was talking, Susan would have been slightly annoyed, for though she saw clearly her mother's weakness for being admired, she found it rather touching and felt maternal towards her. So many young men and older men too had gently fallen in love with Mrs. Dean and she had accepted their homage placidly and remained devoted to her husband. Perhaps, as her son-in-law Charles Fanshawe, the Dean of Paul's, had remarked, she was so stupid that she did not understand anything, an ox-eyed Juno whose mission in life was to be admired and give nothing in return. She was fond of her large family, but her husband remained her favourite child, and all her children knew it and did not resent it in the least. So Susan told Jessica not to be silly and they went downstairs.

In the drawing-room, raked by the golden western light which was placidly registering five thirty P.M. though by the clock it was half past seven, Mr. and Mrs. Dean were talking to Mr. Needham, the vicar of Lambton, and his wife, formerly Octavia Crawley.

"Hullo, Susan," said Mrs. Needham, giving her friend what Jessica afterwards described and imitated for the benefit of Aubrey Clover as a Mothers' Meeting kiss, "Hullo, Jessica. I say, you do look awful with your hair done like that, doesn't she, Tommy?"

"Don't drag Tommy into it," said Jessica. "It is just Gaston's latest craze. It doesn't mean a thing. Underneath I am just the same dear little Jessica who used to cheat at noughts and crosses. How is your arm, Tommy?"

For Mr. Needham, who had left most of his arm in North Africa, had been persuaded by one of his wife's many brothers-in-law, a very wealthy archdeacon, the same who had given to the Dean the very expensive radio-gramophone which was his pet aversion and the delight of all his grandchildren, to try at the archdeacon's expense the newest kind of artificial arm, much against Mr. Needham's wishes, who had trained himself to do very nicely with the arm that remained to him.

"I don't know," said Mr. Needham, "and what is more, as Octavia's brother-in-law is not here, I don't care. I can't tell you, Jessica, how awful that thing was. I couldn't get it on by myself and Octavia wasn't much good at it, and when I did get it more or less fixed, it was extremely painful. And there was a horrible hand on the end of it," said Mr. Needham shuddering, "that always had to have a glove on it and quite apart from the physical discomfort I have never felt such a fool in my life. So Octavia wrote to the archdeacon and he was awfully decent about it and he got the people who made it to take it back and gave me a set of old sporting prints instead. You must come and see my study, Jessica, it looks splendid with the prints up."

Then in burst, for no other word is suitable for the fashion of her entrance, Miss Lucy Marling, followed by her elder brother, Oliver.

"Mother," said Susan, leading her new guests to Mrs. Dean, "this is Lucy Marling and this is Oliver. It was awfully nice of him to come, as we were a man short."

Having painstakingly made this explanation to her mother as if speaking to an idiot who happened to be deaf, Susan took Lucy Marling into a corner to talk about the Marling Red Cross Fête.

"Do sit down here," said Mrs. Dean to Oliver Marling. "I have a heart, you know, and I mustn't stand much."

It occurred to Oliver that no one had expected Mrs. Dean to stand, but he obligingly took her cue and said he was very sorry and it must make life rather difficult with things as they were.

"Well, really," said Mrs. Dean with the greatest candour, raising her beautiful ox-eyes to Oliver's ordinary eyes, "I am not in any danger or pain, but I have to be a little careful. I know you will understand," she added with an appealing look.

Oliver Marling did not as she possibly expected suddenly fall prostrate before the tragic goddess. He had been turned down for active service on account of his eyes and had seconded himself for the duration of the war into the Regional Commissioner's Office in Barchester, and was now back in London with the firm in which he was a partner. As far as he knew, he had never been in love; certainly not with that very pretentious woman Frances Harvey though she had done her very best to make him think he was. And he had no intention of falling in love, even for fun, with a woman who had a large family the eldest of whom was his own age or older. He answered Mrs. Dean with the right amount of sympathy and then talked about her daughter Jessica, whose acting he had admired in London, after which Mrs. Dean, who at heart found praise of her children quite as good as platonic declarations, forgot to look appealing and they got on very well.

"Jessica, darling," said her mother as Jessica approached with a tray of cocktails, "come and meet Mr. Marling. He adores you."

"Do you really?" said Jessica, putting on the muted voice that several thousand schoolmistresses, typists, and female Civil Servants practised in their bedrooms.

"Adore," said Oliver Marling, "is hardly the word. But I went thirteen times to *Home Is Best* and do not yet know whether the heroine was an angel or a she-devil."

"I asked Aubrey Clover the same question," said Jessica, offering Oliver a drink and then very skillfully poising the nearly empty tray on one hip, with her body in what everyone in the room was forced to recognize as a very carefully studied and exquisite curve.

"And what did he say?" said Oliver. "Let me have that tray. You will drop those two glasses." And before she could make a protest he had gently taken the tray from her and put it on a table, leaving her still in the same lovely curve, like an ivory Madonna.

"Do you know, you are quite amusing," said Jessica, without changing her attitude.

"If I thought you knew your Shakespeare I know what he would say," said Oliver.

"'Bear your body more seeming,'" said Jessica, straightening herself and looking at Oliver.

"I apologize," said Oliver. "You do know your Shakespeare. When will you act in him?"

"When I am about forty-five," said Jessica, "and ripe for Rosalind. Till then I shall continue my masterly interpretations of our modern Shakespeare, Mr. Aubrey Clover."

"Which reminds me," said Oliver, "that you were going to tell me what Aubrey Clover said about the heroine of *Home Is Best*."

"I will tell you his exact words," said Jessica, looking up at him and unconsciously appraising him as too tall and slight for the stage. "He said: 'The answer is Jessica Dean.'"

Leaving Oliver to reflect upon Aubrey Clover's words, she turned to her sister Susan, who was pulling at her sleeve.

"I say, Jessica," said Susan. "Richard Tebben hasn't come yet and father is beginning to ramp. I'd better ring up."

"Much better just go in to dinner," said Jessica. "Come along, mother darling. Wittles is up."

"First it's Shakespeare and now it is Dickens," said Oliver Marling, who found himself placed next to Jessica.

"Really not surprising," said Jessica, who had detected, or thought she detected, a slight patronage in Oliver's voice. "I was brought up by the dear nuns at the Convent School and they read English Literature aloud to us during lunch and high tea."

To which Oliver, suppressing in a gentlemanly way his first impulse, which was to answer "Little Liar," said he was beginning to understand what Aubrey Clover meant. Jessica threw him an amused, conspirator's glance and favoured him with the wink that she had so successfully used as Mrs. Carvel in Aubrey Clover's *Attitude to Life*.

"I say," said Octavia Needham in a loud voice, "there's no one on the other side of me." And indeed at her side was Richard Tebben's Banquo seat. Susan, who was on the other side of the gap, made a face at Octavia, but it was too late. Mrs. Dean, comfortably settled between Oliver and Mr. Needham, suddenly woke up to the fact that they were one too few and appealed to her husband for enlightenment.

"Don't fuss, Rachel," said Mr. Dean, always steady and competent, from across the round table. "Richard Tebben is late, that's all."

And even as he spoke, the old parlour-maid reproachfully ushered Richard into the dining-room and saying coldly: "The young gentleman, madam," went away with some dishes.

At the sight of so many people Richard, who had expected a family party, almost stood on one leg with embarrassment, but Mr. Dean, getting up, shook hands warmly and expressed his pleasure at seeing him again.

"We haven't seen you since before the war, Richard," he said.

"You will find your chair next to Susan. I think you know everyone else."

Richard found his chair, shook hands with Susan, and looking round realized to his horror that quite half the guests were unknown to him. Owing to his work in the Argentine and the war and then his new work in Sweden he had lost touch with Barsetshire and it was a good many years since he had seen the Deans though he had heard of them in letters from his gentle sister Margaret, who had married the Deans' eldest son, Laurence. When he had first known them they were living in the Dower House at Worsted, let to them by Mrs. Dean's much older brother Mr. Palmer, the squire. Now the Birketts were at the Dower House and the Deans were living at Winter Overcotes and Richard went bright red inside as he thought of the foolish reason that had made him late.

"It's very nice to see you again, Richard," said Miss Susan Dean, the very competent Depot Librarian of the Barchester Red Cross Hospital Libraries. "You must tell me all about your new job."

One never knows quite whom or what one has expected to see till the seeing has been done, and then one suddenly becomes conscious that it is quite different from what one expected; though by that time what one did expect has become the baseless fabric of a vision and one will never recall it. Richard had carried memories of Susan Dean to the Argentine with him. They had written each other a few dull letters and the correspondence had died. Now he was suddenly faced with this entirely unknown young woman, who must be twenty-six if she was a day, possibly more, who was almost patronizing him, and he did not quite like it. Petrea Krogsbrog, he thought, would have shown more interest in a friend whom she had not seen for many years.

Susan was equally at sea, for the Richard sitting beside her was very naturally not the Richard who had saved Jessica's life on what the Deans still called the Day of Misfortunes. She had liked that Richard after a hearty schoolgirl fashion. He had been kind to her while Jessica was lying unconscious at the Dower House before the doctor came. He had even offered to call his little car, bought with the fifty pounds that Mr. Palmer had given him as a thank-offering for Jessica's rescue, Susan, after herself. She had written to him and gradually stopped writing because she had nothing to say, and in the years of war work and peace work she had almost forgotten his existence. She rather hoped that he had forgotten the episode of the car and wondered why girls had romantic notions about unromantic people.

"I say," said Richard suddenly. "What happened to Modestine?"

Susan looked at him questioningly. Then she began to laugh.

"Nurse wouldn't call him Modestine, he was always Neddy," she said. "Your mother sold him to my mother and he was useful in the garden and about the farm. Then the war came and we sold him to an evacuated nursery school. I believe he is still alive. What an awful day it was when we met the bull and Jessica fell off Modestine! You must have behaved very bravely, Richard. I was too young to realize at the time."

"I don't think it was brave," said Richard. "It was probably pretty silly. But when I saw Jessica on the ground and the bull coming down the lane, the only thing to do was to get Modestine between her and the bull. As a matter of fact the bull wasn't mad at all. It was only that Lord Bond's cowman didn't lead him into the half-acre paddock in time. He never tried to hurt anyone when Mr. Palmer had him. What happened to that nice kitten you had? The one that Robin was always brushing and combing with his own brush and comb and it made Nurse so cross."

Susan said they had left her at the Dower House and probably she was a very great-grandmother by now.

"Oh Lord! the Dower House!" said Richard. "Do you know what I did, Susan?"

Susan said she didn't.

"I forgot you had moved to Winter Overcotes and I went to

the Dower House," said Richard. "Mother did tell me, but she tells one things so often that one doesn't listen. I felt a frightful fool when I realized what I'd done, and that was why I was late. I came along as fast as I could, but the country has changed so much with aerodromes and houses and things and I nearly got lost again. Anyway, I got here."

Susan said it didn't matter a bit and inquired in a rather perfunctory way about Sweden, which Richard said was a splendid place. He knew some delightful people, he added, called Krogsbrog. Susan, he added, would like Petrea Krogsbrog very much.

But before Susan had to perjure her immortal soul over Petrea Krogsbrog, Octavia Needham from Richard's other side insisted on his attention and demanded from him a detailed account of Swedish nursery schools. For owing to the Barsetshire grapevine, or shall we rather say to Mrs. Tebben talking to Mrs. Palmer, who talked to Lady Bond, who talked to Lady Waring, who mentioned it to Octavia, everyone appeared to know that young Tebben had much interesting information about State-controlled ways of shifting responsibility for one's young.

"Isn't Octavia splendid?" said Mr. Needham to Lucy Marling on his left. "I don't think there's a single thing she doesn't know about parish works. I always go to her for help and information. Our two elder children are to go to the village school as soon as they are old enough, and she wants them to go to a nursery school now, only there isn't one, so she is collecting facts about them and is going to start one in Lambton. I don't know anyone like her."

"She looks awfully nice," said Lucy; very generously, for Octavia in a decent plum-coloured dress, product of one of those mysterious people called a "little woman," was looking so like what she would look like when her husband became a bishop, as he undoubtedly would in time, that it made one's heart sink.

"Miss Pettinger told me Octavia was the best Head Girl she had ever had at the Barchester High School," said Mr. Needham, continuing to praise famous women, "only Miss Pettinger calls it a Girl of Honour instead of Head Girl because it is more democratic. I think it's rather a fine idea."

"It sounds a bit affected to me," said Lucy Marling. "But I'll tell you what, Mr. Needham, we are going to have a Red Cross Fête at Marling in July and the vicar will be away and I wonder if you could come and do the opening prayer. Lord Pomfret is going to open it really, but we thought as it was the Red Cross we ought to have a prayer too, just in case. And you not having one arm would be splendid because it all goes with the Red Cross. And then if your wife would like to have a tent and look after the children under three, because their parents *will* bring them and they are always sick, it would be awfully good practice for a nursery school."

Mr. Needham almost blushed. In Miss Lucy Marling he had found a unity, a firmness of purpose equal to, if not greater than that of his wife. That the whole idea was a skilfully conceived plan of Miss Marling's he had no doubt, not realizing in the least that seeing the materials at hand she had at once evolved a most ingenious fantasia upon them, not the least skilful part of which was the appeal to his one arm. For though Mr. Needham was as modest and earnest and hard-working a Christian pastor as anyone would wish to see, it could not be denied, and he even admitted it at times to himself, that he had one besetting sin. And that sin, as he had recognized when doing spiritual gymnastics in his own mind every day for ten minutes before the breakfast bell rang, was spiritual pride in having left one arm upon the shores of North Africa. Indeed, such was his simple modesty that in a way he valued his useless stump more than his good right arm, because the left arm had, as it were, laid down its life in the service of its country. And if anyone thinks this mode of reasoning was far-fetched, we do not think it was, though we admit that we should be incapable of it ourselves.

"That's splendid," said Lucy, taking his assent for granted.

"I'll talk to your wife after dinner." And then they went into talk about other matters, and Oliver Marling, who had heard scraps of the conversation, felt a pang at his heart as he watched his sister, so fiercely benevolent, so violently competent, so essentially kind, so hard-working and tireless, and wondered what was going to happen to her. Seeing her now and less often than during the war when he had lived at Marling and worked in Barchester, he found her getting harder. Never hard to him, nor to those dependent on her, but seeming to feel increasingly the importance of her county and local work and brushing aside the gentler side of life, driving herself to the limit. If only, he thought, she could relax among friends as that nice Susan Dean did, how glad he would be. And he wondered for the thousandth time whether she had really cared for Tom Barclay, who had married her elder sister. But these are things one cannot ask the nearest and dearest of sisters, so he held his tongue and unhappily watched his sister banging herself against life.

A noise that had been steadily rising now overflowed and stopped all other conversation, the noise being Jessica and Charles Belton, who were having a most unbridled and un-blushing love affair on first sight and were both laughing so much that Jessica choked over her pudding. Charles had been rather alarmed at first to find himself next to a famous actress, but when he shyly mentioned that he had seen her acting with Aubrey Clover in India and said how he and the other fellows had loved it, Jessica, being a true actress, was as pleased as if it had been praise from a high authority and turned on her full blast of charm, excited by which Charles had let loose all his youthful good spirits and love of fun and he and Jessica had rapidly become the greatest friends and plunged into a perfectly abandoned flirtation. While they both paused to take breath, Richard Tebben took occasion to say to Susan: "By the way, what is little Jessica doing now?"

Jessica, overhearing these words, favoured the whole company with Mrs. Carvel's wink and choked all over again while Charles Belton sympathetically beat her on the back.

"But that's Jessica!" said Susan, to whom it had not occurred that Richard might not recognize in the star actress with her modish, outlandish coiffure the little girl who had fallen off the donkey so many years ago, long before the war. "Didn't you know she had gone on the stage?"

"Mother did write about her once or twice," said Richard. "But I didn't realize—I mean is she a *real* actress?"

These artless words reached Jessica, who began to choke again.

"Shut up, Charles, and stop hitting me," she said. "Darling Richard, when you threw yourself in front of the bull to save little Jessica, you didn't know that the brilliant young star of the Cockspur Theatre would be the result. I am London's matinée idol."

"Didn't you ever see her act?" said Charles, who had, as far as such a thing was in his friendly nature, taken a dislike to this Richard Tebben. "She and Aubrey Clover were acting to the troops all over the place."

Richard said they had mostly had ENSA shows where he was, and it was his job to round up the men and make them go to them.

"You wouldn't have needed to round them up if Jessica had been there," said Charles. "We adored her. Didn't we, Jessica?"

Jessica said she thought Aubrey Clover's plays were a bit lowbrow for Richard, at which Richard disclaimed so high a standard but said that the Swedish theatre had perhaps spoilt him for the English stage.

"Oh, do you know Selma Lundquist?" said Jessica, mentioning a Swedish actress of immense repute for acting in a highly naturalistic way (which appeared to mean not acting at all) in very dull plays that consisted in the characters' developing the author's views on life and economics in long set speeches.

Richard said he had had the pleasure of seeing her act several times and he had been much struck by her attitude to drama. It was, he said, just what he felt an intelligent woman's approach to drama should be, especially the plays of Hjalmar Gunnarssen.

"You ought to see Selma off duty," said Jessica, who in spite of Richard's having saved her life felt less and less sympathetic towards him. "She does the most shattering imitations of Hjalmar's plays. I've never laughed so much in my life," which remark appeared to shock Richard, as indeed she had meant it to do. "And Hjalmar laughed like anything," Jessica added reflectively, "only he was so drunk that night that I don't think he knew what he was laughing at. You must come and see me, Richard. I'll send you stalls for Aubrey's play."

Richard would have liked to explain that Clover's sophisticated approach to life did not appeal to him, though exactly what he meant by "sophisticated" neither he nor most of the people who use the word would have been quite able to explain. But luckily he was claimed by Octavia, who wanted a really good talk about nursery schools and obtained from Richard a promise to ask Petrea Krogsbrog to send her all particulars about State control of young children.

And then Susan and Charles began to talk about the Priory School and how nice the Winters were, so that Jessica was free to continue her rapier play with Oliver Marling, discovering that they had a common hatred in Geoffrey Harvey of the Board of Tape and Sealing Wax and his sister Frances.

"I nearly asked her to marry me once," said Oliver. "And it was just as well I didn't, for I think she was going to accept me."

"She is an extraordinarily stupid woman," said Jessica. "So many of those clever women are. And they usually end by marrying their boss and becoming Lady Somebody, but don't have any children, which saves such a lot of trouble."

Oliver remarked that judging by their age, which he could only do by photographs of them in the papers, they were more likely to have grandchildren if they had anything. He hadn't heard of Frances Harvey, he said, since before the end of the war.

"Well," said Jessica, "you know what she is doing now."

Oliver said he didn't, adding, Thank God.

"She is secretary, I mean the kind of high-class secretary that can't do typing or shorthand," said Jessica, "to Lord Aberfordbury."

"I know I ought to be impressed," said Oliver, "but I'm not. If I knew Lord Aberfordbury I expect I would be."

"He was Sir Ogilvy Hibberd," said Jessica. "He got a peerage when this lot came in and called himself Lord Aberfordbury of Wopford in Loamshire. His son stood for East Barsetshire, but of course Mr. Gresham beat him."

"Hibberd?" said Lucy, three places away. "He's the outsider that tried to buy Pooker's Piece only old Lord Pomfret frightened him off. What were you talking about him?"

Oliver, a little ashamed of his sister's manners in talking across their hostess, said Miss Dean had just told him that Frances Harvey was his secretary, only now he was a Lord, to which Lucy replied that she supposed Frances would marry him, and serve them both right. For she had not forgotten Frances Harvey's attempts upon her brother Oliver when the Harveys were living in Marling village during the war, and had never forgiven her. Not that she would have minded if Oliver had married a really nice girl, though she would have missed him very much, but Frances was, in Miss Lucy Marling's view, neither nice nor a girl. She then apologized to Mrs. Dean for butting in and returned to a very interesting talk she was having with Mr. Dean about artificial insemination of cattle, giving it as her considered opinion, with her elbows on the table and her voice, so her host thought, perhaps unnecessarily loud, that it remained to be seen what the calves would be like in three or four generations if the cows hadn't had their fun.

"Oh, Mr. Marling!" said Jessica, using her dark starry eyes on him in a deliberately shameless way, "do you *have* to say Miss Dean? It sounds quite *dreadfully* old. And anyway Susan is Miss Dean. I'm only little Jessica."

"You are a shameless baggage," said Oliver, "but I will call you

whatever you like. Dear little Jessica, what is this story of a cock
and a bull?"

"How too, *too* literary," said Jessica. "The bull was Lord
Bond's bull who was visiting Mrs. Palmer, and I was on the
donkey with mother and father and Susan and Robin and
Richard, and the bull snorted and I fell off over the donkey's
head and had concussion. And Richard with really *terrific* presence of mind, though you mightn't think it to look at him," said
Jessica, eying her saviour critically, "got the donkey across the
road and then the men took the bull into his field. So I have got
to be so grateful whether I like it or not."

"Allow me to do the gratitude for you," said Oliver. "I am
eternally grateful to anyone who saves your life."

"Right, darling," said Jessica, and then there was a tumult of
dinner being over and people getting up and the party reas-
sembled itself on the terrace to enjoy the evening sun.

Richard, between Octavia's rather bullying questions about
nursery schools and Susan's unfeigned want of interest in him,
had so far not much enjoyed his evening. He had possibly
expected too much. Coming back to England after many years
abroad, he had vague expectations of being something of a hero,
of a great reunion with the Deans, who would all fall on his neck
and welcome him as their benefactor and possibly, though on
this his imagination did not insist, offer him one of their
daughters in marriage with ten thousand pounds in golden
sovereigns. Far from this, he had first been late for dinner
through his own fault and had then been much disappointed in
Susan and Jessica. The little girl who fell off the donkey had
become a popular actress and was, so Richard felt, quite spoilt;
Susan, after whom he had once intended to call his first car, had
turned into a dull, secretaryish sort of girl, the sort that in his
opinion England was far too full of. The whole conversation at
dinner had been frivolous and aimless. Jessica and that young
Belton had behaved like children. He thought nostalgically of
evenings at the Krogsbrogs', where serious literary and social

subjects were discussed and iron magnates quoted Shakespeare in Swedish.

"Well, Richard," said Mr. Dean, offering him a cigar, which Richard had the courage to decline, "I hope your new venture with Adams is going well. His methods are distinctly piratical, but I have considerable respect for him. The party look upon him as one of their coming men."

"Do you mean the Labour Party, sir?" said Richard, recollecting that his employer was member for Barchester and had got in on an overwhelming Labour vote.

"No, no," said Mr. Dean pityingly. "Our party. The Conservative Party."

Richard said he was a Communist, with the air of a Christian martyr demanding more and better lions.

"Quite right at your age," said Mr. Dean, for which Richard could have shot him. "You'll get over it. Much better begin that way than start as a traditional Conservative and then go parlour Communist because you were unhappy at Eton, or because your father is a law lord and you want to show your independence. Adams has been a thorn in the side of his party ever since that ill-starred General Election. The trouble is that they can't bribe him. He has all the power he wants and all the money he wants and down here and in his works all the popularity he wants, and he will have all the independence he wants. I think it is pretty safe to say that he will remain member for Barchester as long as he wishes, and will vote exactly as he pleases. A very remarkable man. And now tell me about your work in Sweden."

Dearly would Richard have liked to argue every sentence that Mr. Dean had spoken, but an inner voice must have told him that it would be useless and that if only in gratitude to the man who had given him a good start in life he must answer his question. So he told Mr. Dean all about Stockholm and his travels in Sweden, and Mr. Dean was pleased by Richard's intelligent grip of business and felt that he had done well when he backed this unknown young man who had rescued his Jessica from the bull.

"You must talk to Rachel now," he said. "It has been most interesting to hear of your experiences, but I mustn't be selfish. Rachel, I am going to leave Richard with you."

"I thought you were never going to let him go, Frank," said Mrs. Dean. "Come and join us, Richard, and tell me all about yourself."

Mrs. Dean was sitting in a low, comfortable garden chair, with Susan, Jessica, Charles Belton, and Oliver Marling round her. Not far away Lucy Marling was talking to the Needhams and for once meeting her match in the younger daughter of the Deanery, whose gifts for bullying people for their good and organizing them in spite of themselves Lucy recognized unselfishly as being even greater than her own. Mr. Dean, having established Richard near his hostess, felt he had done enough for the young people and went off to his study to be quiet and read some important papers.

It was not without emotion that Richard found himself after so many years sitting by Mrs. Dean. In that black summer when he had got a poor third in Greats, Mrs. Dean had gently moved into his orbit, a goddess made manifest. Being really a nice boy in spite of his rudeness to his parents, and brought up as far as his parents had found possible in a tradition of self-control, it had never occurred to him to declare his passion for Mrs. Dean. Enough for him that she existed, that her lovely sleepy eyes occasionally turned towards him, that she had appealed to him in her need, that when she felt faint after seeing Susan and Robin scrimmaging, as Nurse put it, on the roof of the Dower House, she had taken his arm to support her; that he had supported her slightly lifeless form to a chair and heard her noble dying words: "Don't tell Frank"; how he had wondered if she would let him kiss her hand as she lay there, so lovely in white velvet, with violet-shadowed eyes. There had been it is true a searing moment in which, an involuntary eavesdropper, he had heard her tell her husband that though she would be forever grateful to Richard for saving Jessica, she found his devotion rather trying. That moment he had tried to forget and had on the whole succeeded and Mrs. Dean still remained in his mind the image of perfection, though he had liked and loved more than one girl of his own generation.

Now, after so many years, he approached the goddess's shrine once more and had to admit that the callow Richard, a young man who seemed almost a stranger to him now, had not chosen amiss. Mrs. Dean was, very naturally, a good deal older. Her long dark hair that she had never thought of cutting was an extremely becoming silver knotted simply on her neck, her still composure, her beautiful eyes were unchanged, her skin exquisite, and she remained in Richard's eyes and indeed in the eyes of most people a very beautiful woman, contented with her life and her family as few people, in Richard's experience, were since the war.

"Sit by me, Richard," said Mrs. Dean. "Jessica darling, give Richard a chair—oh, thank you so much, Mr. Marling. We must have a long talk about old times. I do wish the children were all here. Laurence and our dear Margaret and the children are coming here next week, which is lovely," and she then gave him news of her large brood in elaborate detail, winding up with an inquiry as to whether Richard was married yet.

"You were in love with Susan then, weren't you?" said Mrs. Dean. "I mean in a boy and girl way. She used to write to you. She has done wonderfully well in the Red Cross and it is so nice to have her at home. All the others have gone, even my little Jessica." With which words her lovely eyes demanded sympathy.

"My dear mother, you have got it all wrong," said Jessica. "Richard was in love with you, weren't you Richard? That was why he saved my life, to curry favour with you."

"Everyone was in love with mother," said Susan, "and they still are. She can't help it."

Jessica listened. There was no bitterness at all in Susan's

words, but Jessica, wise beyond her years, had watched her elder sister doing her duty through war and peace, being good daughter at home and efficient worker in the Red Cross, and it had occurred to her more than once that Susan had never had a real chance. Noble though the Red Cross work was, it was no inheritance as far as settling in life was concerned, and in Jessica's opinion Susan was heading straight for being one of the thousand good, capable English spinsters who will never be anything else. Last year she had thought that Colin Keith, that perennial bachelor, might be a possibility, but Colin had philandered with the pretty widow Peggy Arbuthnot, who had finally married Francis Brandon. And Colin appeared to Jessica to be, in the jargon of her age, what one could only call wet. If there were any man for whom Susan had a fancy, Jessica would cheat, rob, and murder to help her sister; but Susan appeared to have no fancies and probably had a permanent inferiority complex from living with a mother who was so attractive.

"Really, Jessica!" said Richard, red in the face and outraged. "How can you say such things? You weren't old enough to know anything about it."

There was a slightly uncomfortable silence during which Charles Belton, suddenly transfixed by a thought of Lady Graham, felt sympathy for anyone who loved a woman old enough to be his mother, because that was a very holy and beautiful feeling.

"You are all very silly," said Mrs. Dean. "Of course Richard wasn't in love with anybody, he was far too young. He was," said Mrs. Dean, striking out a perfectly original idea, "more like a son to me and quite like a brother to the children," which piece of idiocy put a stop to the subject. And then the Needhams surged back to the terrace with Lucy Marling, and the two parties coalesced and talked of county matters.

"You must come to the Conservative Rally," said Octavia Needham to Richard. "It's to be at Staple Park in July and the Barsetshire Pig-Breeders are having their show there the same day. It ought to be great fun."

Richard said, though perhaps with less conviction than earlier in the evening, that he was a Communist.

"Oh well, heaps of people say that," said Octavia pityingly, from her unassailable position as a loyal daughter and wife of the Church, "but it's only just to say something. You'll be a Conservative when you are older," which slighting reference to his age, or possibly to his still youthful appearance, annoyed Richard very much and he would have made a protest except that the whole party were now talking at once and telling each other how the rally ought to be run.

"The real stroke of genius," said Oliver Marling, "was to get the Pig-Breeders' show at Staple Park on the same day. If anything will revive the Conservative Party, that will. I don't know who thought of it but he was a genius."

"My brother," said Charles Belton, and then blushed fiercely.

"Good man," said Oliver Marling from the height of his thirty-odd years. "But how? I don't mean I don't believe you," he added hastily, "but I just wondered."

"It was only because my father was in such a temper because the Conservatives and the Pig-Breeders had got the same day for their show," said Charles, rather nervous at finding the whole company's attention was upon him. "So Freddy said wouldn't it be a good idea if they stuck to the date and had both the shows at the same place, because it would jolly well show people that Conservatives stood for Pig-Breeding, and he didn't get it, but then he did and he rang up Sir Robert Fielding and Lord Stoke and Lord Bond and it was all fixed. That was all."

"Well done, Belton," said Mr. Dean, who had come out of the house and heard these last words. "The joint affair ought to be worth a good many votes to us. Jessica, someone wants you on the telephone."

Jessica went indoors but was not long away.

"It was Aubrey," she said. "He's going to drive me to London and he will be here in a few minutes. I must fly and collect my things."

"I say," said Lucy Marling as Jessica went indoors again, "is that *the* Aubrey Clover? I saw one of his plays when I went to stay in London with Aunt Grace last year and it seemed a bit queer. I mean people aren't really like that. I'll tell you what," she added, addressing her new friends the Needhams, "one could write an awfully good play about a Conservative Rally, I mean you could have all the different people that come and the sort of rot they talk and that sort of thing. I could do it myself if someone would vet it for me. I mean getting the commas right and that sort of thing. And we could have something about a nursery school in it."

Octavia Needham said it was the sort of thing that would go down very well with the Women's Institute and why didn't Lucy try.

"All right, I will," said Lucy. "And then the W.I. can act it at the Competition Festival. I say, will you come and talk to the Marling W.I. about how to run a vicarage? They'd simply adore it, because most of them have done a bit of cleaning at the vicarage and they know what a job it is. And I'll come and do a talk to your W.I. on anything you like."

Both these handsome offers were accepted by Octavia and a subject for Lucy was under discussion when suddenly the air was rent by the hideous wail of a siren rising and falling, rising and falling. The war was long over, the raids organized by the Government on food, health, money, freedom, nerves, couldn't be avoided by getting under the kitchen table or into an air-raid shelter. Charles and Richard, by a common impulse, turned their coat collars up and every member of the party felt his or her stomach turning over, as Lucy inelegantly put it.

"That's only Aubrey," said Jessica, appearing on the terrace with a coat and a suitcase. "He had that siren fitted to show Americans the horrors of war, but I think it has stopped being funny. Oh, here you are, Aubrey. Come and talk to mother."

To the Deans and to Oliver, who went about a good deal in London, a real live actor-manager-playwright was nothing out of the way. But to the Needhams and to Charles, who had already had the excitement of meeting a real live actress, this was romance made visible. From the drawing-room there stepped onto the terrace a nondescript man, a man who might be anybody, whom one could meet a thousand times and not know again. Luckily all the Deans were old friends and had no difficulty at all in recognizing him, but the rest of the party could hardly suppress their disappointment at the famous Aubrey Clover in the flesh. Lucy, with recollections of the play that had seemed a bit queer to her, felt a pang of disappointment. If that Mr. Clover could write all those queer plays and act in them too, he ought to look a bit queer himself. But he looked so ordinary that she felt distinctly defrauded. And when he spoke she was even more disillusioned.

"How are you?" he said to Mrs. Dean, not even kissing her hand. "I hope I'm not breaking up the party, but if Jessica is ready we must start at once. I have my accompanist with me and you know he always likes to get back to his mother at Ealing if possible. We shall drop him there on the way up."

This, Lucy thought bitterly, was not the way for a writer of witty and daring plays (though she hadn't thought that queer play of his witty) to talk, which sentiment she confided to Octavia Needham, who said Mr. Clover had acted for the Barchester Red Cross for nothing last summer, so it showed he was a decent sort. Mr. Needham said he felt sure he had seen his face somewhere, but couldn't place it. Then Jessica began saying good-byes, kissing everyone with her famous non-contact kiss, which surprised the Needhams a good deal. When she came to Oliver Marling she remarked: "Too tall," and simply stood with her face lifted. Oliver with great presence of mind took her hand and kissed it instead.

"Coward!" said Jessica, and putting her arms round Charles Belton's neck embraced him warmly. "Aubrey," she called, "meet Charles Belton. He saw us act in that too too Poona place in India and has never forgotten it."

"Was that the time when that dreadful Sonia got ill and Peggy Arbuthnot took her part?" said Aubrey Clover, his putty-like face assuming an air of faint interest.

"It was at Umbrella, sir," said Charles. "We were bored stiff there after all the fun in Burma and your show bucked us up like anything. All the men were singing and whistling 'Up to my ankles in love' till we were absolutely sick of it."

He then stopped abruptly, conscious that he had not said the right thing.

"You must come to our show at the Cockspur," said Aubrey Clover. "Jessica, see that Belton doesn't forget."

"Oh, thanks most awfully, sir," said Charles, going scarlet with hero-worship.

"Not 'sir,' darling," said Jessica, "it's too too schoolmaster. We all call him Aubrey. Charles is a schoolmaster, the lamb," she added to Aubrey Clover, upon which that gifted creature by a slight contortion of the face suddenly became all the schoolmasters in the world and as suddenly relapsed into his usual uninteresting appearance and told Jessica to hurry up. At the same moment the old parlour-maid came out and announced to the world in general with an expressionless face that the gentleman (a word which she pronounced with an intonation that clearly showed her opinion of his claim to the status) in the car had sent in word would Mr. Clover please be quick because his mother was expecting him at Ealing.

"Oh, bother the man," said Jessica. "All right, Aubrey. I'm coming. Good-bye, mother darling. Good-bye, Susan darling and father. Oh! Richard! I had nearly forgotten you. Aubrey, this is Richard Tebben, who saved me from a mad bull and a donkey when I was a horrid little girl and has friends in Sweden called Krogsbrog, too too Nordic, so you must love him for my sake. And he knows Selma Lundquist, but that's not his fault. Good-bye, Richard, and next time you see a mad bull for God's sake don't save me again. You see what it has brought me to."

She pointed dramatically at Aubrey Clover, who had paid no

attention at all to what she said, embraced Richard, and vanished into the house.

"Good-bye, Aubrey," said Mrs. Dean, unmoved by these parting scenes. "Next time you come I shall have three more shirts for you with the collars turned."

To which Aubrey Clover replied that he was most grateful and his mother was very grateful too for she simply couldn't do her mending now because of her arthritis, and so went away.

Lucy Marling may have disapproved Aubrey Clover and his plays, but when he and Jessica had gone, even Lucy felt that brightness had fallen from the air and said to her brother Oliver that they ought to be getting back. Oliver also found the air less bright, so with thanks to the Deans and a promise to the Needhams to ring them up about the Marling Red Cross Fête, nursery schools, and other enthralling topics, the Marlings went away.

"I'll tell you what," said Miss Lucy Marling to her brother as they drove along the country roads in the unnatural light of double summer time, "the Needhams will be a terrific help at the fête, especially him having only one arm. Octavia is going to have six children she says. Have you got to go back to town tomorrow?"

Oliver, pulled from some private dream, said he had.

"Oh, bother," said his sister. "I meant to tell you I wanted the car myself to go over to Holdings."

Oliver, still half in his dream, said that was all right and he would walk to Melicent Halt and get the early train to Barchester. Then they arrived at Marling Hall, put the car in the stables, and walked up to the house, where they found their parents writing letters.

"We had quite a good evening," said Lucy, sitting down ungracefully. "I had a very interesting talk with the Needhams. He's the parson at Lambton, father," she explained in a friendly bellow, "and she is the Dean's youngest daughter and she's going to have six children and Mr. Needham has only one arm."

"All right, my dear, all right: no need to shout," said Mr.

Marling, "I'm not deaf," which provoked his daughter to say under her breath that he was; a remark which he did not hear. "I want the car tomorrow morning. I'm going to the Towers to see Pomfret about that cow of his."

"Well, I've got to go to see Cousin Agnes," said Lucy, "so I can drop you at the Towers and pick you up later."

Mr. Marling grunted in a displeased way and said that wouldn't do. He didn't know how long he would be at the Towers and he knew what it was when Lucy and Agnes got together, gabble, gabble, gabble.

"Perhaps," said Oliver, who disliked more and more these wrangles between his father and his sister, wrangles that we may say meant very little and did not affect the hearty nerves of the disputants. "If you took Ed with you, Lucy, you could go to Little Misfit first and he could drop you there and then take father to the Towers and—no, that wouldn't help."

Everyone then spoke at once, at considerable length.

"Stchupid!" said Mr. Marling, who had been looking at a pocketbook. "It's not tomorrow I'm going to see Pomfret, it's Friday. Can't think what put tomorrow into my head. All right, Lucy, you can have the car."

"Gosh!" said Lucy, "I've just remembered it's the Junior Conservatives tomorrow, so I can't go to Little Misfit. I'm giving the J.C.'s a talk about pigs. I'll tell you what, father, Charles Belton's brother Freddy is the one that got the Conservatives and the Pig-Breeders to have their shows on the same day."

"That will be old Belton's son at Harefield," said Mr. Marling, who was himself several years older than Mr. Belton. "Nice woman his wife. One of the Thornes. You know her, my dear," he added to his wife, who had been pursuing her county correspondence and not paid much attention to the talk.

"Lucy Belton," she said, turning her head. "She is a kind of connection by marriage of mine. I think one of my father's uncles married a Thorne. His girl Elsa made a very good marriage. Lucy, Mrs. Smith has written to ask if she can borrow at least that's the word she uses—a broody hen to sit on some duck's eggs."

"Not on your life, mamma," said Oliver. "You know perfectly well that what Mrs. Smith borrows she keeps. She still has that lampshade that she borrowed last Christmas and a perfectly good clothes brush out of the boot-room. Say you haven't a broody."

"She saw the broody on Thursday," said Mrs. Marling, obviously a fatalist about Mrs. Smith.

"I'll tell you what," said Lucy. "Ed Pollett's wife wants a broody, Ed told me so. I'll take the broody down to his cottage tomorrow and then Mrs. Smith can't have her. Millie is going to have another baby."

"Is that the sixth or the seventh?"

Lucy said she wasn't sure, but thought it was the seventh counting the twins. And probably she was right, for as Ed Pollett the handy-man and Millie his wife, formerly maid to Mrs. Cox who let lodgings, were distinctly wanting as far as intellect was concerned, they naturally had a large family who were all radiantly good-looking under the dirt and all slightly subnormal with a genius for tending animals.

Oliver said he was going to bed.

"Not a headache?" said his mother with quiet anxiety.

"No, darling," said Oliver. "You know I hardly ever have headaches since my dear Mr. Pilman came back from the war and gave me proper spectacles. No, I just feel like bed."

So he kissed his parents and his sister and went to bed, where perhaps he found his dream again in a dream. We cannot say.

The rest of the party at the Deans' went indoors and so gradually dispersed, the Needhams going first because Octavia insisted on her husband being in bed by eleven o'clock if he must get up so early in the morning. Mr. Dean disappeared again, leaving his wife and elder daughter to entertain Richard and

Charles. Susan would have been glad to go to bed herself, but her instincts as a good hostess would not allow her to, the more especially as her mother had practically gone to bed in public and was in a comfortable coma on the drawing-room sofa.

"Do you still write poetry?" said Susan to Richard.

"Oh, just now and then," said Richard, "but I haven't thought of publishing. How did you know?"

"The poem you wrote about mother," said Susan.

Richard looked at her uncomprehendingly.

"You know. The one about strewing no roses. Margaret told it to me. I thought it was awfully good."

Richard's mind went back to the summer when the Deans had first come to Worsted and love had inspired him to write a short poem about his hostess, who now lay half asleep on the sofa. This poem he had communicated to his sister Margaret under seal of secrecy and Margaret must have passed it on to the Deans. He was half annoyed, half flattered.

"I say," said Charles Belton, "can you really write poetry? I've tried sometimes but there doesn't seem really to be anything to say."

Richard said it was just a trick, while Charles thought of Lady Graham and how gratifying it would be if one could write a poem to her, only there wasn't a rhyme to Agnes. Skegness would be the nearest he could get and even Charles felt that it was not the highest poetical flight.

"I'd quite forgotten that poem," said Richard airily. "How did it go?"

Susan said she couldn't remember it, which was quite true, but Richard chose to take it as a deliberate affront and was offended. However, no one noticed his offence and Susan said she knew there was a copy of it somewhere that Margaret had written for Mrs. Dean. She went to a large bureau and after opening several drawers found the poem and brought it back.

"You read it, Richard," she said. "I'm no good at poetry."

To Charles this was real life. A poet was going to read an

unpublished work; like people who read poetry in pubs in London, a thing he had heard of but never experienced.

"If you insist," said Richard.

Susan, who thought the remark rather pretentious, said not a bit and she'd love to read it herself. Richard said there were perhaps some nuances—

"Right, you read it," said Susan good-naturedly. "I wanted to mend my stockings anyway. You don't mind, do you Charles?"

Charles said rather not and his mother always did the mending after dinner while his father went to sleep over *The Times*, which seemed to Richard to denote in Charles a nature not attuned to higher chords.

"Yes, I remember it now," said Richard, with what might almost be described as a gratified simper. "I called it 'Strew No Roses.'"

"Just one moment," said Susan. "I left a pair of stockings in the bathroom and I know one of them has a hole."

She got up and went out of the room while Richard remained in a state of offended and suspended animation.

"Now you can start," she said, sitting down again.

> "Strew no roses round her bed,
> Roses are too white, too red;
> But the cloudy violets bring,
> First-fruits of a tardy spring."

Here Richard had to stop and swallow, owing to the emotion roused in him by his own words.

"It's jolly good," said Charles generously, remembering how Lady Graham had worn a bunch of violets pinned to her coat when she came to Harefield.

Richard said in a pained voice that there was another stanza.

"Do you mean verse?" said Susan. "I thought stanzas were long things like the *Faerie Queen*, or Byron."

As Richard had not the faintest idea what the word "stanza" represented he ignored the remark and continued:

> "All the roses now are fled,
> Rue must deck her lonely bed,
> And upon those scalèd eyes—

—there must be something wrong there," he said, interrupting himself.

"I expect it's Margaret's writing," said Susan. "We can never read her letters properly. Let me look."

There are few things more annoying than to have someone looking over your shoulder when you are reading aloud, and Susan's kind and helpful action made Richard slightly shrug his shoulders in a pitying way.

"It's not 'scalèd,' it's 'sealèd,'" said Susan.

> "And upon those sealèd eyes
> Violets fall, from Paradise—

That's how it ought to go. Isn't it good, Charles?"

Charles Belton, still thinking of Lady Graham, said it was splendid. Absolutely crashing, he added.

Richard said one was young then. And then Mrs. Dean suddenly came to and yawned so unashamedly that both men got up and began to say good-bye.

"I've got a car," said Richard to Charles Belton. "We both go the same way, don't we?"

"Richard can drop you at the Priory," said Susan to Charles, to which Charles objected that he had a bicycle, but Susan said all right, put it in the back.

Richard did not particularly want a bicycle in his car, and Charles did not particularly want to be driven, but the Depot Librarian of the Red Cross organized them into it before they could argue and so they drove away in the still strange summer twilight.

"Go to bed at once, mother," said Susan. "You are a disgraceful hostess going to sleep in your guests' faces."

Mrs. Dean obediently collected various small pieces of personal property and trailed across the hall.

"Richard is rather dull, isn't he?" she said inquiringly.

"Dreadfully dull," said Susan. "I suppose he was pretty dull then too, only one didn't know it. Charles is nice."

Her mother agreed and trailed herself upstairs. Susan saw that everything was shut up and went to her room. The strange light lay on the world and Susan suddenly felt old and tired. To see Richard had taken her back so many years, and for the years between there seemed to be nothing to show. All her brothers and sisters were married or settled in various ways. She had remained the daughter at home, working hard, respected and valued by the Red Cross; but to be in the Red Cross was no inheritance. Last year she had wondered a little about Francis Brandon and quietly schooled herself not to think. Colin Keith had appealed to her for kindness and she had been kind, for it was her nature, but did not wish to be more. Charles was a delightful creature, but to her almost a child. It had been a long day of work in Barchester and a dinner-party at home, and it would never be possible to explain to her employers or her family how exhausting the divided life could be. Yet behind it all there was something pleasant, only she felt too tired and stupid to remember what it was, so she went to bed. Lying awake in the dark, for at last the unnatural light had faded, a comforting thought came to her. Charles's mother had sent her kind messages and wanted to come and see her. Not that it had anything to do with Charles, of course. It was all his brother's doing, Captain Belton, Freddy. It had been kind of him, thoughtful of him, to come and thank the Red Cross for what it had done for the *Barsetshire*. People were rather apt to take the Red Cross for granted and a personal expression of gratitude was very welcome. She hoped Mrs. Belton would not forget.

The journey from Winter Overcotes to Lambton did not take long. Charles was delivered at the school and his bicycle unloaded. Richard, declining a drink, at which Charles was really rather glad because he didn't know if his headmaster would approve guests after hours, drove on to Worsted, leaving Charles to reflect what a jolly evening it had been and what fun Jessica was—not a bit like an actress. In which view he was of course quite wrong. Then he thought of Lady Graham and went to bed.

As Richard drove homewards he also reflected upon the party and how dull the Deans were. Not Jessica, but he did not think Jessica had improved and was almost tempted to wish he had not saved her from the bull, except that it had given him the start in life he needed. But for Lord Bond's bull and his mother's donkey, Modestine, he might have had to be a beggarly usher, or try for the Civil Service, or get into a publisher's office, though what he thought he meant by this last we cannot exactly say, any more than we can say what all the other young men with this ambition think they mean. We can only imagine from their conversation that they envisage an ideal life in which they entertain famous writers and even writeresses every day at lunch at their firm's expense. The one really pleasant part of the evening had been the reading of his poem, though Susan had spoilt it by interfering. How very dull Susan was. Not for a thousand pounds would he call a car Susan. How different would an evening at the Krogsbrogs' have been, with brilliant and intelligent conversations on politico-economical subjects and the deposits of manganese ore in the Ragbag Hills. And Petrea Krogsbrog would play old Swedish airs on a modern harpsichord and there would be quantities of excellent food and wines and spirits and coffee.

His spirits had been high during these beautiful thoughts, but suddenly as he turned down the few yards of drive, they fell to zero. There was a light shining from the sitting-room window and that meant that his father possibly, his mother certainly, would be sitting up for him. And to be sat up for was what no son could tolerate. Had he been an adventurer in foreign parts for many years, an independent bachelor earning a good salary, with his own rooms at a hotel and later his own flat, simply to be sat up for at his age as if he were a schoolboy? The fact of his not having a latch-key was no excuse, for the front door was never locked unless his parents were away, and even if both front and back door were locked, there were at least three other different ways of entering or breaking into the house with no trouble at all. In black dudgeon he left his car in front of the house, for there was no garage, and opened the front door. The hall was in darkness, but as he came in, the drawing-room door was opened and his mother came out.

"Hush! Not a sound!" said Mrs. Tebben, pointing dramatically to the ceiling. "Father went to bed. He was rather tired. But I have kept vigil for you and there is a delicious night-cap for you in front of the fire. Come in."

Where the undergraduate Richard would have almost pushed his mother away and gone sulkily up to bed, the older Richard so far controlled himself as to follow his mother into the sitting-room and make up his mind to humour her, though pretty certain that he would not succeed.

"Cods' roes!" said Mrs. Tebben, pointing to the hearth, where some damp logs were smoking, a small saucepan precariously balanced on them. "A part of a food parcel generously sent by the President of the Snorri Society of Zenith University. Your father and I had them for supper and what we did not eat I mixed with a little of the sauce left over from the fish we had on Saturday and have been keeping it warm for you. Now for the feast!"

"I'm awfully sorry, mother," said Richard, making most laudable efforts to keep his temper, "but I really don't want any supper. We had heaps at the Deans'."

"Smell it," said his mother, taking the lid off the saucepan. "Ah! delicious! Just a tiny bit burnt, I fear, where it has stuck to the bottom of the saucepan, but what of that?"

"I'm awfully sorry, mother," said Richard, feeling it wiser to choose an excuse and stick to it, "but I really couldn't eat anything. Honestly I couldn't."

Mrs. Tebben replaced the lid on the saucepan and put the saucepan down on the hearth.

"I do miss Gunnar sometimes," she said, and to his horror her eyes filled with tears.

"But, mother, cats can't live for ever," said Richard, "and Gunnar was sixteen years old. Why don't you have another cat? Mrs. Phipps always has kittens to give away."

"Gunnar didn't like kittens," said Mrs. Tebben, blowing her nose.

To this final argument there was no reply.

"Well, if you really don't want the cods' roes," said Mrs. Tebben, "I will give them to Mrs. Phipps tomorrow. Dear Gunnar! He always finished everything for us. And now let us forget our troubles. Did you have a delightful evening at the Deans'? And who was there?"

Again Richard felt descending upon him the old annoyance with parents who would ask questions. On the way back he had formed a virtuous determination to make an interesting story of his evening for his parents' benefit, to expatiate on Jessica's charm, Susan's efficiency, and Mr. and Mrs. Dean's kindness, the agreeable company of Charles Belton, the Marlings and the Needhams. But no sooner had he entered the house than the old discomfort and irritation came back as strongly as if he had never left Worsted.

"Oh, it was very nice," he said unwillingly, "Jessica was quite amusing, but I think the stage has coarsened her, and as for Susan she talks nothing but Red Cross. Mr. Dean was very nice to me—" and then he broke off as the telephone rang. His mother was going to answer it, but he got to the telephone first.

Whoever it was seemed to be asking a good many questions, to which Richard replied in a voice that his mother didn't know.

"It is quite impossible to talk here," said Richard to the unknown, "with everyone listening. Can I ring you up from the office in town tomorrow?" and he added some words in what sounded to Mrs. Tebben like gibberish, but what Mr. Tebben would at once have recognized as Swedish words conveying an impression of affection. Mrs. Tebben went slowly out of the room and Richard was uneasily conscious that he heard something like a sob. He finished his conversation and hung up the receiver. He had put his mother in her place, but he did not enjoy the victory.

CHAPTER 4

Owing to her many engagements, all of them taking the form of service of some kind to the county, it was not till the following Sunday that Miss Lucy Marling found herself free to visit her cousins at Little Misfit. It was a warm sunny day, the car was running well, and her only regret was that her brother Oliver was not with her, for now that he was living in London he did not always come home for the weekends, sometimes going to friends in the country, sometimes staying in London. This weekend he was in London, which roused his sister's kindly scorn for in Lucy's opinion London was only invented for people to get away from; and since the disaster of peace there is something to be said for her attitude.

She got to Holdings about half past twelve and found the Grahams just back from church. Chairs were on the flagged pavement before the large room known since the eighteenth century as the Saloon, with its four long windows looking over the garden to where the Rising winds among the rushes. During the war the Saloon had been shut up, but a few months earlier Lady Graham had managed to have it cleaned and had refurnished it scantily but beautifully with family portraits and some old furniture, and her second daughter, Clarissa, had with her elegant hands touched up some of the gold on the carved pilasters and plaster swags, so that the whole room had a look of faded nobility and was very pleasant in the long warm summer days.

Lady Graham was seated on a wooden bench with her embroidery. Not far from her Lady Emily Leslie was installed in a chaise-longue, while the three younger children were grouped round their grandmother, who was drawing pictures for them.

"Darling Lucy," said Lady Graham, making no attempt to rise, but lifting her lovely incredibly soft face to Lucy's. "How lovely to see you. Where is Oliver?"

Lucy said with scarcely veiled contempt that he was spending the weekend in London.

"That is too sad," said Lady Graham. "They all work so hard. I am so disappointed that Robert can't come down this weekend. He has something very important in London. I dare say he and Oliver will see each other. One always does see people in London. And here is Merry."

And out of the house came Miss Merriman, once secretary to old Lady Pomfret, now for several years guide, philosopher, and friend to Lady Emily Leslie, whom she managed with consummate tact and quiet determination.

"Hullo, Merry," said Lucy.

"How are you, Miss Marling?" said Miss Merriman, who had never yet failed to put a mysterious barricade between herself and her employers and their families and friends. Everyone called her Merry, but never did she use a Christian name or a pet name to any but the children, or a few grown-ups whom she had known as children. Once only had she lowered the barricade but had retired behind it again. That was in the days when old Lord Pomfret was alive and the present Lord Pomfret was only Mr. Foster. Old Lady Pomfret may have seen what was happening but no one else did and Miss Merriman had buried that part of her life as deep as Lucy Snowe buried her thoughts of that really very dull Dr. Bretton.

"Oh, I'm all right," said Lucy. "Oh and mother sent you her kind regards."

Miss Merriman said that was very kind of Mrs. Marling and she was sure Lady Emily would like to talk to her; so Lucy went over to the chaise-longue. But it was not very easy to get near Lady Emily on account of the number of things and people that she always managed to collect round her. Books and embroidery were strewn on the shawl that covered her respected legs; a small table on her right was laden with pencils, paper, and coloured chalks, and a kind of cane stool on her left bore a large cardboard box with bits of coloured paper and two pairs of scissors in it. John Graham was hanging over the back of his grandmother's chair looking at the pictures she was making, Robert Graham was perched on one of the flat arms of the chair, while Edith Graham was sitting beside her grandmother's feet, industriously sharpening a pencil with a pencil-sharpener and enjoying the way the curls of thin wood came out of it.

"Dear Lucy, how nice to see you," said Lady Emily looking up, her beautiful thin lips curling into a warm smile of greeting. "Sit down and tell me everything about Marling. I have been wanting to come over for a long time, but they say I am not up to it, which is ridiculous. But I do get tired now: more than I used to. Sit down and we will have a long talk."

Lucy was perfectly willing to sit down, but did not see a single square inch unoccupied in Lady Emily's neighbourhood unless she sat on the warm flags of the terrace.

"Do have my arm," said Robert, getting up from the arm of the chair. "It squeaks a bit, but it isn't bad."

"Darling Robert is having his half-term holiday," said Lady Emily, "and James and John have long leave from Eton. Where is James?"

Robert said that James and Clarissa had stopped on the way back from church to look at Mr. Scatcherd's drawing of Holdings which was going to be reproduced in the Christmas number of the *Barchester Chronicle*.

"And Emmy is coming to lunch with Martin and Sylvia," said Lady Emily. "It is so nice to have them all together. It reminds me of Rushwater in the old days when the house was always full of young people. Sit down, Lucy dear."

Her ladyship hauled herself up, if we may so speak without appearing disrespectful, into a less recumbent attitude and in so doing pushed the table on her right. The table, which had only three legs, was unequal to rebalancing itself and fell over sideways, while pencils rolled all over the terrace and chalks broke into coloured fragments on the flags.

Robert came up with a garden chair which he silently offered to Lucy and then busied himself with picking up the pencils, while James stood the table on its head and hammered a loose leg back into place with the heel of his shoe, which he removed for that purpose.

> "James is mending the table
> As far as he is able,"

said Edith, who owing to her grandmother's change of position now had more room to sit on the foot of the chaise-longue.

Lucy sat down on the chair, her legs planted wide apart, and dragged the chair and herself as near Lady Emily as possible.

"Mother sent her love, Cousin Emily," she said, "and so did father. Father is awfully pleased because the Barsetshire Pig-Breeders are going to have their meeting at Staple Park the same day as the Conservative Rally. He says it is the best thing for the county since the Government came in."

"I haven't seen your father for a long time," said Lady Emily. "He brought your mother to Rushwater when they were first married. That was long before my eldest son was killed or John's wife died. Happy, happy days."

Her voice was muted, her hawk's keen eyes were looking far into the distance. Lucy had an uncomfortable feeling that she was eavesdropping and was puzzled by some of Lady Emily's words. That the eldest Leslie had been killed in Flanders she knew; but that John Leslie's wife should be dead surprised and rather frightened her. Surely if Mary had died they would have heard. Miss Merriman, always quietly in the right place at the right moment, was now gathering a few of Lady Emily's personal belongings which had fallen overboard in the general confusion.

"Please, Merry," said Lucy in an undertone. "Cousin Emily was talking about Martin's father that was killed and she said John's wife was dead. She isn't dead, is she?"

"Lady Emily meant his first wife," said Miss Merriman. "I never knew her, but I believe she was charming. Her name was Gay. Do you want your bag, Lady Emily?"

Her ladyship, who had now resumed her usual spirits and come back from her journey to the end of the night, said she would like her bag and a scarf.

"Not the blue one, Merry," she said, "because I have made some fishes on it with red chalk and I am sure Sir Robert will find a way to fix the chalk when he comes down. The pink one; the dirty pink one, I mean," she added, as Miss Merriman offered her two scarves, one ice-cold pink, the other a soft dusty pink, which Lady Emily twisted round her head over the black lace scarf she was already wearing.

"And now I must go and get ready for lunch," she said, flashing her brilliant smile at everyone. "Will you tell Conque, Lucy dear?"

While her ladyship with Merry's aid disentangled herself from the cocoon of shawls in which she had during the morning enveloped herself, Lucy obediently went to find her cousin's French maid, Conque, whom she ran to earth in Lady Emily's bedroom, where she was making everything a little more untidy than it was.

"Hullo, Conque," said Lucy.

"I know. Er ladyship want me," said Conque, who had successfully resisted any but the slightest infiltration of the English language during the many years she had been in Lady Emily's service. "Quotter of an hour ago, à la bonne heure. Now it is lunchtime and we shall be late. Enfin on est toujours en retard avec miladi. Le jour ou elle paraîtra devant le bon Dieu, ce sera celui-là qui aura à attendre," said Conque, who was extremely devout. And taking no notice of Lucy she went to attend her mistress.

Lucy, who was used to Conque's rudeness and quite undisturbed by it, wandered round Lady Emily's room, which was not unlike Sir John Soane's Museum, or the apothecary's shop in *Romeo and Juliet,* in its crowd of miscellaneous and apparently unrelated objects of all kinds. Watts's beautiful head of Lady Emily soon after her marriage; hundreds of photographs, from studio portraits signed by crowned heads and great statesmen and the Leslie children at every stage to snapshots of the third housemaid's wedding; a set of asbestos mats on which her ladyship had painted red and gold birds; shawls, icons, Madonnas, a drawing of cats by Louis Wain, Sargent's charcoal head of her eldest son, books bristling with pieces of paper left in them by Lady Emily to mark favourite passages, a large bureau covered with letters and bills with corners of papers sticking out of every drawer, occasional tables covered with flowers, pencils, paints, and stationery, a canary in a cage, an old-fashioned cheval glass which showed the room at an alarming tilt; and yet in spite of the muddle such a triumphant sense of the fullness of life, such a bringing together of time past and present, that the rash beholder felt the spirit of the room even more than she saw its untidiness and went back to the terrace reflecting on life.

Here she found James and Clarissa Graham, whom she had not seen for some time, and greeted them warmly.

"I'll tell you what, James," she said, "you're awfully like David," and indeed James bore a good deal of resemblance to his uncle, Lady Emily's favourite child if so large a love as hers could have a favourite among her adored brood.

James said he hoped not, because Uncle David was quite bald on the top now, and then turned the talk to the more interesting subject of his military service, which would begin that very autumn in his father's old regiment. And then Martin Leslie with his golden wife, Sylvia, and Lady Graham's eldest girl, Emmy, who lived with them and even more with their cows, came in the rattling old Ford van from Rushwater and there was such a noise and babble of Leslies and Grahams that Lucy felt rather out of it. She thought of her home, of her quiet father and mother ceaselessly occupied in local or county work, of Oliver now in London, of herself living it is true in the home she deeply loved, happy in her work and in the feeling that she was needed, but almost in a backwater compared with Holdings, where there were so many young and hopeful people. Lucy suddenly saw Marling Hall as a place of old age. Her father and mother were not young. Her elder brother, Bill, a professional soldier, lived at Camberly with his wife and family and would probably never be able to afford to live at Marling even if he wished to. Her sister, Lettice Barclay, was happily married in Yorkshire. She and Oliver were the youngest and neither of them was very young. And neither of them was married. Lucy thought of the night when she had told her widowed sister, Lettice, that she was not fond of Captain Barclay, because she was so sorry for Lettice being a widow and wanted to comfort her, and how after making this renunciation, which though it had not wrecked her life was none the less real, her tears had mingled with the bath-water. She had not regretted her generous action, she was busy and quite as happy as anyone could expect to be with the present Government. But like old Miss Lily Dale who used to live at Allington, she felt that Lucy Marling, spinster, was written on her heart. Then her robust common sense took command and made her confess that life had a great many pleasures and that the whole success of the Marling Red Cross Fête depended on her, in which of course she was wrong, for not one of us is indispensable however much we may flatter ourselves that we are.

How Lady Graham managed to give lunch to so many friends and relations, a good baker's dozen Lucy computed if not more, was her ladyship's secret. As far as human eye could see she managed it by letting it manage itself and incidentally by having cows and pigs and poultry and ducks and vegetables and fruit. She also had a sublime faith that everything would be all right and as she was despite her exquisite appearance and apparently easy-going ways a very competent organizer and arranger, nothing that she did was less than perfect. Her loving nature overflowed in many practical ways and her only slight grief was that her husband could not always get down for the weekends. One other small sorrow she had. Her beloved and sometimes maddening mother had found the long bitter black winter very trying and had lost some of her vitality. With the summer and the warmth she had become almost her old self, but Lady Graham and Miss Merriman had both noticed that Lady Emily was a little slower in her movements, a little less clear in her mind. Nothing to trouble one; but sometimes past and present would mix in her mind and she would call her elder grandson by the name of her son who had been killed in Flanders, or wonder if mamma was feeling the cold, when the Countess of Pomfret, who was her mother, had not feared the furious winter's rages for nearly fifty years. But there was nothing ungracious in these lapses and Lady Emily was still most beautiful, especially when she was quietly musing, her exquisitely chiselled face like alabaster, her handsome kind hawk's eyes veiled, the inner light of her love and kindness shining like a lamp through a window in the dusk.

At the present moment her ladyship after a short rest was in excellent spirits and enjoying with all her heart the crowded lunch-table where everyone was a relation; all except Miss Merriman, who with extreme skill managed to be indispensable and to be liked by everyone while keeping her private life inviolate. The noise and chatter were loud and continuous. News from Little Misfit and Rushwater was exchanged. Ducks and new potatoes and green peas vanished, as did gooseberry pies and junket and early strawberries. Among the voices Lucy

Marling and Emmy Graham were the loudest as they argued about the Barsetshire Pig-Breeders' Association's attitude to White Porkminsters, which everybody knew were created for the sole purpose of being crossed with Crop-backed Crunchers, thus producing more streaky bacon to the square inch than anyone had yet produced. But the B.P.B.A., for by these mystic initials was the Association known among the friends of pigs, was rent from top to bottom on this question, a noisy minority most regrettably taking the view that Norfolk Nobblers would be better for crossing.

"It's just the Government," said Emmy, both elbows on the table and both legs, if anyone had looked, hooked round the legs of her chair. "They don't *want* streaky bacon. They want bacon that's all lean so that we'll have less fats, and that's why the President of the B.P.B.A. is backing Norfolk Nobblers. Nasty lean pigs they are and you can feed them till they burst but they won't fatten. If only Sir Edmund Pridham was still President, he wouldn't stand any nonsense. This man is a rank outsider. He only got in by telling lies about how the Government was keen on pigs. Next year Sir Edmund will be in again for certain. Anyway the secretary's good. He's one of Gillie's farmers and his people have been Pomfret tenants for more than a hundred years."

"I'll tell you what," said Lucy, leaning right across Martin Leslie the better to talk to Emmy, "what this Government wants is to starve us all so that we'll be too weak to stand up for ourselves."

This very reasonable theory was received with applause. Lady Graham said she thought everything had got a bit beyond the Government, but she did think it a shame not to give schoolboys extra rations.

"If they did, the schools would nobble them," said James. "And the colleges too. Some of our lot who went up to Oxbridge last year are nearly starved. And look at Henley. The Yanks can give our crews a stone each, and the Yanks are only schoolboys."

"And the poor starving Dutch are the same," said John. "A stone heavier all through the boat."

"I must say," said Martin Leslie, "that it seems very silly to have Olympic games here. To begin with we shall be the only real amateurs and to go on with our teams will be perfectly undernourished. Still, if that's what the Government wants—"

Lady Graham and Miss Merriman were by now having a kind of private debating society about how well schools and colleges could feed their pupils if anyone had any sense, and what they would do if they had anything from one to three hundred ration books to draw on, till Lady Graham, glancing at her mother, saw that she looked perplexed and at once diverted the talk back to the original theme of the Pig-Breeders' show and the brilliant plan of combining it with the Conservative Rally, which would undoubtedly show Them what They were up against. Rushwater, Holdings, and Marling were showing pigs and there was much speculation as to what Lord Bond, Lord Stoke, and Mr. Palmer would be showing, for the private rivalry, which was intense though friendly, would be sunk against any common enemy such as Lord Aberfordbury.

"Lord Who?" said Sylvia Leslie, emerging from her own thoughts, which were whether Miss Eleanor Leslie, aged not yet one, was going to spit out her lunch again today as she had yesterday.

"He was Hibbard," said Martin. "The one that tried to get Pooker's Piece but Uncle Giles frightened him away. I say, Gran, did I tell you we've had the crack in the Temple mended and the inside whitewashed and the windows rehung? When are you coming over to see it?"

"You haven't whitewashed the drawings, have you, Martin?" said his grandmother, for all her children had drawn and chalked on the walls of the Temple, a pyramidal monument on the hill behind Rushwater, and many of her grandchildren as well.

"Of course not, Gran," said Martin. "I do love David's picture of the princess with long hair in a tower and the knight riding past. Oh, and Uncle John's poem."

"What was Uncle John's poem?" said his cousin Clarissa, who had been quietly looking after her grandmother.

"It was awfully good," said Martin. "It said,

> Ding, dong, bell,
> Fräulein goes to hell,"

at which brilliant witticism the younger Leslies laughed a great deal. Edith, the poet of the family, murmured the distich abstractedly, evidently memorizing it with a view to future use.

"I remember John writing that quite well, mamma," said Lady Graham. "It was that horrid Fräulein Hagenstolz that we had one summer and John wouldn't sing 'A B C Die Katze lief im Schee' and she kept him in the schoolroom and made him write it out ten times, so he made a poem about her. I tried to rub it out but he had licked his pencil for every word and it wouldn't come off."

"Frawlein, your father always called her," said Lady Emily, who had got a gold chain, a pair of eyeglasses on a purple ribbon, and a pearl necklace into hopeless confusion and was trying to disentangle them with a fork. Clarissa took the knots in her neat fingers and loosened them all, while her grandmother continued: "and he would call all the French governesses madermerzell. I shall always think of him at Lord's. He did so love the cricket, which was almost duller than anyone could believe, except the Eton and Harrow match when darling David carried his bat."

These jottings from Lady Emily's memory were listened to in respectful silence, broken by Emmy, who asked how many runs Uncle David had made.

"I don't exactly remember," said Lady Emily with an air of great candour. "Oh, thank you, darling Clarissa. Now I can use my glasses, though there is really nothing I want to see through them at the moment. He went in last and before he had done any batting the other batter was out. We dined at Claridge's and I saw the Hartletops and the de Courcy's drinking cider cup. It looked so delightfully cool."

"When we lived at Hendon," said John Leslie aloud to himself, "Barnes's gander was stolen by tinkers."

"I never thought of it before," said Martin, delighted. "Of course, darling Gran *is* Mr. F.'s aunt. Gran, will you come and see the Temple when Uncle John and Aunt Mary and the boys are with us? We could have a kind of reunion at Rushwater. How many Leslies could we manage?"

The whole table except Miss Merriman and Lucy Marling then began talking at once, making elaborate calculations of Lady Emily's descendants and descendants-in-law, and after a great deal of arguing it was generally agreed that counting everybody it would be about twenty.

"Too few," said Lady Emily, half to herself, so that only Clarissa on one side and Robert on the other heard her. "The Flowers of the Forest."

"Why too few, Gran?" said Robert, who was perhaps nearer to his grandmother's heart than any of the other grandchildren.

"There was Martin's father," said Lady Emily. "And there was Gay. Beauty vanishes, beauty passes."

"I'll remember them, Gran," said Robert. "We will have a private remembering together," at which his grandmother looked at him affectionately and put a spoonful of salt into her coffee.

Her granddaughter Clarissa quietly removed the cup, fetched a fresh cup of coffee, and put the sugar-basin in front of Lady Emily.

"I thought I *had* put sugar into my coffee," said her ladyship, puzzled. "Now I am going to rest and at teatime we will have a long talk about the Rushwater party. And you and I must have a talk," she said to Lucy as she got up.

With Clarissa and Robert as bodyguard she managed to get

out of the room without any serious loss of portable property and was grudgingly wafted away by Conque.

Emmy, who lived, slept, ate, and breathed cows at Rushwater, then suggested to Lucy Marling as a delightful change that they might go and look at her father's cows and generally visit the farm and have a talk with the bailiff, who always spent Sunday afternoon looking at the pigs. Lucy closed with the suggestion at once and they strolled in a manly way towards the home farm.

Cow and pig talk makes us all equal if we know our subject, and so much on an equality were the two girls that Lucy began talking of the Barsetshire Agricultural Show as it was when old Lord Pomfret was alive, before the war.

"I never went then," said Emmy. "At least mother did take us, but I was in the schoolroom and didn't really know about cows. It must have been ripping. Do tell me about it."

At which words Lucy suddenly realized the gulf between Emmy and herself, a difference of twelve years or so in their ages, which at the present rate of the world's so-called progress meant that they belonged to different generations. Luckily cows are a common denominator, and age did not much matter with anyone like Emmy, who had the root of the matter in her, but Lucy again felt the chill she had felt when thinking of life at Marling Hall. She must seem to Emmy nearly as old as her parents. Though in this she was wrong, for Emmy, who dealt entirely with facts, looked upon Lucy as an authority on farming and was not in the least puffed up by her own more intimate knowledge of cows.

"I say, Lucy," said Emmy as they went into the home farm-yard, rich in delightful smells of manure, "do you remember when you showed me how to wring a chicken's neck? That winter Lettice married Tom Barclay and you and your mother came over to Holdings. I practised with a scarf, the way you showed me, and then I got Goble to let me try it on a pullet that had broken its leg and I did it right first time. It's been awfully useful, because quite a lot of people don't like wringing their necks. I can't think why," said Emmy reflectively. "I mean they practically feel nothing, because all that flapping is just reaction or something. Let's see if Goble is at the other side."

They walked across the yard, baking in the hot sun, and went through the great stone barn on the opposite side. Both the great doors were wide open. Sunlight streamed across the openings, full of golden dust. Warm comfortable scents of straw and sacks filled the air. They passed through the dimmer light and came out again into the full radiance of a midsummer sun, beaten back from the stone walls. At right angles to the barn lay what might almost be called a pig colony, with neat brick-paved sties kept in apple-pie order and above each sty the name of the present occupier.

"Hullo, there's Goble," said Emmy, shading her eyes with one hand. "Come on and we'll get him to show us the new litter."

Followed by Lucy she hastened her steps to where Mr. Goble, the bailiff, in his Sunday blacks, was leaning over one of the front gates in fond contemplation of an immense sow. What looked like twenty or thirty piglets were fighting and squealing for their lunch. Goble was scratching the sow's back with a stick and appeared to be in a kind of blissful Nirvana, so that Emmy had to call him twice before he looked round.

"Hullo, Goble," said Emmy. "This is Miss Marling. Her father has some decent pigs."

"Good afternoon, miss," said Goble, touching his bowler hat with his disengaged hand. "I remember Mr. Marling's little lot at the Barsetshire Agricultural in 1919, just after the war. As nice a lot of pigs as ever a man wanted to see. He had a good pigman too. Pucken his name was, from over Skeynes way. Yes. Pucken took a first that year and I only took a second. Ah, pigs was pigs then. None of these mucky, begging your pardon, miss, Norfolk Nobblers then. Now there's a pig as I wouldn't call a pig, that Nobbler. Mark my words, miss, you'll never get good bacon from a Nobbler, not if you were to cross them with the King himself."

He gave the sow a sympathetic scratch behind her ear, which caused her to shake with ecstasy and several of her brood to squeal with terror and rage.

"Pucken's awfully rheumaticky," said Lucy, "but he gets about still. Father's sending a White Porkminster to the B.P.B.A. What are you sending?"

"Ah!" said Mr. Goble. "That's what they all want to know. You come this way, miss. All right, old lady," he added to the sow. "I'm coming back."

He then led the way to the end of the street of sties of round the corner to a rather larger sty, in which was standing the largest and squarest White Porkminster that Lucy had ever seen. When we say that it was standing, we can only conclude from the position of its back and its ears that it was on its feet, for its immense bulk almost filled the sty and almost touched the ground.

"I say!" said Lucy reverently.

"Clarissa says he's a double cube," said Emmy. "She's always talking about cubes and things. I think he's more like a pantechnicon. Isn't he an *angel*?"

Words failed them as they gazed at the huge mass. The White Porkminster looked malevolently at them out of one small eye and shifted his position slightly.

"That's right, old fellow," said Goble. "I know what you want," and with his stick he drew arabesques on the monster's back, prodding him delicately in likely places and scratching him slowly down the spine. The White Porkminster snorted quite terrifyingly.

"There, miss," said Goble, leading them back to the sow's sty. "That's our man. Just under fifty score."

"Well, he'll beat ours hollow," said Lucy generously. "I say, Mr. Goble, how *do* you do it?"

At which question Goble laughed in a low rumbling way and said that was asking questions.

"You'll tell Pucken to come over and see me some day, miss," he said. "I'd like to see Pucken again. And my respects to your father, miss, and may the best pig win."

He touched his bowler hat and began scratching the sow again, so absorbed in her and her squealing, pushing, stout children that Lucy's good-bye did not reach him.

"He's all right, isn't he?" said Emmy in an offhand way. Lucy, too deeply moved for speech, nodded violently.

"The sow's all right, too," she said as soon as she could speak. "She's like a British Restaurant. I say, Emmy, I *do* like Holdings."

"Oh, it's all right," said Emmy, "and the pigs are fun. But I like Rushwater better. Sylvia and I are going to buy some more cows and get the big cowshed repaired and go in for milk on a big scale. It's too much for Martin with his leg. But he's most awfully good at accounts and he's standing for the County Council. And we've a fine two-year-old bull coming on, Rushwater Churchill. He'll be the best since great-grandfather's Rushwater Ramper."

Again Lucy felt the ache at her heart. Her father was still a farming squire, still breeding his cattle and his pigs, but it was probably the end. When he died Bill would not care for farming, nor would he be able to keep the place up. With luck Marling Hall might be let to nice people, or taken over for some county work. There was a pleasant enough red brick house in the village let on a yearly lease, and to this Mrs. Marling would probably go and Lucy might live with her, or she might set up house with Oliver, though not in London. She would always love Marling and work for it. But there seemed to her nothing to come. Emmy and Sylvia were quite young. Sylvia already had a child and would doubtless have more. Emmy would probably marry, and the line of Leslies would go on and there would always be youth somewhere. She had a vision of Rushwater, placid and contented in the sun, full of work and life. Then she saw Marling under a grey sky, all the old world tumbling down and no new world to replace it. Willingly would she have confided her trouble to a friendly person, but Emmy would never understand. Oliver would understand, but he was powerless to do anything, a younger son earning his own living and preferring London. As for Tom Barclay, she defied anyone to say that she had ever really cared for him much, and that was that. Oh well. She forced herself to talk to Emmy about Rushwater, and they continued their tour of the home farm.

Meanwhile James and John and Robert had gone to bathe in the river, accompanied by several dogs. Edith and Nurse had gone to tea with Mrs. Panter in the village, wife of the Halliday's carter, where Nurse was speaking with great condescension of how nice Mrs. Martin Leslie looked and it was to be hoped they would hear of another in the family before very long. After which she and Mrs. Panter indulged in various calculations of the goddess Lucina's views, but we may say on no grounds at all at present. Lady Emily and Lady Graham were resting, Miss Merriman had gone off in the little car to help Lady Pomfret to sort some horrible furniture at the Towers, dating from the year of the Great Exhibition, so that it could go to a Mammoth Auction in aid of the Red Cross. Martin and Sylvia had gone to see her parents, the Hallidays at Hatch End.

So Clarissa found herself alone, a most unusual state of things at Holdings; and also a little lonely. She could not in any sense be called the misfit of the family, but she did not always feel quite at home in it. Her mother was gently and ceaselessly occupied. Her grandmother was the most delightful of companions and Clarissa felt for her almost the protective feeling of a mother for a child, but Gran was so often sleepy now, or talking about a world that Clarissa had never known. Emmy was completely absorbed in Rushwater, and the boys all at school. After some mild opposition from her parents Clarissa had about two years earlier got herself sent to school and had now, as we know, taken a mathematical scholarship and was to go to college in the autumn with the ambition of getting into an engineering firm as a draughtswoman, if such a word exists. To those who did not know her well her extreme elegance, her poise, her good looks, gave the impression that she would be what is mistakenly called a society butterfly. But there is alas little enough sun for the sadly few butterflies now. There must have been in Clarissa something of her father's ambition and steadiness of purpose, something of her Leslie grandfather's business instinct, transmuted in her from prize bulls to engineering draughtsmanship; something too of her great-uncle, old Lord Pomfret's ruthless egoism. She had charming manners by nature and training, but if really annoyed she could on occasion use a small sharp dagger with great accuracy, as her uncle, David Leslie, had found to his cost when he tried to patronize her.

Not often did she feel lonely, for her life was filled by her family and school, and during the holidays she was ceaselessly occupied and her clever elegant fingers were always at work, sewing, embroidering, drawing, painting, carving, in which tastes she resembled her grandmother, Lady Emily, on a smaller and neater scale. But during this summer the world had changed to her. A threat of infantile paralysis, which was adding to the general horrors of peace, had made her school break up early, and though she was delighted to be at home, she had the unreal feeling one knows so well of having already left a place that one knows one is going to leave.

To outward eyes she was Clarissa Graham in her parents' house, but her spirit was already at college furiously pursuing the higher mathematics and engineering, and she found this divided existence more than a little perplexing. Of boys and young men of her own generation she had seen plenty and had a large circle of friends, but so far none of them had penetrated to the real Clarissa, nor perhaps had she herself. The person who probably understood her best was her uncle David, Lady Emily's youngest and best beloved. There had been a time when David and his niece Clarissa had not got on well together. David had, so Clarissa considered, given himself airs, and in David's view Clarissa had been a precocious and spoilt monkey. But time and

David's delightful wife, Rose Bingham, had much improved the relationship between uncle and niece, and he and Clarissa had a kind of private family bond.

If only Uncle David were here, Clarissa thought, as she began industriously to darn the socks that her brothers had brought back from school, one could tell him lots of things and he would understand that one was really grown up, not a nice little girl with good manners. But David and Rose were in Paris, so she must keep her growing pains to herself and concentrate on James's socks, contemptuously unpicking some of the darns and doing them again in the pattern of the ribs as Conque, an exquisite needlewoman, had shown her. So she sat on the terrace in a not unpleasing melancholy, her fingers industriously employed, her thoughts wandering in many directions, and some of them to that nice Anne Fielding who was to marry Robin Dale, a housemaster at Southbridge, this summer, and how Anne had half promised to introduce her to Mr. Adams, the wealthy ironmaster at Hogglestock, into whose designing-rooms Clarissa had decided to go. She knew that her parents did not quite approve of Mr. Adams, or rather did not wish to have the honour of his further acquaintance beyond the meetings in public places that were inevitable, but she saw no reason why Clarissa Graham, a person in her own right, should not know a man who might be very useful to her career.

The sun was warm. The rich golden air was full of garden scents, no breeze stirred, bees hummed steadily as they went about their shopping, and Clarissa fell into a kind of dream of warmth and light with her elegant hands idle in her lap. So entranced was she that she did not hear a car at the front of the house and was greatly surprised to see three people coming round the corner of the house onto the terrace, which people revealed themselves to her sun-dazzled eyes as Mrs. Belton and her two sons.

"I hope we didn't surprise you," said Mrs. Belton as Clarissa got up, dropping a lapful of socks and upsetting her workbasket.

"We did ring but nobody answered. It is so often like that at home on Sundays. So we came round the house."

Clarissa, by now completely mistress of herself, said her mother was resting and everyone else had gone out, but there would soon be tea and how nice it was of Mrs. Belton to come.

"I know mother was expecting you," she said, "because it's all down in her engagement book. I'll go and find her."

But Mrs. Belton begged her not to disturb Agnes just yet, so Clarissa took the guests for a walk round the garden and played the hostess very prettily. Very prettily indeed, thought Captain Belton, observing her elegant form, her studied deference to his mother, her easy and natural way of talking. And his mind went back to a colder and more windswept garden on the east coast where an Admiral's daughter who was a Wren used to come on leave till German raiders dropped death from a cloudy night, and his heart stirred with an old ache and the sunlight looked grey. Then he exerted himself and talked to Clarissa and observed with private amusement that his mother had matchmaking in her eye.

"And this," said Clarissa, pausing before a large stone basin set against a wall, where water bubbled up among green slime and slimy weeds, "is where we always thought the Frog Prince lived. Emmy and I got a tennis ball and painted it with gold paint and threw it into the pool, but the Frog Prince never came, which was very sad."

She had been dabbling in the water with one hand as she spoke and suddenly gave a little cry.

"Here it is," she said, opening her hand to show a decayed tennis ball with a gleam of tarnished gold clinging to it. "That must have been before I went to school."

"But no Frog Prince," said Captain Belton.

"Only you and Charles," said Clarissa, with a little air of mockery, and she dropped the slimy ball into the pool.

"'King's daughter, fairest,'" said Captain Belton, "'let me eat from your golden plate and drink from your golden cup,'" and then they all laughed and went back to the terrace, where Lady Graham came towards them, cooing apologies for having been asleep. On seeing Lady Graham, Charles Belton fell in love all over again, which Clarissa watched with detached friendly malice. And then what she had foreseen took place, for Lady Emily appeared at the door of the Saloon leaning on her stick like an exquisite witch and, as Captain Belton afterwards expressed it to his mother, mopped up the gentlemen body and soul. All of which did not affect Lady Graham in the least as she poured out the tea at a long table in the Saloon and the young people came trooping back from farm and field and river.

How Lady Graham found food enough for all the young we do not know, but the loaves and fishes are multiplied every day by the good inarticulate housewives of England and will be as long as there are young to be fed and housewives to plan for them and, in most cases, to give up their own share. Lady Graham was a good housekeeper and had a sympathetic cook who believed, as she said, in filling young stomachs and if we can't give the young ladies and gentlemen a proper tea, your ladyship, and beat all those old Hitlers with ten ration books too, we did ought to be ashamed of ourselves. To which Lady Graham, who had been getting some American flour and shortening and dried fruits out of what she called her hoarding cupboard in what used to be the housekeeper's room, answered that at least we hadn't a Hitler.

"Well, my lady," said Cook, "their name mayn't be Hitler, but that's what the Government are, a set of Hitlers. I'd just like to see Them standing in queues and making one rasher do for a week," said Cook vengefully. "Meals at clubs and restaurants and all that, that's the way They live, and there They'll stay as long as They get the money. And tinned sausages have gone up on points, my lady, so Mrs. Hubback at the shop was telling me. And the Schools just as bad. If it wasn't for us sending parcels to the young gentlemen they'd be skin and bone. Ulcerated stomachs too," said Cook with gloomy relish. "I've made some nice

rock-cakes, my lady, and six sponges. I s'pose they'll be putting
hens on points soon," said Cook sarcastically, "to stop us getting
any eggs."

At this point Lady Graham had melted out of the housekeeper's room, leaving Cook to argue with an invisible opponent
about Them, after which she went back to the kitchen, where
she found the kitchen-maid, aged fifteen, reading a newspaper
of semi-official character given to her by a young man who
believed in Moscow.

"Ow, Cook, it says the King and Queen have gold plates,"
said the kitchen-maid. "Doesn't it seem awful? I wish I had a
gold plate, Cook."

"Now how often have I told you not to waste time reading,"
said Cook. "Give me that paper, Marlene, and get on with your
work and don't you meddle with what doesn't concern you.
Have you done the potatoes the way I said?"

"Yes, Cook," said Marlene. "Oh, Cook, it says in a piece in the
paper that every kitchen should have a nautomactic potato-
peeler, so as girls wouldn't get their hands dirty."

"Now, my girl," said Cook, bundling the potato peelings into
the newspaper, "just put that in the dust-bin and that's about all
that paper's fit for. Dirty hands indeed. My hands have been a
lot dirtier than yours'll ever be, and no red nails neither. Just take
that stuff off your nails at once, Marlene, and use plenty of Vim,
or we'll all get blood-poisoning. Good dirt never hurt nobody,"
said Cook, "but nasty dirt, that's a thing I can't abide. When
you've cleaned the scullery I dessay I'll give you a rock-cake. I'm
making some for tea and they're made with American flour and
mind you remember it, because the Americans have sent her
ladyship all the things this Government won't let us have."

"Ow, I *do* like the Americans, Cook," said Marlene. "One of
them gave me—"

"Now that's enough, my girl," said Cook. "It's not for a girl of
your age to talk about Americans and you'll be lucky if it's no
more than talk," said Cook darkly. "But if you do say your

prayers at night, and I hope you do because if you don't you know where you'll go, just you remember the Americans. Anyone that thinks about their stomach the way you do," said Cook, "ought to go down on their knees for real flour and not that stuff the Government gives us. Now, that's quite enough chatter," which last criticism was manifestly unfair, but Marlene accepted it meekly with a nice rock-cake in view.

On the terrace conversation was running on much the same lines as the older guests praised the rock-cakes and the fair-faced sponge sandwiches. As for the younger guests, quantity not quality was their motto and they were just as happy with the sandwiches of Government grey india-rubber bread and Holding's jam which cook had lavishly provided.

"I can't think," said Captain Belton, "when I last saw a proper rock-cake. What lovely complexions they have."

"And the Victoria sandwich," said Mrs. Belton, "a perfect dream with real castor sugar on it."

Emmy asked what a Victoria sandwich was, to which Miss Merriman replied that two rounds of sponge with jam between them were always known as a Victoria sandwich in her youth, but now she came to think of it the word Victoria had dropped from usage; why she couldn't tell.

"The sugar is from American friends," said Lady Graham. "It is real sugar, not this odious beet. And the flour is from America and the currants, and the butter too. Everyone in America has been so very kind," which remark her ladyship's friends rightly interpreted as meaning not that every American was kind, but that all Lady Graham's friends were kind. "The dreadful thing is," said Lady Graham plaintively, "that there is absolutely *nothing* I can do to thank them except to write and thank them."

Mrs. Belton, who had also had some food parcels from the United States, joined her regrets to her hostess's.

"And if any of them do come over," she said, "you can't do anything for them except ask them to stay with you and give them no central heating and no hot baths and not enough to eat."

"And they ask you to lunch in London," said Captain Belton, "and always manage to get good food and if you take them to your club you can only apologize for it."

Lady Graham said she was quite sure they didn't mind things like that.

"I'll tell you what," said Lucy Marling. "Someone ought to write to the President or somebody to say that we all think the Americans are absolutely marvellous for going on sending us food. I mean anyone could send a person a parcel once, but when you keep on doing it you must be jolly kind. If I were the King I'd cut newspaper heads off if they try to make us not feel friends with America."

"And they send one nylons," said Clarissa. "Martin's mother sent twelve pairs of nylons to Sylvia and luckily they were too small so she gave them to me," and she exhibited in proof of this a very pretty leg in its fashionable coat.

A discussion then took place about (*a*) the word "nylon" and (*b*) nylons.

"I cannot get used to the word," said Lady Graham plaintively, "because it seems like nonsense. If it were 'pylons' I'd know what it meant."

"But you can't wear pylons, mother," said James, pausing for a moment in his attack upon the Victoria sandwich.

Lady Graham said she wondered if pylons and pyjamas had anything to do with each other, which foolish remark made Charles Belton's heart beat faster, as showing how exquisitely untouched by the world she was.

"Well, nylons are no use to *me*," said Emmy jovially. "They'd be in rags in ten seconds if I wore them in the cowshed. But I've got a nylon slip and it gets dry the minute you've washed it. I say, Sylvia, have you seen Goble's pigs? The White Porkminster is terrific. He's about the size of the *Queen Elizabeth*. Come on."

Followed by most of the younger people she went off to the

pig-sties again. A sudden peace descended upon the Saloon and the older people felt how delightful it was when the young went away, provided they did not go too far.

"I am so glad, Lucy," said Lady Emily to Mrs. Belton, "that you have both your dear boys safely at home now. I remember the first war so well and what one's anxiety was. And my eldest boy did not come back. Tell me about your boys. Freddy has the dearest face, but it is a face with a secret. Your Charles has no secrets and his face is his fortune. He is happy, isn't he?"

Mrs. Belton, overjoyed by this praise of her sons, said that she had never seen Charles unhappy except over things like a dog dying or losing his new gun in the lake when the punt sprang a leak, and he was so happy at the Priory School and brought such nice masters over to see them.

"And Freddy," said Lady Emily, "what is his secret?" And this was said with such loving interest in a cousin's son that Mrs. Belton could not resent it.

"It is a very old story, Cousin Emily," she said. "So old that I sometimes hope it is forgotten. I try to forget it, because I can't bear to think of his unhappiness," and tears forced themselves to her eyes as she spoke.

"I know, I know," said Lady Emily, who was putting the remains of a jam sandwich and half a rock-cake into the slop basin, moistening them with the remains of her cup of tea and mashing the whole with a teaspoon. "They think their hearts are broken because they can't have their wish, but young hearts don't break. Ours break to see theirs ache. Don't let yours break, my dear."

"Did you let yours break when Gay died and John was so unhappy, Cousin Emily?" said Mrs. Belton.

"Touchée," said Lady Emily, a gleam of amusement shooting through the remote sadness in her eyes. "It would have broken, my dear, except that I couldn't let it, because John needed me."

"And now he has been happy with Mary for a long, long time," said Mrs. Belton, "and all your heartbreak wasted."

"I don't know," said Lady Emily, abstractedly adding some cream to her mixture. "Perhaps if one's heart breaks a little, a piece of it goes to the child that is hurt and helps it: and what one gives one has. You know, Lucy, I miss Henry more and more. I thought I wouldn't. I thought I was so glad that he would never have a heart attack again. But you can't be married for so many years and not miss your companion. You will find that perhaps. All our women live very long, almost terrifyingly long. Now why am I making this mixture?" said her ladyship, suddenly aware of the horrid kind of porridge she had been stirring. "I simply cannot think. Yes I can. Conque's dog. She has got a French poodle who has mange and had been sent to the kennels. One of the Free French left him with her and he is called de Gaulle, but quite unlike. And I feel sure, my dear," said Lady Emily, coming back as she always did in the end to her starting-point, "that your Freddy will forget his secret or find it again. I know he will. As for Charles, a star danced when he was born. He has been happy in war and will be happy in love."

Mrs. Belton, unreasonably cheered by her cousin's soothsaying, or what her son David Leslie called Mother being the Original Gypsy Lee, said that the second part was coming true already, as Charles was head over ears in love with Agnes.

Lady Emily's bright eyes flickered with amusement as she looked towards her daughter, who was uttering dovelike idiocies about the unusual qualities of her children: the keen wish for soldiering of James, the fine agricultural sense of Emmy, the brains of Clarissa, the goodness of John, Robert's wonderful sense of words, and Edith's real poetic talent.

"When Robert had only just gone to prep school," said Lady Graham, her soul in her eyes, "he saw a picture by Mr. Scatcherd, who is an artist in the village, really quite an unusually bad one even for an artist," said her ladyship earnestly trying to explain herself, "and he said it was an admiring picture."

She paused for these remarkable words to make their full effect.

"By Jove!" said Charles Belton reverently. "I suppose he meant the artist admired the—the whatever it was he was painting."

"Not quite that," said Agnes, slightly disappointed. Charles noticed her disappointment and wished he could shoot himself for being gross and clumsy and then have himself stuffed and made into a doormat for the goddess. "It was just the way he put it. An admiring picture."

"I know," said Charles, an echo of a song heard in his childhood coming to him. "He meant it was a picture for admiring; the fine song for singing."

"*How* well you understand things," said Agnes gratified. "And what is so dreadful, Charles, is that in the autumn I shall have only Edith left. James will be in the Army, Emmy lives at Rushwater, Clarissa will be at college, and John and Robert at Eton. I expect you know their housemaster, Mr. Manhole. He comes for the weekend sometimes."

Charles did remember Mr. Manhole and his mild contempt for his old housemaster was roused to active hatred by the thought of old Manhole being privileged to sleep under the same roof as Lady Graham, to have meals in her company, probably to go for a walk with her, and even, though this was almost more than flesh and blood could bear, sit next to her in church.

"Clarissa must be awfully clever," he said.

"I suppose she is," said Agnes. "You know, Charles, it is a little sad that Emmy and Clarissa don't want to go to dances or have a season in London—not that there is much season left, but it is a good way of seeing friends. I did take Emmy to a garden party, but it was hard work because Martin was expecting a new tractor and she was thinking of it all the time. And I want to take Clarissa next year, but if she is at college I am afraid she may wear spectacles and despise me. I hope darling Edith will be more social. You know, I was engaged at a dance," her ladyship continued. "Did I ever tell you about it?"

Charles said she hadn't and felt a stab of jealousy for Sir Robert Graham, K.C.B., who had won this rich prize, this peerless jewel.

"It was a very nice dance at the house of some friends of mama's whose name I don't remember," said Agnes, "somewhere off Belgrave Square or was it Grosvenor Square, but it doesn't really matter except that it was a very fine, warm night."

She paused, overcome by this interesting recollection. Charles hung breathless on her words.

"And Robert took me down to supper," Agnes continued, looking pensively into the past, "and a waiter spilt some coffee all down his shirt-front and I said: 'Oh, Colonel Graham, that coffee will stain your shirt!' So he asked if he could have the next dance but two and he went straight back to his rooms and put on a clean shirt and came back and proposed to me."

"I say!" said Charles. And as his hostess had apparently finished her story he ventured to add: "What did you say?"

Agnes looked gratified.

"I don't exactly remember," she said, "but Robert said something very nice about mamma and I said that sounded very nice, so we got engaged."

Charles let out the breath he had been holding. Not only was the story deliciously exciting, but the whole atmosphere was high romance. An exquisite woman, wife of a distinguished general, was confiding in him, Charles Belton, a younger son and a schoolmaster, the inmost secrets of her life; her courtship and her hopes and fears for her children.

"I say, Lady Graham," he said, with a slight impediment in his speech due to love, "I do wish I could help you. I mean do something for you. I mean *anything*."

"Perhaps you could," said Agnes, "only it is rather dull. Poor Clarissa is a little lonely I think. There is no one of her age here when Emmy and the boys are away and she is so clever at arithmetic and things. Do come over when you can and amuse her. She is quite good at tennis and we have two horses and there is the farm and the river. I know you are *very* busy in the week, but perhaps your school would let you out at weekends. And I do so want Robert to meet you. It is such hard luck that he cannot come down this weekend. I must see what mamma is doing."

Throwing a dazzling smile at Charles, she went over to inspect her mother's activities.

"Oh, mamma, what have you been doing?" she asked, looking at Lady Emily's mess of pottage.

"It is for Conque's poodle," said Lady Emily. "The poor creature is at the kennels with mange."

"But the kennels are three miles away, mamma," said Agnes.

"I thought," said her mother, who had trailed an end of her scarf in the jam and was pouring the tepid dregs of the silver kettle over it and flooding the tray, "that when Lucy and the boys go home they could just drop the bowl at the kennels. There is no one there who speaks French and the poodle must be hungry."

Even Agnes for all her mild addlepatedness was struck by the want of reasoning in her mother's suggestion.

"Let me have it, mamma," she said, taking the bowl, "and I will ring up the kennels and tell them to be *sure* to see that the poodle has plenty of food."

Lady Emily, though unconvinced, gave way and said she thought she would rest now. Conque was summoned and Lady Emily bade farewell most affectionately to Mrs. Belton and Charles, left her love for Freddy, and disappeared under Conque's implacable eye.

"We really must go," said Mrs. Belton. "I wonder where Freddy is," and then Nurse and Edith came back from tea with Mrs. Panter.

"Say how-do-you-do to Mrs. Belton, Edith," said Nurse, "and to Captain Charles."

"How do you do," said Edith.

"Mrs. Belton
                Had a belt on."

"That's quite enough, Edith," said Nurse, not at all hiding her
pride. "And tell mother we saw Captain Belton and Clarissa as
we were coming back by the river path."

"Do go and fetch Freddy," said his mother to Charles, who
accordingly went off across the lawn to the little gate that leads
into the water meadows and so down the river path, where he
met the wanderers.

There was something very kind in Captain Belton that made
him listen to people when they talked about themselves. This
trait can give a good deal of trouble to its owner, as people who
want to talk about themselves scent it miles away and lose no
opportunity of benefiting by it. What Captain Belton had not
heard in the way of confidences, from the Admiral to the lowest
rating, from Lady Pomfret to Wheeler the chimney-sweep, is
hardly worth mentioning. To all these outpourings he gave
deliberate attention and usually refrained from giving advice
because he did not think it would be wanted and certainly would
not be taken. On the rare occasions when he had uttered his
views he had usually mended matters, or at least had not made
them any worse, which is about all one can expect. Once he
knew he had been able to help, in the case of Heather Adams,
daughter of the wealthy M.P. ironmaster, who had blurted the
secrets of her silly heart to him and ever since been very grateful,
though without sentiment, for his practical way of taking it.

No two people could be more unlike than the fat, awkward,
plain Heather Adams and the elegant, well-born, well-bred
Clarissa, but both girls were growing up in a troubled world.
Heather was suitably engaged and Captain Belton had not seen
her for some years, but Clarissa was about the age that Heather
had been and in spite of her poise and her instinctive worldliness
was not taking things easily.

Walking by the Rising, watching the dragonflies like blue

jewels shimmering over the river, Captain Belton congratulated Clarissa on her scholarship. Clarissa thanked him gracefully, but gave him to understand that scholarships, God forgive us, were ashes, cinders, dust, to which Captain Belton very reasonably replied why on earth had she gone in for one.

"I want to go into an engineering works as a draughtsman," said Clarissa. "Nobody understands. Mother and father were very kind about it, but they don't understand."

"You can't have your cake and eat it," said Captain Belton. "You have got your scholarship and I expect you will do very well at college. People don't understand one, you know. Even the dearest people in the world," said Captain Belton, thinking of his mother, "don't always understand. But one thing they can do and that is to go on loving one. So with your father and mother loving you and doing the work you like, it oughtn't to be too bad. Probably they are proud of you too. I have noticed with parents that they have a peculiar gift of turning anything they don't like in their children into a subject for pride. My people weren't very keen on the navy, but when I did pass fairly well into Dartmouth I believe they boasted like anything."

Clarissa looked at him with a quick piercing glance and liked what she saw.

"All right. I *am* a beast," she said. "And I'm going to work so hard that father and mother will boast. I shall get a first in mathematics and mother will cry and father will give me fifty pounds." To which Captain Belton replied that she was not at all a beast and what was she going to do when she had got her first.

"I don't quite know yet," said Clarissa. "You see none of the family know anything about engineering. Do you know Anne Fielding? She is going to marry Robin Dale before Christmas, he is a master at Southbridge and a great friend of Martin's, because they were both at Anzio, and she knows Mr. Adams's daughter and I'd love to get into his works, so I thought I would ask her to help me. Only by the time I have got my degree she may have forgotten," said Clarissa rather unhopefully.

"Perhaps I can help you," said Captain Belton. "I know Heather Adams and her father too."

Clarissa stopped, turned, and stared at him. That Freddy should know the Adams family was entirely unexpected and in the nature of a miracle. Suddenly she saw an open door where she expected no door to be.

"Oh, Freddy!" she said, clasping Captain Belton's arm with both hands. "But too marvellous, my dear. How?"

Captain Belton, amused at her sudden affectation and touched by her gesture, extricated himself courteously from her grasp and said he had known Heather Adams for some years. She had, he said, been at the school that was evacuated to Harefield and had been a good deal at Arcot House. "Mother likes her," he said, "and you know she doesn't easily like people that aren't of her world."

And then Charles came hot-foot in search of them and they went back to the house. Clarissa, forgetting her grown-upness, prattled happily to Charles about her plans and how Freddy was going to arrange for her to meet Mr. Adams's daughter so that she could ask for a job in the works.

"Heather!" said Charles, with the natural and quite healthy snobbery of the young. "Good Lord, Clarissa, you don't want to know that great suet pudding. She's perfectly ghastly. I say, you don't *really* want to go into old Adams's works, do you?"

"Oh, but yes, my dear," said Clarissa, suddenly drawing her stiletto. "One mightn't get married you know, and so one might as well have a job. You are schoolmastering, aren't you? I am going into Mr. Adams's works. I want a career, not to be a stick-in-the-mud, and I think Heather Adams sounds nice, and your mother likes her."

Poor simple Charles was entirely taken aback by this new Clarissa, and being a modest young man, thought that by stick-in-the-mud she probably meant himself and his school-mastering. Possibly it wasn't a career. Schoolmasters didn't make fortunes, not assistant masters at any rate. But the Priory School was such fun and Philip and Leslie so kind and the other masters good sorts and the boys jolly little beggars, and he was jolly lucky to be there. Lots of men he knew had spent their gratuity and were living on their parents and still wearily hunting for jobs, but here was he, by the greatest of good luck, independent of his parents and enjoying his work, and if Clarissa called him a stick-in-the-mud he liked the mud and proposed to stick in it, which thoughts made him keep silence as they walked back to the house. His brother saw what was happening and felt sorry for both of them. Charles was all right though, and Clarissa wasn't. Holdings was not at the moment the right place for her. She was beating her wings against imaginary bars and thinking too much of jobs and careers. It was not her fault. It was the fault of the spirit of unrest and dissatisfaction that was abroad. Lucky were those like Charles and himself whose lives were decided for them.

The navy was his life, his duty; and to Charles the education of little boys might be the same. Poor Clarissa, with no clear duty before her. Poor Clarissa so sure of herself, not yet knowing misfortunes or rebuffs. He hoped she never would, but felt anxious about the elegant, clever, wilful child.

Then they reached the terrace and were submerged in a great flood of farewells and plans for the future. Lady Emily was in the drawing-room, where the Beltons went to say good-bye, reclining on the big sofa, Edith at her feet, and getting some embroidery silks into a spider's web of muddle.

"Dear Lucy, come again soon," said Lady Emily, kissing Mrs. Belton affectionately. "We will have a delightful talk about your boys. Henry always liked them. We must have all sorts of plans for Freddy and make his secret come true. And Charles must go on being happy. It is the greatest gift," said Lady Emily. "I have been very, very happy. Mamma always said that even if there wasn't any happiness one must try to be happy without it. You remember how she spread happiness round her. Last winter I was worried that she might be feeling the cruel cold, but Agnes said there was central heating at Pomfret Towers now. Come again, soon."

Mrs. Belton kissed Lady Emily. Freddy and Charles with an unconscious gaucherie, all the more charming for being unconscious, raised her thin beautifully shaped fingers to their lips.

> "Good-bye, Freddy,
>   Come again, as soon as you are ready,"

chanted Edith.

> "Good-bye Charles—"

She paused.

"I thought that would beat you," said Charles, and picked her up in his strong arms, kissed her, and put her down.

> "Good-bye, Edith,
>   What a life she leadeth,"

he added, upon which Edith made eyes at him so shamelessly that Nurse coming in said really anyone would think Edith had been brought up like a little Hottentot and it was time for her supper. As the Beltons got into their car Clarissa appeared and begged Captain Belton not to forget his promise. To Charles she said in her most grown-up voice: "Amuse yourself nicely, my dear," and then kissed Mrs. Belton affectionately.

As they drove back to Harefield, Mrs. Belton expressed a certain anxiety about Lady Emily, but did not pursue her subject, for she was a sensible woman and knew that her old friend was surrounded by loving care.

"I am almost inclined to agree with Elsa that Clarissa is getting spoilt," she said, "but I dare say college will cure it."

"She wants to meet Heather," said Captain Belton, "so that

Adams will give her a job in his firm. Will you arrange it somehow, mother? I think she has grown up too fast, that is all."

Mrs. Belton, always delighted to please any of her children, at once agreed, wondering as she did so whether Freddy might find forgetfulness of his secret with that pretty child, so young and yet so mature. As for Charles, he said he couldn't understand girls and didn't want to. If Clarissa wanted to know that ghastly spotty Adams girl she was welcome, but he thought Lady Graham ought to be consulted, because she was so kind and wonderful and might be upset by that awful Heather. To which Mrs. Belton, who was quite aware of Agnes's fine imperturbability about everyone and everything so long as her family were well and happy, said she would see.

The party at Holdings was rapidly breaking up. Martin and Sylvia and Emmy tore themselves away from the farm and came to say good-bye to Lady Emily upon her sofa.

"Don't forget you are coming to Rushwater, Gran," said Martin. "I thought we might have the great family reunion on my birthday. Do you remember my seventeenth birthday, Gran, and the dance and how John got engaged to Mary next day, and those awful French people? What fun it was!"

"Darling Martin," said Lady Emily. "And Rose and Hermione were there with Dodo. We never thought David would marry Rose then. He has married Rose, hasn't he?"

Martin saw his grandmother's perplexed look and assured her that David and Rose were safely married and had two babies, and Lady Emily smiled her content. At the door he met Miss Merriman, just back from her afternoon at Pomfret Towers.

"I say, Merry," he said anxiously, "Gran wanted to know if David and Rose were married. Is that all right?"

Miss Merriman assured him that these lapses of memory meant nothing and all old people had them, so Martin, who was very fond of his grandmother, went away quite happily. Lucy Marling, who was waiting her turn to say good-bye, had heard the confusion and suddenly realized that at Holdings, for all the light and youth and happiness, there was a shadow. And though she did not wish anything to touch Holdings, she felt a vague comfort that Marling was not the only place where shadows fall. Then with her usual honesty she was ashamed of herself for selfishness and resolved that she would work harder than ever for Marling and not let herself indulge in forebodings. And she would have a nice comfortable talk with Oliver next weekend.

When she had gone, Miss Merriman and Agnes sat with Lady Emily, who was all agog to hear what furniture Lady Pomfret had decided to dispose of, and displayed a lively recollection of various hideous chairs and an ecclesiastical sideboard and a gigantic dumbwaiter.

"And there is that quite dreadful German bronze statuette of a knight in armour with long moustaches," she said. "We always called it Aslauga's Knight. It is in mamma's dressing-room."

Miss Merriman said Lady Pomfret had sent a special message to ask if Lady Emily would mind it being jumbled in a good cause.

"How kind Sally is!" said Lady Emily, her beautiful eyes shining with gratitude and affection. "And I am sure mamma didn't mind. Merry, I think I will have my dinner here. So many people make my old bones ache a little."

Miss Merriman said she thought this a very good plan, as supper was apt to be noisy with the children at home. So Lady Emily had a tray and then got her embroidery silks into a worse muddle than ever till Clarissa, with neat elegant fingers, disentangled them and wound them onto pieces of cardboard. Outside, the boys shouted and laughed in the late sunlight, and Lady Emily lay with an amused loving look on her face till Conque descended and took her away for the night.

About half past ten Miss Merriman looked in on Lady Graham, who was writing letters.

"Conque says Lady Emily is reading in bed and quite comfortable," she said, "and I thought you would like to know. Good night, Lady Graham."

"Good night, Merry, and thank you so much," said Lady Graham. "I will go and say good night to her."

But this was not in the least what was in their minds.

CHAPTER 5

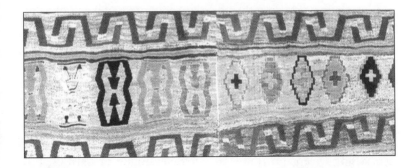

Mrs. Belton had not forgotten that her son Freddy would like her to make a personal call on the Red Cross Hospital Libraries to thank the librarian for looking after H.M.S. *Barsetshire*, but for some time she had no opportunity of getting to the city. This may sound unreasonable, but life is now so shortened and hemmed in that the things one ought to do accumulate in a Sisyphus ball, and even more the things one would like to do, which last one usually ends by giving up as a bad job. What with her duties to Arcot House and Harefield, a visit to Elsa and her grandchildren in Scotland, the exhausting resumption of duties at home, the difficulty of petrol, the way in which no day however long had enough hours in it, and the increasing fatigue of life, she had put off going to Barchester again and again. But the annual meeting of the Women's Institutes she could not miss, so she determined to make a day of it in Barchester; call at the Deanery, lunch at the Women's County Club, have her face cleaned, perhaps run in to see Lady Fielding, and in general go to the devil. Having resolved to do all these things and committed herself by letter and telephone, she then lay awake for several nights wishing that she hadn't and suffering mentally in advance the fatigue and frustration that the day would probably bring. In which she was only behaving like most other people who had taken six years of war with uncomplaining courage and were now being starved, regimented, and generally ground down by their present rulers, besides the deep hidden shame of feeling that England's name had been lowered in the eyes of all lesser breeds.

This condition was so widespread in England that people had to recognize it and to try rather unsuccessfully to laugh themselves into a happier state of mind; but it was not easy to keep it up. Sleep that did not refresh, the endless struggle to get food and clothes, and the nastiness of the food and the clothes when you got them, the gradual disappearance from the shops of everything except horrible fancy articles made of plastics, the surging crowds of foreigners everywhere, the endless waits at the Food Office and the Fuel Office; the overcrowded buses and trains, the daily humiliation of one's country and oneself, the gradual decay of houses and gardens for want of labour and materials, the increasing difficulty of finding anywhere to live when the Government stopped building plans, the increasing inquisitioned prying of officials into private affairs, were all bringing people into a state of dull resentful apathy with no hope of relief.

"Lots of people say they are going to emigrate," said Mrs. Belton to Mrs. Sidney Carton, who was also going into Barchester by the bus that morning, "but I don't think I could and candidly my husband wouldn't. I wonder if we could go into the village aims-houses when we are a little older. My husband's great-grandfather built them, so it would be quite reasonable."

"I'm quite sure you couldn't," said Mrs. Carton. "Homes for the aged middle class won't come in our time, and by the time they do come there probably won't be any middle classes. And when They have exterminated the middle classes, England won't be any the better."

Mrs. Belton said hopefully that perhaps by that time there would be a new middle class, but she said this with a kind of deferential inquiry in her voice, for Mrs. Carton before her marriage had been the headmistress for the Hosiers' Girls' Foundation School and had the unusual opportunities of watching the development of a new upward-surging class without much background.

"You are probably right," said Mrs. Carton. "Our girls are an extremely nice lot. Their parents are very nice too and the most of them very good citizens and rather well off. It is only a question of time, as it always has been."

"And of languages," said Mr. Carton, who had up to now not been able to join the conversation, partly because of being pressed like a flower in a prayer book between two immense, jovial cottage women with bags and baskets who overflowed him from each side, partly because of the dreadful grinding noise of the motor-bus's exhausted gears. "I sometimes think that a Mansion House Fund for supplying Fowler's *Modern English Usage* to the secondary schools would be a fruitful scheme. His article, prejudiced and venomous you may say but going to the root of the matter, on genteelisms would in itself do considerable good."

"You mean like saying 'couch' for 'sofa,' and 'lounge' for 'sitting-room,'" said Mrs. Belton, being obliged to shout her remarks owing to the noise. But at this point the bus thankfully reached the top of the hill and could take breath for the long run down into Barchester.

"And worse," said Mr. Carton. "Scholars are coming up to Paul's, young men of considerable ability, who whenever they cough say 'Pardon.'"

His wife said one of the most difficult things to teach was the right way of being polite, for there was no common standard, and if you tried to explain that one knocked at a bedroom door but did not knock at a drawing-room door, it began to sound rather silly and pretentious. That attitude, said her husband, was a lapsing, a falling away, strongly to be deprecated, and then the bus stopped at the Westgate and the two fat women rose majestically from their places, almost drawing Mr. Carton up with them by suction.

"Sorry, dear," said one of the fat women, to which Mr. Carton raised his hat and said not at all, and the bus with a nervous start got under way again.

"They're all right," said Mrs. Belton. "They are the ones that are going to keep us steady. In fact I'm not sure if the future of England isn't in the Women's Institutes."

"I agree with you," said Mrs. Carton. "They are as competent as they can be and very wide-minded. If you are a lady they don't mind a bit."

"Which all goes to prove," said her husband, looking at her with scholarly affection, "that women are better than men when it comes to rebuilding a country. Men in Parliament to keep them out of the way, women to do the real work."

The bus then arrived in the Market Square and the passengers got out and went about their various avocations. Mrs. Belton did some small household shopping, or to put it more correctly she went to at least six different shops without being able to get anything she wanted, and what with walking from one shop to another and either standing in a queue or waiting in vain while shop assistants conversed in a superior way with each other, or disappeared to have cups of tea, it was half past twelve before she knew where she was, and as it is one of the joys of the Revolting New World that you must practically start trying to get your lunch directly after breakfast though even so the chances of getting it are small, she decided to go straight to the Women's County Club.

Before the war the club had very good premises of its own, next to the real County Club, but as soon as officialdom got well into its seat, both clubs were commandeered for the Ministry of General Interference. Owing to very strong pressure from its influential members, the men's club had been released some time ago, but They had no intention of giving up the women's club, where three hundred and sixty-five cups of tea a day were understood to be consumed by the staff and most of the handsome public rooms, for it was a fine stone eighteenth-century house, so knocked about that it was doubtful whether they could be repaired for many years to come. The men therefore, with unusual chivalry and mostly driven thereto by the ceaseless badgering of their wives and elder sisters, had thrown open the small dining-room and one drawing-room to the Women's County Club, who were also allowed to bring one guest provided they gave twenty-four hours' notice. It was not bliss, it was not rapture, but there was no other female club in Barchester and one had to make the best of it.

By great good luck Mrs. Belton found a small table in a corner occupied by Lady Pomfret, who was alone and delighted to have her company.

"You can't sit there, madam," said a waitress, "it's only for one. You can wait outside till this lady's finished if you like."

We all obey these Jills-in-office now, and curiously enough we obey them because we despise them, an attitude that I do not think they are capable of understanding. Even as Mr. Fanshawe, the Dean of Paul's College, argued with his female pupils with logic and without rancour while with his intellectual equals he used every weapon fair and unfair and nourished scholarly feuds that overflowed into every learned journal, so do we cut our coat to the cloth of our mental inferiors, while with our equals we would fight fairly or unfairly to the death. So Mrs. Belton with a smile to Lady Pomfret and a light shrug of her shoulders was about to retire when Lady Pomfret said: "Mrs. Belton is lunching with me: the Countess of Pomfret."

"Ow, of course if I'd known it was your ladyship," said the Jill-in-office. "There's liver today if you fancy it."

"Is there any tripe?" said Lady Pomfret. "Sit down, Lucy dear."

"Well, there *is* tripe, my lady," said the Jill-in-office, implying that tripe was low.

"Two tripes then, please," said Lady Pomfret, "and then the apple pie. The chef really understands tripe," she continued to Mrs. Belton. "We can never get it from our butcher, so I always have it when I come here. I don't like throwing my weight about, but thank God a title still helps."

The tripe was à la mode de Caen, delicious, brown; not that we would for a moment deprecate the fine national dish of tripe and onions, for which we have a deep affection, but as the rose is beautiful, so is the lily, and we admire sometimes the one, sometimes the other. While Lady Pomfret gave a bird's-eye sketch of her family and its doings Mrs. Belton reflected upon what she had just said about throwing one's weight about. Old Lady Pomfret would have been incapable of doing such a thing, but she had never had to face a world at peace. Perhaps, Mrs. Belton thought idly, Sally would not have been so able to stand up for herself had she not been Sally Wicklow, unsurpassed in her handling of horses and dogs, good minor county stock but not what the heir to the Pomfret earldom was expected to marry, though never had there been a better marriage. Perhaps Sally was a living proof of what Mrs. Carton had said about a new middle class which only needed time to make good. Possibly the kind of woman that Gillie Foster, as he was then, was expected to marry would not have done as well as the estate agent's sister. She certainly could not have done better. Possibly every class of society needed reinforcing by the best from below. But it was all too difficult. If Freddy or Charles married say Heather Adams, who had health, brains, and money, she would do her very best to pretend and to make the best of it, but how much she would prefer that one of them should marry one of Agnes Graham's girls, possibly Emmy, for Clarissa, though charming, was so young; at any rate a girl of their own set, real county. It was the not-quite-county that she feared, though she admitted it was pure prejudice. And then Lady Pomfret asked about Harefield and she had to give news of her husband and children and how much Charles was enjoying his schoolmastering.

"We went over to Holdings yesterday," she said. "I needn't say that Charles is in love with Agnes."

Lady Pomfret laughed and then asked Mrs. Belton how Lady Emily was.

Mrs. Belton said very handsome, very kind, but perhaps not quite up to the mark, for she did not wish to be a scaremonger.

"Merry was over with me yesterday," said Lady Pomfret, "helping me to sort out some things for the Red Cross Mammoth Auction—what a name. She said Aunt Emily wasn't quite so well."

"I don't think she is unwell," said Mrs. Belton. "She is just getting older. I remember my mother mixing up people and the past and present, but it was only a kind of surface woolliness. Underneath she was absolutely all right. And she is so well looked after at Holdings. Don't worry, Sally."

"I must go and see her soon," said Lady Pomfret. "I found an old album with photographs of Old Lady Pomfret—I don't mean Gillie's Aunt Edith, but Aunt Emily's mother—and the big houseparties they used to have at the Towers. She has a bustle and Gillie's uncle has a shooting-jacket buttoning right up to his chin and there is Agnes, her sister who died, with a poodle. It all looks so incredibly old. I want to take the album to Aunt Emily and ask her who some of the people are. His Royal Highness one recognizes, but there are what are obviously minor royalties. She could tell me who they are. You really don't think she is ill, Lucy? I don't want to worry Gillie."

Mrs. Belton said she was quite sure it was only a gradual coming of old age and that Lady Emily was not in the least an invalid or going mad, and was Sally going to the W.I.

"Is she not," said Lady Pomfret, "seeing that she is the President. But I've got to go back to the office first. Will you come with me, and then we will go on to the W.I."

Mrs. Belton said she wanted to see the Depot Librarian, so that would suit her very well.

"Miss Dean?" Said Lady Pomfret. "An excellent worker. I don't know her people, except her father, who is on some of my committees and very helpful."

There it was again. In this fascinating hierarchy of Barsetshire and of all counties that were not metropolitan, there were degrees. Sally's people were the right kind of people in a small way, and because of this Sally was a suitable bride for the heir to the Pomfret earldom, although not of noble blood. The Deans, from the little Mrs. Belton had seen of them, were nice people. Mrs. Dean's being Mr. Palmer's sister, though much younger, gave her a definite background. Mr. Dean was an engineer, known to be very successful. Barsetshire did not mind much about the success, for it all took place in the outside world, but it was coming to value Mr. Dean as an absolutely reliable man on county committees; one who would not take on a job until he knew all about it and, once having taken it up, could be trusted to see it through. His daughter Susan was just as prudent, just as reliable, and if there were such a thing as being elected to the county she would have got in with no difficulty at all, carried by acclamation. Of this Susan Dean herself had no idea until her younger sister lightly mentioned it.

"Does it ever occur to you," said Jessica, when Susan, after a long hard week at the office, said she wished the Red Cross was at the bottom of the Atlantic, "that you are the famous sister here?"

Susan stared, for she had a deep affectionate admiration for the brilliant actress who was really only little Jessica, and knew that Jessica's name was high in her profession.

"Squint eye, square eye, can't catch a butterfly," said Jessica, remembering a rhyme of their nursery days. "Also blind bat, my lamb. Miss Jessica Dean of the Cockspur Theatre is all right in London and next year she will probably be all right in New York, but to Barsetshire she is just the Deans' daughter who has gone on the stage, while Miss Susan Dean will go on doing her duty so well that she will probably marry Sir Edmund Pridham, or one of the Greshams."

"Don't be silly," said Susan.

"And also suckle fools and chronicle small beer," said Jessica.

"But, darling goose Susan, you really are worth fifty me's and that's that. If Lady Pomfret burst, you could carry on without turning a hair. If the Dean family takes roots in Barsetshire, and it is high time it rooted somewhere, you will be the one. Dear, dear, I don't seem to express myself well. Aubrey does it so much better. I'll get him to tell me exactly what it is that I mean."

Susan knew her sister's impulsive, exaggerating mode of speech and discounted most of what she said, but she did begin to wonder in a modest way if she was perhaps being useful to Barsetshire and to feel a gentle pride in it and to resolve that nothing on earth would make her give up the Red Cross as long as they truly needed her services.

"I once saw her sister at the Cockspur Theatre," said Mrs. Belton to Lady Pomfret. "A very clever actress, though I didn't much care for the play. I wonder if Mrs. Dean likes having a girl on the stage."

"From what I have heard of her she is so stupid that she wouldn't notice it," said Lady Pomfret, not spitefully, but dismissing from her mind a woman who did not take part in any county work. "Come upstairs, Lucy, and I'll send for Miss Dean."

So they went up to Lady Pomfret's office and Susan was summoned. She appeared with military promptness.

"This is Miss Dean," said Lady Pomfret. "Mrs. Belton wants to see you, Miss Dean. I have to go to the Mayor's Parlour about those papers, so you will have my room to yourself. Good-bye Lucy."

And the County Organizer, very smart and business-like in her neat uniform and becoming hat, went away, leaving Mrs. Belton and Susan alone. Even as they shook hands Susan felt that she had met Mrs. Belton before, though she did not know where.

"I hope I am not taking up too much of your time," said Mrs. Belton, "but my elder son asked me to come and see you. He was in the *Barsetshire* and I know how very much he and the whole

ship appreciated your kindness with books. He so often mentioned it in his letters to me and I am truly grateful. And now
you are carrying on your good work in peace-time."

Susan made suitable acknowledgments of this pleasing tribute, stressing the fact that the organization was responsible and
not any one person, and even as she spoke she knew where she
had seen Mrs. Belton before, or at least a reflection of her. It was
when Captain Belton, not Charles but Freddy, had come into
the office and she had had a strong impression that he must be
very like his mother though she had never seen her. The same
face but older and cast in a feminine mould, the same eyes
deep-set and blue, though Mrs. Belton's were not so clear a blue
as her son's.

"It seems like boasting," said Mrs. Belton, "but I did quite a
lot of book-binding for the Red Cross during the war and I liked
it very much, only it was so difficult not to read the books one
was binding. I remember having one of Mrs. Morland's Madame Koska books and I simply couldn't stop reading it and I
got the paste all over the last page and bound it upside down.
When I told Mrs. Morland, she was so amused that she asked if
she could have my copy and she gave me six new copies for the
Red Cross."

"Do you *know* Mrs. Morland?" said Susan.

Mrs. Belton said she had known her for quite a long time
though not very well. Mrs. Morland's younger son and her
second boy had been at Southbridge School at the same time.

"I *love* her books," said Susan. "Is she nice? I've never met
her."

Mrs. Belton, who had quick sympathy with the young and
was in any case prepared to like anyone who had been kind to
one of her children, said if Susan would like to meet Mrs.
Morland she was sure she could arrange it, at which Susan went
pink with pleasure and to show her gratitude offered to show
Mrs. Belton the library. Mrs. Belton had a heavy afternoon
ahead of her, but she recognized that Susan was offering her the

best she had to give, so she dismissed from her mind the hope of an hour at the beauty-parlour under Miss Miranda's soothing hands and said she would love to see it, pleased to notice Susan's gratification. But, as so rarely happens in this Piljian's Projess of a mortal wale, virtue was at once rewarded in the shape of a message from Lady Pomfret to ask if Miss Dean could bring the green file to the Mayor's Parlour at once.

"Another time then," said Mrs. Belton, "and I won't forget about Mrs. Morland," and went on to Miss Miranda, where for an hour she lay relaxed and had cream and cleansing lotions and hot packs and cold packs on her face and was skilfully and suitably made up with just the right amount of powder and rouge for a middle-aged lady who is going to the Women's Institute annual meeting. She then went to the meeting, and as the part which concerned Harefield came early in the proceedings she was able to slip away with a clear conscience and found herself free just as the Cathedral bells sounded four o'clock. She turned into the most beautiful close in England and was at once lapped in peace. Motor traffic was forbidden in the precincts except for the inhabitants and their visitors and tradesmen, and in any case very few people were using their cars now and there were horrid rumours that petrol would be cut down ferociously before long. The elegant red-brick houses lay basking in the sunlight with the pale beauty of the Cathedral beyond. A very old gardener was cutting the grass with a mowing machine drawn by a very old pony with bedroom slippers on his feet, and at this sight tears suddenly sprang to Mrs. Belton's eyes. Here was a relic of the lost age, of a time when the first long spring grass fell in lovely moiré stripes before the gardener's scythe and then followed the weekly mowing by pony lawn-mower, with grass and the heads of daisies whirling from the blades and being cast into the green bin which was unhooked and emptied at the end of every two or three turns, so that damp, fragrant heaps of grass were piled high for little Freddy and Elsa and Charles to jump on and roll in till their nurse told them not to. Gone were the slippered ponies, gone the gardeners now. Some people had little motor-mowers, of which her husband's opinion was almost blasphemous. Others could not afford motor-mowers and could not get gardeners, and the grass grew first thick and rank and then as alien seeds were dropped in it by birds or by the wind, turned to a tangle of sorrel, nettles, dandelions, couch-grass, each year making it less possible to reclaim the lost lawns. As she stood, wrapped in piercing memories, Lady Fielding, who had also been at the meeting, caught up with her and stopped to speak.

"Every time I see that I wonder what we are all alive for," said Lady Fielding, who was not as a rule given to sentiment nor to repining.

"The land of lost content," said Mrs. Belton, quickly dabbing her eyes with her soft old handkerchief, because she had a kind heart and knew it would have pained Miss Miranda very much to see her exquisite handiwork marred. "I was just going to see if you were at home before I went to the Deanery. Are you?"

Lady Fielding said she was and the two ladies went into the Fieldings' house, known to everyone as Number Seventeen (for it was a peculiarity of the close that every house had a number and no house a name, except the Deanery, which was allowed, as it were, a courtesy title). Here they had a peaceful cup of tea in the beautiful drawing-room on the first floor whose tall sash windows looked out over the sun-bathed close.

"Old Tomkins used to mow the close with a scythe," said Lady Fielding. "But it is too much for him. The Bishop, though the close was not in any way under his jurisdiction," said Lady Fielding, who was a staunch partisan of the anti-Palace party, "made a very impertinent suggestion of a motor lawn-mower, which the Dean very rightly refused to consider, and by great good luck, Dr. Crawley's archdeacon son-in-law, who is very well off, found that old Lady Norton had a pony-mower that she wanted to get rid of because she was turning her lawn into an Alpine rock garden. Dreadful woman."

"Whenever I see Victoria Norton," said Mrs. Belton feelingly, "I want to get under the dining-room table. She shops in Harefield every Saturday in the brougham and one really daren't go out in case she wants to come and be rude about one's garden."

"She always makes me think of someone very wicked in history," said Lady Fielding vaguely. "What was I saying? Oh yes, the archdeacon bought Lady Norton's machine and her pony and presented it to the Chapter."

"And those divine over-boots?" said Mrs. Belton.

"Those came from Northbridge," said Lady Fielding. "The Noel Mertons' agent, Mr. Wickham, picked up a set in Norfolk and we heard of them through my future son-in-law, Robin Dale, who had met Mr. Wickham at Southbridge Vicarage, so my husband made Mr. Wickham an offer for them. You know Anne is to be married at the end of July, so that she and Robin can have the holidays together, and then she goes to Southbridge as a housemaster's wife."

Mrs. Belton, who did not know the Fieldings very intimately though she liked them, expressed general pleasure at this news and said her younger son had just begun being a schoolmaster at the Priory School, which news did not particularly interest Lady Fielding. But both ladies, though without much in common, had a liking for each other. Presently Mrs. Belton said she had promised to go to the Deanery before she caught the bus back to Harefield. Just as she was saying good-bye the front-door bell was heard and the elderly parlour-maid Pollett opened the drawing-room door and announced Mr. Adams.

As the Labour M.P. for Barchester walked into the room, Lady Fielding had a moment's discomfort. She and her husband had come to know the wealthy ironmaster rather well one summer during the war when they were living in their house at Hallbury and Mr. Adams and his daughter were lodging during the holidays in the new town at the foot of the hill. The acquaintance had not been one that the Fieldings particularly desired, but their daughter Anne, who had been rather an invalid, had somehow made friends with Heather Adams. The friendship between the girls had not come to anything in particular, for their natures and ways lay far apart, but the parents had again been brought into contact when Sir Robert and Mr. Adams contested Barchester at the General Election. Sir Robert, who had never had any hope of getting in, had seen a good deal of his opponent before the election and the two men had got to understand each other pretty well and to the horror of their respective election committees often lunched together at the Club. Having got into Parliament with a huge majority, Mr. Adams, who had never paid the faintest attention to his committee, announced that he was going to vote exactly as he saw fit and had consistently done so, with loyalty to His Majesty's Government but at the same time often commanding the delighted horror of His Majesty's Opposition, so much so that several people who knew nothing about it at all said that the Opposition Whips looked upon Mr. Adams as a likely man. He and Sir Robert, and later Lady Fielding, had come to like each other, and Mr. Adams often looked in at Number Seventeen for what he called a chat.

Lady Fielding shook hands with the newcomer and was just going to introduce him to Mrs. Belton and wondering if she could explain Mr. Adams, when to her surprise he seized Mrs. Belton's hand and in a ponderous but not undignified way bowed slightly over it.

"Well," said Mr. Adams, "if anyone had told Sam Adams this morning who he was going to meet this afternoon, I'd have given him sixpence," though whether this sum represented a suitable reward for prophecy or was merely a general expression of surprise at the queerness of things, we cannot say.

Lady Fielding was so obviously surprised at her guests' knowing each other that Mrs. Belton quickly explained.

"Mr. Adams's daughter was at the school that took our house," she said, "and we saw a good deal of her. My husband likes her so much, and so do I."

"But what Mrs. Belton doesn't say," said Mr. Adams, releasing her hand and sitting down, "is that when my little Heth went through the ice, all through her own disobedience, Commander Belton, he's a captain now but I always think of him as Commander, got her out and saved her life, and Mrs. Belton treated her as if she had been her own daughter. My little Heth thinks the world of Mrs. Belton and so do I."

To Lady Fielding, who had gently discouraged friendship between the two girls although she liked Mr. Adams personally, this was quite a new light on Mr. Adams, also on Mrs. Belton. Being a very intelligent and capable woman, much occupied on committees and more of Barchester than of Barsetshire, she had vaguely thought of Mrs. Belton as a pleasant woman who lived in a village and did not take much part in activities outside her neighbourhood. To find that she was, if not a close friend of Mr. Adams, certainly looked up to and admired by him made her revise her appraisal of Mrs. Belton, and to do her justice she generously admitted to herself that she had been wanting in discernment. And curiously enough at the same time her opinion of Mr. Adams went up because he knew Mrs. Belton.

"When is Heather coming to see us at Harefield?" said Mrs. Belton.

"That's exactly what my Heth wrote to me in her last letter," said Mr. Adams. "'Do you think Mrs. Belton will ask me to come to Harefield this summer, Daddy?'—that's what she said. So I wrote back and said: 'Don't you worry, Heth, because Mrs. Belton's a friend that doesn't forget. You do your examinations well, I said, and trust Mrs. Belton.'"

Mrs. Belton said, quite truly, that she wanted Heather to come to Arcot House for a few days and her husband was looking forward to it, and then she asked if the date for Heather's wedding was settled, for Heather had contracted, about the time of the General Election, a most suitable engagement with young Ted Pilward, son of Pilward and Co.'s Entire.

"Well, Mrs. Belton," said Mr. Adams, "I thought it over. I

said to myself: 'Sam, what would Mother say if she was here,' for my little Heth having no mother I have to do my best to do like Mother would wish. And I think I know what Mother would have said to me. 'Sam,' she'd have said, 'you were never one to turn back from anything you set your hand to, nor is our Heth. She's gone to college and she's a clever girl with brains and knows how to use them, and three years is what she went for and three years she must stay.' So me and my Heth we talked it over and she said: 'I'm very fond of Ted, daddy, but I'm going to get a first-class, because that's what I set out to do.' So I had a talk to old Pilward and he said he wanted to send young Ted to America for the winter to study brewery plants there, so the wedding is to be a year from now. And I can't say I'm sorry, for I'll miss my Heth when the House isn't sitting."

Mrs. Belton applauded the plan and said she would write to Heather. And then, for she was very conscientious and had trained her memory to remember details, she added: "My son Freddy has a young friend who wants to meet you, Mr. Adams. When Heather comes I will ask her over and I hope they will make friends."

Mr. Adams said with a not unpleasing kind of heavy gallantry that any friend of Commander Belton's, he meant Captain Belton's, or Mrs. Belton's would find a friend in Sam Adams and then Mrs. Belton said good-bye and walked across the close to the Deanery.

"So Heather is to be married next year," said Lady Fielding to Mr. Adams. "You must find out what she would like for a wedding present from us."

"And Miss Anne is to be married quite soon," said Mr. Adams, who stuck to this old-fashioned form of address, which suited him very well. "She's not as old as my Heth by years, but she's older by nature. They're different. That's the way I see it. My Heth can stand on her own feet if the worst comes to the worst, but your Anne needs a man's arm, Lady Fielding. I've brought a little present from Heth and me."

He felt in a pocket of his well-cut coat and Lady Fielding wondered with an uneasiness for which she blamed herself what the present might be, for she had not forgotten a birthday that Anne had celebrated at Hallbury in the year when she had first made the Adamses' acquaintance, and overpoweringly expensive and unsuitable presents of scent and orchids that Mr. Adams and his daughter had brought.

"I saw it in one of those Bond Street shops," said Mr. Adams, "and I said to myself: 'That is Miss Anne Fielding, and have it she shall,' I said to myself, 'if it costs a hundred pounds.' Well, I may say it didn't," he added, "because I had a talk with the counterjumper in his black suit and I told him Sam Adams might be a fool, but he wasn't so big a fool as he looked, and I beat him down to seventy-five."

He produced a velvet-covered box in which lay a crystal heart surrounded by a wreath of tiny rubies with diamond leaves, as small as the jeweller's art could make them. A winter chill breathed from it, a chill of crystal-clear skies and frost shining like diamonds in the cold sunlight and red holly berries hard to the touch.

"It's second-hand, of course," said Mr. Adams, "or it would have been anything you like with the purchase tax, but I don't think Miss Anne will mind."

Lady Fielding assured him that she would never think whether it was old or new and would be delighted by it. Then Mr. Adams showed her how it had little prongs behind it and could be used as a clip on a jacket or a frock, or be worn in the hair.

"The moment I saw it," said Mr. Adams, who never minded saying a thing twice or three times if he thought it of interest to himself or anyone else, "I said: 'That is Miss Anne Fielding.' I'm not much good at explaining what I mean," said Mr. Adams, "and if I said Miss Anne was like those frosted Christmas cards it wouldn't in the least convey what I mean to convey. But being her mother, I dare say you get my meaning."

Lady Fielding thought she did, though she would have been

as puzzled as Mr. Adams to put it into words. The word that came to her mind was "virginal," but it is a word one doesn't use as a rule and she felt self-conscious about it. So she contented herself with thanking Mr. Adams and saying how delighted Anne would be, and Mr. Adams went away. Lady Fielding remained in the drawing-room and looked at the cold crystal heart and thought about her only child. Why the chill jewel should be so suitable she could not explain to herself, for Anne was an affectionate daughter and deeply though quietly in love with her old friend Robin Dale. Perhaps her ill health as a growing girl had something to do with it, setting her a little apart. At any rate Anne would like her jewel.

By this time Mrs. Belton was absorbed into the Deanery, where as usual there was a good deal of life and coming and going, for not only had the Crawleys a very large family, all married, and nearly twenty grandchildren, but their house was a kind of headquarters for visitors to Barchester. Fain would the Bishop and his wife have received as guests the various people distinguished by birth or intelligence who came to the Deanery, but owing to the episcopal housekeeping no one who had once spent a night under its grudging roof and partaken of its cold comfort ever came there again, and what is more, visitors who had escaped from the Palace without being quite starved or frozen or both, not to speak of the odiously uncomfortable beds with one blanket and a nasty flat eiderdown and tepid hot-water bottles, forgot in their fury all the guest's code of honour and betrayed their hosts right and left.

Among the recent sufferers was Mr. Johns, partner in the well-known firm of Johns and Fairfield, who had been tempted to the Palace by a possibility of getting an option on the Bishop's recent broadcasts, including his talk on Sweden entitled "Germans in Human Shape." But Mr. Johns, though a publisher, was in the second place a patriot, and what he had heard at the Palace had made him determine not to have any dealings with it.

"Not only was the food scanty and execrable," said Mr. Johns to Mrs. Crawley and Mrs. Belton, "but the Bishop, or rather his wife, kept me up till half past twelve to hear a broadcast from Moscow of which I could not understand a word."

Mrs. Crawley asked if the transmission was very bad. It was, said Mr. Johns, not so much the transmission, though he dared say it was as bad as anything that came from that country and he would not count the ballet because that belonged to the old Russia, as that it was in Russian. At least he supposed it was Russian, as it was a language that he couldn't make head or tail of.

"Are we to conclude," said the Dean, "that his lordship understands Russian? It would be more to the purpose if he could speak, or write, English," for the bishop, to the great admiration of such people as were misguided enough to like him, had taken to writing religious articles for a tendentious weekly, in a preface to which he said that the Shibboleths of religious writing repelled many otherwise devout Christians, and had affected a kind of hearty schoolmaster's style which, he said, could be understanded of the people. And if a bishop says things like that, it is very difficult to contradict him.

"His English was clear enough," said Mr. Johns. "He wanted the kind of terms we give Mrs. Morland or that very troublesome Mrs. Rivers. I told him he had better approach Bungay. He likes anything to do with Russia, or indeed," continued Mr. Johns, who had no love for the firm of Bungay, though they rarely came into contact, "anything at all if it is bad enough. Did you know, Dean, that he has a contract with the Mixo-Lydian Government which gives him translating rights of every State-published book in Mixo-Lydia?"

The Dean asked what about books not published by the State.

"There aren't any," said Mr. Johns. "Authors and publishers have to be pro-Government or they are deported."

The Dean said that was very interesting. He did not realize, he said, that deportation was still possible.

"Well, they call it that," said Mr. Johns tolerantly. "All that happens is that the Government put anyone they don't like into locked horse-trucks with no windows and take them to the top of the electric railway over the Gradenko Pass. Then they uncouple the trucks and let them run down the other side."

"But they must all be killed!" said Mrs. Belton.

"Not all," said Mr. Johns. "But the ones who aren't killed are massacred by the Slavo-Lydians on the other side of the pass. Bungay is doing quite well out of the contract at the moment and buying large country houses. It is a kind of folie de grandeur, I imagine. But now, Dean, what about your Congleton Lectures?" for Dr. Crawley had during the past year delivered at Oxbridge the Congleton Divinity Lectures, the blue ribbon of the literary-philosophic-ecclesiastical world. It is true that he had delivered them to an audience consisting, when it consisted of anything at all, mostly of women and coloured scholars from Lazarus, including the Head Chief of Mngangaland's eightieth son, who felt a temporary call to take orders and be the first native bishop of his subequatorial country, but they were acclaimed by all scholarly journals and would undoubtedly sell. And then the Dean and Mr. Johns began to talk about the prospects for Henley, so Mrs. Crawley and Mrs. Belton could talk about sensible things.

"Charles tells me that he met your Octavia and her husband at the Deans'," said Mrs. Belton. "I do wish they weren't called Dean, it is so confusing with you and Dr. Crawley." But Mrs. Crawley said no one who knew her husband could possibly confuse him with the Deans as they were quite newcomers to the county.

"Of course we all know that Mrs. Dean is Mr. Palmer's sister," she added. "They have been here once or twice for meetings, but we have never been to their house. One of the daughters is very well spoken of. She works at the Red Cross Libraries and Lady Pomfret says she is an excellent organizer."

"I like her very much," said Mrs. Belton. "She sent books to the *Barsetshire* when Freddy was in her."

Mrs. Crawley said with slight severity that it was time Freddy thought of marrying; for all her large family had married and she enjoyed being a grandmother very much and considered that one's children were only born to the end that they should provide grandchildren.

"I think so too," said Mrs. Belton with a sigh. "But all the nice girls are so busy now. Even Agnes Graham's Clarissa is going to college. And some of them are getting on. Lucy Marling for instance. It is all rather depressing. I suppose I ought to be thinking of my bus."

"Nonsense," said Mrs. Crawley. "It doesn't go till six fifteen. Besides I am expecting Mrs. Morland. She is in Barchester today for the Women's Institute meeting and she said she would come on here when she had done some shopping."

"How stupid of me," said Mrs. Belton. "I did see in the time-table that the bus was six fifteen, but I thought it meant five fifteen because of summer time."

"It easily might," said Mrs. Crawley, who considered that she held a watching brief for the Church in the matter of tampering with the hours of daylight. "The Cathedral clock cannot be altered, I am thankful to say, without wrecking the works, so it goes on striking the real time. Laura! I began to think you weren't coming. You know Mrs. Belton."

Mrs. Morland, her hair rather loose after three hours at the Women's Institute meeting, for she had stayed the whole course, was delighted to see Mrs. Belton again and agreeably surprised to meet Mr. Johns. A good many years previously she had been approached by Mr. Johns, who had seen a future in her early novels and tried in a quite gentlemanly way to detach her from her own publisher, Adrian Coates. Mrs. Morland, who liked Adrian Coates, had explained to Mr. Johns that if he, as he had suggested, advertised her books on a larger scale, some of the money he spent on advertising would come off her royalties, at which striking view of the uses of advertisement Mr. Johns had been so staggered that he gave up the unequal struggle. But he and Mrs. Morland had remained very good friends and on more than one occasion he had taken her advice about books.

"And how is the latest book going?" said the Dean.

"Very well, thank you," said Mrs. Morland. "At least I get very large checques, which always frightens me, because of pride going before a fall and that kind of thing. So I always put half of it into my number-two account."

From her voice it was obvious that she was almost bursting with pride at this remarkable achievement, and when the Dean asked her why she did this she received his question coldly.

"Because of Them," she said simply.

The Dean asked who.

"You know, They," said Mrs. Morland, who seemed to share with the more primitive races a dislike of mentioning unseen powers by name for fear of attracting their unfavourable attention. "If I put half what I earn into a separate account I can pay Them the income tax out of it and not feel it," at which ostrich-like piece of self-deception Mr. Johns and the Dean exchanged looks expressive of their opinion of intelligent women, but Mrs. Crawley and Mrs. Belton were much struck by the idea.

"I suppose, Laura," said the Dean, "that you get a very large fan mail?"

"Good gracious, no!" said Mrs. Morland, nearly losing a hairpin in her surprise. "It is only people like Mrs. Rivers that get fan mail. She always tells me how many letters she gets, whenever I see her. But I have some very good hate letters," said Mrs. Morland with modest pride.

"Hate letters?" said Mrs. Belton.

"Yes. People who think we ought to stand in queues for ever and the friends of the U.S.S.R., whatever that means, for all these initials for everything are *quite* beyond me," said Mrs. Morland. "I have a couple in my bag. Would you like to hear them?"

Her audience, much interested in this version of fan mail, begged to be enlightened.

"Now where are they?" said Mrs. Morland, picking up her bag, which was not shut and immediately disgorged its contents onto the carpet. The company assembled came to her aid and an incredible number of small objects, including several hairpins, an india-rubber band, a drawing-pen, a powder case, a comb with three teeth missing, a crumpled handkerchief, a note-case, several keys, a penknife, a fountain pen, two pencils, one with a broken point, a quantity of loose change, and the stopper of a hot-water bottle were retrieved.

"I did think I had them," said Mrs. Morland. "Oh, I know, they are in the secret compartment." She pulled a zip fastener outside the bag and revealed a pocket out of which she took some letters.

"The difficulty is," she said, pushing her hat sideways and then hitting it down upon her head, "to remember what it is you have said that annoys people. If only the would say page 108 line 7, one would know what they were talking about. Now, here is one from somebody called E. G. Towel about a dog and I haven't the faintest idea what I said about a dog because they don't say which book. Would you like me to read it to you?" she added rather shyly, as if she were going to read aloud something of her own composition. Everyone said yes.

"'Dear "Laura Morland,"' it begins. But why Towel put Laura Morland into inverted commas I cannot think. It is my name and I have never pretended it wasn't. It does sound like a name, doesn't it?"

Her hearers assured her that it sounded exactly like a name. Much reassured she went on. "'I have just read a book of yours and upon reading the line "Women feed their *odious little dogs* on pounds of meat" I gather you are just an "odious little woman" and so un-English.' I do not know," said Mrs. Morland breaking off, "whether she means I am *so* un-English or and so, comma, un-English. The Towel goes on: 'There's something rotten about a man or woman who does not love animals as their faithfulness and loyalty is superior to any human being. I do hope the time will come when you experience real hunger. Thank God for the R.S.P.C.A., the P.D.S.A., and all societies to ensure the welfare of man's greatest pal—the dog.'"

A respectful silence followed this reading, broken by Mrs. Belton, who asked what the P.D.S.A. was. Mrs. Morland said she had always supposed it was Our Dumb Friends' League, only the initials didn't seem right.

"And what, may I ask, do you do about such communications, Laura?" said the Dean.

"Well, I do believe in answering letters," said Mrs. Morland, "because one ought to. So if it is a hate letter I just send a postcard and thank then for their kind communication. The card has my name and address on it so I don't sign it and then they don't get an autograph."

Mr. Johns said Mrs. Morland was even cleverer than he had believed, and that the difficulty he had in preventing Mrs. Rivers trying to bring libel actions no one would believe.

"But you couldn't bring a libel action against somebody called Towel who doesn't give any address," said Mrs. Morland simply. "Besides it might be a pseudonym. The other one," she continued rapidly in case her audience might get up and leave before the end of the performance, "was about a book I wrote with a school in it—not that I know anything about schools except that all my boys were at school," she added to disarm any possible criticism. "It was from somebody in Maida Vale called V. Lefter—people do have the most extraordinary names—who says: 'You should know that most London secondary school headmasters are Oxford or Cambridge men and that all are conversant with dinner jackets and sherry. I am speaking from knowledge as I have relations in these professions and a brother who is a senior army officer.'"

Her audience were too much overcome by this staggering statement to make any immediate comment, till Mrs. Belton thought of asking after Mrs. Morland's youngest son, who had been at school with Charles.

"Oh, thank you very much," said Mrs. Morland, "the Tape and Sealing Wax Office have sent him to Mixo-Lydia, though why I do not know, except that they are always sending people somewhere and much to my annoyance he has taken the baby with him."

"Oh dear," said Mrs. Belton sympathetically. "Is he married, then?" After which she felt she might have put it better. But Mrs. Morland did not appear to find the question at all unusual and said that it was so difficult to know whether people were married or not, because if you happened to miss it in *The Times* you might never know about it at all, unless of course it was in your own parish, where as the banns had to be read three times you could hardly miss them all unless you were one of those people who always went to the evening service, and Tony had been married for more than a year now.

"Do you like your daughter-in-law?" said Mrs. Belton, whose maternal mind had often been exercised as to whether she would like her sons' wives when they got married.

"Like," said Mrs. Morland, pushing a wisp of hair behind one ear, "is not exactly the word," which made Mrs. Belton wonder if Mrs. Tony was cross-eyed or cross-tempered as she sometimes feared, on no grounds at all, that Mrs. Freddy or Mrs. Charles might be. "I don't want to boast, but I sometimes think I am fonder of her than of Tony, which," said Mrs. Morland with the air of one who has been brought up with Euclid from the cradle, "is of course impossible. And as for the baby, it is the most angelic tomfool in the world."

This may not to our male reader seem a compliment, but both Mrs. Crawley with nearly twenty grandchildren and Mrs.

Belton with as yet a bare two realized that this baby must be a paragon and almost though not quite as good as their own, and the conversation became so nauseatingly feminine that the Dean and Mr. Johns had to talk about Mr. Birkett's great work on the Analects of Procrastinator, which the Oxbridge University Press were going to publish.

"I wouldn't have minded taking it myself," said Mr. Johns, "though it isn't exactly in our line. It's a good selling title—makes people who don't know anything about it wonder. But I've got my eye on a real winner. There's a man called Winter, a schoolmaster, though I don't suppose you would have heard of him, who has done a new Latin grammar. Now anyone who can get the schools to take a Latin grammar is on velvet, and from some exploratory work I have done I think the time is ripe. Lorimer's Grammar has held the field for a considerable time, but the classical men want something more up to date and I think this is. It will also," said Mr. Johns meditatively, "be one in the eye for Bungay, who has practically cornered Latin for the last forty or fifty years."

Only good manners kept the party silent till Mr. Johns had finished, for most of them had known Philip Winter far longer than the publisher and all knew him better. Philip had been an assistant master at Southbridge before the war, and the Crawleys were close friends of the Birketts. Mrs. Morland's younger son had been in Philip's class and had studied his classical master's weaknesses with a detached scientific eye, finding considerable entertainment in his ill-starred but brief engagement to the headmaster's daughter Rose. As for Mrs. Belton, she had seen enough of her son's headmaster to like him very much and also his wife. So they all burst out at once with rather boasting accounts of their intimacy with him until the Dean, using his pulpit voice, asked if Mr. Johns had decided upon a title, which in its turn led to reminiscences of Latin grammars under which they had variously suffered.

"I remember papa trying to teach me Latin out of a book called *Via Latina*," said Mrs. Crawley, "and how I hated it."

The Dean said that he was one of the few people who had been started on Roby.

"I was never much good at Latin," said Mr. Johns. "I think it was North and Hillard who put me off."

"Well, I wasn't much good either," said Mrs. Morland, "but I did rather like Kennedy and Scott because of the poetry."

The Dean's bushy eyebrows went up in a questioning manner that would have terrified a curate.

"Poetry, Laura," he said. "I do not follow you."

"You know quite well what I mean," said Mrs. Morland severely. "The poetry part at the end," and assuming a Sibylline expression she began:

> "Common are sacerdos, dux,
> Vates, parens et conjux—"

but at this point the men could not restrain themselves.

> "Gives, comes, custos, vindex,"

said Mr. Johns loudly.

> "Adolescens, infans, index,"

boomed the Dean.

"Something or other artifex," said Mr. Johns. "Dear me, how does it go? I shall forget my own name next."

"The one I like," said Mrs. Belton unexpectedly, "is:

> Dies in the singular
> Common we define,
> But its plural cases are
> Always masculine,"

and then apologized, saying that she used to help Freddy to learn them when he had a tutor for a term before going to Dartmouth.

"A woman, island, country, tree," said the Dean. "What a beautiful juxtaposition of words! But perhaps the poem on the motor-bus by the late Public Orator remains the finest monument to Latin.

> Domine defende nos,
> Contra hos motores bos."

"Good gracious," said Mrs. Belton. "The bus. I must go at once if I am to get the six fifteen. Good-bye, Mrs. Crawley. Good-bye, Mrs. Morland. Oh, I had forgotten. Do you hate people meeting you?"

Mrs. Morland, perhaps because she was used to living with words, was pretty good at understanding them and said she would like to meet anyone who was a friend of Mrs. Belton.

"Thank you very much," said Mrs. Belton, who felt humble before people who wrote books, except of course before Hermione Rivers because she always roused her worst feelings. "It is a very nice girl called Susan Dean, who works at the Red Cross here and she is longing to meet you because of your books. She used to send books to the *Barsetshire* when Freddy was in her and there isn't much I can do for her," said Mrs. Belton rather sadly, "because everything is so difficult now."

To her great relief Mrs. Morland, instead of being haughty or offended, as she had feared a famous writer of thrillers might be, said the Red Cross had sent books to all the camps, ships, aerodromes, hospitals, where her various sons had been during the war and nothing would give her greater pleasure than to meet Susan Dean, of whom she had heard through the Francis Brandons, and then Mrs. Belton went down to the Market Square and got the last empty seat in the bus, next to Miss Holly, the headmistress of the Hosiers' Girls' Foundation School. Talk was impossible while the bus clanked and groaned and shook itself up the long rise of the downs, but when it reached the top, comparative quiet succeeded the racket. "I'm sorry I can't make more room," said Miss Holly. "It's partly being so stout myself and partly the man next to me, whose pocket is bulging with bottles and most painful."

Mrs. Belton said she had plenty of room, and knowing that Miss Holly was interested in her ex-pupil Heather Adams, she told her about her meeting with Mr. Adams at Number Seventeen and his plans for Heather's future.

"I coached her one summer holidays," said Miss Holly, "before Mrs. Carton retired, when I was mathematics mistress. She has an unusual head for what one might call the philosophy of figures and might go far in pure mathematics, but she wants to go into her father's business. However, I dare say marriage will settle all that."

"But don't you want her to do whatever it is she wants to do?" said Mrs. Belton, who was rather vague about what going into her father's business meant.

"She doesn't know what she wants to do," said Miss Holly calmly. "Girls don't. Young Mr. Pilward will settle all that. Marriage is what she wants."

"But I thought," said Mrs. Belton, trying to put what she wished to say so that it would not sound offensive, "that really good schools like the Hosiers' wanted their girls to get degrees and things, not to get married."

"Any intelligent girl can do both," said Miss Holly, "and the sooner she gets onto being married the better. That's her real stuff," and seeing Mrs. Belton's look of surprise she added: "I would have been a nicer woman if I had married, but you see I didn't. As a matter of fact no one asked me. But this I will say about not being married," said Miss Holly, "that once you have got over the mortification it is a very pleasant life."

At this frank avowal Mrs. Belton couldn't help laughing and Miss Holly most good-naturedly joined in her laughter.

"I have got to be quite fond of Heather," said Mrs. Belton, "and so has my husband. It is extraordinary how much she has improved. And I like her father more and more."

"Largely due to you," said Miss Holly, "Heather and her father both have extremely gentlemanly instincts. I don't know how to put it better. Mr. Adams is very intelligent and he uses his brains and is never above learning. Heather is the same. When I remember Heather as she was when she first came to us, I wonder that we took her. It wasn't only her being so fat and so spotty, but her temper and her sulks were quite dreadful. It was the winter we acted *As You Like It* that she began to improve. And then next summer when I was coaching her at Hallbury she saw a good deal of little Anne Fielding and she learnt something there. But Arcot House has made Heather what she is, Mrs. Belton, and in the words of our M.P. Heather thinks the world of you, and so does her father. I get out here."

She said good-bye and went in at Harefield gates while Mrs. Belton went on to her stop in High Street and was glad to be home and have a bath before the simple evening meal. And if any reader wishes to know how she managed to have a bath, we will explain that the boiler in the cellar was not too proud to burn wood if a little coal was added as a relish and that wood was plentiful on the estate and there were still a couple of elderly men to cut and carry it, for except to the very rich or the so-called poor who live in large blocks of flats from which central heating belches for the greater part of the year, baths are infrequent luxuries, as too well most of us know.

To Mrs. Belton's great pleasure her elder son had come down for a long weekend as there was some business to be done with their lawyer, Mr. Updike, for which his presence was necessary. She would dearly have liked to have Charles as well, but as he told her on the telephone it wasn't his Sunday off, and it was considered bad form to ask for special leave, because Mr. and Mrs. Winter were so kind that as likely as not one of them would stay in so that a master could go out.

"I saw your nice Miss Dean today, Freddy," she said after supper, when they were sitting in the garden under the big cedar. "I liked her so much and Sally Pomfret says she is such a good worker. We must ask her here and get Mrs. Morland to come. Apparently Miss Dean loves her books. I can't think why we don't know the Deans. Do you think I ought to call on Mrs. Dean?"

"You ought to have called on her years ago when they first came to Barsetshire," said Mr. Belton. "It is rather late now, isn't it?"

"Perhaps it is," said Mrs. Belton, "but I never thought of it before, I don't know why."

"I don't know why you should," said her husband. "We don't know the Worsted people much, I mean her brother, old Palmer. But it's never too late to be civil, my dear. You remember we saw their youngest girl in that play at the Cockspur. Jessica, that's her name."

"Oh, perhaps I had better not call," said Mrs. Belton, at which her husband and son unchivalrously laughed. "And I don't mean what you think I mean," she added.

"Depends what you think we think, my dear," said her husband.

"Well," said Mrs. Belton, "I don't mean that I don't want to call because of their daughter being an actress, because I thought she was very clever and I would love to meet her. But I thought perhaps lots of people wanted to know them just because of Jessica Dean, and they might be rather sick of it."

"Bless your simple soul, mother," said Captain Belton, "from what I know of the Deans I should say they took the whole Jessica business in their stride, and certainly wouldn't attribute any lion-hunting motives to you. Ask Charles. He knows them better than I do. He dined there, didn't he?"

"He not only dined, he also got on very well with Jessica," said Mrs. Belton. "She sent him tickets for her play and he got a weekend off from the Priory."

"Well done, Charles," said his elder brother, amused. "I hope he took her out to supper afterwards and drank her health in champagne out of her slipper."

"Not exactly," said Mrs. Belton. "It's all so upside down now. She took him out to supper. At least she asked him back to her flat and he said it was great fun. Oliver Marling was there."

Captain Belton said he hadn't seen Oliver for ages, adding that he liked Oliver's sister Lucy, who was a remarkably fine woman with no biggodd nonsense about her.

"When we saw her at Cousin Emily's that Sunday," said his mother, "I had a kind of despairing feeling."

Her son inquired if there was any reason for this. He himself had seen nothing despairing about Lucy.

"Only that she isn't married," said Mrs. Belton. "She *is* such a nice girl, Freddy."

"I hate to disappoint you, mother," said Captain Belton, "but I am not going to marry Lucy Marling, nor anyone else as far as I know. And certainly not Jessica Dean."

He said these words with such force that his mother looked alarmed.

"It's all right, mother," said he smiling. "But I am not thinking of getting married. Charles can take that on. If he is going to be a schoolmaster he will need a suitable wife and I am sure any school with Jessica as headmistress would be a great success."

Then he said he would do some watering, for as always happens in England the shortest spell of fine weather produces a drought and this fine weather had been going on for some time and showed no symptoms of abating. His mother watched him as he went to and fro with the watering-can and knew that Freddy had put her in her place, so kindly, and not for the first time, and she wondered, again not for the first time, whether Freddy would ever forget his long-lost love. But she was too well-trained a mother to ask, so she tried to comfort herself by thinking of all the unsuitable girls that Freddy had not married, from young Lady Norton's dreadful daughter who lived in a state of feverish activity over the Help for Slavo-Lydia fund and was said to be living in highbrow sin in Chelsea with a Slavo-Lydian intellectual, to Heather Adams. At which last thought she couldn't help laughing aloud. Her son, who was passing her on his way to the rain-water butt, stopped to inquire what it was.

"I was only thinking," said Mrs. Belton, "how funny it would be if you married Heather. After all, you did save her life."

"I might do worse," said Captain Belton. "She has improved enormously and I imagine she will be an heiress. Either Charles or I will have to marry money and rescue Harefield from the clutches of the usurers," but seeing that his mother was taking him a little too seriously and looked alarmed, he added: "Don't worry, mother, I give you my solemn word of honour that I won't ask Heather to marry me. And I know she wouldn't if I did."

"Because of being engaged to that young man, Pilward?" said Mrs. Belton.

"That of course," said her son. "But I wasn't thinking of that, mother. I think we ought to wake father and tell him the bad news. The rain-water butt is nearly empty. That's all the reward we get for having some warm dry weather at last."

"What's that?" said Mr. Belton, whose light after-dinner slumbers though impervious to aeroplanes overhead, heavy lorries in the High Street, or any amount of conversation were always dissipated at once by any allusion to the estate. "I knew that would happen. The butt always runs dry just when we need it. You'd better fill it from the hose, Freddy. This weather won't break for weeks and I don't want the barrel to split. Old Wheeler can patch it, but if it really goes I don't know where to lay my hands upon a cooper now, nor a blacksmith," he added angrily, "nor a wheelwright. They used to have all their own on Pomfret's estate, carpenters, blacksmiths, brewhouse, laundry, everything you wanted. So did my old grandfather at Harefield. Now you can't get a horse shod or a wagon retired, and soon there won't be any horses or any wagons. All this damned motor business. Sorry, my dear," he added to his wife, who said mildly that he would never have been able to keep up the home farm without the tractor and what a blessing the potato spinner had been.

"Oh, I grant you that," said Mr. Belton grudgingly, "but our soil's too heavy for the potato spinner. All very well in Norfolk, where you get a light soil."

His wife said mildly that it would be very expensive if they had to grow their potatoes in Norfolk just to please a machine, which piece of reasoning caused Mr. Belton to get up and walk in an offended way to the rain-water butt. Captain Belton put the garden hose into it. The water slowly rose. Here and there was a trickle between the staves, but Mr. Belton pronounced that the wood would swell by the morning and no damage was as yet done.

"And now of course it will rain," he added, looking suspiciously at the cloudless deepening blue of the summer evening sky. "We'd better be getting over to Plassey House, Freddy."

So Mr. Belton and Captain Belton went to visit Mr. Updike and the business was satisfactorily settled and inquiries made for Mrs. Updike, who had fallen over a broom in the passage and skinned an elbow.

"I think I shall go for a walk, father," said Captain Belton as they walked back up the High Street. "Don't lock the door."

"All right, all right," said Mr. Belton. "And thank you for your help, Freddy. I sometimes think I'd have done better to sell the place outright. The Barsetshire County Council would like it for a housing estate, though I must say I wouldn't."

"Nor would I, sir," said his son. "Try not to worry, father. The estate isn't doing too badly."

"Nor too well," said his father. "I suppose things will last out my lifetime. Selfish way of looking at it. Good night, Freddy."

Mr. Belton went into Arcot House. Captain Belton remained on the pavement listening, with a look of amusement on his face.

He heard the bolts being pushed home, and the chain slipped into its groove, and the double turning of the ponderous house-key, and then, knowing at least three easy ways of breaking into the house, he walked back down the High Street, crossed the little bridge over the Rising, and so up onto the downs.

Double summer time is but a fiction and a very confusing one, for although we all know that at eleven o'clock at night it is really only nine, nothing will prevent our childish minds from finding the late evening light a miracle. To Captain Belton, walking on the high ground with Barsetshire spread beneath him, the well-known landscape was strange and beautiful. A little frightening too, as if in a land where it was always early evening with long shadows and slanting light and incredible quiet, broken only by the far-borne sound of the Cathedral bell proclaiming to the world that it was nine o'clock, for all experts were agreed that to try to alter the chimes might cause irreparable damage. Now all was peace in the air and on the land. No death would fall from the sky to shatter and to burn as it had fallen on that East Anglian coast, destroying Captain Belton's hopes. His mother knew what he had lost, but only one other person, Heather Adams, to whom he had once generously told his story to save a fat, silly, ugly schoolgirl from making a fool of herself. He had never had cause to repent his generosity, and he had watched with a kindly interest Heather's gradual improvement as she gained self-confidence and mixed more with the world. Much of it, he knew, was due to his mother's kindness and he felt almost a glow of pride at the thought of what Arcot House had done for Heather.

Then as the strange magic twilight deepened he came down from the hills wondering as he went what the fate of Harefield would be. His brother-in-law Admiral Hornby had been very generous in helping, but no help could do more than stave off the evil day during his father's lifetime, after which he and Charles would probably be homeless. Charles, dear fellow, was sure to marry and would inevitably marry a nice girl without much money, which was what his mother had been when as Lucy Thorne she married his father. As for himself the navy was his life and beyond that he did not look, except to contemplate retiring to a small house near Harefield if such a house could be had and boring people about the war. Not that anyone would want to hear about operations off the North African coast, or the escort on D-Day, or the icy Atlantic. One must learn to hold one's tongue. And as he crossed the bridge and came quietly up the High Street his thoughts turned to those happy years of war spent first in H.M.S. *Gridiron*, then in H.M.S. *Barsetshire*. Sometimes dull, sometimes dangerous, always happy, and friends, work, and books when he had time. God bless the Red Cross for that, and he was glad that he had been able to thank that nice librarian personally and glad that his mother had taken a liking to her. It was not every girl who looked well in uniform, but Miss Dean undoubtedly did. And he thought of the Wren's uniform and how perfectly the right girl was suited by it. Better not to think. He went in by the side gate, climbed onto the coal-bin and with his pocket knife prised the scullery window open and entered the house. All was quiet. There was a light in his mother's room, but he was not going to see her this night.

CHAPTER 6

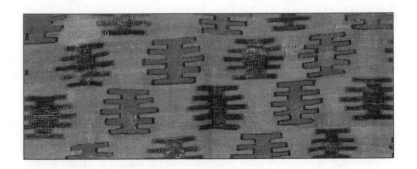

The Marling Red Cross Fête was to take place at a peculiarly auspicious moment. The Conservative Rally and Pig-Breeders' Association were already occupying many people's minds and keeping them busy, but this double event was still at some distance and the Marling Fête just filled the gap nicely. It was to take place in the grounds of Marling Hall and some people said that Lucy Marling was being rather like Mr. Toad in her masterful way of doing everything herself, but the fact remains that in every county enterprise one person of immense vitality, tact, and driving-power is needed. The first and last of these qualities she possessed in full measure. The second was not her forte, but in its place she brought a large and tolerant kindness to bear which did almost as well.

The opening ceremony was to be performed by Lord Pomfret, with a kind of benediction by Mr. Needham, whose one arm commanded respect and affection everywhere. Packer's Universal Royal Derby, in other words a roundabout with a steam organ, had been persuaded to alter the date of its visit to Hogglestock and come with its almost pre-war glory of boats, horses, and prancing birds, and its post-war charge of sixpence a ride and that a short one, where once one had revolved in glory for nearly ten minutes for twopence. There were other side shows, all of substitute variety, a mild vegetable and cottage garden exhibition, a tent for rabbits and birds, and a platform for the opening. This platform had been quite illegally made by Mr. Marling's carpenter, abetted by the ticket clerk at Melicent Halt, who was also the porter and in a fit of deliberate absent-mindedness directed, for this is the current jargon, a number of planks intended for repairing the station platform to go up to the Hall in a lorry and do their best for the Red Cross, with instructions to come back to the station when the fête was over.

"That's a tidy job," said the ticket clerk to the carpenter, on the evening before the fête. "Wish we had old Winnie on that platform," which friendly allusion to England's great Prime Minister of the war was heartily echoed by the carpenter and by Ed Pollett, who was distinctly half-witted but had a genius for cars and any form of machinery. Ed, who had before the war been under-porter at Worsted Station owing to family influence, his uncle Mr. Patten being then the station-master, was friendly with the ticket clerk and often did a little light duty at the station to oblige, which was again entirely illegal. "If old Winnie was on the platform," said Ed in his pleasant slow Barsetshire voice, "Ed would salute him."

"That's right, Ed," said the ticket clerk. "If old Winnie was Prime Minister we'd get some decent engines. The engines they send out on this line it's cruel. All dirty, poor things and every bit of machinery past work. When the *Gatherum Castle* came down yesterday I could've cried. Like an old shunting engine she looked. And that Bert Crackman in the driver's cab he wouldn't even take a handful of waste and polish her name-plate up a bit. I dunno what his uncle would say, old Sid Crackman that's been a guard on this line for thirty year and more."

A very old gentleman with a Newgate frill, his wicked old face seamed with the dirt and wrinkles of a long, disgraceful life, who had been sitting on an odd bit of timber smoking a very nasty pipe, said old Winnie'd never done nothing for him and he wasn't going to do nothing for him.

"Now, Mr. Nandy," said the ticket clerk, "that's just talk. You don't mean not the half of what you say, we all know that."

If this remark was meant to placate Mr. Nandy's animosity against Mr. Churchill it was singularly ineffective.

"No more old Winnie don't mean what he says," said the old gentleman, spitting in a quite odious way. "None of 'em do. Not old Winnie, nor Clem Attlee, nor that Strakey. You show me a man as is in Parliament and I'll show you a liar."

"You hadn't ought to call anyone a liar, Mr. Nandy," said Ed. "My Millie she gives the kids a good one if they talk like that. It's not right."

"How many kids is it now, Ed?" said the carpenter, which was a perennial joke owing to the Polletts' quite lavish way of having babies, who were all beautiful, healthy, very dirty, and not quite all there: in fact exactly the kind of children that a community still largely agricultural needs and ought to have.

"That's asking," said Ed, a proud yet sheepish smile on his good-natured face. "Let me see. We was married in the spring. Millie and me, that's five years last April and the twins came in July, then there's Luke and Ol; then there's Will and Belle and then there's Cassie and we're expecting," at which his audience laughed in a very coarse way, but somehow with respect for Ed and Millie and their acceptance of life.

"I never had no children nor didn't want none," said old Mr. Nandy rising from his seat. "Lot of bawdy, that's what it is. I'm going down to the Hop Pole. Beer's all the children I ever wanted; beer and baccy."

As no one took any notice of him, he hobbled off.

"Wodjer going to call the next one, Ed?" said the ticket clerk.

"That's just it," said Ed. "There's the twins, they're called Donald and Mickey, then there's Luce after Miss Lucy and Ol after Mr. Oliver; and then there's Will after Mr. Marling and Belle after Mrs. Marling. Mrs. Marling she was fair pleased when Millie asked her to be godmother, but Amabel's an outlandish name begging Mrs. Marling's pardon, so we call her Belle. Then there's Cassie, that's after Lady Bond and her ladyship has a queer name too, Lucasta they call it, so Millie said we'd make it Cassie. Millie she says we did ought to call the next one Winnie."

"You ought to have done that before, Ed," said the carpenter reprovingly, "but we all know you're not quite all there. What'll you do suppose it's twins again?"

Ed, to whom mental effort was almost physical torture, made a painful effort to concentrate. Then his face lightened as he said: "Winnie and Millie if it's girls and Winnie and Ed if it's boys."

"Now," said the carpenter, "don't let anyone tell me that Ed hasn't got some sense. Well done, Ed. We'll go down to the Hop Pole and drink their health as soon as I've put my tools away."

And the carpenter, handling his tools as reverently as a priest handles a chalice, put each into its place in his shed and locked the door.

"Either of you remember Bill Morple?" said the ticket clerk, who had been industriously reading three square inches of the *Barchester Chronicle* while he waited.

"A nasty piece of goods," said the carpenter. "Used to be ticket clerk down at the Halt and then he went to Winter Overcotes. He was supposed to be mixed up with that gang that stole the Cup from the Station. Near broke the station-master's heart they say—old Beedle, that's the name."

"That's right," said the ticket clerk, "and then the Cup turned up again and no names were mentioned, but Bill Morple left the railways. Well, he's been in with a bad lot and they've all got seven years for robbing a post office and half-killing the post-master. I always said Bill Morple wouldn't come to no good. His mother was old Patten's niece, the station-master at Worsted, but his father—well, Ed'ard Morple was a foreigner."

"Loamshire?" said the carpenter darkly.

"Not as bad as that," said the ticket clerk. "But somewhere over the other side of Barchester. He must be a cousin of yours, Ed, seeing his mother was Mr. Patten's niece."

But so distressed was Ed by the suggestion that it was agreed a relationship so remote did not count, and the party dispersed.

The first excitement of the fête was the arrival on the previous evening of Packer's Universal Royal Derby in a caravan and two enormous lorries, which were parked at the end of the field. In normal summer time the work of erecting the roundabout would have been finished by the light of flares or the lorries' powerful headlights, which would have made the spectacle doubly exciting to the village children, but even by the unreal evening light the work caused such excitement that Donald and Mickey and Luce Pollett after gazing their fill went home without Ol and Will and Belle, who were supposed to be under their care. Luckily Marling was exceptionally free from kidnappers, who in any case would not have wanted three small dirty children, so when a distracted Millie came onto the field to rescue her offspring she found them having cocoa and bread and margarine in Mr. Packer's private caravan. At this sight Donald, Mickey, and Luce, who had been dragged back by their mother to the scene of the crime, began wildly to demand their rights.

"Belle's got a cup of cocoa, Mum," said Donald. "I want a cup of cocoa too," which cry was taken up by Mickey and Luce till their mother cuffed them.

"Evening, Mrs. Pollett," said Mr. Packer, who on his yearly visit to the neighbourhood had had several amorous passages with Millie, consisting, we hasten to say, of gallant salutations from Mr. Packer followed by coquettish slaps from Millie Poulter as she then was. "Come to look for your young 'uns? They're a fine lot. These yours too?" he added, looking at the elder children.

"That's what Ed says," said Millie. "And there's Cassie at home and I dare say there'll be someone else before long," she added with a giggle.

"Looks like it," said Mr. Packer. "No offense. I'm a family man myself. Come in and have some cocoa and bring the kids."

The three elder Polletts, enraptured at the idea of being in a real caravan, climbed the steps and settled themselves on the floor among the company's legs, aided by a few good-natured slaps from their mother.

"He's got a black face," said Luce, pointing at Mr. Packer and beginning to cry.

"So've you," said Millie, rubbing a dirty handkerchief across her eldest daughter's face. "And don't you give cheek."

"That's all right," said Mr. Packer. "It's oil, that's what it is. They say oil's good for the skin and if it wasn't I'd be oily all the same. Hullo, Ed! Looking for the missus?"

Ed, who now appeared wheeling a perambulator, said he'd come home and there was Cassie screaming like a peacock in her pram and nobody about, so he brought her up to the field.

"I knew where old Millie'd be," he added meaningly.

"Mum, Cassie's crying," said Mickey.

"You mind your own business," said Millie, smacking him. "It's her supper she wants. Come on then, Cass."

In a moment Cassie was in her mother's arms and voraciously supping, while Ed and the children all had more cocoa.

"How's things?" said Ed to Mr. Packer.

Might be better, might be worse, Mr. Packer said. There were so many places where a man used to have a stand, but where were they now. Before the war there was a flower show somewhere every week and twice a week and a man could make an honest living at twopence a ride. Gatherum there was, and Pomfret Towers, and Courcy Castle, big shows they were. And there was Harefield and Pomfret Madrigal and Allington and Hallbury and Worsted and many more, and a man had the whole summer booked. But now, he said, half the big houses was shut and the gentry mostly hadn't got a field to let and all these new houses there were, taking up good ground where a man could put the Royal Derby.

"Why, when I was a boy," said Mr. Packer, "and used to go about with my old dad, there were villages round Barchester that'd have a flower show every year, and now it's all houses. Nasty little houses, too," said Mr. Packer. "I wouldn't change my caravan for none of them nasty little houses. People don't want a proper Royal Derby now. They're all for the pictures. Now, if you want to enjoy life, you don't go and sit in the theayter and see a lot of photos jiggling about; you get a horse, or a cock, or a nostrich, or two in a gondola if you like, and the organ plays and away you go, and all for twopence."

"It was you said twopence, Mr. Packer," said Millie quickly, who was not wanting where money was concerned.

"Ah, it was thinking of old times," said Mr. Packer. "Sixpence I did had ought to have said. Never mind, Millie. We're old friends and your kids can have all the rides they want tomorrow when we start. People are always a bit backward at the beginning of the afternoon, and if they see all those kids on the roundabout it'll be as good as an advertisement."

"Mum," said Donald, who had finished his cocoa and gone to look at the assembling of the roundabout, "there's a norse and he ain't got only the one ear."

"Don't talk nonsense," said his mother. "Horses have two ears and I'll box one of yours if you tell lies."

"All right, Millie," said Mr. Packer. "I know what he means. It's Lord Raglan, our dapple-grey. Those boys over at Hogglestock they're a rough lot and they got three on old Lord Raglan and knocked his ear off. There's a swan with its beak gone too, and the ostrich with a nasty crack in his neck and Barchester Belle, that's the first gondola after the ostrich, the schoolchildren at Northbridge they broke one of the seats. It's no use complaining to the police. They're frightened of the children themselves and the magistrate's all for the children. Poor little things, they say, they don't know no better and they won't do it again. Now, I ask you, it's encouraging them to do it again. I'd encourage them with a belt if I had my way."

"That's right," said Millie, who had, while Mr. Packer was speaking, given her son Will a hearty clip over the ear for fighting with his brother Ol.

"And I'm short-handed and my own odd-job man," said Mr.

Packer, continuing his lament for past glory. "And as for wood, They'd as soon give you gold. I sometimes think I'll burn the whole thing on Guy Fox day and have done. I've my old-age pension and I'll live in the caravan."

"Seems those horses ought to be mended," said Ed, in whose slow brain some process remotely connected with thinking had been going on. "I'll talk to our carpenter. He's somewhere about, putting a railing on the platform."

He went away at his labourer's slow slouch and presently came back with Mr. Marling's carpenter, still in his apron of office.

"Evening, Mr. Packer," said the carpenter. "Pleased to see you here again."

"Pleased to see you, Fred," said Mr. Packer. "Have some cocoa. You have some too, Ed. It's Packer's special." He winked.

A curious noise as of cocoa being poured out of a bottle was heard from one of the recesses of the caravan and the three gentlemen drank each other's healths in teacups.

"Ed, he says you're in trouble about some bits of wood," said the carpenter. "I don't know but I mightn't have something. Let's have a look."

Accompanied by Ed, the two men went over to the Royal Derby. Its framework was now erected and the organ in place and the various animals or boats lay in rows on the grass waiting to be fixed to their stands.

"Dear, dear," said the carpenter. "Poor old horse. That's Lord Raglan, isn't it, Mr. Packer? I remember him well. Mr. Bill and Mr. Oliver and Miss Lucy they used all to ride him at once. Dear, dear."

The three men looked sadly at Lord Raglan.

"Well, we'll see," said the carpenter. "I haven't shut my shop yet, and it's not much past ten and I've a good light in there. Let's see what we can do. What time do you start tomorrow?"

"Two o'clock," said Mr. Packer.

"Well, we'll see," said the carpenter. "You take Millie home,

Ed. It's time those youngsters were in bed. No, my lad," he added, as Ed showed signs of protesting, "if it was the steam organ I'd say 'Ed's the man,' or likewise the machinery. But when it's wood, or a bit of paint, I know what I'm talking about. Now, if you give me a hand, Mr. Packer—"

Disconsolate but obedient, Ed went back to the caravan, woke up his children, who were by now mostly asleep, and told Millie to come along. As many children as possible were crammed into the perambulator. Millie carried the baby, Ed pushed the perambulator, and the Pollett family staggered off into the night.

We will not say that a light burned all night in the carpenter's shed, for it did not. But by seven o'clock next morning the carpenter was again at work, mending, painting, and gilding, with a continued grumbling comment on the badness of all materials and how They didn't want a man to do good work, and how a man could do good work without good tools and good materials he didn't rightly know. But in spite of these hindrances the carpenter worked steadily through the morning, while other side shows were put up, judging went on steadily in the garden produce and livestock tents, and a part of the field was roped off for various sports and races. By twelve o'clock the Universal Royal Derby was fully populated and the licks of paint almost dry, and the carpenter at Mr. Packer's invitation went down to the Hop Pole while the dirty man, for many years Mr. Packer's assistant, took charge of the roundabout.

At Marling Hall there was to be a lunch-party for some of the principal guests or performers at the afternoon's festivities, and owing to the farmyard and the garden and the pig that had been killed earlier in the year, Mrs. Marling was able to produce a very creditable meal. That is to say she had exactly the same food as everyone else in her position. The chicken, ham, vegetables, cream, and fruit, being off the estate, were very good, while the bread was like a damp loofah that had spent the night in a slate quarry. The first to arrive were the Pomfrets, whose sense of duty made them so punctual that they nearly always had to wait. As it was a Red Cross Fête, Lady Pomfret had come in uniform, and as Mrs. Marling looked at the countess and her conscientious, tired husband, she felt that a Red Cross nurse's uniform would be even more suitable, but naturally did not say so.

"Hullo, Sally," said Lucy Marling, who was dressed for the occasion in a linen coat and skirt which she wore with a cavalryman's stride and swagger. "How's Gillie?"

"He is better in the warm weather," said the countess, her ever watchful maternal eye on her husband. "At least it makes him very tired, but he doesn't have the horrid cough and he sleeps better. Dr. Ford says he ought to get abroad, but everything is so uncomfortable and he would worry if he weren't here for the Conservative Rally. How are your Young Conservatives?" for Lucy, whose unbounded energy perpetually required fresh worlds to conquer, had recently established a Young Conservative Party in Marling and Melicent Halt and had been giving instruction to its members according to her own lights.

"Pretty putrid," said Lucy. "They'll turn up if it's a dance in the Village Hall or a whist drive, but when I got Sir Edmund to speak about local government hardly anybody turned up. I suppose it's because nearly everyone's a Conservative here so they think they needn't bother. Do you think Gillie would give us a talk about the House of Lords? If it's an earl speaking, the people who voted Labour last election will come too. None of them know they voted red, and most of them won't admit they did."

"No, Lucy," said Lady Pomfret. "If Gillie makes one more engagement before Christmas I shall take him to Cap Martin whether he likes it or not. We still have old Lord Pomfret's villa there. But I'll tell you what," she added, falling unconsciously as so many of Lucy Marling's friends did into that excellent creature's way of speaking, "we may be having a guest at the Towers for the Conservative Rally. I can't say who it is, or whether that guest will come, but if things go as I hope, your Young Conservatives will see something to remember at Staple Park. I hope the opening today won't take long, because Gillie has to get back for a committee in Barchester."

Then the Needhams came and the matron of the Cottage Hospital and the vicar of Marling, who was not jealous of Mr. Needham for opening a Marling Fête but all the same was determined to keep an eye on him. In old days there would have been anything from sixteen to twenty guests for such an occasion, but now ten seemed to Mrs. Marling a large number to feed, though she blamed herself for the feeling.

"Hullo, Matron," said Octavia Needham, shaking hands with the matron. "Do you remember that Caesar, the year Lettice married Captain Barclay? I mean the one that went so well. It was my first and I was frightfully bucked about it, but there weren't any complications at all, and I was *furious*."

Matron said, with some dignity, that complications were things she would not allow, adding brightly that she did remember a day when V.A.D. Crawley forgot to put the little vase of flowers on a patient's tray. It was little things, like a tiny vase of flowers, or even a little bit of green in the winter, she said, that just made the difference in the sick room. And now, she said, she was just longing to meet Mrs. Needham's husband, because a friend of hers had been night nurse at the convalescent hospital where Mr. Needham was and told her Mr. Needham was a wonderful example of pluck, always so cheery, though it stood to reason it must quite come over him sometimes that he was minus an arm.

"Hi! Tommy," said Octavia, "this is matron where I worked with Lucy at the Cottage Hospital. She knows the night nurse at that convalescent hospital."

Matron, her eyes so professionally fixed on Mr. Needham's empty sleeve that he began to wonder if she would ask him to take his coat off, said it was a great privilege to meet Mr. Needham, and Nurse Macpherson had said he was the life and soul of the ward. And very luckily, just as Mr. Needham was beginning to feel embarrassed, she began to tell him about Octavia's work as a V.A.D. at the Cottage Hospital and Mr. Needham's face lighted up at this praise of his wife and to show his gratitude he told matron all about his arm, to which matron listened with portentous gravity and pursed-up lips, implying that while Sir Omicron Pie knew his job quite well, it was entirely due to Nurse Macpherson that Mr. Needham had made such a wonderful recovery. Mrs. Marling, who had been wondering how much longer Mr. Needham could stand it, then intervened to offer her apologies.

"I can't tell you how sorry I am," she said, "that we couldn't get loudspeakers put in for the opening. I do hope you won't mind, and I am sure they will hear you."

"I hate the things," said Mr. Needham, quite vehemently for one so kind and tolerant. "I went to an open-air theatre in London lately, and first we had to sit on deck chairs, which means you can't see and lean back at the same time, and then the actors' voices came at me from the back of my neck and my left shoulder instead of from the stage. I can assure you I quite envied my arm for not being there," said Mr. Needham looking at his empty left sleeve. "And on another occasion I was among the congregation in—well, I had better not say where, as some of these up-to-date clergymen are very touchy about criticism, and the beautiful words of the morning service came simply roaring and bellowing at me from every side."

Mrs. Marling said she quite agreed and would rather not hear the service properly than have it out of a box, and it would be much better to teach the clergy to speak properly.

"What's that?" said Mr. Marling from across the table. "You get gentlemen into the Church and then the Church will be all right. My old uncle, Fitzherbert Marling, was Rector of Courcy Abbas for sixty years and you could hear every word he said. Hunted till he was eighty, too. I remember him sayin' to a curate, one of these mealy-mouthed young fellows: 'The words of the Lord can't be too loud or too clear. How do you think Moses would have heard the Lord if he'd mumbled as you do? The Lord speaks up and he expects you to do the same, young man, and what is more I expect it.' The whole Hunt turned out for his funeral."

Oliver and Lucy exchanged glances. Their respected papa was in his Old English Squire mood and his offspring felt they were on the verge of having the giggles.

"Pray excuse papa," said Oliver to Lady Pomfret.

"I like it," said the countess. "We haven't enough eccentrics. Gillie's uncle was first-rate at it. I have heard him curse the foot-men at the Towers, when Gillie and I were engaged, in a way that did one good. It was quite like reading history."

"Unfortunately," said Oliver, "we can only curse or be rude to our equals now. If we say an unkind word to our inferiors we find ourselves in the police-court, whereas they can be and often are as rude as they like with impunity. How is the Red Cross going?"

"Very well," said Lady Pomfret, "and largely thanks to my secretary, Miss Dean. You know her sister, don't you?"

Lucy, who was silent at the moment, happened to glance at her brother and saw him with a look on his face that she did not know.

"Oh, yes. I mean which sister?" said Oliver.

"The clever little actress," said Lady Pomfret. "Jessica Dean. I saw you with her at the Wigwam last Sunday, didn't I? I'm hardly ever in town at the weekend, but Gillie's cousin George Rivers had a party, and as we hardly ever seen him now, we couldn't say no."

Lucy, who did not mean to stare but was stranded with each neighbour talking away from her, saw her brother Oliver's face assuming an almost sheepish expression and could not understand it.

"The Wigwam isn't much in my line," said Oliver, "but Jessica asked me to take her and I couldn't very well say no."

"I should think not," said Lady Pomfret. "She is quite charming, on the stage I mean, and I gather from her sister that she is delightful in private life. I admired you both. I had no idea you danced so well, Oliver."

Oliver, wondering if his face looked like what it felt like, said it was easy to dance with so good a dancer as Jessica. He hardly ever danced now, he said.

"Then you must keep it up," said Lady Pomfret. "I shall be having some young people at the Towers at Christmas and I shall count on you. Cousin Amabel, ought we to be moving?"

In anyone else Mrs. Marling might have resented such a question put to her at her own table in her husband's house, but no one could be offended by Sally Pomfret, who gave herself freely and endlessly to others, if she occasionally marked that she had a position in the county. Besides, Sally was quite right, they ought to go down to the field, for it was almost half past two.

Accordingly the party walked down to the home field, where the fête had already been unofficially open for the last half-hour. The Pollett children were making use of Mr. Packer's invitation to act as decoys and had already had between them the equivalent of at least ten shillings' worth of cock, swan, horse, and ostrich exercise, and two of them had been sick. Most of the grown-ups were in the tents, openly gloating over their first prizes, or saying people as had cousins in the nursery-garden line hadn't ought to be allowed to exhibit. At the sight of what Oliver called the vice-regal party several bowler-hatted, rosetted stewards bestirred themselves to collect the audience, and by the time Lord and Lady Pomfret, Mr. Needham, and Mr. Marling had climbed onto the little platform, there was a good crowd on three sides of it with a reserve line of children and impedimenta, these last being mainly perambulators which were used by the mothers more to keep Em and Sid and Daise within bounds than with the idea of giving them carriage exercise. Beyond the pale there was a good deal of noise where a number of big boys and young men were tinkering with the engines of their motor-bicycles for the gymkhana that was later to be held, and the air was torn by every noise of which machinery is capable.

Mr. Marling advanced to the front of the platform and shouted: "Ed! Ed Pollett!"

"I wish papa would say 'Ho, varlet!' and have done with it," said Oliver irreverently to Lady Pomfret, who smiled, but more he felt from kindness than because she really understood him.

All Ed's friends obligingly joined in the outcry and within a few moments Ed appeared at the foot of the platform and grinned.

"Here, Ed, go down to the sports enclosure and tell those boys if they don't stop that noise I'll cancel the races," said Mr. Marling. "Have to be firm with them," he added to Lord Pomfret, sitting down again as a token that the meeting was not yet open, "or they take advantage every time. When I was a boy it was pony gymkhanas and all the farmers' sons had a pony of some sort. Now it's all these filthy motor-bicycles."

Lord Pomfret said, with great truth, that his uncle, old Lord Pomfret, often said the same thing. Meanwhile Ed had walked placidly down to the sports enclosure and singled out young Joe the carpenter's son, to whom he delivered himself to the effect that the old squire didn't like the noise because the gentleman couldn't hear himself speak and if all that noise was a-going to go on he Ed Pollett wasn't going to give a hand with some folks' motor-bikes when they ran them without oil and the bearings seized. After which words, spoken in his usual mild and slow way, the popping and grinding and roaring died down and Ed slouched back to the platform.

Mr. Marling then hoisted himself to his feet again and announced to the crowd, which by now was encouragingly large, that Lord Pomfret, the Lord Lieutenant of Barsetshire, had kindly come down to declare the show open and he needn't say anything about Lord Pomfret as they all knew him and that was that. He then sat down.

"You've forgotten about Tommy, papa," said his daughter Lucy.

"Eh?" said Mr. Marling. "What's that?"

"You've forgotten about Tommy," said Lucy, speaking quite distinctly but not troubling to raise her voice as she knew from experience that he would only tell her she needn't shout and he wasn't deaf. "He's going to pray."

"Going to pray, eh?" said Mr. Marling. "What for? Oh, Needham, you mean. All right, all right. Give me time."

He then hoisted himself up again and said Mr. Needham from Lambton was going to address them and everyone could see he had lost an arm in the war, at which there was an outburst of cheering, for Mr. Needham's fame as the owner of one arm and a justly popular vicar had spread even to Melicent Halt.

"That's all," said Mr. Marling and sat down.

Lord Pomfret and Mr. Needham rose to their feet and even as they did so realized with acute embarrassment that no one had told them which was to speak first.

"Is there a program?" said Lord Pomfret helplessly to the world in general.

A steward rushed up and said the programs had only just arrived and were being unpacked. Lord Pomfret and Mr. Needham looked at each other and Lord Pomfret, too tired and conscientious to find much in his life to laugh at, smiled almost audibly. Even Octavia Needham, who considered it her mission in life to tell other people what to do and mostly, we must admit, with beneficial results, was at a loss, when she caught sight of her father and mother, who had just arrived, and, working her way through the crowd, told them what was happening. The Dean by sheer force of personality, which included a good deal of physical strength, made his way to the front of the platform and spoke to Lord Pomfret. His lordship nodded and spoke to Mr. Needham, who courageously sketched the action of advancing to the edge of the platform, though it was obvious that one step forward would have precipitated him onto the heads of his audience. Mr. Marling stared like a bull beset by toreadors and might have interrupted had not the steward returned with a sheaf of programs, which he thrust into Mr. Marling's hands. Mr. Marling put on his spectacles, glanced at the program, and turned to Mr. Needham to say it was all right. But it was too late, for the audience, seeing Mr. Needham's empty sleeve, were moved as one man by the truly English love of everything crippled, from a canary with an artificial leg to a politician who scores heavily at the poll owing to having a paralysed arm, and burst into cheerings and clappings. Mr. Needham was by now used enough to this kind of popularity, which he took with sincere humility attributing it, and quite rightly, to no merit of his own but rather to his Creator, who had kindly seen fit to let him have his arm blown off by a shell-splinter in the Libyan Desert. As soon as the noise had stopped he spoke, asking blessings upon the work of the Red Cross and speaking a little of England. There was then silence and before the audience could get out of hand again Lord Pomfret made a very short speech, composed for him by his wife, and declared the fête open.

"That's all," said Mr. Marling in a loud voice to himself, and the crowd after rather perfunctory applause, for Lord Pomfret though liked and respected was far better on committees than in public meetings, which he loathed and only undertook from a sense of duty, drifted away to amuse itself.

The vice-regal party, as Oliver had called them, then de-scended into the arena and were taken in tow by the stewards, at which point Lady Pomfret said to Mrs. Marling that she was afraid she and Gillie must leave as they both had committees in Barchester and how much they had enjoyed their lunch and how nice that the weather was so good for the fête.

"That's all right, Sally," said Mrs. Marling. "Will and I are very grateful to you both, and Gillie spoke so well. Don't overdo things, my dear."

To which Lady Pomfret replied with great honesty and

simplicity that if she didn't overdo things nobody else would ever do them.

"You must sometimes wish that Gillie were still a landscape painter," said Oliver, who had overheard this conversation. If Miss Anne Fielding, so shortly to become Mrs. Robin Dale, had been present she should at once have taken the allusion from her favourite poet, Lord Tennyson, but Lady Pomfret looked politely puzzled and said it was old Lady Pomfret that did those water-colours of the Alhambra in the green drawing-room, and with repeated thanks took her husband away.

"There go the best couple in Barsetshire," said Mrs. Marling to Mrs. Crawley, who quite agreed, and then told Mrs. Marling as they walked across the field to the tents about the forthcoming wedding of the Fieldings' girl in the Cathedral and how the dates had been chosen with great cunning when the Bishop would be at Zurich attending a meeting for the furthering of Mixo- and Slavo-Lydian unity: which, said Mrs. Crawley, was impossible, for quite apart from centuries of racial hatred, one country was Orthodox and the other belonged to the Church of Rome, and neither would concede an inch religiously or politically to the other; vastly preferring a carefree mediæval life of cattle-maiming, varied by arson, robbery, and assassination.

As the vice-regal progress continued, it was joined by other county contingents. The rabbits, pigeons, fowls, and other livestock were admired. Mr. Marling pretended not to see that his gardener had a first prize for the mixed vegetables and loudly congratulated the ticket clerk from Melicent Halt on his prize table decorations, which were tasteful in the extreme though overcrowded by maiden-hair.

"All very nice," he said, "all very nice. When my dear mother had people to dinner she had the table done much in the same way, only it wasn't these fern things, it was—Amabel!" he called to his wife.

"Yes, my dear," said Mrs. Marling, tearing herself away from a delightful Commination Service that she and Mrs. Crawley were holding about the Palace.

"What was the stuff my mother always had at her dinner-parties?" said Mr. Marling.

"Which course do you mean?" said his wife.

"No one's talking about courses," said Mr. Marling. "Dinner-parties I said. You know, Amabel, creepin' all over the table."

Oliver nearly said caterpillars, but checked himself.

"You mean smilax," said Mrs. Marling, to whom peculiar powers of divination were granted.

"That's what I said, smilax," said Mr. Marling. "Proper dinner-parties those were. Eight courses and the right wines. People don't do that sort of thing now. Don't know what we're comin' to. Not that my father ever drank too much himself, but my Uncle William used to make his butler sit up and see him to bed. Can't expect that sort of thing with this Government."

Oliver looked at his sister for sympathy, but she was taking an interest in the schoolchildren's faded bunches of wild flowers in jam-jars and he could not catch her eye, when suddenly he saw an answering gleam in a very pretty pair of eyes and looked down from his height upon Mrs. Francis Brandon, whom a good many of her friends still thought of as Peggy Arbuthnot.

"I *adore* your father," said Mrs. Francis, as everyone found it more convenient to call her, if they did not call her Peggy.

"So do I," said Oliver. "It's rather sad all the same."

"I know," said Peggy Brandon. "But it would be almost worse if he did move with the times, wouldn't it? Like that dreadful Hibberd man whose name one *never* can remember, pretending he is the working-classes and then taking a title."

Luckily, said Oliver, his papa had the form of snobbery that thought a title on the whole a come-down when your people had been squires in a place since the Heptarchy, whatever that was, otherwise he might have found himself the Honourable Oliver and would have had to learn etiquette.

Peggy Brandon said the one thing about being an Honourable was that it made it much easier to marry well.

"Oh, by the way," she added, "Francis and I were in town this weekend and went to see Jessica in her new play. She sent you heaps of love and says don't forget the Wigwam next Tuesday. She said would you call for her after the curtain."

There is a stage when one is caring for people, when you can, or so you think, quite easily remove them from your thoughts, for you are not really thinking about them at all; oh no indeed not. But if you hear their name, or any scrap of talk connected with them, your heart leaps up and hits you in the stomach, which may sound unscientific but is as near as we can get to the feelings involved. Oliver did not go red or pale, nor did he start nor show any symptom of confusion, but undoubtedly he was in a lift which suddenly began to descend, leaving most of his inside on the top floor. So he thanked Peggy Brandon for the message and said he would remember.

"Colin Keith is coming too," said Peggy.

So this, reflected Oliver bitterly, was what one got for trying to be agreeable to people. They asked one to take them to a night club and then invited Colin Keith. Hah! So he said how nice, and inquired after Mrs. Brandon.

"She is very well," said Peggy, "and making the moist divine clothes for the baby. We haven't decided whether it's a girl or a boy yet."

As it was well known to the whole county, and quite obvious even if they hadn't known it, that the pretty Mrs. Francis Brandon was going to have a baby, Oliver took this news calmly and asked when it was to be. Peggy said about the end of September because the Bishop would be in New York trying to convert the American Protestant Episcopalian Church to Christianity during October, so they could safely have the baby christened in the Cathedral.

"We would have loved the christening to be at Pomfret Madrigal," she said, "but unfortunately Mr. Miller will be having his holiday then. He was so sweet and said, Indeed, indeed he would willingly forgo his holiday for the privilege of conducting so delightful a ceremony, but mamma said he must really control himself and not be unselfish and Mrs. Miller needed a holiday badly. Which was rather casuistical of mamma, if that is the word I mean, because she really wanted a cathedral christening frightfully. Oh here she is."

And up came Mrs. Brandon, now mostly known as Mamma, looking though tired extremely pretty and obviously studying the Art of Being a Grandmother with all her might.

"What a delightful fête!" said Mrs. Brandon. "I have spent fifteen and sixpence already and nothing to show for it. You must see Jessica's new play. We all went and she is better than ever. We went to the Wigwam with her afterwards and Charles Belton was there. What a nice boy he is! It was so lucky that he could come. His headmaster is very kind about letting them out, and we all motored down afterwards because it does seem so important to use all the petrol we can before there isn't any."

The old Oliver would have been amused at Mrs. Brandon's inconsequent speech, but the Oliver of today was a different man. He had of course no real interest in Jessica Dean, no right to criticize the life of one who was a Servant of the Public, but first Colin Keith and now Charles Belton; it was intolerable. He would telephone to her, no not telephone for one would hear her voice and forget one's justifiable indignation. He would write to her and say how sorry he was that circumstances made it quite impossible for him to take her to the Wigwam, but he was sure she would not miss him as Colin Keith would be there. Then he realized how silly and pettish this would sound and he decided to keep his appointment and show by his attitude that his presence was merely an act of courtesy because a gentleman does not go back on his word. Then his sense of humour asked him how on earth one expressed so many fine shades by an attitude, and he began to laugh at himself. Mrs. Brandon, who liked people to laugh and never expected to understand why, smiled

enchantingly and approvingly on him and passed on with her
daughter-in-law to the sports ground.

By this time the roundabout was packed and a large crowd
was gathered round it, some waiting their turn, some longing to
go on it but knowing fatally that the circling movement combined with the rhythmic rise and fall of the horses on the
beautifully polished twisted brass poles on which they were
impaled, and the rich odour of hot oil from the engine, not to
speak of the ear-splitting noise of the steam organ, would
infallibly make them seasick. To Oliver himself, though æs-
thetically he found complete satisfaction in a roundabout regarded as a pure fusion of the Arts, the very sight spelt nausea
and he was preparing to go when he caught sight of his sister
Lucy seated astride upon an ostrich with the face of one who
follows the gleam. It was so seldom that Lucy allowed herself
time for amusement, though it must be admitted that she did
not miss it, that Oliver had almost forgotten how young and
how handsome she could look. At that distance and with his
rather poor sight she looked as handsome as he had ever seen
her, and for once doing something of supreme unusefulness and
with no moral purpose at all. He wondered, as he had often
wondered before, whether Lucy would ever get married, whether
she had ever cared for anybody, for brotherly affection can be
very blind, and it had never occurred to him that she had begun
to like Tom Barclay when Tom Barclay was falling in love with
their widowed sister, Lettice Watson. And even if it had occurred to him he would have thought, quite sensibly, that it was
a long time ago, far back in the year after Dunkirk, and told
himself not to be silly. He had vaguely thought that their distant
cousin David Leslie was a good deal at Marling that year, but
David was safely married to Rose Bingham and already had two
children. Thank goodness it hadn't been that revolting poseur
Geoffrey Harvey, and Oliver shuddered at the thought of his
own narrow escape from Geoffrey's dreadful sister Frances, now
happily engaged in persecuting underlings in a Government

department. Men of a suitable age had not been wanting, but Lucy treated them all, so he felt, as probationers, while she was a fully qualified nurse, and one could not force one's sister who was a far more forceful character than oneself into a suitable marriage. He came to the conclusion that it was after all more Lucy's business than his own. As he turned away he bumped into a man of about his own height and hastily putting on his spectacles saw that it was Captain Belton. As children they met at parties, and for a brief time at a preparatory school; then Dartmouth on one side, and Eton on the other, had separated them and of late years the war, and the worse-than-war peace that had followed, had not only sent Freddy Belton to sea for several years, but had made casual visits between Marling and Harefield increasingly difficult. A childhood shared makes it very easy to pick up threads, and after each had got over the slight shock of seeing in the other exactly how much he had aged, they were exchanging news and gradually came round to the subject of "What are we to do about our parents?"

"You know we had to give up Harefield," said Captain Belton, "and a girls' school got it. Luckily my people have got a very nice house in the High Street, and father has sold a good deal of land to the Hosiers' Company to build a new school, so he and mother are all right. What happens next I don't know."

"Mine still live at Marling," said Oliver, "but that's the end. I hope a County Council may buy the house and some land, even if it's for a lunatic asylum. There's a little house in the village that would do for mother, but I can't imagine Lucy without the farm and the garden. If there would only be another war she could go somewhere with an ambulance, but this beggarly peace cramps her style everywhere. How is Elsa?"

Very well, Captain Belton said, mostly at their place in Scotland with the children, and Charles was being a schoolmaster at the Priory School and enjoying it.

"You know," said Oliver, who wasn't really interested in Elsa and had been quietly pursuing his own train of thought, as indeed we so often do while our friends are talking, "you know, Freddy, we always arrange for our fathers to die first. What happens if one's mother dies before one's father?"

"I hadn't thought of that one," said Captain Belton. "It's a bit of a facer. If mother died first I think my father would go melancholy mad. Of course he might marry our old nurse Wheeler, who is the cook now. With Elsa in Scotland there wouldn't be anyone else to look after him. I do wish you wouldn't think of such things."

"Sorry," said Oliver, "but I do. I don't think papa would go melancholy mad, but Lucy would have a pretty grim time alone with him. I'm back in London now, at my old job."

Captain Belton said oh yes, but did not commit himself further because he either didn't know or couldn't remember what Oliver's job was. And as we are in exactly the same predicament ourselves we will not go into the subject, merely adding that we do not care, for we are perfectly certain that whatever job Oliver Marling held was a good one, and that his brains and reliability were paid for at a suitable price.

While Captain Belton spoke, his eyes wandered to the round-about, which was slackening for its passengers to get off and make room for newcomers.

"Who is that good-looking girl on the ostrich?" he said to Oliver.

"Lucy, you great fool," said the heir of Marling to the heir of Harefield, just as Marling Minor had said it to Belton Major at their prep school. "Lucy," he shouted.

His sister heard his voice and waved her hand, but was carried once more round before she could alight.

"It's Freddy Belton," said Oliver when Lucy joined them. "He's at the Admiralty now."

"Lord! so it is," said Lucy shaking Captain Belton's hand with a ferocious and friendly grip. "I did just see you at Holdings the other day. I'll tell you what, Freddy, come and have tea. They're only just beginning and if we're quick we'll get a table. Come on."

With manly strides she led the way to the select tent reserved for the Marlings and their friends, laid violent hands on a rickety table, sat down with her knees well apart and her sensibly shod feet well planted on the floor, and stared at her old friend.

"Are you an admiral yet?" she inquired. "Oh well, captain's quite good. I mean it's about equal to a full colonel, isn't it? I say, Packer's Derby is as good as ever. Come on with me after tea. Packer's keeping the ostrich and the cock for me at five o'clock."

"Like Lord Nelson I am always sick on a roundabout," said Captain Belton, at which remark Lucy stared.

"Oh, I suppose you mean because he was always sick when he went to sea," said Lucy, "but he stuck to his job, and if you come on the roundabout you'll soon get over it. I'll tell you what, I'll let you have the ostrich. He's steadier than the cock."

But Captain Belton declined this handsome offer, suggesting that Lucy should come and show him the prize rabbits instead, so they went off together leaving Oliver alone, of which he was rather glad as the sun and the heat and the noise were making him tired. So he remained in the tea tent, watching people and smoking rather more cigarettes than were good for him till a party of Deans came in. Most of them were unknown to him, but Susan Dean detached herself from the family and came over to greet him.

"Hullo, Oliver," she said. "Before I forget, I've got a message for you from Jessica. She says not the Wigwam because she's sick of it, and will you go back to her flat for supper because she and Aubrey have got to talk some business."

This was better. At the Wigwam one simply spent money and felt out of it, except for Jessica, who followed one's steps so beautifully and was always gay. As for Clover, one didn't think about him one way or the other. Obviously Jessica had to discuss things with her author-manager-producer. Then jealousy raised its green head. What about Colin Keith? Was that insufferable young prig of a barrister also invited? As if she had known his thoughts Susan went on: "And to tell you Colin isn't coming. She put him off because of having to talk business, but she said you wouldn't matter."

Another man, a man who was not Oliver Marling, might, so that gentleman felt, have been slightly offended, or hurt, or froissé should one say, by Susan Dean's version of her sister's explanation, but so welcome was the news that Oliver received it gratefully and did not criticize. It served young Keith right, and the sun, even inside the tent, appeared to shine more brightly.

"Lady Pomfret was awfully nice," said Susan. "She gave the office a holiday so that we could come to your fête. At least the ones that live in West Barsetshire get their day off for the Gatherum Castle Red Cross Fête in August. My secretary lives over there, so she's doing my work today. Come and sit with us."

Oliver, whose head was beginning to ache with the heat of the tent and the babel of noise from the strident, high-pitched voices of well-bred English county people, would willingly have made an excuse. But Susan Dean was a very nice girl, her family had given him a very good dinner, and one must be polite in one's own grounds, so he followed Susan to where what looked to him like about three hundred large, good-looking people of all ages were pitching into the tea.

"This is Oliver Marling," said Susan. "Mother, you do know Oliver because he came to dinner," at which words Mrs. Dean roused herself from a drowsy contemplation of her tea and smiled.

"Mother's exactly like the Dormouse at the Mad Tea-Party," said a tall, dark, handsome young woman to Oliver. "I'm Betty."

"She's really Mrs. Woolcott Jefferson Van Dryven," said Susan, "and they live in New York, and Woolcott is over here on peanuts, and this is Laurence and Margaret, and the twins and Gerald and Robin. And that's the whole family except Helen and Charles and of course, all the children."

Oliver's brain reeled, as indeed tougher brains than his had reeled before the large Dean family, their in-laws, and their children.

"Oh, and Jessica," said Susan, "because she's never here except at weekends. Oh, and father of course, but he's nearly as busy as Jessica."

Betty's husband, who with the skill only given to American citizens had at once memorized Oliver's name, though Oliver had imperfectly grasped his and forgotten what he did grasp, then kindly came and sat by Oliver to ask his opinion of the peanut cartel. Luckily for Oliver he prefaced his question by so long a statement of his own views and those of Senator Smith and Judge Brown that the waitress began to remove the remains of tea and clink the teacups in the washing-up basins in a very threatening way, and the party felt they had better leave before the revolution began.

The Dean family, who in spite of usually being scattered over the globe, were extraordinarily united and, like so many large families, never so happy as in one another's company, moved as one man to the Royal Derby. Captain Belton and Lucy coming up at the same moment were co-opted, and Mr. Van Dryven, addressing Mr. Packer as Captain, handed him a pound with a request to let him know when the money ran out. Oliver refused all invitations to mount an animal or ride in a gondola and went to see what his parents were up to, whom he found quite innocently engaged in talking to Millie Parker and her children, while Ed stood proudly and sheepishly by.

"Well, father, it has gone very nicely so far," said Oliver.

"Eh? What's that?" said Mr. Marling, but Oliver refused to be drawn, so his father said he had seen flower shows that went worse.

"Not a flower show, William," said his wife. "A Red Cross Fête."

"What I said," said Mr. Marling, "I've seen plenty of Red Cross Fêtes go worse than this. All your doing, my dear."

Mrs. Marling said: "Nonsense," but Oliver could see her

pleasure over his father's admiration, and he thought of his talk with Freddy Belton about "What to do with our parents" and felt that if heaven would kindly arrange for both his parents to die in their sleep, though not for a long time, simultaneously, it would be a kind deed and worth heaven's consideration. But he had noticed that heaven appeared to be more and more occupied with its own affairs, or perhaps had given up trying to help when this Government had so obviously got the upper hand, and told himself that wishful thinking did nobody any good.

"Do ask that nice Freddy Belton to stay to dinner," said his mother. "It's only a scratch meal, but I'd like to see something of him. One wants to know the children of one's old friends, but it's so difficult to see anybody now."

"Right, mother," said Oliver. "And we might ask Susan Dean," because, Oliver reasoned with himself, one doesn't really care about Jessica, but Susan is her sister and one oughtn't to neglect people's sisters. His mother, who thought far more than anyone guessed about her younger son's future, approved the plan. The Deans were not perhaps exactly what she would have desired, but the actress sister was pretty, famous, and well-mannered, and Susan was a nice girl of whom Sally Pomfret thought highly. And though one didn't mention it, Susan would probably have money. So Oliver went back to issue the invitations while Mr. and Mrs. Marling made a kind of patriarchal progress among the tents and side shows and looked at the end of the motor-bicycle gymkhana, not without loud criticisms from Mr. Marling on internal-combustion engines as compared with ponies.

The crowd was now thinning, for everyone wanted their tea, supper, or dinner, according to what they chose to call their evening meal. The rabbits, pigeons, and other livestock were being taken home, cross and sulky that their day of glory was over. Mr. Marling's cowman's Speckled Willesdon, who had won first prize for cockerels, had a very unpleasant argument with the carpenter's Islington Brooder, who had in her time hatched at least a thousand chickens, or so she said, till their respective owners shoved them into boxes too small for them, banged the lid down, and took them home. As for the fruit, vegetables, and wild flowers, they were left to their fate for the present. The smaller side shows were packing up and only a Hoop-la and Murdstone's Wild West Shooting Gallery remained, and of course Mr. Packer's Derby, which was spending the night at Marling.

"'Night, Packer," said Mr. Marling stopping beside the Derby while the passengers changed. "Not like old times. Fellers drunk all over the place when I was a boy."

Mr. Packer, wiping his hands and face on a handful of cotton waste said: "Ar," adding: "that's right, sir."

"What's your what's-its-name, that infernal musical box, playing now?" said Mr. Marling, pointing with his stick at the steam organ. "It was 'Ta-ra-ra-boom-de-ay' when I was a boy, and 'Tommy make room for your uncle.'"

"Bit before my time," said Mr. Packer, quite respectfully, but omitting the sir according to Modern English Usage. "When I was a nipper it was 'Tommy Atkins' and 'Sweet Marie.' But our patrons like to be up to date. Just wait a moment, Mr. Marling, and you'll hear our latest—not that it's very new," he added apologetically, "for the prices they ask for the new populars you'd be surprised. 'Handhold in the Twilight' it's called," at which Mr. Marling went so purple in the face that his wife and son, closing in on him, walked him away like Eugene Aram.

"It's no worse than 'Just a song at twilight,' papa," said Oliver. "Nurse used to sing it to us after tea in the winter and we nearly died of nostalgia." But Mr. Marling was not the man to be put off by such paltry casuistry, and went on being Old-fashioned Squire to his own complete satisfaction till they reached the Hall.

Captain Belton, who had come by bus, said he was afraid he must catch the seven thirty back, but Miss Susan Dean, Depot Librarian of the Barsetshire Red Cross Hospital Libraries, had

used the Red Cross car to come to the fête and said she had
plenty of petrol and could drive Captain Belton home, so the
invitation was gratefully accepted, and being far from up to date,
each telephoned to tell their families not to expect them. And if
our reader cavils at this use of the words "their" and "them" we
can only respectfully ask him to try the sentence himself, for we
confess it has completely baffled us.

The scratch meal was of course as good a meal as times can
afford, and as long as people are allowed to keep cows and hens
and grow vegetables there will still be presentable food; as for
pigs the whole subject is under such tyranny that we would
prefer not to speak of them. Apart from Mr. Marling's cornering
Captain Belton to tell him about his experiences in France with
the Barsetshire Yeomanry in the '14 war, experiences which he
felt must be particularly interesting and instructive to a naval
captain at present working at the Admiralty, the conversation
was general and dully pleasant. Lucy, after condemning loudly
and not perhaps without cause the ruling of the judges about
runner beans and Lopsided Angoras, tried to settle down with
Susan Dean to a really searching talk about the Red Cross, but
Susan with the firm and gentle tact that her official work had
taught her, refused to be bullied and talked very prettily to her
host, who liked young women with no nonsense about them,
especially if they happened to be good-looking as well, and
Susan like all the Deans had plenty of good looks. Captain
Belton had seen her in uniform and now he saw her in a summer
dress and he thought both suited her well, but he had not much
opportunity to speak to her at dinner for she was across the table
and he was annexed by Lucy Marling, who wanted to know
what his father was doing about the swedes this year. Though
Captain Belton had been a sailor for most of his life, you cannot
be the son of a country gentleman without imbibing something
about your father's estate. As a boy and until he first went to sea
he had spent most of his holidays with the bailiff, or the
cowman, or the men on the home farm, and had learnt and

remembered a good deal. And as for the business side he knew sadly far too much about it and the increasing difficulties under which the estate laboured. He had done his best to help his father, and had voluntarily relinquished certain rights of his own, for he had no intention of marrying, and thought that his father might as well be happy while he lived. So he and Lucy, having begun to talk of these matters, went on with their talk after dinner, when they all sat on the flagged path outside the house, and he found Lucy singularly free from illusions about the future of Marling Hall.

"It will just have to go," said Lucy looking to see that her parents were well out of earshot. "My elder brother is a soldier and anyway he won't be able to afford to live here. It's either the County Council or a Government department or a big business firm, and I wish," said Lucy, her eyes suddenly brimming, "that *everybody* was dead. The Government first of course, just to show them, and then everybody else, because I have tried so hard, and so has father and we can't do anything."

There was really nothing to say. The same thing was happening all over England and no one could stop it. In many cases the final crash had been staved off during the war by letting the big country houses to the public bodies of whom Lucy had spoken, or to one of the lesser breeds, who although by their own account penniless expatriates mysteriously had huge sums of money at their disposal. But this flood was ebbing and half Barsetshire, which means half England, were wondering if they could have the roof reslated, or send Tommy to Eton, or manage to keep up their bounty to old pensioners; and many of them were trying to reconcile themselves to the conviction that apart from the last-named commitment, which was a debt of honour, they did not know how to carry on.

Captain Belton as representing the British Navy wondered if he ought to offer his handkerchief, clean it is true but darned in two places by Wheeler, to Lucy, and was relieved when she pulled from her jacket pocket a large manly handkerchief and blew her nose, and said she was sorry.

"So am I," said Captain Belton. "I couldn't be sorrier. They have put us where they want us and that's that. And I don't see what we can do except carry on till we can't."

Lucy said she wished there would be a General Election, to which Captain Belton very sensibly replied that *(a)* the same lot would probably get in again, *(b)* could she say with her hand on her heart that their own lot had a real program or a real leader, and, as an afterthought, that *(c)* he really didn't know what the Liberals had been invented for except to split votes.

"Cheer up, Lucy," he said. "It will last for our parents' time and that's all that really matters. After that we can look after ourselves. I shall probably be an admiral by then and have a pension when I retire, unless of course the Government stop all pensions above the rank of petty officer."

"I say," said Lucy, alarmed. "Don't say that. They might hear and They'd absolutely jump at the idea."

"That's true," said Captain Belton smiling, "and I dare say there is a dictaphone behind the wainscot and whoever is in charge of liquidating landowners taking it all down in short-hand. However, as I was saying. I shall probably be able to live in one of father's small houses in Harefield and have one arm and a flagstaff and hoist the Union Jack when the sun tops the yard-arm and drink rum. That is, if one can get it by then," he added.

At the beautiful word "rum" the party suddenly coalesced like beads of quicksilver to mourn over the decay of drink. Mr. Marling took up a firm stand upon claret and port, saying that in his great-grandfather's time, who laid the foundation of the Marling cellars, cocktails hadn't been invented and he didn't know why anyone wanted to drink them. But the younger people, more interested in the present, fell into a discussion of the various ways and means of getting drink, some advocating sticking to a firm who knew you, others recommending a wider field.

"There's only one way as far as I can see," said Oliver, "and that is to begin ordering immense amounts of drink the moment you are born and never stop ordering, and then when a war comes you get a little attention from your wine merchant."

Susan, who was very special, said if it came to that that one might start accounts with every shop one could think of at an early age. Grocers, she said, and tailors and shoemakers and linen-drapers and hardware shops and glass and china shops and furniture shops and stationers and *everything*. Which idea seemed so reasonable and yet so impracticable that they were all left much where they were. Mr. and Mrs. Marling, who were very obliging parents, then took themselves indoors to write letters.

"I know what mother is saying," said Oliver. "She is telling my father that the young people like to be left alone. Young people! Do you realize, Freddy, that you and I could easily have growing families now?"

If there was a faint hesitation before Captain Belton answered, no one but himself was conscious of it.

"Taking it by and large, I could conceivably be a grandfather," said Captain Belton, "but it would have meant marrying when I was about eighteen and expecting my eldest son or daughter as the case may be to do the same. My people are just the same. They allow Elsa to be grown up because she is married, but Charles and you and I shall be the young people till we die."

"Or till we marry," said the practical Lucy.

"Or till we marry," Captain Belton repeated.

"I'll tell you what," said Lucy, to whom abstract speculation was abhorrent, "let's go down to the field and look at the roundabout again. Packer's rather a friend and he expects me to have a talk. Come on."

As a sailor and a gentleman Captain Belton could not refuse, though he would have preferred to sit in the long twilight and talk with that nice good-looking Susan Dean about books, but a hostess's word is law, so he got up good-naturedly.

"We'll come presently," said Oliver. "You don't want to go, do you, Susan?" to which Susan's natural kindness made her say she didn't, though really she would have liked to follow Lucy, partly to see the fun, partly because she had a premonition of what was going to happen. Nor was she wrong, for Oliver, in what he erroneously took to be a perfectly offhand manner, led or rather directed the conversation towards the Cockspur Theatre and that brilliant ornament of the English stage Miss Jessica Dean.

"What is such fun about Jessica," said Oliver, "is that she isn't a bit like an actress," to which inanity Susan hardly knew what to reply. It had been pretty obvious to her, and to anyone with eyes in their head, she thought, that if Jessica was like anything it was an actress. By some freak the youngest of the Deans had been born with a sixth stage sense and had also the faculty of complete absorption in the work, endless patience in learning and improving, and, luckily for her, excellent health and a body impervious to fatigue. Certainly it was partly luck that had put her in neon light on Shaftesbury Avenue so young, but her luck was backed by her character and her gifts.

"I don't know," said Susan doubtfully. "I don't know any actress except Jessica. I should have thought she was pretty good."

"Good heavens, I didn't mean that," said Oliver. "Of course she is good. I mean she understands things so well. One can talk to her."

Alas for Oliver that the kind Susan was his audience. Had it been Lydia Merton, or Peggy Brandon, or almost any of the younger women he knew, they would have explained to him very clearly that it was part of a good actress's job to be able to turn on the sympathetic tap at will, and that if a pretty actress listened attentively to what one said, it meant either that she wasn't listening at all or that she was thinking of something quite different; or possibly memorizing some look or phrase for her own use. But all Susan could say was that Jessica was a darling and so kind to rather dull people like Colin Keith.

Stung by this hated name, Oliver said bitterly that possibly Jessica found him dull too. Susan stared. Oliver Marling, whom she liked, who seemed to her a very pleasant and a peaceable kind of person, who could be very amusing when he wished, as he had been when he and Lucy dined with her family, appeared all of a sudden to be conducting a one-sided lover's quarrel. She was quite sure Oliver couldn't be in love with Jessica and certainly Jessica wasn't in love with Oliver or with anyone else, but something queer was happening and her honest heart was troubled by it.

"I say, Oliver," she said. "Don't be angry. You aren't dull a bit really. I expect we all seem a bit dull to Jessica, because she practically lives with Aubrey Clover."

Oliver knew perfectly well that there was no implication behind Susan's words and indeed was ashamed of himself for imagining an implication, but even so the contrast between the company of that fellow Clover and himself was bitter to him. Calf-love should reach one young. If one doesn't catch the disease till one has come to forty years one is going to make the very most of what capacity one has for suffering. Susan sat dumb, not knowing what more to say, and silence did not help. Oliver lit a cigarette, thinking angrily as the little flame burned in the still twilight air how theatrical it all was.

"Let's go down and have a look at the roundabout," he said. "I'm sorry."

Rather like one of the periodical difficulties with the women at the Red Cross, thought Susan wearily. Those were part of one's job. As soon as you got a few women together they began to ferment, though when she came to think of it the men could be quite as bad as the women, and she recalled the scene between the Hogglestock Red Cross Librarian and the Barchester General Hospital Librarian about a bookcase twelve by six and how there had almost been tears and hysterics till she had put on her rarely used voice of authority.

"We all get tired sometimes," said Miss Susan Dean, "and I know you are worried about your people. Do let us go and see the roundabout."

Never in his life had Oliver felt so completely put in his place. He did not resent it for he knew perfectly well that he had been silly and, what was even worse, lacking in consideration for a guest in his father's house, but he was deeply mortified by his own want of self-control. That was not how a gentleman should behave. The best amends he could make was to say no more about it. So he walked with Susan across the lawn, through the walled garden, past the potting-sheds and so through the vegetable garden to the field where romantic lights were shining from the Royal Derby and the steam organ throbbed nostalgically through the warm darkening air. A line from a Victorian song that his grandmother used to sing came to his mind, "Eve, gentle eve, it is the hour for love." But things weren't like that now. Jessica was probably in the Cockspur Theatre enchanting and amusing the packed house. He was escorting Jessica's sister to see a roundabout in his father's grounds and that was that. And as they approached the roundabout the noise of the organ, the smell of the warm oil, and the shrieks of the riders and audience, now reinforced from neighbouring villages, made all finer feelings vanish.

"'Evening sir," said a voice at his side, and turning he saw Mr. Packer himself, unusually clean.

Oliver inquired how the roundabout was doing.

"She's doing fine," said Mr. Packer. "Not a hitch all day and the old engine running as sweet as you'd wish and a nice crowd. Not a lot of old Hitlers like the Hogglestock lot that knocked Lord Raglan about and broke the swan's back. Lot of Russians they was if ever I saw one," said Mr. Packer, who appeared to have a comprehensive view of England's enemies. "Can I offer you and the lady a ride? There's a nice gondola just empty, or there's the ostrich and the unicorn. On the house."

Oliver declined the compliment with many thanks, on the ground of being too soon after a meal, and pressing a piece of paper into Mr. Packer's hand, which was conveniently near, begged him to have one on Marling Hall at the Hop Pole.

"Well, I don't know as I won't," said Mr. Packer, not rudely, but merely following a Brave New Custom of never showing gratitude. "I'll be stepping along now with some of the boys. I've got an assistant on the Derby. Back in half an hour!" he shouted across the noise.

From the bowels of the Derby an oil-blackened face appeared with a wide grin and shouted Okay.

"It's only Ed, sir," said Mr. Packer. "It isn't everybody I'd leave with that engine because there's a piston-head as likely to blow off as not. But she's all right with Ed," and he walked rapidly away towards the village, collecting the carpenter and another friend as he went.

Lucy and Captain Belton now emerged from Murdstone's Wild West Shooting Gallery carrying a large cheap doll, a necklace of red beads, and six striped cardboard trumpets. Captain Belton was loud in his praise of Lucy's marksmanship and said he wished he could get her to his brother-in-law's place in Scotland for the shooting.

"Well, try," said Lucy. "I'd love to come. I'll tell you what, Freddy, we'll give Millie Pollett these things for the children. She's sure to be about."

With unerring instinct she led the party across the field to Mr. Packer's caravan. On the steps Millie was nursing the baby, while the rest of her young family, grimed with oil and sodden with cocoa, were blissfully and sleepily fighting each other.

"Hullo, Millie," said Lucy. "I've brought you some prizes. I got them at the Shooting Gallery. How's Cassie?"

"She's lovely, miss," said Millie, proudly exhibiting her youngest daughter, who was so determinedly attacking her supper that all the visitors could see was the back of her head with beads of perspiration on it caused by the violence of her greed. "Mr. Packer's gone off to the Hop Pole, miss, so I said I'd stay here and then him and Ed's going to have their supper. I've got it on," and she pointed to a small witches' cauldron that was simmering over a wood fire near by.

"It's like the gypsy's stew that Toad had," said Lucy.

"More like your young rabbits and partridges," said Captain Belton.

But on hearing the word "supper" all the young Polletts stopped fighting and began to say they were hungry, and as there was no means of stopping the noise the gentry said good night. Susan then took Captain Belton on board and drove away, leaving Oliver and Lucy alone.

"Freddy's a good sort," said Lucy with a huge yawn. "Oh Lord! Turk's out. Be an angel and find him. I'm going to bed."

Not for the first time did Oliver wish that his sister's dog Turk were dead, or chained in the yard, but it had to be done. He wandered through the garden whistling and calling in vain till in disgust he came in, shut the doors, and went to bed. He did not easily go to sleep, for when one has been rude to a guest it rankles within one. And on Tuesday he was to fetch Jessica at the theatre and have supper with her at her flat. And with Aubrey Clover, but he didn't count. And then he remembered how Susan had said that anyone who saw a lot of Aubrey Clover would naturally find ordinary folk dull: only those were not exactly the words she had used. So he tormented himself and took a sleeping-pill which had no effect at all and tormented himself again till at last in the grey dawn he fell asleep and dreamed that Aubrey Clover had locked Jessica into a room and taken the key and she was beating the door trying to get out and he was paralysed, as one is in dreams, and couldn't rescue her. Then he woke in terror and heard Turk whining and scratching at his door, having probably got into the house by the scullery window, which no one would shut because there wasn't a scullery-maid now. Unwillingly he let Turk in, cursed his maud-lin fawnings, and tried to go to sleep again. And when he did go to sleep it was only to dream again and wake with one of his headaches.

Captain Belton said he could not possibly take Miss Dean so far out of her way as Harefield, which was a silly remark as there was no other way for him to get home unless he walked. Susan said she loved night-driving and anyway it wouldn't be dark much before midnight. They did not talk much. But there was no discomfort in their silence and Susan had a curious impression that the half-hour spent in that little wheeled abode had been very safe and comfortable, and when Captain Belton said good night his handshake made her feel that she could rely on him.

"Would you lunch with me in Barchester one day?" he said. "I get down here a good deal at present."

"Rather," said Susan. "Ring me up."

She drove away and Captain Belton told his parents, who were still up, what an amusing afternoon it had been, and how Susan Dean had kindly brought him back and was going to have lunch with him one day. Mrs. Belton at once began to wonder, for nothing could cure her of wondering and hoping, but Captain Belton had no more to say.

CHAPTER 7

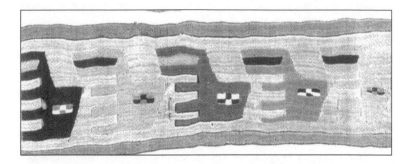

Barsetshire continued to swelter under the first really warm summer since Dunkirk. All sensible people enjoyed the sun. A great many other people complained ungratefully of the heat and said there was bound to be a bad winter. But as any winter occurring while They were in power was bound to be bad, the sensible people went on enjoying the warmth and tried to take short views. Quantities of people went abroad in great discomfort and spent most of their time worrying about whether the money they were allowed to take out of the country would see them through. Our formerly lively neighbours the Gauls were showing the unconquerable Spirit of France by being even ruder and more grasping than before the war. In Switzerland the national spirit was also unbroken in that while en pension terms were reasonable, a cup of coffee or a funicular ride crippled a week's finances for good, while the hotel-keepers openly deprecated the spending of good English money in shops. People who went to Italy said it was so wonderful and friendly and what fun the crowded trains were with everyone so jolly and *quite* kind to animals now. And in the middle of it all They cut down the travel allowance except for Themselves and the vast army of people who mysteriously do well for themselves under all conditions. Captain Belton was at Harefield a good deal and twice took Miss Susan Dean out to lunch.

"My mother was wondering," said Captain Belton, "whether

your mother would mind being called on. I gather that the visit would be in the nature of an act of reparation as by all canons she should have called at least fifteen years ago."

"I don't think mother would mind at all," said Susan. "In fact she'd rather like it, only I don't think she'd remember to return the call. She doesn't notice things much," at which Captain Belton, who had now been in Winter Overcotes several times, laughed.

"And how is the divine Jessica?" said Captain Belton. "My brother Charles is quite besotted about her. It must be a bit trying for the Winters, but they are very nice about it. Are you going to their Parents' Day?"

Susan said she hadn't been invited and wasn't a parent.

"But you've got a nephew there," said Captain Belton, "which makes you a parent at once. Why not come with mother and me? She's not a parent either, unless you count Charles. It's on Saturday week."

"That's the day after Anne Fielding's wedding," said Susan. "Lady Pomfret has given me the afternoon off for it. Yes, I'd love to come. I might make mother go too as Laurence's boy is there, and your mother could call on her in the tea tent," which seemed to Captain Belton a very sensible suggestion, and they went on talking of this and that and how Mr. Dean had been to call on Captain Belton's department at the Admiralty's request and how struck the department had been by his suggestions. All of which Susan was pleased to hear, for one likes people one is fond of to like each other and Susan was fond of Captain Belton in a gentlemanly way. If she had troubled to analyse her own feelings she would have discovered that she felt as if she had known him all her life, but she was not by nature introspective and was one of those lucky people who get into bed at night and turn out the light and go to sleep.

The dining-room at the White Hart was by now very full and the head waiter had more than once cast a jealous eye on the empty seat at their table, which was a small table for three in a corner. He now approached and speaking to Susan, whom he knew quite well, asked if she would mind him putting a lady and gentleman at her table as what with the trade delegation from Mixo-Lydia and the Barsetshire Pig-Breeders' Association's special show committee meeting he didn't know which way to turn. She could but say yes, and the head waiter brought up another chair and a lady and gentleman who turned out to be Lydia Merton and her brother Colin Keith in disguise.

Lydia and Susan had known each other for a long while, and Susan had helped Lydia through a measling period in the previous summer, which had made a bond between them of kindness freely and capably given and gratefully received. Their part of Barsetshire had its eye on Susan Dean and Colin Keith, but it had also had its eye on Colin Keith and Mrs. Arbuthnot, now Mrs. Francis Brandon, and almost had it on Francis Brandon and Susan Dean: a kind eye, interested, on the gossiping side, but not in the least malicious. Of all of which Susan was aware though Colin, only down for occasional weekends, had no suspicion that he was under the county microscope. As so often happens in real life, the ladies talked to each other very comfortably and the gentlemen had to make conversation for themselves, which was not difficult as both were used to meeting people and both had county interests outside their work. But, as Captain Belton was not slow to notice, Colin's attention was but speech-deep and his eyes wandered more than once towards Susan while she was asking Lydia for the latest news of Miss Kate Merton, now aged two months, who had ousted Master Harry Merton from the position of head baby. Barsetshire had not been wrong a year ago when it had its eye on Colin Keith and Susan Dean, but Barsetshire had not been present when Susan, wearied by Colin's mooning about after Mrs. Arbuthnot, or so she inelegantly phrased it, had told him not to sulk and she would like to see him again when he had done a little more growing up, adding that his sister Lydia was probably right when she said she thought Colin was a permanent uncle.

This, however, was a year ago and Susan may have had cause to change her mind about Colin, who was increasingly successful at the bar and much in demand at London parties. The talk then shifted to Anne Fielding's wedding, to which they were all going, for the Fieldings had many friends in the city and a good many acquaintances in the county, while Robin, being connected with the Dales of Allington, would have his side of the church better filled than the bridegroom's usually is.

They were not talking very loudly, but all had the voices of educated people who were used to command, and Lydia vaguely noticed that a woman lunching with a large party near by turned and looked at them several times.

"I say, Burden," said Lydia to the old head waiter, jerking one shoulder in the direction of the lunch-party, "who are they?"

"Trade delegation from Mixo-Lydia, madam," said the head waiter. "Foreigners. Was the steak to your liking, madam?"

"Well, I couldn't chew most of it," said Lydia. "At least I couldn't cut it with my knife, so I just left it."

"I assure you, madam," said the head waiter, who had been at the White Hart before human memory began, "that I could cry when I see the meat we have to serve. When I remember the old days, madam, and my hot joints and my cold table, I could cut my throat. I assure you, Miss Lydia, if your father could see the meat They give us now, he would rise from the grave."

Lydia, though a little confused by his chain of reasoning, said she was sure he would and Burden mustn't take it to heart, because it wasn't his fault.

"Ah, if we'd had Mr. Churchill, he'd have seen that the sirloins and the steaks were tender, and the mutton, miss. What sweet will you have, Miss Lydia? I couldn't recommend the semolina pudding, nor the pastry, and the cheese is off. I'd have an ice if I was you. It goes down quick and you don't seem to taste it."

On this doubtful recommendation they all ordered ices and coffee.

While the ices went down quick without tasting, Lydia was more and more conscious of the woman at the large table, and was rather alarmed when she got up and came to the little table.

"You speak of Prodshkina Anne?" said the stranger menacingly.

Colin and Captain Belton rose, for an English gentleman should not remain seated while a lady stands even if she is obviously not a lady and is talking nonsense. Susan, used to dealing with peculiar visitors at the Red Cross, asked the stranger to sit down, which she did, pulling her own chair across with her foot.

"You speak of Prodshkina Anne?" the stranger repeated. "Ah, I see you do not onderstand. The daughter of Lady Fielding. She is to be spoused, yes?"

"Yes, she is to be spoused," said Susan, finding herself to her horror adopting the stranger's manner of speech. "In the Cathedral."

"Which is not a wedding at oll," said the stranger. "In Mixo-Lydia the hosband, which you say the groom, must bring a male cock and a female hen which does not yet lie eggs and slit their necks and if the blood gushes over the bride's mother it is good luck."

"What happens if it doesn't?" said Lydia, fascinated by this religious ceremony.

"Then is the dowry returned and the bride's friends fight the groom's friends. So is all joy," said the stranger. "Do you know Lady Fielding? Good. Then will you tell her that Prodshkina Gradka will come to the wedding. It is quick?"

"About three quarters of an hour," said Colin.

"She doesn't mean quick, she means soon, you idiot," said his sister Lydia. "It's next Friday at half past two."

"Then shall I not assist," said the stranger. "I go to Smoozepore with the Mixo-Lydian trade delegation tomorrow. God wills it so. Man arranges, God disarranges."

She remained silent, apparently thinking over this proverb.

Each of her hearers was mouthing: "Who is she?" at the others, when the waitress came up with their bill. She stopped to stare.

"If it's not Grad!" she said.

The stranger looked up and stared back.

"You've not forgotten me, Grad?" said the waitress. "Greta Tory. My auntie's Admiral Palliser's cook at Hallbury and I was post-woman there. Remember the time we all had tea in the kitchen on Miss Anne's birthday and the old governess came down in her dressing-gown? Poor old lady. She's got a nice bit about her on the wall in Rushwater Church. Me and Ernie Freeman went over on our bikes to look."

"Bog!" said the stranger. "Which pleasure! Which joy! I embrace you. I embrace all the world for joy to see an old friend."

"No you don't, Grad," said the waitress. "Not when I'm on duty. Tell you what, come and have a nice cup of tea with me at the Crabbe-Apple tea-rooms and bring your boy friends along. I'm off duty today."

"I shall comm," said the stranger. "Bot alone. It is more costful for you if I bring the others, olso I do not like them, for they wish to admit Slavo-Lydia to the United Nations, which repugnates me. Nor are they boys, they are old-age men, which you call pantaloons."

"All right, Grad, have it your own way," said the waitress, offering Captain Belton his change. "Thank you, sir," which rapid change was caused by the approach of the old head waiter. The stranger went back to her party.

"That must be the Mixo-Lydian maid that was with the Fieldings in the war," said Lydia. "There were a lot of them at Southbridge. I wonder where Smoozepore is."

Captain Belton said probably Portsmouth.

Lydia got up and gave herself a shake, though not so violently as Miss Lydia Keith would have done. "Coming, Colin?" she said.

Colin said he would walk round to the Red Cross with Susan and meet Lydia at the station.

"We can quite well go and see the Bohun Memorial another time if you like," said Captain Belton, addressing Susan.

Susan, whose straightforward nature had during her Red Cross work learned some of the shades of social guile, told Colin Captain Belton had promised to show her the memorial tablet lately put up in the Cathedral cloisters and he must ring up and come over to Winter Overcotes for tennis soon.

"Oh, come on, Colin," said Lydia. "I've got to collect those khaki runners for Nanny Twicker. Good-bye, Susan. I'll see you at the wedding," and she hustled her brother away.

Captain Belton and Susan walked up the High Street in the hot sun. Dogs were sprawling on doorsteps. Large cats were luxuriously lying behind shop windows, basking in a kind of hothouse. Even the bluebottles outside the butcher's were dozing upon a blood-smeared placard bearing the inscription: "SORRY NO OFFAL TODAY. DO NOT ASK. A REFUSAL OFTEN OFFENDS." Barchester was still in its siesta or lunch-hour. They passed under the close gateway, where the air was cool, and came out into the golden warmth of the close. So soft was the air, so still, that Susan did not speak for fear of breaking the circling calm. They passed slowly in front of the Deanery and so up to the magnificent east front and in by a heavy leather-covered door to where the great Cathedral rose in white beauty, brilliant with sunlight, to support the roof of the nave and the great spire. A door from the south transept led to the cloisters, which were empty except for a few birds flying in and out and the murmuring of bees in the clover-strewn grass, which was being slowly mown by old Tomkins with his scythe.

"And here is the memorial tablet," said Captain Belton.

Susan Dean looked at the marble with its inscription and said she didn't really know Latin.

"Nor do I," said Captain Belton. "But this isn't too difficult. It only says that the Reverend Thomas Bohun, M.A., was Canon of Barchester from 1657 to 1665 and wrote some rather unreadable love poems. Oliver Marling could tell you all about them.

He found a book of his that nobody knew and wrote an article about it. I believe it was all rather awkward because his poems were distinctly erotic and the Dean had to take a good deal of trouble about the wording of the tablet."

"I think it's awfully dull," said Susan. "I say, Freddy, why did you pretend I had promised to go and see it? I backed you up but I didn't understand."

"For two reasons," said Captain Belton, standing very still and looking to Susan taller than usual. "I didn't think you wanted to go back to the Red Cross with Keith and I did want you to walk with me."

"But why?" said Susan, knowing how foolish she was being.

"Need I explain?" said Captain Belton. "Need I, my darling?"

"No," said Susan in a very small voice, looking very hard at old Tomkins while the white clover flowers fell before his scythe. "No, please don't explain. I don't think I could bear it. Not yet."

With which words she looked up and then looked away again and Captain Belton thought she was trembling.

"Very well," he said at length. "When you would like me to explain, will you tell me?"

Susan bent her head in agreement, and colour rose to her face, but Captain Belton seemed satisfied and they walked silently round the cloisters while the grass and white clover fell in swathes as the old gardener swung his scythe in his own rhythm and the bees murmured aloud. They went back into the high whiteness of the Cathedral and slowly over the black and white marble pavement and so out into the golden warmth of the sun. The Dean was seen approaching.

"I ought to be back at the office," said Susan. "Good-bye." She looked at him for a moment, her soul in her eyes, and left him, going by the far side of the close.

"Good afternoon, Dr. Crawley," said Captain Belton. "I have just been showing Susan the Bohun tablet. I am ignorant of these matters, but the Latin is very elegant, isn't it?"

"It is not for me to say," said the Dean, who had composed the inscription himself and suspected Captain Belton of knowing it, but was none the less pleased by the tribute. "Do you know that the Palace did its best to have a chapel erected to his memory? A chapel! Incredible. But we have never had a scholar and a gentleman here since Bishop Grantly. We shall all meet at Anne Fielding's wedding on Friday I hope."

Captain Belton said he and his parents were coming and he expected it would be a very pretty wedding, especially if the weather remained so fine; and then felt that Nelson would have thought but poorly of his self-control. But the Dean, who was not Nelson nor in any way like him, did not think about it at all and they parted.

There is not much to be said about Robin Dale and Anne Fielding. They had loved each other when very young without being conscious of it and had become engaged without any change in their feelings unless it were an even more complete sense of safety. Robin Dale, now for the last year junior house-master at Southbridge School, with a home for his wife and an adequate salary to support her, besides his private means and the dowry Anne would bring from her parents, whose only child she was, loved Anne so much that he was sometimes afraid. Anne had been very delicate as a growing girl, but thanks to Dr. Ford, the old governess Miss Bunting, who had guided her through the awkward age to a shy self-confidence, and the ever watchful care of her parents, there seemed to be no reason why she should not be perfectly well and strong. When he thought of his approaching marriage, it is true, he felt that so much happiness could only tempt the Gods to destroy him, but having been well brought up in what very few people now like to call religious principles and being as sane as anyone can expect to be, he decided that for Anne and himself to be so happy must be a good thing for everyone, as indeed we think it was. For with the exception of the Palace, who were as we know not to be in residence at the date of the wedding and sent a second-hand fish-slice, and old Lady Norton, who said these were not times for marrying or giving in marriage with the income tax what it was, everyone was delighted. A wedding is always fun. One wears what good clothes one has, meets one's old friends and plays the delightful game of seeing what they have given, and comparing it favourably with what one has given oneself. Also there may be champagne.

Anne had moved through the weeks before her wedding in a dream, dutifully going to London with her mother to shop, trying on clothes, writing to thank everyone for the presents and especially people who had sent her clothing coupons. And these people, and it is greatly to their credit, were mostly Anne's contemporaries, who frightfully wanted new clothes themselves but felt that a bride must come first. She had also helped her mother to select house linen from the store that Lady Fielding had wisely been laying in from the moment war seemed imminent and had marked most of it herself. As for furniture the junior house had a kind of permanent foundation of useful uninteresting furniture, Robin had any of his late father's furniture that he wished to keep, and Anne would not come to him with empty hands.

"I think," said Anne to Robin, who had been allowed to come and see her the evening before the wedding, "that Tennyson knew everything."

"Did he, my darling?" said Robin. "I don't think he knew I would have to spend the night at the Deanery. I have got that enormous room with the two brass bedsteads in it and a huge looking-glass that swings forward and makes you feel drunk. And I am sure the Dean will want me to say my catechism before he marries us."

Anne smiled and put her cheek against his arm. "What I meant," she said, speaking into his coat sleeve so that it was rather difficult for him to hear, "was 'Now folds the lily all her sweetness up and slips into the bosom of the lake.' Only you aren't a bit like a lake *really*, Robin."

"My precious angel," said Robin, more moved than he liked to show, "you don't know what you are talking about and I adore you."

And then Lady Fielding came in and said she was so sorry, but she had heard the Deanery gong across the close and perhaps Robin ought to be going. So he kissed Anne and ran to the Deanery, and Anne, who was watching him from the drawing-room, saw him as he went and felt her heart bursting with love because he always limped a little but never, never complained. Then she had dinner with her parents and did some packing and went to bed and to sleep.

Sir Robert and Lady Fielding also went to bed early, partly because they had little to say, partly because they didn't want to say it.

"I suppose it had to come," said Sir Robert through his dressing-room door, "but I'm damned if I look forward to it. I like Anne."

His wife said what she could, but her heart was also heavy at losing her only child. It was all very well to like Robin, in fact to be very fond of him; to trust him, to feel that Anne would be safe with him. But nothing could alter the fact that Anne's bed would be empty, her place at table not laid, her voice not heard. Lady Fielding could willingly have shed tears, but alas that relief becomes impossible to most of us as we get older and suffer more. And then she blamed herself for selfishness, because Robert must be just as unhappy as she was and had not the secret joy that she was cherishing, the prospect of grandchildren. No man, she considered, had the proper feeling for grandchildren. He might want heirs for his name, but Anne's children would be Dales. Only a grandmother could enter fully into the joys of a nursery; broken nights, a perpetual airing of small objects, teething, vaccination, sterilizing bottles, untimely and unquench-able shrieks; being naughty at the most inconvenient moments, deliberate tyranny, gross selfishness; in fact, all that makes our young utterly adorable.

"I was thinking," said Sir Robert, walking about her room, looking out of the window, and taking an unusual interest in the organist, who was coming back from a private orgy of music in the organ loft, "that when Anne and Robin come here, later on I mean, we might have that door between the white room and the little white room reopened and those shelves removed. They would make a very good day and night nursery. I mean if one were needed," he added, to show his detachment.

Lady Fielding confessed herself convicted of spiritual pride. Finer feelings were all very well, but Robert's feelings had led to something real, something one could look forward to and work for, something too that would help their beloved Anne in time to come. So she applauded his suggestion and they went upstairs to look at the two rooms and before they went to bed had turned a third small room into a bathroom, installed a service lift and a speaking-tube from the kitchen, and put a low cupboard with a tiled top and a gas ring on the landing.

After this profligate expenditure of the future they yawned and went to bed, but Lady Fielding had not finished the first chapter of Mrs. Morland's new novel when her husband appeared, dressing-gowned and rather haggard, in the doorway.

"What is it, Robert?" said Lady Fielding, who had always known that some quite dreadful thing would happen to spoil the wedding and that this was probably it and Robert was going to have acute appendicitis.

"I was thinking, my dear," said Sir Robert, "that we had forgotten one thing. We must have the nursery gate put back."

His wife praised him for his forethought and he went back to his room and fell asleep quickly, conscious of duty done. But Lady Fielding did not sleep so soon, for the thought of the nursery gate was too much for her. Behind the gate her little Anne had lived. Her first real crime had been to unbolt it and go down to her mother's room, where she had felt frightened at what she had done, hidden in a dress cupboard, and gone to sleep, while a distracted nurse searched the house and garden.

Lady Fielding remembered her agony when she came home and was told that Miss Anne couldn't be found, her frenzied inquiries from neighbours and the reaction when Anne reappeared with a very dirty face and much refreshed by her nap. So vividly did she relive these scenes that tears came to her eyes and she cried as she had never thought to cry again. "Elderly fool!" she said angrily to herself and opened Mrs. Morland's book again and went to sleep with the light on.

The wedding was not to be a large one. At least that was what Lady Fielding said, for only an imperial or royal wedding could have filled the huge edifice, so high, so drenched in light. But what with Sir Robert's friends and the Hallbury friends and the Barchester and county friends, it was evident that the audience would make a good show and that the resources of Number Seventeen would be taxed to the utmost.

"Not that 'audience' is quite the word," said Lady Fielding to Mrs. Crawley, who as the mother and grandmother of a large marrying family had come over to offer assistance before the ceremony, "but one can't say 'congregation' for a wedding, because it isn't religious."

The wife of a dean might have taken it upon her to be shocked, but Mrs. Crawley, possibly relying on her husband's dignity and his gaiters in the next world, was a woman of this world and sympathized with Lady Fielding's difficulty, adding that she found the word "guests" covered the ground quite well.

Madame Tomkins, the Barchester dressmaker who had made for Miss Fielding (a trade expression) since she was a little girl, now sent down to say that Miss Anne was ready and would Lady Fielding come up and look. So Lady Fielding took Mrs. Crawley with her. Anne was standing on a sheet in the middle of her mother's bedroom in a cloud of white, the pearl necklace that her parents had given her on her seventeenth birthday round her neck, and in her hair, holding her veil in place, a crystal heart wreathed with tiny rubies and diamond leaves, shining like stars on a clear frosty night.

"Lovely, my dear. Quite lovely," said Mrs. Crawley, to whom Anne was for the moment merely an actor suitably dressed for one of the church's best performances. "What is the little ornament? Is it old? Rather unusual for a wedding to have rubies, but it suits Anne admirably. It seems to express her if I make myself clear. Well, Madame Tomkins, I must congratulate you."

"I nevair fail," said Madame Tomkins. "You geeve me the material, I deeliver the goods, hein? You walk round her, you will see."

Anne, composed and serious, stood quite still while her mother and Mrs. Crawley admired from every side. Then the elder ladies went away, for it was time that Lady Fielding should take her place in the front pew. In the drawing-room Sir Robert was looking at the champagne and talking to Simnet, butler to the headmaster of Southbridge School, lent by the Carters for the occasion.

"Very nice it looks, my lady," said Simnet. "When Miss Rose was married we had twelve dozen champagne, but times are changed."

Lady Fielding said that was very true and she must be going.

"And you won't forget, Robert, will you," she added anxiously, thinking as she did so how very distinguished her husband looked.

"Forget what, my dear?" said Sir Robert. "*I* don't have the ring, it's the best man."

"I mean to take Anne to the Cathedral," said Lady Fielding.

Sir Robert, his feelings at the moment much like a vegetarian's who finds himself landed with a lamb and instructions to take it to the butcher's, might have lost his temper had not Simnet, from his long experience, come respectfully forward and said to Lady Fielding: "There is no occasion for anxiety, my lady. I myself will take charge of Sir Robert."

So Lady Fielding and Mrs. Crawley walked over to the Cathedral and Lady Fielding took her seat in the front left-hand pew and after kneeling in prayer for a moment, or rather, as she told Bishop Joram afterwards, being able to think of nothing but whether the housemaid had remembered to press Anne's grey flannel skirt, arranged herself in the pew and looked at the guests. On the other side of the aisle Robin, looking exactly like Robin, was standing with his best man, a Dale cousin. Robin smiled at her and she smiled back and felt less fluttered. In the bridegroom's pew were some Dale aunts and uncles, not interesting nor particularly good-looking but obviously the right people. Behind them were friends from Hallbury, where old Dr. Dale had been vicar, a large contingent from Southbridge School, and quantities of Leslies and Grahams. To look round on her own side of the aisle would have been too marked, but she knew her adherents would do her credit and the Deanery was supporting her. A cousin in the pew behind her leaned forward to say something. Lady Fielding turned slightly and as she listened she became aware of a rather large but distinctly striking girl, well dressed, with a good hat that must have cost money. She could not at the moment think where she had seen her and in any case had to bring her attention back to her cousin's very dull remarks, and by the time the cousin had finished, the girl had been hidden by Lady Norton.

The organist was now making the musical experiments which betoken a gap to be filled and Lady Fielding suddenly felt so sick, so certain that her husband had forgotten to bring Anne, who would therefore never get married, that she thought no more of the girl. Then the organist broke into a hymn, the choir advanced in ill-assorted couples up the red carpet, and Miss Anne Fielding on her father's arm came up the aisle with two Deanery grandchildren for bridesmaids. The Dean, assisted by the Southbridge School chaplain, better known as Holy Joe, then began the marriage service, using the words we all know in a fine sonorous voice as though defying any persons who revised or deposited any part of the Church of England service. Sir Robert made a slight inclination from the waist, though to whom he had he had no idea, being by this time convinced that he was dead or dreaming, and relinquished his guardianship of his only child for ever, glad to be safely back in the pew at his wife's side. The Dale cousin produced the ring, Robin and Anne were made man and wife and moved slowly up to the altar to kneel and worship Love while the Dean, who knew perfectly well that no bride and bridegroom are capable of taking in anything but the fact that they are together, abstained from any hortatory words and gave them the Church's blessing.

All old cousins, family retainers, and the people who had come in because they see a wedding going on were now in tears and enjoying themselves vastly. Lady Fielding did not shed a tear, but as she knew quite well that she was not there at all, but was somewhere, possibly in the roof of the Cathedral, looking at Dora Fielding, wife of Sir Robert Fielding, whose daughter was being married, it was not necessary for her to cry.

Then the Dean and the bridal pair disappeared, the organist amused himself with all his hands and feet, and a general emigration took place into the vestry, where several people kissed each other for the first and last time and found themselves very much surprised by what they had done. Presently they all moved back to their places and Robin, doing his best not to limp, brought Anne down the aisle with her cloudy veil of lace thrown back, a cold crystal and diamond gleam in her hair, and a sweet serious face of absorbed happiness.

"Thank God!" said Sir Robert.

"Not now," said his wife in a firm undertone. "Take old Miss Dale out."

So Sir Robert took Robin's elderly aunt, and Lady Fielding was squired by an elderly Dale uncle, the bridesmaids fell into place with the best man and Mr. Traill, assistant master at Southbridge, and so the whole procession came out of God's blessing into the warm sun with bells ringing from the Cathedral and walked across to Number Seventeen, where Anne and Robin had already been arranged in the big drawing-room to be kissed and shaken hands with.

Earlier in the day there had been a high explosive moment when Pollett the parlour-maid, a distant but very despising cousin of Ed Pollett, had said that if Mr. Simnet wished to be boss she was sure her ladyship would understand her giving notice at once. To which Simnet, who concealed his contempt for women servants under a velvet tongue, replied that while he and Miss Pollett both knew the guests, there was one job that no ladies knew and that was how to handle champagne. At a dinner-party, yes, he continued, and he was sure Miss Pollett did it very nicely. But champagne at a reception was a different thing, and it required a MAN to see that some people didn't get more than their fair share, especially if any of the Palace lot were about, added Simnet, who was a thorough-going partisan. So Pollett announced the guests, altering her voice subtly according to their status, while Simnet at the back of the great L-shaped room busied himself with his champagne, aided by his sister-in-law who was formerly in service with Mr. Oriel at Harefield and could not be trusted not to break things.

"Now, Dorothy," said Simnet to his sister-in-law, "all you've got to do is to take the glasses out and wash them and mind you polish them well. And if you've got to break something," he added pityingly, for Dorothy though a devoted wife to Mr. Simnet's brother and a submissive daughter-in-law to old Mrs. Simnet was distinctly subnormal, "mind you break an empty bottle. And if you break one you'd as well break two more, for breakings always go by threes."

"Yes, Mr. Simnet," said Dorothy. "That's what Mrs. Simnet said when I broke the best teapot and the other two next best ones. Mr. Simnet," said Dorothy, who had a confusing habit of calling both her husband and her brother-in-law Mr. Simnet, owing to her great respect for them, "laughed ever so."

"That's enough, Dorothy," said her brother-in-law. "Here's

the company coming and what you want is not to be seen nor heard, but I'll let you look when no one's likely to notice you."

"Oh, *thank* you, Mr. Simnet," said Dorothy.

And now the county and the city began to pour into the room to congratulate and to enjoy the party. Robin and Anne smiled, shook hands, were kissed by people they didn't know, tried to thank people they did know for their presents, but all in a delightful dream where nothing was real except that only death could part them.

"Well, Miss Anne," said Mr. Adams, suddenly towering before them in a very well-cut suit with a flower in his button-hole and looking distinctly like somebody "I have to wish you and your husband a long life and a happy one and I may say Sam Adams was never so pleased as when he saw his little gift being worn by you and on your wedding day too. I picked it as a winner when I saw it in Bond Street and I didn't grudge the money," said Mr. Adams, gazing appreciatively at the frost-cold crystal and diamonds, "and when I see you wearing it I'd give as much again. And here's an old friend."

He moved on to congratulate Robin, and a large but distinctly striking girl, well dressed, with a hat that must have cost money, stood in front of Anne.

"Congratulations," said the girl. "I can't tell you how pleased I am. Dad and I always liked Robin."

"Heather!" cried Anne. "I didn't know you were coming. I am so glad. And you are engaged too, aren't you? Oh, Heather, isn't it all heavenly?"

"Ted's here somewhere," said Heather. "I'd like him to meet you if you have time. He's absolutely one of the best. Dad's clip looks lovely on your veil. I mustn't keep the queue waiting."

She paused for a second and Anne impulsively lifted her face and Heather kissed her and passed on to greet Robin. And more guests surged in and the noise of talking grew louder and louder and Simnet handed champagne, discriminating between those who deserved it and those who, in his opinion, didn't.

To the dispassionate observer the room might have appeared to be dominated by Leslies (including Grahams) and Deans, but this was perhaps not so much because of their numbers, though there were a good many of each, as their good looks, their vitality, and their general air of being able to take on any job and do it well. Lady Graham was holding court, just as her mother had always done, without the faintest effort to attract her friends, magnetically enchanting by her mere existence. The boys were of course back at school. Emmy had torn herself from her cows, pushed herself into a silk dress, and was walking about the room with the air and gait of a farmer on market day appraising cattle. Clarissa, slim and coolly detached, Edith stout and lively, kept close to her mother, looking at the scene with detached interest. Mrs. Belton oozing through the crowd saw Lady Graham and came to speak to her with her two sons in tow. Charles made for Clarissa, as youth goes to youth, but Clarissa slipped under his guard and took possession of his elder brother in a very woman-of-the-world way. Charles did not mind, for he had nothing in particular to say to Clarissa, but for the first time in his life he felt a shadow of envy. A captain in the Royal Navy, a schoolmaster; one was a little handicapped. Then his honest mind told him that Freddy had been at his job for more than half his life while he, Charles, after a delightful interlude with his guns, was only beginning to work, so he devoted himself to one of the Deanery bridesmaids and they laughed and got on very well.

Meanwhile Captain Belton was amused and slightly flattered by Clarissa's unblushing pursuit of him and allowed her to exercise her prentice hand on a mild flirtation, though being fairly shrewd about young women, as any sailor must be unless he has been caught and married young, he had a conviction amounting to certainty that Clarissa was not ogling him for nothing and wanted to see what it was.

Meanwhile Mr. Adams after congratulating Anne's parents was having a few useful words with some of the guests, for Sam

Adams, as he rather too often said, wasn't one to let the grass grow under his feet and many a deal had been begun or satisfactorily settled by meeting the right people on an informal occasion like this. So he had a few words with the Mayor of Barchester and the Chief Constable and Mr. Pilward of Pilward's Entire, his future co-father-in-law, and Councillor Budge of the Gas Works who had done such useful work during the General Election. And then he talked to Mrs. Belton, which gave him great pleasure, not only because she was real county and Sam Adams by no means despised the social side of life, but because he truly liked and admired her and never forgot her kindness to his daughter.

"It's a very pretty wedding, Mrs. Belton," said Mr. Adams, "and a very pretty bride, and I'm picking up a few hints because when my little Heth gets married next year I haven't Mother to help me," for so Mr. Adams always spoke of the wife who had died when Heather was a little girl, "and I'll have to be father and mother too. I'll tell you one thing, Mrs. Belton, I'm as pleased as Punch to see little Anne wearing my and Heth's wedding present in her veil. A cool seventy-five pounds that cost me, Mrs. Belton, but I don't grudge it."

Mrs. Belton, who would have been genuinely shocked by such a statement from any friend of her own sort, not that any such friend would ever have spoken such words, accepted Mr. Adams's point of view without blenching and said all one could do for the young people nowadays was to give them all the happiness one could and think how different the world was now, to which point of view Mr. Adams gave his hearty consent.

"But mind you, Mrs. Belton, one must be firm," he added. "Now my little Heth she's got the idea of what I call a hole-and-corner wedding, as if she was one of those Communists. But I say no. If there's to be a wedding, I say, it's to be a real wedding like Mother would have wished, bridesmaids and wedding cake and all, and Ted Pilward, that's Heth's fiancé, thinks the same. Heth's only going to be married the once as far as I'm concerned, he said, and I want her to remember it. So we're going to have a slap-up wedding at Hogglestock and a day's holiday at the works and everyone turning up with a sore head next day if they can turn up at all," said Mr. Adams philosophically.

To all of which Mrs. Belton listened and her sympathies were on the whole with Mr. Adams, because there is not much fun in life now and with any luck a girl is only married once and might as well have all the excitement, just to show Them that we are not broken.

"Don't go away without saying good-bye to me, Mr. Adams," she said, "as I have something to ask you," to which Mr. Adams, with a kind of rough deference which she thought suited him very well, said if Mrs. Belton wanted anything, Sam Adams was the man to do all he could for her, and then moved on to buttonhole Dr. Crawley about a small matter of a job for old Tomkins's grandson. Dr. Crawley was talking to Mr. Dean and the two gentlemen opened their ranks to admit the wealthy ironmaster, of whom they had a high opinion.

"Pleased to meet you again," said Mr. Adams to Mr. Dean, "though two Deans is a bit confusing," at which Mr. Dean laughed and said it was even more confusing when the Deanery bills were sent to Winter Overcotes, or the other way round, and nothing could induce him to pay for Dr. Crawley's new gaiters, after which Dr. Crawley was seized by old Lady Norton, and Mr. Dean and Mr. Adams had short but important talk about a very large engineering contract that Mr. Dean's firm was hoping to get.

"Wait a minute now, Dean," said Mr. Adams. "I don't often talk business out of the office, but we might as well get this straight now, only I can't remember the exact figures of that chromium-manganese super-annealed girder steel. I'll tell you who'll know though." He looked round the room, saw his daughter hemmed in by two elderly prebendaries, neatly cut her out, and brought her back.

"You know my little Heth," said Mr. Adams.

Mr. Dean said he had not had the pleasure of meeting her before, shook hands, and thought how unexpected Adams's daughter was. Tall, well-built, face a bit heavy perhaps, but his own daughter Betty erred in that direction, well dressed and looked clever. Still Adams himself was a remarkable man, so no reason why he shouldn't have a presentable and intelligent daughter, and Mr. Dean blamed himself for snobbery; quite unnecessarily, we think, for though the world is full of sows' ears there are very few of them that can be made into silk purses, but here the transformation appeared to be almost complete.

"I want you to help your old dad," said Mr. Adams to his daughter. "What was the last quote for those C.M. super-annealed girders—the ones we put in at Bombay?"

Heather frowned in thought.

"I don't remember the exact discount, dad," she said, "but the price F.O.B. was three-two-five eighteen less seven and a half," or if these were not the exact words they give the impression of what she said and who are we to inquire further?

Mr. Dean, secretly very much impressed by Heather's knowledge of her father's affairs, thanked her and said he must congratulate Miss Adams on her head for figures.

"Heth and me were going to be partners," said Mr. Adams, taking his daughter's arm and speaking half jokingly, half reproachfully, "but she's going into partnership with Ted Pilward instead, aren't you, girlie? Never mind, your old dad has some life in him yet and he'll see a young Pilward in the firm before he dies."

At that moment Susan was borne by the press to her father's side, who to tell the truth was now anxious to get away from Mr. Adams and speak to other friends. So he rather meanly made the two girls known to each other and slipped away.

"You're at the Red Cross, aren't you?" said Heather. "I saw you with Lady Pomfret at the Red Cross Bookbinding Exhibition last year."

Susan said she had heard about Heather from the Beltons and

should they try to get near the window because it was so hot and talking made one feel even hotter? Heather agreed and by dint of gently leaning against the people who were in the way they reached the embrasure of one of the long sash windows which was wide open to the sun, and sat down on the window-seat. Susan felt a liking for anyone that the Beltons liked and was prepared to find Heather agreeable; Heather had admired Susan's handsome business-like appearance at the Red Cross and they talked together quite comfortably while the party roared and surged.

"Champagne, miss?" said Simnet suddenly materializing in front of them with a tray and addressing Susan.

"No, thank you," said Susan.

"I do not wish to intrude, miss," said Simnet, "but as the bride's health is about to be drunk you may wish to participate."

"I've had one glass," said Heather, "but as it's a wedding I'll have another, specially if it's to drink Anne's health."

Susan also took a glass.

To Simnet the one mistake in a party which under his supervision was necessarily almost perfect was that there were to be no speeches, for it had long been his ambition to say: "My lords, ladies, and gentlemen, silence pray for the toast to the bride." But the Fieldings had been adamant on this point and rightly too, for as Sir Robert said, once people began making speeches there was no end to it besides usually making fools of themselves, to which his wife replied that she entirely agreed, but wouldn't it be a little difficult to get everyone to stop talking at the same moment if no one told them to, and Sir Robert, whose temper had sometimes worn a little thin as the wedding preparations went on, said it would be all right on the night, or words to that effect. But as the roar of the party rose louder and louder it was obvious that nothing short of a professional city toast-master could make itself heard.

Simnet, looking discreetly at his temporary employer, saw that he was at a loss. The butler was not an unkindly man at heart, but human nature is human nature and he felt much as Earl Percy must have felt when he saw the Douglas fall. At this moment Dorothy dropped one of the best wineglasses on the floor, where it shivered into fragments. Horrified by this mishap, but always conscientious, she seized two empty champagne bottles and dashed them upon the stone hearth of the back drawing-room fireplace, thus shocking a number of guests into momentary silence, which silence then spread so far that the Dean, who having made a voluntary sacrifice of the address felt he had arrears to make up, seized the moment and asked the company to pledge the newly married couple's health, which was done with polite murmurs of "God bless them." Anne and Robin, frightened but pleased, smiled their thanks to everyone, and the roar once more engulfed the party.

Susan, who did not care for champagne, sipped to their health and set her glass aside. Heather drank hers at a draught in a dashing way and continued her conversation with Susan, which not unnaturally was about the Belton family, their common link.

"Mrs. Belton is the kindest person I know," said Heather, whose face was a little flushed by her two glasses of champagne and who felt a pleasant exhilaration. "She was awfully good to me when I was at the Hosiers' School and dad is devoted to her."

Susan agreed that she was very kind and so were her two sons, and then Heather told her how Captain Belton had pulled her out of the lake one Christmas when she had deliberately skated too near the place marked DANGER.

"Miss Sparling said I would have had pneumonia if Freddy hadn't made me put his coat on and run up to Arcot House. I felt frightfully ashamed of myself."

Susan, her secret heart swelling at this praise of Captain Belton, said Charles was very nice too.

"Oh, he's only a kid," said Heather, who had a permanently low opinion of Charles owing to a slight he had once inflicted on a fat, spotty-faced unattractive schoolgirl. "But Freddy's different. I used to make up a story to myself about how I was going to marry him, but of course that was schoolgirl rubbish. And anyway he can't marry anyone."

Susan had not been paying much attention to Heather's account of her calf-love, but suddenly her heart stopped beating; or else it beat harder than it had ever beaten before, she could not tell which. If Freddy Belton could not marry anyone, why had he said to her what he had said in the Cathedral cloisters. Or had she misunderstood him. Oh, why had she not let him speak his full mind? What did Heather mean? One had heard of sailors having a wife in every port, and there was no reason why he should not have several; one in Bombay perhaps, one at New York, and why not one at Smoozepore, she thought, an echo of that far-off peaceful lunch sounding in her mind. Her world was suddenly dark and reeling. She tried to speak, to ask Heather to explain, but no sound would come.

"It's because of the girl he was engaged to," said Heather, her tongue loosened by her second glass of champagne, a faint desire to dazzle Susan Dean, and the need we all feel to share a secret, however we may repent afterwards. "She was a Wren and her father was an Admiral and they lived on the east coast and there was an air-raid and she was killed. I said would he forget her and he said Never. But," she added, with belated caution, "don't tell anyone, because it's a secret."

"Of course I won't," said Susan, quite surprised at the natural sound of her own voice, longing to ask why Captain Belton had told Heather his secret, too proud to do so; though Heather had probably never realized his real reason, which was to stop the very silly schoolgirl she had been from thinking herself romantically in love with him. "I think I ought to find my mother now. I'm driving her home."

"Wait a minute," said Heather, who had taken a liking to her new friend, "here's Ted. I'd like you to meet him," and up came Ted Pilward, a very nice young man who had had two years at Cambridge, five years of war, and another year of his old college to take his degree and was now going into his father's brewery combine.

Susan spoke with Ted Pilward, thought well of him, said she hoped they would both come and see the Red Cross Library one day, and went away to look for her mother. It was not easy to get through the crowd, but time had ceased to exist and nothing was of any particular value, so when Oliver Marling appeared at her side she smiled.

"What a nice party," said Oliver. "I got off early and came down by the midday train. Have you recovered from the round-about?"

If Susan had spoken the truth she would have said that the giddiness and nausea caused by the Royal Derby was as nothing compared with her present feelings, but one does not intrude one's own troubles on friends, so she smiled and said she hoped Oliver had had a nice evening on Tuesday. Oliver, with the ostrich-like idiocy of men who are a victim of a tender passion said: "Tuesday? Let me see. Oh yes of course, Jessica gave me supper. Yes, it was very nice. Aubrey Clover was there, but he was very quiet. I expect he is often thinking of a play he is writing."

Yes, he is, thought Susan, and if you looked even half as self-conscious as you are looking now he was probably making notes of you and will have you in his next play. You won't know it, but Jessica will. And in spite of her own heavy heart she felt troubled, for Oliver was a nice creature and probably thought that Jessica was ready to care for him whereas, as Noel Merton would have borne witness, Jessica was in a way heartless. Never unkind, thought Susan, who loved her young sister very much, only uncaring, but that will be bad enough for Oliver. And then she felt afraid. It had been bad enough to hear what Heather Adams had told her of a heart that was true to a lost love; now her own unhappiness seemed to have given her a clarity of vision hitherto unknown and she wanted to save Oliver from the splinter of ice that kills one's joy. But one cannot save one's friends any more than one can save oneself, especially if they are pushing their heads further and further into the sand. So she said she hoped he would come to dinner again soon and pressed on to where her mother was sleepily not listening to Bishop Joram.

"As I was saying to your mother, Miss Dean," said the Canon of Barchester, ex-Bishop of Mngangaland, "this delightful party reminds me so much of a Mngongi."

Susan, taking her cue, kindly asked what a Mngongi was.

"Mngongi," said Bishop Joram, "Mngongi is a word that belongs to a different tribe whose members are, I regret to say, Baptists. A Mngongi is a ceremony that takes place every year when the river is in flood. It really means the Uniting of Two, because the land and the water are quite indistinguishable at that time, and it is a point of honour for every chief to let as many of his barren wives as possible be drowned. By the way, have you heard about the Bishop's socks?"

To Susan at the moment there was nothing left remarkable beneath the visiting moon, but news of the Palace was something that no true loyalist could put aside, especially when the news came from an anti-Palace source.

"It appears," said Bishop Joram, "that the Palace has been employing unmarried mothers, though whether as an act of charity or because they are cheaper, one cannot say. And when the Bishop and his wife went away, they left twelve pairs of socks with instructions that they should be washed."

"Twelve pairs!" said the Dean, who had overheard these interesting words. "No one has twelve pairs now, unless they buy coupons on the black market."

"What Joram has just told us," said Mr. Miller from Pomfret Madrigal, who although the gentlest of men became quite violent about the Palace, "does not preclude the possibility of dealing with the black market. As for myself, I should not have the faintest idea where to begin to look for a black market, but it may be that those in high places are better informed. But indeed, indeed it is a sad state of affairs when we are forced to suspect such things."

"No one forces you, Miller," said the Dean. "You quite rightly suspect those who invite suspicion. What happened to the socks, Joram?"

"I am not conversant with such matters," said Bishop Joram, "but I am told that one of these unfortunate women put his lordship's socks to soak in a strong solution of washing soda, in an aluminium saucepan."

At these dreadful words Mrs. Dean woke up.

"But soda *ruins* aluminium," she said plaintively. "And Woolcott will call it aluminum."

"They do in America," said Mrs. Miller, who had joined them. "They can't help it. Like calling biscuits crackers."

Mr. Miller said he supposed what they used at school to call fly-biscuits—Garibaldi was, he believed, the real name, though why Garibaldi he did not know, as biscuits did not have red shirts—would in America be called bug-crackers, and Mrs. Dean said she would ask her son-in-law.

"But," said Bishop Joram, determined to get on with his story, "that was not the worst. They boiled the socks and—"

"Good God!" said the cheerful voice of Francis Brandon, "even I know that you don't boil socks. How are you, Mrs. Dean?"

Mrs. Dean roused herself from a pleasantly comatose condition to ask after his wife, to which Francis replied that she was very well, and was just going to give a last-moment report of her health when Bishop Joram overrode him with the voice that used to make even the Head Chief of Mngangaland's very spoilt eightieth son quake in his rooms at Balliol.

"They not only boiled the socks, but they went to a cinema and left the saucepan on and the socks were burnt to a cinder and the saucepan ruined," said Bishop Joram.

"Glory Hallelujah!" said Francis Brandon piously.

Mr. Miller said indeed, indeed it was deplorable that good

socks should be burnt, and saucepans too, at this time when it behoved each of us to be careful with the talent entrusted to him, and then several friends joined the party and the story was told again, and when Francis Brandon said he meant to subscribe at once to the nearest institution for unmarried mothers, it was generally felt that he had the root of the matter in him.

Susan then roused her mother, who had lapsed into her usual abstracted condition, and took her to say good-bye to the Fieldings. There was a crowd round them and Susan found herself close to Captain Belton.

"I have hardly seen you," he said, looking down at her. "Can we have lunch when I come down next weekend?"

Susan would have given the world to say yes, but she knew she must say no. It was not that she was angry, or hurt. On the contrary she loved—yes, the word must be faced—she loved him more than she had thought possible. But if his heart was with the Wren that the Germans had killed, it could not be with Susan Dean. She must have misunderstood him in the cloisters. It was friendship that he was offering of course, and though friendship would, she hoped, in time bring peace and content-ment with it, she needed love. If they had been alone she might have had the courage and the sense to ask him if what Heather said was true, but here they were in the Fieldings' drawing-room in a press of people and she must decide at once what to say.

She looked up and met his eyes and all her love flew to her own, but her tongue obeyed her silly tormented mind and said, quite calmly and nicely, that she was afraid she would be very busy for the next two or three weekends as Lady Pomfret would be away. Captain Belton, to whom duty was duty, said he quite understood and would she come to Harefield one Sunday and he would show her the little decayed rococo pavilion called the Garden House, and they might go for a walk. And the very competent Depot Librarian of the Red Cross Hospital Library instead of saying yes, or at least saying that she wanted to ask him something when there weren't so many people about, explained politely that all her weekends would be occupied at present.

"But, Susan," said Captain Belton.

And at his voice all her resolutions melted. She did not care. Nothing mattered except his happiness, and if he still wanted her companionship he should have it, though every step she took was on red-hot ploughshares. Let his old love have his heart. She could not be his love, but she could be his friend and walk and talk with him. And then, as happens at parties, they were suddenly separated by an onrush of guests. Politeness claimed her. The Fieldings must be thanked, her mother must be taken home. So she thanked the Fieldings and drove her mother back to Winter Overcotes. Nothing mattered now.

The crowd was thinning. Robin's foot wished it could go off duty, but had determined to see the thing through. Anne was still in a quiet dream which the party, the noise, the excitement could not disturb. Her mother came to her and said she had better go and change. In her quiet dream she smiled and went.

"This is the first time I have been alone since we were married," said Robin thoughtfully. "I don't know how to thank you enough, Lady Fielding. You and Sir Robert couldn't have been kinder if I had been a duke, or a black-market profiteer. I shall do my very best to deserve it."

"I know you will," said Lady Fielding. "And I cannot think of anyone to whom I would more willingly trust Anne. Robert feels the same, I know."

"I can't say that I do," said Sir Robert. "The most I can say is that I let Anne go to you with less reluctance than I would feel in the case of any other husband. As a matter of fact," he added grimly, "I believe Anne will be safe with you, but I would far rather she were safe with us."

Robin said he understood, which was not exactly true, for a young man cannot enter into the feelings of a middle-aged man whose child he has won. Sir Robert turned away and looked out of the window and wished the Crawleys and the other lingering guests would go. But the Crawleys and the Beltons, and the Grahams, and a few more old friends lingered to wish the young couple Godspeed. Clarissa, who had spent a pleasant afternoon impressing various young men by her precocious worldliness, mostly we may say deliberately assumed for the occasion, had never lost sight of what was secretly her chief aim in coming to the wedding and now approached Mrs. Belton.

"Well, my dear, are you looking for Charles?" said Mrs. Belton, to whose mind it rarely occurred that young people wanted to see her for herself rather than for her sons.

"Oh no," said Clarissa. "We did have a talk and I am going to Parents' Day tomorrow. Charles seems to be amusing himself quite nicely. Of course he thinks he is in love with mother, too, too young. And I wanted to talk to Freddy, but he was rather remote, so I came to ask you if you could do something very kind."

Her affectation of grown-upness had suddenly slipped and Mrs. Belton did not like her the less for it and asked what it was.

"Well," said Clarissa, suddenly and surprisingly a girl in the schoolroom, tracing a pattern on a chintz-covered chair with one elegant finger in an embarrassment most unusual in her, "it was Freddy. He said he would introduce me to Mr. Adams because I want to get a job in his works when I have taken my degree, but when I asked him this afternoon he was a bit putting-off. I don't mean unkind, but really too too absent-minded, as if he saw something a long way off and couldn't quite see what it was."

A clever child, Mrs. Belton thought. Possibly, in her own catch-word, too too clever. For she had apparently seen in Freddy what his mother had in earlier days too often seen: the complete withdrawal into the past of a heart and mind that have been deeply hurt. Ever since Freddy had told her about his one and only love whom the Germans had killed, she had learnt to know his remote mood and pretend not to know. Heavens knows her own heart had felt near enough to breaking at times when she saw him alone in his controlled anguish, but if a pretence of not seeing it, a pretence that he must always have seen through, could help him, she would go on pretending. For a long time now she had not seen him withdrawn and she believed that the past had ceased to claim him. Now at Clarissa's words she felt as if the ground had moved beneath her feet. If Freddy were still grieving she was beaten.

Clarissa with her quick eye and intuition saw that she had said something wrong and wondered where she had erred. Perhaps Mrs. Belton thought her impertinent to criticize a captain in the Royal Navy who must be quite twice her own age.

"I only meant that perhaps he thought me a bit bothering," said Clarissa, trying to put the blame, if any, on herself. "So I thought perhaps if you didn't mind you would introduce me. I asked mother if it would be all right and she said she would ask father because he always knew what to do."

Clarissa's slight mimicry of her mother's way of referring every decision to her husband made Mrs. Belton smile, and Clarissa, having scored her point, added: "But father isn't here and he won't be down till tomorrow evening, so if it wouldn't be too much bother—"

She left her sentence unfinished on an upward inflexion.

"Very well, my dear," said Mrs. Belton. "Here comes Mr. Adams, so this is a good moment. Mr. Adams, earlier this afternoon I said there was something I wanted to ask you and you were kind enough to say you would help me."

"That's right," said Mr. Adams. "Sam Adams doesn't forget."

"This is Clarissa Graham," said Mrs. Belton. "Her mother is an old friend of mine and Clarissa is going to college with a mathematical scholarship and wants to take up engineering draughtsmanship. If you have any use for women in that kind of work, may Clarissa come and see you later on?"

"So you're after a job like the rest of them, young lady," said Mr. Adams good-humouredly. "What college is it?"

Clarissa, all affectation banished, named it.

"Well," said Mr. Adams, "that's where my Heth is. She's going to get a first-class next year, aren't you, Heth? Now, I can't do anything for you at present, Clarissa, but Heth here will keep an eye on you at college next year, and if she says you'll do, then you will do. For my Heth and me are partners in a manner of speaking, aren't we, Heth?"

"How do you do?" said Heather, shaking hands with the younger girl. "I'll do my best for you and I'm glad you are coming up. Dad's bark is worse than his bite, and if you make good I'll see that he doesn't forget about you. Would you like to see over the works?" to which Clarissa could only say a long-drawn "Oh" of pure joy, every trace of grown-upness gone.

"Right," said Heather, "I'll ring you up." And then Lady Fielding came to tell her friends that Anne and Robin were just going, so the company went downstairs and clustered on the steps round the front door. Something of Anne's serene happiness seemed to have passed into everyone present. She kissed her father and mother very lovingly, smiled upon all her friends, each of whom felt that the smile had been for him or her alone, took Robin's arm, and then dropping it ran back to hug her parents once more.

"I love you," she said, and went down the steps. Robin handed her into his shabby little car and got in beside her. There was a general waving of hands, a few tears were suppressed, the car disappeared through the close gateway, and the guests dispersed. Sir Robert and Lady Fielding went back into the house and thanked the servants and Simnet for their help.

"A pleasure, sir, I assure you," said Simnet, "to officiate at a proper wedding, for really the kind of people that get married now are not what one can wish. What is it, Dorothy?"

"Oh please, Mr. Simnet," said his sister-in-law, "do you think I could taste the champagne? I've never tasted it, but Mr. Simnet says it's lovely."

"Well, really, Dorothy, I don't know what's come over you," said her brother-in-law, "talking as bold as brass about drink, and dropping those bottles on the fireplace. What Sir Robert and Lady Fielding must think of you I wouldn't like to say."

"If it was your sister-in-law who dropped the bottles, we are very grateful," said Sir Robert. "It made people stop talking just in time," and then he and Lady Fielding shook hands with Dorothy, and Sir Robert gave Simnet a suitable tip.

"Thank you, sir," said Simnet. "The champagne was just right, sir. Only the one bottle left," to which Sir Robert answered that Simnet had better take it with him.

"Thank *you*, sir," said Simnet. "I am spending the night with my old mother and my brother and they will greatly relish it. And you can have some too, Dorothy," he added patronizingly to his sister-in-law, "and don't forget to thank Sir Robert and Lady Fielding too."

But Dorothy, probably afraid of being consumed by fire if she approached such godlike beings, backed out of the drawing-room and knocked over a small table. A crash of glass was heard.

"Really, Dorothy," said her outraged brother-in-law.

"It's all right, Mr. Simnet," said Dorothy. "I've broken three glasses, the way you said."

Neither Sir Robert nor Lady Fielding wished to go upstairs, where Anne's room was tenantless. Their car was at the door, their luggage in it, and they drove away to spend a few weeks with cousins in another county. Later they would join Robin and Anne at Hallbury, where most of the honeymoon was to be spent.

Robin and his bride reached Hallbury and there, in her parents' house, their quiet story comes for the present to an end. After dinner they sat in the garden among the scent of sun-warmed flowers and were happily silent. The moon was rising over the poplars, and a star fell in swift silence through the darkening sky.

"Robin," said Anne out of the dusk, "I think Miss Bunting would be pleased."

Robin remembered the old governess and her wise handling of Anne, her last pupil.

"I know she is," he said firmly, "and pleased that we are at Hallbury now."

> "And I think oft if spirits can steal from the regions of air,
>   To revisit past scenes of delight, thou wilt come to me there,"

said Anne softly, quoting for once not her favourite poet, Lord Tennyson, but a bard of lost Ireland.

CHAPTER 8

The life of a preparatory school during the summer term is of passionate interest to the little boys concerned, to assistant masters, to the headmaster and his wife if any, and in a considerable degree to the household that sweeps, dusts, bedmakes, and cooks. But to the outer world it is merely a preparatory school that is kind enough to take one's adored little boys off one's hands; though as the holidays become longer and the fees higher, its benefits are not so apparent to the English, whose philoprogenitiveness takes the peculiar shape of paying more money than they can well afford to be relieved of their beloved children during the greater part of the year.

The Priory School had had on the whole an uneventful summer term and no infectious diseases. Philip Winter and his staff had worked very hard, the little boys, fiends angelical, had run as true to type as little boys do. Selina had done marvels with the rations, her husband had made the garden produce so many vegetables that it paid for itself besides feeding the school, and Marigold had on the whole given satisfaction. The school year was now to culminate in Parents' Day, with which had been amalgamated the prize-giving and breaking-up, because it was so difficult for parents and friends to travel under a Government which had so satisfactorily made the world safe for big business and the common man; and the commoner the better as far as this lot were concerned, said the senior master in Charles

Belton's room, where Charles and his two fellow ushers, for so they liked to call themselves, were discussing the cricket for Parents' Day. And when we say they were discussing the chances of the school eleven, we must be understood to imply that they were talking and not for the first nor the last time about the golden days of the war and all the places where they had just missed meeting each other.

"Well," said the senior master, who had a list of names before him, "we've pretty well settled our team, except for young Dean. Do you remember the match we had at Sadd-el-bac, Belton, against Signals? No, you weren't with us then. Gosh, how hot it was!"

"That's enough grouse in the gun room," said the junior master, who happened to have been a captain whereas the senior master had only got his second pip by the skin of his teeth before peace, that separator of companions and terminator of delights, had blasted his career. "Come on. We've got to decide about Dean. He's a good steady bowler with brilliant patches, but if his nose bleeds he won't be much use to us."

"It bled again in the Scripture exam," said the senior master. "I think myself he is born lucky and you'd better have him. What I'd have given if my nose had bled in the Scripture exam, or the French, or the maths for that matter!"

"I don't feel too sure about that nose-bleeding," said Charles, "nor does the Old Man," for by this endearing and respectable appellation Philip Winter was mostly known to his staff, a fact that speaks volumes for his character. "I'll bet you five bob that young Dean's nose won't bleed tomorrow if he's bowling. No I wont," said Charles, taking two florins, a threepenny bit, and five pennies, the total contents of his pockets, and spreading them on the table. "I'll bet half a crown, though."

"Done," said the senior master.

"Then I'll hold the stakes," said the junior master, grabbing one of the florins, the threepenny bit, and three of the pennies, upon which his colleagues fell on him and the leg of a chair was broken.

"Never mind," said Charles. "That leg was due to break. I'll ask Selina to ask Higgins to mend it. Lord! I must go and take prep. What waste of time on a lovely day when one might be at the Woolpack!" For though the Sheep's Head at Lambton was nearer, the Woolpack at Worsted was considered more dashing, though as both were clean and well conducted and neither could retail anything but the most watery of beers, and both were mostly out of cider, gin, whisky, and all interesting forms of liquor, there would seem to the outsider but little to choose between them except that distance lends enchantment to the view.

"This one mightn't," said the senior master. "All this term whenever I've been to the Woolsack on a Friday night or a Saturday night either, I've had to listen to that insufferable man Tebben. I can't stand fellows that run their people down in public. Of course my father can be perfectly ghastly when he likes and mother will look at me as if she could see right through my waistcoat to where there's a button off my shirt, but I must say they are jolly decent and even if they weren't I wouldn't bleat about it."

The junior master said his mother was all right except that she made him ashamed at restaurants by getting flustered over the tips, to which the senior master retorted that if he had ever paid for a lunch himself he would think more charitably of his mother, so that the leg nearly came off the chair again and Charles had to hurry away and take prep. And as he sat in the classroom, sometimes filling in reports, sometimes thinking of the novel he was going to write when he could think of (*a*) a name, (*b*) a plot, and (*c*) anything for any of the characters to say, he also thought of his own father and mother and how, given their limitations, their great age (or so it seemed to him), and their incredibly Victorian (by which he meant late Edwardian and nearly Georgian) attitude to life, they were extraordinarily

nice. And through the word "nice" his mind wandered to Lady
Graham and her beauty, charm, and intellect, and how wonderful it would be to serve her, though what he meant by serve we
really do not know, nor did he, except that it was all very very
beautiful. And while he thus drank the milk of Paradise the
young gentlemen under his care made little pellets of paper and
dipped them in the inkwells and flipped them at each other, as
schoolboys have done ever since ink was invented and long
before, the whole in dead silence from kind consideration of
their master's feelings. It was this silence, highly suspicious on
the last evening of term, which made Philip Winter suddenly
open the door and come in. At the sight of a number of small
boys industriously doing their Latin prep, at least two of them
with French dictionaries as his professional eye noticed, he
stood quite still. His pupils, respectfully following his example,
stopped writing and Charles Belton, coming out of a dream of
telling Lady Graham all his soul's adoration and feeling her soft
hand smooth his fevered brow as she murmured: "Dear Boy,"
went red in the face and could not speak. The headmaster then
withdrew and for the rest of the period the little boys worked
and Charles wondered if he would be given a week's notice.

At supper the conversation was general and Charles hoped
his absence of mind had passed unnoticed, but after supper
Philip asked Charles to come to his study. It was not unusual for
the headmaster to invite one of his staff for a private talk, but to
Charles it seemed that his last hour at the Priory School had
probably come.

"Have you thought about your future at all?" said Philip with
what Charles considered hypocritical mildness.

"No, sir. At least not particularly," said Charles. "I mean I like
it awfully but I thought perhaps you would not think I was good
enough."

"You will find it a good plan," said Philip, but quite kindly,
"not to waste time thinking what other people may or may not
have thought. You have done very well this term, Belton. Our

arrangement was for a term, both sides on approval. I gather you have approved?"

Charles mumbled something about awfully jolly.

"Good," said Philip. "Then I suggest that we make it a permanency, by the year. I would like to feel that your people will agree, but this is not essential."

Charles delivered himself of a confused statement which boiled down to his own gratitude and his certainty of his parents' pleasure.

"Good," said Philip again. "And now that is settled. I may tell you that I am very much obliged to you. We have enough applications on hand to double our numbers if we wanted to. We don't. But the Priory is going to be a larger school than I ever thought and I shall need the right men to help me. As for those young devils this afternoon, you will get even with them in time, and when they find you don't take them seriously they will stop. When I was an assistant master at Southbridge under Mr. Birkett, there was a boy called Swan who had to wear spectacles, and because I was an inexperienced and very conceited young master he used to put on his spectacles and look at me deliber-ately as if I were something queer, as indeed I was. I even went so far as to complain to the housemaster about him, which shows how silly I was. Of course as soon as I had the sense to keep my temper Swan lost interest. I wonder what has happened to him," he added, as if speaking to himself.

"I'm sorry, sir," said Charles, much relieved that this subject was done with. "I was thinking about—things," he finished lamely.

"Are you in love?" said Philip. "This is off the record, of course."

"Yes," said Charles without hesitation. If the headmaster liked to sack him on the spot he could, and Charles would glory in being sacked for thinking of HER in prep time.

"Good," said Philip. "I gather that you have been to Holdings a good deal this term. Affection, real affection, can help one a great deal. I had a foolish entanglement when I was about your age. She was very young and very lovely and a perfect nitwit. In fact the only sensible thing she ever did was to throw me over. And then I met my wife," upon which word he rested lovingly.

Charles went scarlet. Word had gone round the county of his visits (two, to be exact) to Holdings. He had confessed himself in love. Probably her name would be dragged in the mire and Sir Robert Graham's grey hairs brought in sorrow to the grave, though if he had ever seen Sir Robert he would have known that the distinguished General's hair was still almost black. He would willingly lay down his life for her, but with a faint gleam of sanity realized that this would not simplify matters in the least.

"I haven't seen the Graham girls for some time," said Philip. "Emmy struck me as very nice; so good-looking and competent. Well, Belton, that's all, I think. I hope we shall have some good cricket tomorrow. The ground could have done with some rain."

Charles thanked his headmaster and went into the garden, where he found Leslie Winter reading *The Oxford Book of English Verse* and darning socks.

"It's a kind of vow I made," said Leslie, moving some of the socks so that he could share the seat. "When my brother was at school they always sent him back with buttons off his shirts and his socks in holes, so I swore if ever I married a schoolmaster I'd send the boys back with their clothes mended. It must be bad enough to have them at home now with all the rationing, without having to mend for them. Did you and Philip have a nice talk?"

"Very nice, thank you," said Charles. "But I expect you know what about. I am to stay on here. I do hope I'll give satisfaction."

Leslie said she was sure he would and what fun it was to see the school getting bigger, and how in course of time she and Philip would probably live in the far wing of the house and they would make married quarters for two housemasters.

"I expect you will be our senior housemaster in time, Charles," she said, "only you must find a wife first. You know Lady

Graham is coming tomorrow with Clarissa. It seems peculiar for one of her girls to be going to a university, but everything is peculiar now. Except little boys," she said, her voice warm with affection. "They are always the same from their dirty hands to the way their hair twiddles round from a kind of whirlpool on the back of their heads, bless them. Clarissa is very pretty, isn't she?"

Charles liked Leslie very much, but this was going too far. It had been bad enough for Philip, though a man and a headmaster, to hint that one might be in love with Emmy, that large cowminded young woman, and now here was Leslie hinting that he might consider Clarissa. Clarissa, who wanted to know that dreadful Heather Adams and go into a works. They might as well suggest that he should marry Jessica Dean, whom Charles in a friendly way adored, but of whom he had never thought except as a delightful and amusing companion. Still, perhaps it was for the best. If he amused himself with Jessica and Emmy and even that stupid Clarissa, it would throw dust in people's eyes and he could worship his own goddess in peace. It made him feel very poetical and he felt sure there was a piece of poetry somewhere about pretending to love one person when you really loved another so that people wouldn't know.

If Leslie noticed that Charles was rather silent it did not trouble her. Her hands were occupied with socks, her mind with tomorrow's celebrations, her heart with her husband and her young son. So she spoke when the spirit moved her, and Charles answered amiably. The insistent sound of the telephone was heard, muffled, from the house.

"It's the one in Philip's room," said Leslie. "I know by the sound because I put a bit of stuff round the bell so that it wouldn't startle him. People who were in the war sometimes mind noises. Do you?"

"Lord! no," said Charles. "But sometimes if I hear an aeroplane I find myself wondering whose it is. Funny the way things are."

Philip came out of the house and sat down and then:

"Jessica Dean," he said. "Trunk call from London. These actresses! She says she wants to give her nephew a treat, so she is coming down for the beginning of the sports with Aubrey Clover in an aeroplane and wants to know if they could land here. I suppose these things are done."

"What fun!" said Leslie. "They could land on the cricket field."

The men stared at her as at one bereft of her wits.

"They might damage the pitch, Mrs. Winter," said Charles.

"My dear girl, you don't know what you are talking about," said Philip. "Ten weeks' drought has been bad enough without an aeroplane trying to land and probably ripping up the turf or getting on fire and making a mess. Certainly not. There's a perfectly good aerodrome near Winter Overcotes and they can motor from there. Much better to motor the whole way. You don't fall so far."

His wife said Jessica would undoubtedly do exactly as she liked and what fun it would be to have her and began a scrimmage of plans for providing a meal for Jessica and Aubrey Clover, which plans had to be based upon the hour at which they had to be back in London for the evening performance. "It's seven o'clock," said Charles who had been to the play.

"Well, I can't do anything tonight," said Leslie, resigning herself to Jessica. "Philip darling, read us some poetry. It will calm our spirits," and she pushed her work at him.

"If one asks what one shall read," said Philip, "one never gets anywhere. We will try the sortes Oxfordianæ."

He shut his eyes, opened the book, put a finger on the page and opened his eyes again.

> "The merchant, to secure his treasure,
>   Conveys it in a borrowed name;
>   Euphelia serves to grace my measure;
>   But Chloe is my real flame,"

he read, in his pleasant, rather deep voice. Charles heard the first stanza, but the rest might as well have been in Arabic, for he had found what he had been searching for. Clarissa should serve to grace his measure, but Lady Graham was his real flame. He did not say Agnes, even in his thoughts, because he was modest and would have died rather than presume. And so overcome was he by this exquisite conceit that he did not benefit by the moral of Mr. Secretary Prior's charming vers d'occasion.

As we all know, the summer of that year was so warm and dry that it was almost possible to make open-air plans as long as two days ahead. A good many people said that if we didn't get some rain the ground would be too hard to plough, and others predicted a potato famine. Both were right, and the potato question was to be very much complicated later by rationing, which led to an almost total disappearance of potatoes, but during these warm comfortable days it was foolish to brood over what might happen later, for against the combined powers of Nature and Them ordinary people are powerless.

The sun rose hotly on Saturday morning, though without the lovely early morning mist which accompanies England's most perfect summer weather. The cricket pitch was as hard as marble and as slippery as waxed boards, the field was almost brown. All the little boys were wildly excited and Addison, he who had earlier in the summer been stung by a wasp, was nearly sick at breakfast, while Pickering, demonstrating to some admiring friends how he was going to demolish all the parents' wickets with his famous yorker, tripped and fell on the gravel sweep in front of the school and took most of the skin off his nearly healed knees. As for young Dean, he was looking forward with cool certainty to the cricket match and Charles felt sure that not even Mother Nature could make his nose bleed till Parents' Day was over.

By ceaseless work Leslie, ably seconded if not firsted, as she afterwards said to her husband, by that stalwart and masterful daughter of the Deanery, Octavia Needham, had managed to make a very good buffet lunch in the school dining-room, formerly the billiard room. A good many parents had kindly brought their own lunch with them and picnicked with their offspring in the grounds, while the thoughtless and improvident, as so often happens in this world, battened on Leslie's food. Other relations who lived in the neighborhood very thoughtfully lunched early at home, among them the Deans, who came over in force to see their respective grandson, nephew, and first cousin.

"I hope there aren't too many of us," said Mrs. Dean apologetically to Leslie, as Deans poured out of one another's cars like the animals coming out of the ark. "I think you know them all," said Mrs. Dean, who was often a little vague herself about her grandchildren, "and it doesn't really matter because I am sure you are *far* too busy to mind who people are."

Leslie, who all through the war had remembered hundreds of people by name and often by face and had never since the Priory School opened got a boy's name wrong, answered in suitably vague terms, and Mrs. Dean, surrounded by excited grandchildren, was led away to look at the school rabbits, rather like a large kind cow, said Leslie irreverently to her husband.

"A perfect woman," said Philip Winter. "I think we could start now."

So the first part of the program, which was the prize-giving, was advertised by the ringing of a bell in the Priory back yard, formerly used to collect the servants in that huge house for their frequent and copious meals. Parents and little boys filled the great central hall of Beliers Priory, prize lists were read, prizes distributed, a very short address given by Sir Harry Waring, and everyone was free to sit in the grounds or walk over to the cricket field, where the eternal Fathers v. Sons was to be played. More neighbouring families came as the afternoon went on from Worsted, Skeynes, and even Greshamsbury, and by the time the parents were out, the audience was at least two deep about the cricket field and enjoying itself very much, for in spite of two years of so-called peace, life was becoming more bare, more hemmed in, more hopeless if one had the courage to say it, and to sit in the sun and talk to the friends whom one could not visit in the old easy way was a pleasant oasis. And it was pleasant for Sir Harry and Lady Waring to feel that all this excitement, all these nice chattering little boys, all these agreeable neighbours, were really due to them, for Philip and Leslie could not have opened their school unless her uncle and aunt had agreed to let them have Beliers Priory, and if the school had not been opened there would have been no Parents' Day and no meeting of old friends.

"A very nice set of boys, Waring," said Lord Bond, who had come over from Staple Park with his wife. "Well hit, youngster," for Addison had just hit a boundary off Pickering's father's ball. "I want C.W. and Daphne to send their boys to you. Six and four they are. Put a boy down early for a good school, I always say. You know we are having the Conservative Rally and the B.P.B.A. at the Park next month. We've got a White Porkminster that ought to be a good runner-up."

Sir Harry courteously expressed his pleasure that Lord Bond's grandsons would be coming to the Priory and said he didn't know much about pigs himself.

"Nor does Middleton," said Lord Bond, speaking of the distinguished architect who was his tenant at Laverings. "We brought him and his wife with us. I like Mrs. Middleton. I have a great respect for her, and Middleton is as far as I know a good architect, but when he pretends to a knowledge of pigs he is quite out of his depth. When I tell you, Waring, that he doesn't know the difference between a Cropbacked Cruncher and a Norfolk Nobbler—" and here Lord Bond was so overcome by his tenant's gross ignorance that he left the sentence unfinished.

Sir Harry said he feared he did not know the difference himself.

"Ah well," said Lord Bond, "a soldier had other things to think of," and then Mr. and Mrs. Middleton came up, so that conversation had to stop and Lord Bond passed on to greet other friends.

"Sir Harry!" said Mr. Middleton, not in surprise but as one might say Dr. Livingstone I presume. "And Lady Waring! My wife and I came over with the Bonds. We hope to see some young connections here ere long—you will permit us to tarry here awhile? Let us sit down, Catherine, my dear," he added to his wife. "Nephews, great-nephews-in-law, by marriage, I know not which. These relationships are sorely puzzling to one like myself who am in a way unrelated to anyone."

Lady Waring, not exactly interrupting but speaking firmly across the current of Mr. Middleton's speech, said she did not quite understand. One must, she imagined, be related to someone, or where would we all be?

"Mea culpa!" said Mr. Middleton. "My uncontrollable fancy, deceiving elf! leads me astray. I merely meant to adumbrate as it were the difficulties of a relationship in which there is no tie of blood, yet a strong link of propinquity and goodwill, if I make myself clear."

"You don't, Jack," said Mrs. Middleton. "Jack only means," she added, turning to the Warings, "that his sister's stepdaughter, Daphne Bond, is thinking of putting her little boys down for the Priory School. No relations at all, but we are very fond of Daphne."

Sir Harry, reassured by Mrs. Middleton's calm but still a little bewildered, said were those the same boys Lord Bond had mentioned.

"They are," said Mr. Middleton with the air of one who having committed a serious crime is determined to confess it and start the world again. "Yes, I may say, they are. But here are the couple in question. They can explain. I renounce the attempt. Age, Lady Waring, a busy life. If it were not for my wife, my Catherine, I would be as naught, the mental wreck of a once not entirely useless man."

By this time the Warings, who in any case did not know the

Middletons very well and had not seen them since the last Barsetshire Agricultural Show before the war, felt that they would shortly be mental wrecks themselves. But the arrival of the Honourable C. W. Bond and his wife brought sanity with it, and Daphne Bond told Lady Waring that from what she and her husband had heard of the Priory School they very much wanted their two little boys to go there and hoped the school would have vacancies in a few years, which pleased Lady Waring, for she loved her husband's niece Leslie Winter very much and the welfare of the Winters' school was very near to her heart.

"Oh, Catherine," said Daphne Bond, who had always been on very affectionate terms with Mrs. Middleton, "I heard from Denis yesterday. He is coming back. Isn't it *lovely*? Do you remember my brother Denis, Lady Waring?"

Lady Waring said was it the one who was rather an invalid and played so nicely.

"That's it," said Daphne. "He's been in America for *ages*. He went before the war and then he couldn't come back and anyway he wasn't physically fit, so he went on doing music and he has been a *frightful* success in New York. Betty and Woolcott Van Dryven know him and they say everyone *adores* his music. He has had a smashing success with a musical play called *Sweetest Sorrow* and it's going to be put on in London. He rang me up on a transatlantic call and said he was flying over at once. It's too marvelous. I expect he'll be frightfully grand and American."

The Warings, who rarely went to London and would not in any case have gone to an American musical play, were not much interested but said polite things. And then Daphne\Bond, who had a very kind heart, noticed that the Warings looked tired, a phenomenon not unusual in those who came into contact with Mr. Middleton, and took her uncle and aunt away.

By this time Sons were all out for sixty-eight and Fathers had been in for quite long enough in their own opinion, for batting on a very hot afternoon when you are not so young nor so slim as you were with a lot of very active, shrimplike boys throwing balls at you from every direction is a trying job. The last two Fathers were playing and time was nearly up with three runs to win. The talk ceased. Even Mr. Middleton, eloquently expounding the game as played on the village green in his boyhood, was ignored and pushed aside by a great phalanx of Deans, eager for young Dean's success. That young gentleman had been bowling with a self-possession that terrified the Fathers, and with three minutes to go he sent down a slow ball which the hypnotized parent blocked, and followed it by a twisting ball which glanced off the edge of the Father's bat, rose gently, and fell quietly into the wicket-keeper's hands. Shrill applause rose from the little boys, the audience joined in the cheers, and the Fathers thankfully walked off the field. Just as they did so, a large, low, rakish car drove up and with perfect timing Jessica Dean emerged, ravishingly pretty and smart, with Aubrey Clover and a very tall, thin, not quite so young man.

The Winters came up and welcomed her affectionately.

"*How* nice of you to come, Jessica," said Leslie. "Your nephew has just won the match for us. His bowling was *devilish*. He forced that wretched father to snick the ball into Pickering's hands and he took four other wickets. I wish Cecil had been here," for Leslie's beloved brother Cecil had been as keen a cricketer as the navy can allow and she had followed every game with him when they were children.

"My dear, too divine," said Jessica. "Aubrey will be green with envy, won't you, darling? He always wanted to play for England but had absolutely *no* qualifications. Oh, this is Denis Stonor. He arrived from New York in an aeroplane this morning and looked Aubrey up, so we brought him down. He writes divine music. He did all the songs and incidental music for Nat Blumenfield's last show. Nat is such a lamb and he is going to star me in New York, isn't he, Denis?"

"And me too, don't forget," said Aubrey Clover. "If it weren't for my plays, Mrs. Winter, no one would ever have heard of Jessica."

"And if it weren't for Jessica, everyone would have forgotten about Aubrey by now," said Jessica, adumbrating the gesture of putting out her tongue at Aubrey Clover. "Sound the horn, darling," she said to the tall thin man.

An ear-splitting hoot rent the summer air.

"Sorry, Leslie," said Jessica, "it's only to call the boys. Aubrey's car burst a gudgeon-pin or something so Denis rang up the American Embassy and got us this. A bit ostentatious, but the times are hard."

The car was certainly conspicuous, to say the least, among the modest battered cars of the visiting parents, apparently a hundred feet long by three feet high, with glossy black paint and covered with badges. At the sound of the horn and the sight of the monster the crowd of little boys in their white or their grey flannels, the white mostly yellow by now, an ill-fitting inheritance from older brothers or cousins, surged towards the car. Young Dean, suddenly recognizing his Aunt Jessica, ran full tilt across the grass and threw himself upon her with shrieks of joy.

"Come on, you fellows," he yelled to his friends. "It's Aunt Jessica. I bet she's brought something for me."

"Not the way you and I used to behave," said Aubrey Clover to Denis Stonor, speaking in the role of the ex-public-school man, heir to thousands of impoverished acres. "If I had as much as hinted that an aunt might have brought me something, I would have been told that little boys who asked never got anything."

"We had a nasty one at the prep school," said Denis Stonor. "Those who don't ask don't want; those who ask won't get. I thought for years it was an unpublished axiom of Euclid."

"I wonder what's happened to Euclid," said Aubrey Clover. "One never hears of him now."

"He was taken over by some people called Geometry," said Denis. "A nasty lot. They are only Euclid upside down. What I liked was, Which is absurd. I say, what a good name for a play."

"No you don't," said Aubrey promptly. "I've got it down for my next play but three. For Jessica, of course."

"Where are your manners, darlings?" said Jessica, who among the tumult of little boys had missed nothing. "Keeping Lesliie standing while you show off. Do take Denis to say how do you do to your uncle and aunt. Aubrey darling, do you mind being an uncle for a few moments? What is your name?" she said to Pickering. "Right, Pickering, this is your Uncle Aubrey and he wants to know all about the cricket match. Cue, Aubrey."

So Aubrey Clover became a visiting uncle of Master Pickering and did it very well, holding his audience spellbound by an account of a cricket match he had played in a jungle and how they had lions to field because it was so hot and how the lions ate the umpire, while Jessica distributed chocolates. And if anyone wants to know why she had chocolates to give, it was all fair and above-board on account of the presents sent to her by admirers in the Forces all over the world.

"I think my uncle and aunt are on the other side of the field," said Leslie to Denis, and then, not quite knowing what to say to a famous composer of light music who had just arrived in an aeroplane from New York, she said how nice Jessica was and always thought of kind things and being polite to people older than herself.

"She is charming," said Denis Stonor. "Excuse me, but where am I? I only got here this morning and went to see Aubrey and before I knew where I was, Jessica made me ring up the Embassy and ask for a car and said I must come to see a school cricket match. American girls are fairly masterful, but Jessica outdoes them all."

Leslie, who much to her relief found it quite easy to talk to the famous composer, said this was Beliers Priory, not far from Worsted.

"The country has changed so much since I was in England," said Denis. "Houses everywhere. Jessica said we came through Winter Overcotes, but I wouldn't have recognized it. I used to stay at Skeynes. My sister is Daphne Bond. Do you know her?"

"But she is here," said Leslie, thinking how pleasant Mr. Stonor's slight American accent was. "What fun. She was sitting with my uncle and aunt. Do let's find her." Full of zeal she hurried her guest across the field to where the Warings had been, but the seats were empty.

"I expect they are in the house," she said. "The boys and parents are having tea in a marquee, but my aunt isn't up to crowds so we asked a few special parents, I mean friend-parents, not ordinary ones, to have tea in the drawing-room. We can go in this way."

She led Denis up a few stone steps and through a French window. As he stood in the entrance he could see the people within, but to them he was a silhouette against the sunlight outside. Across the room he saw Mrs. Middleton. It was nine years since he had seen her. How often he had thought of her he could not say. At first he had tried not to think, for thinking made his old wounds bleed anew. Then as time passed he often forgot. Far better so. But still, too often for his peace of mind, some turn of a woman's head, some foolish thing would remind him of her. He had landed that morning wondering when they would meet. Now the hour of meeting had come and he was afraid. She had not yet recognized him and he could quickly look at her and remember how few the words they had spoken, how brief the pressure of her hand when he suddenly went away. There was Catherine Middleton and there was Uncle Jack; just as they used to be. But not as they used to be, for he saw that they were much older. Nine years of absence, six of them years of war. His uncle had shrunk and stooped a little. Catherine had not shrunk, she did not stoop, but where he had left a woman no longer very young, he found a woman who was middle-aged and a little shabby, as indeed were most of the women he had seen since his arrival.

"There is Daphne," said Leslie Winter. "Forgive me, I must go and talk to some guests." As she passed Daphne Bond she touched her arm. "Denis," she said, looking towards the window.

"Denis," Daphne shrieked at the top of her voice across the room and almost pushed her way towards him. At the noise that Daphne made, Mrs. Middleton turned her head and saw against the light a tall thin figure. She had schooled herself not to think of the moment when they might meet again, for she was deeply attached to her husband and knew that her feeling for Denis was born of compassion, not love that would bear the light of day. But however calmly one may reflect upon meeting a man whose going once ripped one's heart almost from one's bosom, the moment itself is not easy. His name had often been mentioned by his sister and his stepmother and she had heard it without a pang, for the war made his return impossible and she need not be afraid. Once, the summer before peace broke out, someone had said to her on some country occasion, the meeting of the Barsetshire Archæological at Hallbury it was and it was Jane Gresham who was speaking, that Denis must want to get back to England sometimes. "Perhaps," she had answered, "but sometimes it is better if people don't come back." And as she remembered these words she thought how true they were and wished with all her heart that Denis were in New York, for any meeting must be a renewed anguish or, worse, an anticlimax and a disappointment. And then she blamed herself for cowardice and felt so tired that she could have lain down on the floor and died. But one cannot so easily die on other people's drawing-room floors and she was a courageous woman though desperately afraid. What she was afraid of she did not quite know; love half asleep or love half awake, or to find that all was illusion? And meanwhile Daphne had hurled herself into her brother's arms and word was going round that this was Denis Stonor, who had written music for all the most successful American ballets and musical plays, and everyone was consumed with curiosity in a friendly way. Daphne said something to her brother. Denis turned his head and looked to where Mrs. Middleton and her husband stood, and came across the room towards them.

"My boy!" said Mr. Middleton. "Words fail me."

"That's fine, Uncle Jack," said Denis, though whether he was expressing his pleasure at meeting his uncle or congratulating himself on Mr. Middleton's word-failure, we cannot say.

"And you are back," said Mr. Middleton.

Denis said that he was; he arrived that morning. It all seemed extremely flat and Catherine could not help laughing. The sound of her own voice gave her courage to hold out her hand and say how very glad she was to see Denis again. She could now see him, and as she looked into the sallow melancholy face that had once bereft her of the power of speech, her nine-year-old dreaming died. This was Denis, and she would never dream again. One cannot explain these things.

"My dear Catherine, I have been living for this," said Denis, kissing his aunt by marriage. "I have thought of you so often and how good you were to me that summer at Laverings. What an insufferable young prig I must have been."

He looked down at a woman, middle-aged, a little shabby, with a face that proclaimed good breeding, tired eyes, and a mouth set in a thin line till suddenly it broke into a smile of welcome.

"You have been happy?" he asked.

"Yes," said Mrs. Middleton, speaking the truth not only to Denis but to herself. "And you?"

"Bittersweet," said Denis. "Excuse my affectation," he added, "but it is expected of me. Darling Catherine, this is bliss. You will come to hear my music, won't you? It is the best thing I've done yet. I invented the name: *Sweetest Sorrow*. New York went mad over it."

"You didn't invent the name," said the voice of Aubrey Clover, who, suddenly bored by being Pickering's uncle, had left Jessica with the little boys and was now looking at Denis and Mrs. Middleton with his stage eye, and with the horrid insight of the good playwright feeling the drama that their meeting might have held but luckily didn't. "It was a poet called Keats.

> Come then, Sorrow,
> Sweetest Sorrow!
> Like an own babe I nurse thee on my breast."

"Good God, that's exactly what I meant," said Denis. "How did he know?"

"Experience, my boy, just the same as the rest of us," said Aubrey Clover. "I've got a good tune for it too. All syncopated."

"No you don't," said Dennis. "I'm going to have that. I wanted a new number for my show and that's it. It will be a kind of slow waltz. Beethovenish and very simple. Is there a piano anywhere?"

"No, my lamb," said Jessica, who had also come in, "and if there were there isn't, if you see what I mean. And what's more we must leave in ten minutes to allow for your Yank car getting stuck in Winter Overcotes High Street." She then embraced all her friends and acquaintances, cheek just not touching cheek for fear of spoiling the perfect make-up, and took her cavaliers away. As they walked towards the car a group of three people sitting under a tree got up and came hurriedly towards them. Jessica recognized Richard Tebben and his mother, who in spite of a large drooping straw hat with a dingy green scarf round it and a faded flowered dress looked very hot. The large blonde girl with an expressionless face who was in their company she did not know.

"Joyous meeting," cried Mrs. Tebben. "I am the proudest grandmother in England. Margaret's boy won the day for us. But the dear boy will have told you all about it."

In a large family it often happens that those who come into the family by marriage are absorbed and their origin almost forgotten. Although Mrs. Tebben's daughter Margaret had married the Deans' elder son, they were apt to forget that she was also a grandmother of Laurence's children, and Jessica had to think for a moment before she got her bearings.

"As a matter of fact he was stuffing himself with chocolates," she said, "but he looks frightfully well and you must be frightfully proud. How are you, Richard?"

"I can only," said Mrs. Tebben gazing upwards in holy reverence, "think of one other occasion so joyful. My little grandson inherits his gift for games from his uncle. You remember, Richard, the year you made that wonderful catch against the eleven at Skeynes. I felt the same thrill today."

Richard was heard to say that he was sick of hearing about that catch.

"That's not the way to speak to a mother, Richard," said the large blonde young woman, to which Richard mumbled: "Sorry," which so surprised Jessica that she almost stared.

"But I forget my duties as a hostess," said Mrs. Tebben. "This is Petrea Krogsbrog, who is staying with us. Krogsbrog's daughter," she added importantly.

"Oh, don't fuss, mother," said Richard. "Jessica wouldn't know about Krogsbrog."

Jessica, disliking Richard more than usual, shook hands with the large blonde.

"Selma Lundquist told me about your father," she said. "She adores him."

"My father also adores her," said Miss Krogsbrog. "We go to all her first nights. I do not hear your name."

"Jessica Dean," said the owner of it.

"Richard has told me of you," said Miss Krogsbrog. "He says he saved you from a mad bull, but I think he exaggerates. He is also not respectful to his mother. My father would knock a hundred sons down if they were disrespectful to their mother. Unfortunately he has no sons except only myself, which am not a son."

"I say, Petrea," Richard expostulated.

"Then say you are sorry," said Miss Krogsbrog. "And not in sulking," she added, "but as in real sorrow."

"I'm sorry, mother," said Richard with fairly good grace.

"He is as your English poet says but a child of larger growth," said Miss Krogsbrog, with the air of a competent lecturer dissecting a frog. "Because of all my social work among children which are arrested in development, I understand him. And I shall help the dear mother to understand him," said Miss Krogsbrog, whom Jessica rather expected to put on a helmet and wear a breastplate over her nightgown and sing at the top of her voice, waving a spear.

Jessica, who felt out of the corner of her eye that Aubrey Clover and Denis were about to disgrace themselves, then said she had to rush back to London to act and so escaped. When they got to the car they found Charles Belton reverently admiring it, on the pretext of keeping off the small boys who were longing to blow the horn.

"Darling Charles, how divine!" said Jessica. "And Aubrey you do know, and Denis you don't. He wrote the music for *Sweetest Sorrow*."

"Do you mean he wrote it?" said Charles. "I mean *really*. I've got all the records of it, sir, and it's absolutely wonderful."

"To think that I should live to be called sir, and by a real officer I should guess," said Denis. "You must come and see it. I'll send you tickets. Don't let me forget, Jessica."

"I won't," said Jessica. "And tell me, Charles darling, how is Freddy?"

"Oh, I expect he's all right," said Charles, with the confidence of a brother that nothing is likely to be wrong. "He didn't come down this weekend. Busy at the Admiralty, I expect."

"You know we're coming off," said Jessica. "Not that the play isn't going well, but Aubrey wants a holiday before the new play starts. We're rehearsing now. So I may be down here for a bit and we could go to Barchester Odeon or something dashing. Kiss me, my lamb."

So Charles kissed her, exactly like a brother, she thought with amusement, and she got into the back of the giant car.

"You'll be sick if you sit in the back," said Aubrey Clover. "You don't know how these American cars roll."

"Not half as sick as if I sat in front and you and Denis argued about *Sweetest Sorrow* and he upset the car," said Jessica. "Besides, my heart is broken because Richard Tebben is obviously going to be married by a large Swede and that lamb Freddy Belton isn't here."

So she got into the back seat and let herself relax while Denis drove the car and argued with Aubrey Clover until they got to the Kingston by-pass, after which he had to attend to the driving. When he had left his passengers at their homes, or rather flats, he took the huge car back to its garage and walked to his expensive hotel. And as he walked he thought of the summer at Laverings when he had played duets with Catherine Middleton, and Lord Bond had backed him in his first venture with ballet music, and how he and Catherine had walked in silence and parted in silence. It had hurt him then and for a long time, but for a long time he had forgotten it. Today, at the sight of Catherine, changed but somehow unchanged, those days, that parting, had melted into the past for ever. But from them were born an idea for a ballet whose music was to surpass anything he had done. A ballet of Harlequin and Columbine, a pas de deux of meeting and parting that would break the audience's heart and make it come again and again to be heart-broken. Damn it, why was he in London when Nat Blumenfield, who could handle it, was in New York? As soon as he got to his hotel he settled himself at the telephone and talked across the Atlantic for ten minutes. Then he worked furiously on his new number for *Sweetest Sorrow* till four in the morning, went to bed, and slept dreamlessly.

By this time the uninteresting parents had gone and only friends of the Warings and the Winters remained. Some of the little boys had gone home with their parents and some were to be sent off next day, and now under Selina's eye they were in the marquee engaged upon a second tea, even larger than the first, of everything that was left over. The noise of their ignorant arguing and their boastful chatter came pleasantly across the lawn to where Philip and Leslie were for the first time for several days taking things easily among their own friends.

"I wish mamma could have come down," said Lady Graham, who had come as Charles's guest, bringing Clarissa with her. "She does love seeing people, and now that she can't go about much it is a little lonely. Who is the good-looking girl Charles is talking to?"

Leslie said it was Susan Dean, whose nephew had bowled so well.

"I have heard about her from Lucy Marling and I am sure she is nice," said Lady Graham, who engaged her new friends rather as one used to engage a servant, from good references given by people whom one knew. So Leslie brought Susan to talk to Lady Graham while Clarissa sat silent and looked at her appraisingly. Mrs. Belton, who was also Charles's guest, asked Clarissa if she had heard any more of Mr. Adams.

"Not exactly," said Clarissa, "but Heather took me over the works and it was too too exciting. One has to be frightfully clever to get a good job there. I'm going to work like anything and I shall be friends with Heather because her father will do anything she says."

"And what did your father say?" said Mrs. Belton.

"Well, I don't really know," said Clarissa, looking a little confused, "because I heard something I wasn't meant to hear."

"Then you had better not tell me," said Mrs. Belton quite kindly.

"Oh, it wasn't *wicked*," said Clarissa. "It was only that mother said to father would he mind my going to Mr. Adams's works and he said: 'If you can't manage your daughter, my dear, don't come to me. I look after the boys, and you must do your best with the girls.'"

Mrs. Belton, secretly amused, said that seemed quite reasonable.

"Yes, but father doesn't *know*," said Clarissa. "Robert is going to be a poet, and father would be furious if he knew, because he wants him to go into the Guards. And it was father who made a fuss when Emmy wouldn't have a proper coming-out and went to help with the cows at Rushwater. If one's father and mother stuck to what they wanted and shut one up and kept one on bread and water, it would be so much easier," said Clarissa earnestly, "because then one would know, and you could be obedient or disobedient. But all the fathers and mothers I know say: 'Do what you like, dear, only don't bother *me*,' and that," said Clarissa with her air of precocious worldly wisdom, "is far more difficult than being ordered to do things. It sometimes makes me feel that I'd like to be a *nun*."

This anticlimax made Mrs. Belton smile, though she was too kind to laugh, but it was really no smiling matter. She had been through it all with her own independent self-willed daughter Elsa, and she knew how near Elsa had been to losing Christopher Hornby through her independence and self-will. Marriage was taming Elsa, very slowly, and she was lucky in a good husband. But what of these younger girls who in a world even more difficult than Elsa's world had been, where there were at least clear-cut duties imposed by a war? Agnes Graham could have steered a daughter, dozens of daughters, through the world of balls and parties and Ascot and Scotland, but how was she to steer them, or even help them to choose their own course, in these uncharted, unplumbed seas? She suddenly saw Agnes, who was telling Philip Winter how wonderfully John understood birds, as if she were a stranger and thought how perhaps Agnes's real talent was in home-making and that as soon as the young creatures began to dry their wings her interest, though not her love waned. What Agnes was doing superlatively well was to make a home for her mother, and that was, alas! of little avail now, for Lady Emily could but descend the darkening slope, however slowly. But as for helping her young, all she could do was to be a mother-bird and sit on the emptying nest with warm feathers in case anyone wanted to come back to it.

"Girls ought to marry young," she said aloud to herself.

"I think so too," said Clarissa's polite voice beside her. Philip Winter, who had overheard these last remarks, pulled his chair nearer to them.

"Do go on," he said, "I agree entirely in principle, but one doesn't always catch the right one young. I caught Rose Birkett—you may remember her, Mrs. Belton, her father was the headmaster at Southbridge School—when she was quite young, and we were perfectly miserable till she very sensibly lost her temper and threw her engagement ring at me and became disengaged. Then I caught Leslie, and she wasn't quite young, and it has been perfect, at least as far as I am concerned. What she would say I don't know. Yes, I do," he added. "She would say the same. So my evidence isn't the faintest help in any direction."

"Do you mean," said Clarissa, "that if one is really in love with a person their age doesn't matter so much?"

Philip said he supposed he did.

"Well, I don't suppose I'll ever be in love with anybody who is the right age," said Clarissa, "but I thought I would ask you. I thought Freddy was coming today, Mrs. Belton," she added with her unconscious air of royalty changing a subject on which everything has been said.

"So did I," said his mother, "but he often gets kept at the Admiralty. He hasn't been down since Anne Fielding's, dear me, I must remember to call her Anne Dale, wedding. Charles," she called to her younger son, who was now at liberty, "come and sit with us." So Charles sat down cross-legged on the grass in one swift, well-oiled movement, much to the admiration of the ladies.

"I can do that too," said Philip, "but I hate showing off."

Susan Dean, who had been audience but not participated in this symposium, heard what Clarissa said and she was certain that Captain Belton's absence was her work. Bitterly she had blamed herself and uselessly. If Captain Belton could not, would not marry because his heart was buried on the cold east coast, why had he taken her heart in his hand while the white clover and the green grass fell before old Tomkins's scythe? She could not believe him cruel, but cruel he had been. And if she knew that his heart was for ever lost, what could she do but avoid him, for his sake and for her own?

"Another way," said Susan, "is not to marry at all. But I think one has to be fairly well off to do that."

"Expound," said Philip, amused and interested by these girls and their views on life, though if it came to calling people girls, Susan Dean must be well, very well into her twenties, while Clarissa was still in her teens, though wiser in her generation perhaps than her elders in theirs.

"What I mean is," said Susan, "at least, what I think I mean is that unless the Government takes all father's money I shall always have enough to live on comfortably. Father tells us all about his investments and things. So I can do the job I like, and I do like it. And I shall be an old maid quite respectably; Aunt Susan that all the nephews and nieces love to visit. But if I hadn't father behind me and didn't marry anyone I would have to share a flat with somebody called My-friend-that-I-live-with and be a bore to my nephews and nieces. It sounds rather horrid," said Susan, "but I think it's true."

Philip Winter thought so too and was perturbed by this wisdom from the mouths of babes and sucklings, if such terms might be applied to the highly efficient Depot Librarian of the Barchester Red Cross.

"Do men feel like that?" said Clarissa innocently; too innocently, Philip thought.

"You had better ask Charles," said Philip. "Out with it, Charles. What are your ideas on marriage?"

Charles said he hadn't any. He meant fellows seemed to get married and it must be awfully nice to be married if you liked your wife and children.

"But one wouldn't get married at all if one didn't," said Lady Graham earnestly. "I adored Robert from the moment we were engaged and of course all the children," said her ladyship with the air of one who has finished an argument by a knock-down blow, and Charles wished he were Sir Robert and all the Graham children rolled into one so that he might the better sun himself in her affection.

"Oh please, Miss Leslie," said Selina, who had come across from the tent most becomingly out of breath and dishevelled, her hair like tendrils of a silver vine, "the young gentlemen want to know if they can have a funeral."

Leslie, with the composure that hardly ever deserted her, asked whose.

"It's a hedgehog, Miss Leslie," said Selina. "The poor thing got into the strawberry nets and it must have strangled itself. It was Dean that found it, and he brought it to me and I *was* so upset," in proof of which her lustrous eyes brimmed with bright tears.

"Why was Dean in the strawberry nets?" said Philip, but as Selina did not appear to hear the question he did not repeat it, for it was the last day of term and one could not be bothered to set impositions, nor could one give one's assistant masters the boring task of invigilating. "Tell Dean and the rest of the mourners to come and see me."

Selina sped away to the marquee, from which there shortly issued some dozen or sixteen little boys making the high chattering noise that little boys make, and they came across the grass to where Philip and his guests were sitting.

"Sir," said Pickering.

"Well, what is it?" said Philip. "And what have you got on your knee?"

Pickering looked with interested surprise at his knee, which was tied up in a bloody napkin (the bard's expression, not ours).

"On my knee, sir?" said Pickering. "Oh, it's my handkerchief, sir."

"I thought it was. Nothing else could be so dirty," said Philip. "What were you doing?"

"Please, sir, I was showing Dean how to bowl a yorker and I had such an exertion that it made me fall down," said Pickering in an injured voice, "and my knee burst out again. I'll show you, sir," he added, and began to untie his revolting blood-stained handkerchief.

"I don't want to see it," said Philip. "Go and find Matron."

"But, sir, we wanted to ask you if we could have the hedgehog's funeral," said Pickering. "Mr. Higgins gave us a box for a coffin."

"I don't want to hear about the coffin," said Philip. "Take your knee to Matron at once."

"Sir, can I go with Pickering?" said Addison, his eyes gleaming at the thought of seeing Matron deal with the abraded knee.

"No," said Philip.

"But, sir," said Addison, "he needs someone to go with him. His knee hurts, sir. It's going skeptic."

"I said NO," said Philip. "Off you go, Pickering. Now, Dean, what is this about a hedgehog in the strawberry nets? You know you are not allowed in the kitchen garden."

"Kitchen garden, sir?" said Dean, turning upon him a face blank of all expression except regret that the headmaster seemed to be losing his wits.

"Yes, kitchen garden," said Philip.

"Oh, the kitchen garden, sir," said Dean as though a great light had burst upon him. "I wasn't exactly in the kitchen garden, sir, but I was just looking in to see it and then there was a hedgehog in the net, so I thought I ought to take it out, because it was dead. But it was really Addison that rescued it, sir, because he has a penknife with two blades. Would you like to see it, sir? It has a corkscrew, too."

"I am not interested in red herrings," said Philip, which remark sent the little boys into ecstasies of laughter at what they considered their headmaster's brilliant wit. "I conclude that Addison has hacked the net to pieces with his penknife. You'll have to tell Higgins."

"But *Higgins* got the hedgehog out of the net, sir," said Dean. "He told Addison if he touched the net with his penknife he'd lam the lights out of him, sir. Sir, would you like to see the hedgehog? Bring the coffin along, Addison."

Before Philip could express his distaste for the treat so kindly offered to him, Addison had come forward with a battered cardboard box marked "Genuine Imitation Sponge Pudding Mixture," in which on some grass and daisies lay the hedgehog corpse, its little front paws pathetically limp.

Most of the ladies present said: "Poor little thing."

"So we thought we ought to bury it, sir," said Dean virtuously, "and not leave it lying about. Please, sir, can we have a funeral?"

"All right," said Philip, weary of the unequal struggle. "But you must ask Higgins to help you. Otherwise," he added to his guests, "they will undoubtedly put it where Higgins has just planted something. Charles, will you go with them?"

Susan said she would go too as her nephew seemed to be at the bottom of all this trouble. Addison at once took her under his protection and, slipping a very dirty hand into hers, dragged her away to follow the funeral procession.

"From the persistence of little boys, good Lord deliver us," said Philip.

"They can always wear one down," said Mrs. Belton sympathetically. "Have you heard Mrs. Morland talk about little boys? She understand *exactly* how horrible and exhausting they are and yet how one can't help adoring them."

"I am glad to hear you speak so well of me, mother," said a new voice, belonging to Captain Belton, who had come across the grass while the hedgehog argument was going on.

"Freddy! I never expected you," said his mother. "How nice."

"I didn't really expect myself," said Captain Belton after greeting his host and hostess, "but the Admiralty suddenly got tired of me and I came down to see the end of breaking-up."

He looked round with a sailor's searching eye and did not seem quite satisfied.

"The boys are all burying a dead hedgehog," said Clarissa. "I have been over Mr. Adams's works, Freddy, and they are too too exciting."

Captain Belton, having as it were raked the horizon with his telescope and seen no sail in sight, sat down by Clarissa, which was perhaps what Clarissa had intended.

"When James was quite little," said Lady Graham, whose mind had been slowly working in its own way, "mamma found a dead thrush on the window-sill and James was eating some chocolate pudding and mamma let him bury it in a boot-box."

Such educated members of the party as heard this remark felt that there were still milestones on the Dover Road and rejoiced accordingly, though to an ignorant generation this will mean nothing. Captain Belton, whose attention to Clarissa was, if she had known it, but skin-deep, caught his mother's eye and each knew that the other was thinking of the late Mr. Finching's bequest, for Agnes was her mother's own daughter.

"I made a poem about a dead thrush when I was quite young," said Clarissa negligently.

"Do tell me," said Captain Belton.

"It was quite short," said Clarissa.

> "See our thrush does now arise,
> And to heaven he quickly flies."

"Very nice," said Captain Belton, whose blue eyes were still scanning the vast expanse of ocean. "I wish I could write poetry, it must relieve one's feelings."

And then the funeral party came back rejoicing, with Charles and Susan bringing up the rear, and were joined by Pickering, now neatly bound up by Matron.

"Well, how did it go?" said Philip.

A shrill chorus of little boys expressed their ecstasy.

"It looked *splendidly* dead, sir," said Dean. "Hullo," he added to Pickering. "You *were* an ass to bust your knee again and not see the funeral."

"Well, I didn't want to see the funeral," said Pickering. "You should have seen my knee. Matron put some stuff on it and it all fizzled. It was like ginger-beer."

He was at once surrounded by a crowd of friends anxious for horrid details.

"Now you've had your funeral and it's time for your supper," said Philip. "Dean, you are going back with your people, aren't you? All the rest go indoors."

"I say, Aunt Susan," said young Dean, clinging to his aunt in a most exhausting way, "let's go home now. I'm most awfully hungry. Oh, do say yes, Aunt Susan."

Susan said yes mechanically, but her mind was elsewhere, for there was Captain Belton, whom she had half hoped to see when she arrived, whose absence had been such a mixture of relief and disappointment, whose presence now was such a mixture of joy and pain. There was a general movement to go. Captain Belton greeted Miss Susan Dean. She spoke very pleasantly in answer, but her eyes were a blank wall to him and he could not before so many friends ask her what he most wanted to know: why she had withdrawn herself, why no light shone from her.

So Susan and various other Deans went away with their young relative, and the rest of the party dispersed, Charles going with his mother and his elder brother. Philip and Leslie had an informal supper with the two assistant masters, visited the dormitories, inquired from Matron about Pickering's knee, and at last were free to sit quietly together under the trees.

"A few more years shall roll, a few more seasons come," said

Philip, "but I don't see any likelihood of our being at rest, nor do I particularly wish to be within the tomb, especially when I think of the people one might meet there. Mrs. Major Spender, for instance."

"What made you think of her?" said Leslie, remembering the overpowering wife of Major Spender, who had been at the hush-hush camp with Philip during the war.

"I had a letter from her this morning. I forgot to tell you," said Philip. "She said that she and her husband want to send their youngest boy here because Bobbums always said I was one of the best and believe it or not the headmaster of Coppin's School, where her elder boys are, won't reduce the fees though Billy that's the eldest is the sort of boy that you simply can't stop getting scholarships if I know what she means."

Leslie was amused by Philip's précis of Mrs. Spender's letter and said she must see it later. "And what are you going to say?" she asked.

Philip said The Terewth. "And," he added, "the truth happens to be true if you know what I mean. Unless there's a Black Death among the junior male population, or the Government takes the Priory as a training home for imbecile girls who are entering the Civil Service, I cannot take another boy for two years at least, unless, of course, your uncle and aunt really decided to give up their wing."

"Or if they died," said Leslie, with no want of affection, but as a matter of fact, a thing that might happen though neither she nor her husband wished it. "It's pretty good, Philip, isn't it?"

"If it is, I have you to thank," said Philip. "They are your uncle and aunt, bless them. How I was lucky enough to make you marry me I still don't know."

"You *didn't* make me marry you. I threw myself at your head," said, Leslie, remembering the bitter winter morning when she had engaged herself to Philip Winter through the window of a railway carriage at Winter Overcotes Junction with the engage-

ment ring cast off by his first love, the beautiful sparrow-brain
Rose Birkett, now Rose Fairweather.

"Bless you for it," said Philip and they held hands quite
foolishly till Selina came out to say that dinner was ready.

CHAPTER 9

The reunion at Rushwater which Martin Leslie had light-heartedly adumbrated had actually taken shape. Lady Emily was to be conveyed to Rushwater on her birthday and every possible descendant was to be convoked to the festival. Dr. Ford, privately consulted by Lady Graham and Miss Merriman, said he was all for old people killing themselves in their own way, and provided that Lady Emily spent a day in bed before the party and a day in bed after it, she was more likely to kill her family by her vitality than herself. The Marlings and the Beltons, both connected with Lady Emily through the Thornes, were to be of the party and of course the Pomfrets. Except the old estate agent Mr. Macpherson, who was still threatening to retire or failing that to die and so far had done neither, no outsiders were to intrude, which considering that the guests would amount to nearly forty people was just as well.

To feed forty people in London would mean death and despair or a restaurant, the alternatives being now about synonymous, but in the real country with a farmyard it would be quite possible. Sylvia and her sister-in-law Emmy, putting the baby and the cows out of their minds for the time being, concentrated on bacon, eggs, milk, cream, vegetables, rabbits, home-made jam, honey by private enterprise of the Rushwater bees, who had not suffered so severely in the previous winter as some other local bees, and parcels of real white flour and other food sent by Martin's mother and stepfather from America. The John Leslies were bringing a whole tinned ham that had reached them from Australia. David and Rose promised tinned meat from the Argentine, where David had many friends, and indeed every guest contributed something to the feast.

The scheme as arranged by Lady Graham, Miss Merriman, Sylvia, and Emmy was that Lady Emily should be driven over in the morning and rest before lunch. At lunch her health was to be drunk, but there were not to be any speeches. After lunch she was to rest again till tea in the big drawing-room, unsheeted for the occasion. There was to be a short informal service in Rush-water Church in memory of Mr. Leslie and of their eldest son, Martin's father. Lady Graham had wondered whether her brother John's first wife should also be remembered, but that gentle ghost was so far away and John's life was so calmly happy that she decided to say nothing.

"I don't think darling Gay would have wanted it," said Agnes to Miss Merriman, "she is so very far away from us now," a sentiment that Miss Merriman understood. Some of our be-loved dead feel near us for ever. Some have wandered far, so far that their voices are lost, and we cannot try to reach them, though the love is always there.

After this Lady Emily was to be driven back to Holdings and retire from the world for twenty-four hours; all of which plans were of course subject to her ladyship's delight in rearranging other people's arrangements, though Miss Merriman had no-ticed, without pleasure, that her employer had been less meddle-some of late and more apt to yield to advice about resting.

That golden summer had continued its course unchecked. Some said by a kind intervention of Providence so that people could store up a little warmth against the winter; others said it was just to spite people because the nicer weather was, the nastier They made life in general, so that one couldn't give one's mind to enjoying the sunshine. Also the grass was getting brown with want of rain and the raspberries and the late summer vegetables were less juicy than they should be, which doubtless gave pleasure to Them. But, as Emmy truly remarked, one really could be pretty sure that Gran's birthday would be fine.

And so it was. A day of glowing sun, a dark-blue vault of sky, a breeze so faint as hardly to stir the down on the head of Miss Eleanor Leslie, aged very few months, as she lay in her perambulator under the great tulip tree, light and warmth everywhere. And if the drowsy humming of bees was not so loud as in former years, at least there were bees at work, whereas in many gardens the hives were empty. At the bottom of the garden the little Rushmere brook ran shallow below the brick terrace, shallower than anyone remembered it, even old Cruncher at Hacker's Corner, who remembered hearing as a boy that the Frenchies had been licked by the Prooshans. Mrs. Siddon, the house-keeper, who knew Rushwater House better than any of the family, had been at work with Sylvia and Emmy for several days taking the covers off chairs and tables and pictures in the drawing-room, bringing curtains out of linen cupboards and silver and china out of store cupboards. Clarissa, who had come over the day before, was put in charge of the flowers. Owing to the dry weather they were not as plentiful as usual, but Clarissa was up early to pick the best, and plunged them neck-deep in large jugs and after breakfast arranged them with her elegant skilful fingers about the drawing-room and upon the round table in the dining-room, where Lady Emily and a select part were to sit, the rest of the guests taking a buffet lunch at trestle tables brought in from the servants' hall, now used as a kind of furniture repository. By eleven o'clock all the preparations were finished and the three ladies put on their last year's summer dresses and sat under the tulip tree to await Lady Emily's coming and admire the exquisite and witty conversation of Miss Eleanor Leslie, who had just invented a very good game of making bubbles come out of her ridiculous mouth and then laughing at herself for doing it.

"I say," said her cousin Emmy, who did not look her best in a silk dress and would far rather have been wearing breeches and leggings, "Eleanor's going to be awfully good at cows. When nurse was at Barchester yesterday I took her down to the farm in her pram, and when she saw Rushwater Churchill she said 'Oo' quite distinctly. She meant bull of course. Didn't you, Eleanor? I say, Sylvia, I think Eleanor's a bit grown-up for her. Could I call her Ellie?"

Sylvia said it did seem rather a large name for a baby, but as she was called after her grandmother, Sylvia's mother, and Mrs. Halliday was called Ellie by her friends, it might be a bit mixing.

"Oh, all right," said Emmy. "I see. It's like Rushwater Richard and Rushwater Richmond. If you called them both Rushwater Richie no one would know which was which, unless they saw them, and then of course they'd know. Baby, say Rushwater Richmond."

Miss Leslie smiled a wide toothless smile and said: "Oo," with a deep, rich, romantic intonation.

"Clever girl," said her cousin Emmy, proudly, on hearing which Miss Leslie blew a very large bubble which burst over her face and caused her to be consumed with mirth at her own funniness.

"Angel!" said her mother.

"Little pig!" said Clarissa.

"Juggins!" said Emmy, and it is difficult to say which of these three ejaculations gave evidence of the most besotted affection.

Martin then joined them and was invited by all three ladies to admire the beauty, wit, and intelligence of his daughter. He bent over the perambulator much struck, as he always was, by the way that her hands and feet were finished so neatly with nails like pale pink rose petals. Very respectfully he put his little finger in one of her hands.

"She's holding it," he said in a reverent voice. "Lord! what a grip!"

On hearing this, Miss Leslie relaxed her hold and fell asleep with a soft flush on her cheeks, and her relations went back to their chairs. Presently a car drove up and they all went down to the front of the house to welcome Lady Emily. There was the usual confusion of scarves, bags, and a Spanish silk shawl, but with time and care Miss Merriman and Lady Graham extricated Lady Emily, who advanced leaning on her ebony stick to meet her grandson Martin as he came towards her with his slight limp.

"Many happy returns of the day, Gran," said Martin, suddenly moved to kiss her hand with a pleasant awkward grace.

"Dear boy," said Lady Emily. "You and I are not so good at walking as we were. I used to walk with your father, Martin, when he was a boy. At first I went too quickly for him. Then he caught me up and soon he could outwalk everyone, even the gillies when he went north for the shooting. And here am I, an old woman with a stick, and you with your foot."

She stopped, but Martin had a strong feeling that she had meant to say more, that she was thinking of the father that he could not remember, thinking of him as walking over the moors in the pride of his youth and strength while his mother and his son lagged far behind. Sylvia and Emmy came up with loving greetings and took Lady Emily to see Miss Leslie in the abandonment of a baby's sleep, lying like a warm jelly fathoms deep in her repose.

"And now, mamma," said Lady Graham, who had been into the house to see Siddon, "everything is ready for your rest. Merry will bring your shawl," for Lady Emily had let her Spanish shawl and her bag slip to the ground while talking to Martin. Lady Emily flashed one of her smiles at Martin, a smile which conveyed to him that Agnes and Merry must be humoured and that he and she had a secret understanding.

"We will have a long delightful talk, darling Martin," she said, "but now I must rest or Merry and Siddon will be disappointed."

Whether Miss Merriman would have been disappointed or not it is impossible to say, for that admirable woman had trained herself never to let her face express her private feelings. Gath-

ering an armful of Lady Emily's belongings, she accompanied
her very trying employer into the house, where Clarissa received
her grandmother with loving greetings and a nosegay of tiny
scented picotees and Lady Emily was wafted away to the morning-
room to rest till lunchtime.

"I don't know what it is about Gran," said Emmy, sitting
down again very inelegantly, "but she makes one feel as if one
had had a hard day's hunting. I mean I'm frightfully fond of her,
but sometimes one just can't keep up. I dare say I'm talking
nonsense but it's what I mean."

Martin and Sylvia, both reeling under the first impact of Lady
Emily's personality, said they understood.

"One needs to be an angelic feather-bed like Agnes," said
Sylvia, "to live with Gran."

"Or to take her in one's stride like Merry," said Martin.

"I've seen Merry pretty done in sometimes at Holdings," said
Emmy, "but she never lets you know."

"I know who doesn't mind Gran a bit," said Sylvia. "My sweet
idiot angel Eleanor. Martin, she splashed her bath-water with
both hands this morning," which fascinating subject completely
drove Lady Emily out of their minds.

The John Leslies were the next to arrive. They were so dull,
though quite delightful people, that Lady Emily's friends occasionally wondered how she could have produced such a son. But
John had transmitted to their boys something of Lady Emily's
personality, and Leslie major and Leslie minor had quietly
flowered at Southbridge School till Leslie major, the eminently
respectworthy member of Everard Carter's house in Everard's
own phrase, the apparently dull son of provedly dull parents, had
perpetrated a piece of deliberate and unblushing impertinence
worthy of the highest traditions of the school, which impertinence had led to the final routing of Miss Banks, who was
teaching elementary Latin without the faintest grasp of quantities. To them at Southbridge had now been added Leslie mini-

mus, who was always at the bottom of any trouble in the preparatory school and took life exactly as he found it.

"I say, John," said Martin, "did you know we had cleaned the Temple? But I didn't touch the pictures on the wall or your poem about Fräulein."

"Did I write a poem about Fräulein?" said John Leslie.

"You know you did," said Martin indignantly,

> "Ding, dong, bell,
> Fräulein goes to hell,"

which made the three young Leslies look at their father with a respect that they had never hitherto felt.

"I'd love to see the Temple again," said Mary Leslie. "The summer I got engaged to John when those French people had the vicarage, we had a kind of secret meeting there. They were all Royalists and we were going to conspire against the Republic, and we had our meetings in the Temple. It was so hot and stuffy."

"That was the night of my seventeener," said Martin. "And that French boy, I've forgotten his name, had a flag wrapped around him under his waistcoat and he was to pull it out and wave it at supper-time and somehow it all went wrong. But it was a lovely seventeener. Rose and Hermione Bingham were there."

"And I was dreadfully in love with you, John," said Mary Leslie to her husband, "and David gave me some champagne in the garden and kissed me."

"And I saw it," said John. "And I thought you really cared for David."

"And now David is married to Rose Bingham," said Mary, and as so often happened she and John withdrew into a private world of their own full of affection and trust and every enduring good quality, but excessively uninteresting to the rest of the company.

"I say, Uncle Martin," said Leslie major, "do you think I could climb the Temple?"

"No," said Martin. "Only a steeplejack could climb the pyramid thing at the top. I tried myself when I was your age and fell and sprained my wrist."

"Then can I climb it, Uncle Martin?" said Leslie minor. "I've been right round the school chapel on the parapet and up the spire, but that's easy because there are crockets."

"Certainly not," said Martin.

"But, Uncle Martin," said Leslie major, "there are things like crockets on the pyramid thing on the Temple. We could easily get up. I went up the church steeple at home with the man who was mending the leadwork and he said I had a good head."

"That's enough," said their father.

"Oh, all right, father," said Leslie minor. "But, Uncle Martin, could I *just* climb the pyramid, just *once,* because then I could boast about it at school."

"I said NO," said Martin, and then, as often happened when he was irritated and tried to hide his annoyance, his leg began to ache as if in sympathy. Sylvia, who watched him more closely than he knew, suggested that the Leslie boys should clean out the pond in the kitchen garden after lunch, which met with immediate approval and Leslie minimus, a quiet boy with the easy movements of the born athlete, was told by his brothers that he could bale out the goldfish and not get in the way like a young idiot, which instructions Leslie minimus accepted with great composure.

Agnes Graham and Miss Merriman then came out again and reported that Lady Emily was lying on the sofa in the morning-room with a notebook and several pencils in case anything came into her head, and Siddon on guard in case her ladyship took it into her head to paint the white walls with arabesques or rip the cover off the large armchair to see if the material underneath was what she thought she remembered it was or something else.

"But mamma was quite restful when we left her," said Agnes.

"I think she is inventing some poetry. I always think it would be a good thing to have a poet in one's family, because they give so little trouble."

"Explain," said John, who was very fond of his sister Agnes. "I don't think Shelley's family would have agreed with you, or Byron's, or even Wordsworth's for that matter."

Agnes said if one were trying to find rhymes for words it would make one quiet because one would have to think, because a good many words didn't seem to have many rhymes, a subject so controversial that those who were interested in it all talked at once while the golden Sylvia and Emmy held their peace and thought how far better was a baby, or a cow, than all the poetry in the world. And then Mr. and Mrs. Belton joined them with their two sons, but Elsa could not come because she was in Scotland though nobody minded very much, for she was not so agreeable as her brothers, or shall we say that she needed a fairy Blackstick to give her a little misfortune before her imperious nature could show its true inner goodness.

"Agnes," said John to Mrs. Belton, "has put forward the original theory that a poet in the family is a good thing because they are so busy thinking of rhymes that they aren't much trouble."

"And I know I am right," said Agnes in a way quite provocative in one usually so mild, "because Milton wrote all *Paradise Lost* which I have never read in blank verse, but I think he must have been a most disagreeable person, the kind one would not ask to the house again."

So delightful was Agnes's soft vehemence that Captain Belton was for a moment almost as overcome by her charm as his brother Charles, but the feeling faded before it had blossomed and he watched with detached amusement Charles metaphorically at Agnes's feet with his heart in his hands. The rest of the Holdings detachment then poured on to the lawn, James, Clarissa, John, Robert, and Edith, this last young person feeling rather uppish because Nurse had not come with her. James attached himself silently to his elder Leslie cousins, Clarissa slipped into a seat near Captain Belton, while the three younger children tiptoed to look at Miss Eleanor Leslie still lying in warm soft abandon, her cheeks faintly flushed, her small hands thrown above her head.

Sylvia, anxious lest they should wake her baby, got up and went to the perambulator, but their rapt faces and silence reassured her.

"Mother," said Robert, tiptoeing back to Lady Graham, who had luckily forgotten Milton in admiring her own offspring, "do you like Sylvia's baby?"

Lady Graham said she did.

"She is a festoon of loveliness," said Robert in a reverent voice. "Could I kiss her toes, mother?"

Agnes, who for all her maternal besottedness had a practical nature, said Robert must wait till the baby woke up. Robert listened, nodded his head wisely, and said princes kissed princesses to save them from witches' spells, but he supposed kissing an ordinary baby might make it turn into something else, like a toad, and sat down on the grass near the perambulator to wait, quite happy, trying to blow on a piece of coarse grass held between his thumbs.

"Robert is a poet," said Captain Belton, who had heard this conversation, "but he is a very nice one even if he is in blank verse. Clarissa told me that she wrote a poem about a thrush when she was small. How is your mother?"

"Very well," said Agnes, "but easily tired. Sally dear, and Gillie, *how* pleased darling mamma will be to see you. I want to have a talk with you, Sally, and Martin shall take Gillie round the farm where nobody can get to them."

"Perfect," said Lady Pomfret as she watched her husband walk slowly towards the farm with Martin. "All Gillie needs is not to be talked to except about hay and stock. He is so worn out with this tiresome Parliament and his work in the Lords and all the unrest in the country that he doesn't sleep well. Don't make a noise, children, or you will wake Sylvia's baby."

James and the elder Leslie boys, with that peculiar gift for being nursemaids which young gentlemen in their later teens often show, took Lord Mellings, Lady Emily Foster, and the Honourable Giles Foster in tow and, accompanied by John and Edith Graham, went to a rickety summerhouse on the other side of the lawn and played a private game invented and developed by the elder Leslies about some rather magic people called Gwarzies and Borsicoes in whom all the younger children implicitly believed, and peace again spread her wing under the tulip tree while Miss Eleanor Leslie lay fathoms deep in quiet slumber and Robert sat on the grass by her perambulator trying to blow upon his piece of grass till the Marlings came over the lawn to them, but theirs was not a noisy arrival and they melted easily into the quiet talk.

"Only David and Rose to come," said Agnes, who had been counting the guests, "and they are bringing both the babies. Oh dear, Sally, I do hope mamma won't be overtired. It is a heavenly plan to have everyone here, but I shall be glad when she is safely home again. It is so difficult to know how to keep her quiet sometimes. Merry is the greatest help and I don't know what we should do without her. And of course, *so* annoying, Robert is kept in town. He did so hope to be here, but people are always sending for him. Are Emily's teeth getting straighter?"

And then she and Lady Pomfret fell into a delightful talk about dentists and oculists, and Lady Pomfret told Agnes about Lord Melling's tonsils and Agnes countered with Robert's three stitches on his head when a cricket ball hit it, and still Miss Eleanor Leslie slept the sleep of the self-centred while Robert sat cross-legged on the grass.

"It *is* a lovely place," said Lucy Marling to Captain Belton. "I haven't been here for ages, not since before the war. I suppose," she added wistfully, "they can manage to go on here?"

"I think they can," said Captain Belton. "Old Mr. Leslie was very clever at estate business and Macpherson the agent is a marvel. It cheers me up to see a place looking as prosperous as this and so many children about. I do wish my sister Elsa didn't live so far away. Harefield needs children and young life."

So, said Lucy, did Marling, with her brother Bill and her sister Lettice, the married members of the family, living in distant parts of England.

"The fact is there are too many unmarried people about," said Captain Belton. "I have only just thought of this, but I think it is true. You and I ought to be married."

He said this quite kindly, just as a statement of his views, and Lucy agreed. If she had married someone unspecified ten years ago, she might have a flourishing nursery, and the same held good for Captain Belton. Then his last words sounded again like an echo in her mind. A slow flush came over her neck. Did Freddy mean what he said? Oh, why was English so inexplicit a language. What he had said was that he and she ought to be married; but was he implying that they ought to be married to each other, or the one to X the other to Y? Lucy had thought a great deal about Freddy Belton since the day of the Marling Fête. She was not by nature romantic nor given to vain imaginings, but their talk about the decay of the landed gentry, her hardly suppressed tears, her heart-broken confession that, try as she might, she could not stop the decay of Marling, Freddy Belton's understanding sympathy, his prowess at Murdstone's Wild West Shooting Gallery, had all made a more than favourable impression on her. Ever since her sister Lettice had married Tom Barclay she had schooled herself not to think of love or marriage, for she saw no one in whom these existed as far as she was concerned and was an excellent fellow with all the young men, not so many and not so young, who came into her life. Now, since the Red Cross Fête, she had begun to dream a little and think that it might be pleasant sometimes to give in, to obey; not always to give the orders, to see that things were carried out, to be far more of a master at Marling than her brother Oliver could ever be. To begin to care for anyone was a weakness, and her whole life was a protest against weakness in herself and those she really loved, though to the less favoured she could be a tower of strength. Her memory flashed back to the day of the Marling Fête. They had talked of the attitude of their parents to unmarried children, however old. Freddy had said: Charles and you and I shall be the young people to them till we die. She had answered with her usual common sense: Or till we marry. Did those words mean anything? Had the even more explicit words he had spoken meant anything? It was clear as daylight to Lucy that Freddy would never say anything untrue, anything that could not be brought to the touchstone of his integrity, his honour, whatever one liked to call it. What, what did it all mean?

All these thoughts raced through her mind in a silence that might have lasted for two seconds, while Clarissa, very neat and elegant and cool, looked at them both appraisingly. The silence had not been long, but Lucy felt that it had lasted a hundred hours and it was a relief when Nurse came stumping over the grass and said to Miss Eleanor Leslie: "Ready for your din-din, you sleepy-head?"

Miss Leslie opened her dark eyes, looked at nurse, and realized at once with the appalling perspicuity of babies that the arrival of Nurse meant warm slightly sweetened milk followed by prune purée, which beautiful thoughts dissolved into the stern reality that her lunch was not at hand, that it would be as much as five or six minutes before she had been wheeled back to the house, carried up to the nursery, and was settled to her food. Her disapproval of these facts of life was immediate and took the form of a bright red shining face, a square mouth, shrieks, baffled milk-lust; and even a tear escaped from her fiercely screwed-up eyes.

"Darling," said Robert in a cajoling voice, "don't cry. Is it hurting you?"

Miss Leslie stopped yelling for a second, opened a tear-drenched eye, looked at Robert, and evidently saw in him a direct manifestation of the powers of darkness disguised as a milk-snatcher, so she screwed her eyes tight again and relapsed into a crisis of shrieks.

"Oh, *please*," said Robert, pulling Nurse's arm. "*Please* stop it hurting her. My sweet Eleanor, *please* don't cry."

"She's a bad girl," said Nurse with professional want of interest as she hurried the perambulator towards the house. "You're a bad girl, aren't you, you little Tartar? You're a little greedy, aren't you? Come along, my lady, and we'll pop something nice in that little mouth," and she trundled the perambulator away while Miss Leslie lay screaming with rage and perspiring all over the top of her head, which now showed bright scarlet through the down. As they turned the corner of the house the noise died away and peace descended again upon the lawn.

Emmy, who had been having a last general look round at the lunch preparations, now came out of the house carrying a large gong, which she beat with great vigour. At the sound, children old and young came from all parts of the garden with requests to be allowed to beat too, which Emmy obligingly let them do until Martin and Lord Pomfret were seen approaching from the farm.

The whole company then went into the house, where Agnes and Miss Merriman skilfully sorted out the favoured few who were to sit with Lady Emily. Her own children John and Agnes, Martin because he was the son of the eldest son and had a limping leg, Lord Pomfret because he was Lady Emily's only relation present on her father's side and was always tired, Lady Pomfret because her husband liked her to be near him, the old agent Mr. Macpherson, and John Leslie's wife Mary. There were ten seats at her table and two were still empty.

"I do hope David and Rose won't be late," said Agnes to Miss Merriman in an undertone. "It will spoil everything for mamma."

And undoubtedly her ladyship would have seen the empty places, made searching inquiries and been bitterly disappointed, but that she had brought a number of loose sheets of paper with her in addition to her shawl, her bag, her scarves, and a few other useful articles, among which her son John said afterwards that he had distinctly seen a bird-cage and a large pair of scissors and a chafing-dish, which feat of imagination in one so good and so literal-minded as John must be set down to his credit and to the infectious nature of Lady Emily's jackdaw habits. As she sat down, her portable property fell or fluttered in every direction so that Miss Merriman and Clarissa, who were stationed as a kind of relief party near Lady Emily's chair, had to go almost under the table to retrieve them.

"Thank you, Merry; thank you, Clarissa," said Lady Emily flashing her brilliant smile at them and at the whole table; "I don't know what I was thinking about while I was resting. It was something really important, only I cannot for the moment remember what it was," said her ladyship, pulling two pairs of spectacles out of her bag and looking at them with a dazed expression.

"Those are your reading-glasses, Gran," said Clarissa.

"Thank you, darling," said Lady Emily. "Then it is the other pair I want, because I was thinking about the vicar."

"Mr. Bostock isn't here, Lady Emily," said Miss Merriman. "We thought we would just keep to the family for lunch, if you remember. Mr. Bostock is coming to tea."

"Then why are there two empty places laid for him?" said Lady Emily with the passionless triumph of a logician. "If he doesn't say grace I am afraid he will be so disappointed. Not," she added conversationally, "that we ever had grace before meals, because your father always said it made the meat get cold, John. But I suppose meat is different at a vicarage and keeps hot longer. I must ask Mr. Bostock about it."

Miss Merriman, John, and Agnes exchanged anxious looks. If Lady Emily chose to confuse the vicar by asking him about the calorific powers of the vicarage that was all right. But what they did not like was that Lady Emily had seen the two empty places and they knew, quite fatally, that in a moment she would ask where David was. At that moment Miss Merriman's watchful ear, if we may use the expression, caught the sound of a car and she spoke softly to Agnes. Then the door opened and in came David Leslie, forcing his way with some difficulty and his usual easy charm among the crowd of relations young and old, and in his wake his wife, Rose, looking even smarter and more poised as the mother of two children than she had looked before her marriage.

"Darling mamma," said David, kissing his mother tenderly, "we are a little late. Merry, I salute you. And John and Martin and you, Agnes darling, and everyone. Mother darling, here is Rose."

"I am so sorry we are not punctual," said Rose to Lady Emily in her attractive husky voice. "We were in Paris yesterday and our plane got into a fog this morning, *too* stupid, so I got Johnny Grabshaw to fly us down to Winter Overcotes from the aerodrome, and Gerry Coverdale lent us his racing car and here we are. Many, many happy returns of the day, dearest. And how lovely to see everybody."

Miss Merriman hustled, if such a word can be applied to her methods, David and Rose into their seats. Mrs. Siddon as a tribute to so important an occasion had condescended to be butler for once, aided by Deanna, the kitchen-maid, who was almost paralysed with terror, in spite of which the service did not flag and Agnes and Miss Merriman felt they could sit back and relax.

Lady Emily, with John on one side and her beloved David on the other, was in a seventh heaven of happiness and sent piercing looks of love and appreciation to the rest of the table while she listened to David and made hay with her food. The rest of the guests, sitting or standing, were enjoying the excellent country food and talking among themselves, but their eyes often turned to the round table where Lady Emily sat, her beautiful eyes resting lovingly on one or another of her children, grandchildren, and relations.

"I am glad to see, Mr. Macpherson," said Rose Leslie to the old agent, "that you haven't retired yet. Rushwater can't do without you."

"I'll not say that you're wrong, Mrs. David," said Mr. Macpherson, with a fine Scotch mixture of self-approval and cautiousness. "Young Martin is a fine lad, but his bairn is hardly old enough to manage the place yet. Have you seen our wee Miss Eleanor? She has as fine a temper and as good a pair of lungs as any in the county. I am on old man, Mrs. David, and though I have no weans of my own," said Mr. Macpherson, who was apt to drop into, or perhaps it would be more correct to say assume, the Doric when moved, "I know fine what a bairn should be, and that Eleanor has a grip the like of which I've never known. Let her once get hold of your little finger and she'll no let go till she wishes. If only Martin's father could have seen her," said the old agent, wistfully remembering the eldest Leslie son, killed in Flanders so many years ago.

Rose said they would all need him for many years to come.

"Threescore years and ten," said Mr. Macpherson thoughtfully. "Sometimes I have my doubts about flying in the face of the Good Book at my age, but if the Lord has need of me here, seventy years or eighty years are as one in his eyes. I came to Rushwater when I was thirty, and a cocked-up youngster I was then. Her ladyship was the same age. Well, we have grown old together, she in her station, I in mine, for fifty years. I used to say that once I could see Martin well married I'd be away to Dunbar and lay my bones there, but here I still abide."

"I don't think it much matters where one lays one's bones," said Rose. "Rushwater isn't a bad place. And after lunch you must see my babies. Nannie brought them in the car to Heston to meet us and of course we couldn't let them miss Gran's birthday so they and Nannie flew down with us. She is up in the nursery now with Sylvia's nurse. She brought all their special food with her. She's a marvellous Nannie and lets me go in and out of the nursery just as I like. Her one regret is that I am not even an Honourable, but Uncle Tom often comes to dinner and that bucks her up like anything. Poor Uncle Tom. It's not very funny to be the Duke of Towers and have no money and see all your gardens being dug up for coal. Thank goodness, mamma married big business and papa was rather a lamb in his way."

And then she turned to Lord Pomfret and they had a quiet talk about their relations, a great many of whom they shared in varying degrees of kinship, and Lady Pomfret, looking across the table, felt grateful to Rose for being so good-looking and well dressed and obviously amusing Gillie, and then she turned her attention to John and listened to his very nice dull talk and watched David flattering and amusing his mother.

As for the other guests, they were enjoying their buffet lunch very much, exchanging family news in a gradually rising roar, and discussing the influence of politics on pigs.

"It's my opinion," said Mr. Marling to Mr. Belton, "that there isn't a feller in the Government who knows how to cut up a pig. Any feller with a grain of sense could see that to get the best out of a pig you must cut him up properly. And look at the bacon ration. Enough to make my father turn in his grave. If the Government don't feed the agricultural labourer, that's the end of farming. Extra rations, they say," and Mr. Marling, to the admiration of the Leslie boys, who were standing near, actually said: "Pah! Any man could eat a week's extra rations in a day and still have to draw his belt in. I'd like to see the Cabinet doin' a day's farm-work, summer or winter, on what they expect our men to live on. Well, Belton, I'm gettin' on and I shan't see much more of it. Sometimes I think my grandfather had the best of it. Broke his neck out huntin' at forty and left everything to my father."

Mr. Belton, though he could not quite see the point of this anecdote of philoprogenitiveness, sympathized deeply and said how good his elder son had been in relinquishing various rights so that money could be raised to keep the estate going and how his younger boy was earning his own living as a schoolmaster, so that Mr. Marling, taking up the gauntlet, had to boast that his elder son, although he worked in London, which Mr. Marling seemed to feel rather a slur on the family, never asked for help.

"My Lucy's a good girl too," he said. "Can't make out why she doesn't get married, though. Girls got married young in my time."

Mr. Belton, who felt that the fact of his daughter having married not only for love, but from a worldly point of view extremely well, rather spoilt his hand in the game of grumbling, said he had not seen Lucy for a long time.

"See her now if you want to," said Mr. Marling. "Over there. Talkin' to your Freddy."

Mr. Belton looked and saw Captain Belton with Miss Marling. They were talking earnestly and appeared to be on very good terms and Mr. Belton was struck by a kind of nobility in Lucy's bearing and manner which he did not remember of old. Mr. Marling on his side thought Freddy Belton had filled out nicely. Neither gentleman was in the habit of analysing his thoughts. Each would have been shocked if what was mistily passing through his mind had been formulated in words. Had Mrs. Robin Dale, who was still apt to wonder whom people meant when so addressed, been present she might have said in the words of her favourite poet, Lord Tennyson: "Well, if it prove a girl, the boy Will have plenty: so let it be," though as Mrs. Robin Dale would have been first to admit, there was not plenty in the Belton household and even less at Marling Hall. Both the landowning gentlemen, tied by tradition and duty to their fields and the men who had worked for them and with them, looking with deep unhappiness at a future when they, and even worse their sons after them, would have to leave their fields and their patient workers to alien hands, or to impersonal, bureaucracy-ridden State control, thought for the moment in the simpler terms of the old, free life, and in the mind of each was an echo of the words: "A marriage has been arranged."

"So I'll tell you what," Lucy Marling was saying to Captain Belton, "I'm sure if father would only sell that bit of ground that needs draining, it would keep things going for a bit. I know the County Council are after it for a housing estate, but father won't consider selling. Probably they'll take it in the end anyway. I've talked to father till I'm tired, but he only says he's an old man and wants to be left in peace. Bill is a dear, but he doesn't understand and Oliver won't *do* anything. You couldn't possibly talk to father, could you, Freddy?"

Captain Belton was very sorry for Lucy. He was sorry for the Marling family and the Marling lands, just as he grieved for every family that was being violently divorced from the fields and woods their forbears had cultivated and planted and cared for, but it was not for him to interfere in the private affairs of Lucy's father, even if his private affairs had also become part of the public weal or woe.

"My dear Lucy," he said, very kindly indeed, "I would do anything I could for you, but your father would quite rightly kick me out of his house if I offered advice upon his affairs."

"I suppose he would," said Lucy, feeling to her horror a most unmanly moisture in her eyes. "Oh well, I expect you're right, Freddy. Forget what I said. I won't say it again."

"Good girl," said Captain Belton, touched by the gentleness so unusual in her. "Couldn't you talk to Bill again? After all, he is the heir to anything there is, just as I am the heir of what is left at Harefield, and I really have been able to help my father a little."

"Thank you *awfully*, Freddy," said Lucy, lifting her eyes to his. "I'll try. And anyway Bill has boys, so he *must* want to do something about Marling for them."

"I suppose I ought to have boys too," said Captain Belton, thinking with some self-reproach that he had let a shadow from the past keep him from providing the grandchildren whom his parents naturally desired.

And then other friends were at hand and Lucy talked to one and he to another, till John stood up. The talking gradually died down, and when there was silence, "We are going to drink mamma's health," he said. "I am the oldest now, but Martin's father was my elder brother and Martin is carrying on at Rush-water as his father and grandfather would have wished. Martin."

He sat down again and Martin rose to his feet with a slight hesitancy because when he had been sitting his leg was always difficult. John's words had been entirely unexpected and he looked at his wife for help. His golden Sylvia smiled at him, which seemed to be all he needed.

"Darling Gran," he said. "I wish it was my father making this speech, but as it isn't it can't be helped. Many happy returns of the day and we all love you with all our hearts." And that was perhaps all that needed saying. There was no glory of champagne as there had been on his seventeenth birthday when he had to return thanks at the dinner-party; a little white wine and large jugs of almost non-alcoholic fruit cup were all that the times could afford; but the love and goodwill of everyone present triumphed over these mortifications, and a kind of hum of applause rose from the room as Martin sat down again.

It then became apparent that Lady Emily was preparing to rise and acknowledge the tribute. Agnes and Miss Merriman looked at each other and recognized that they were powerless, but Miss Merriman quietly took her place with Clarissa near Lady Emily, who had now got up, letting a vast amount of personal property slip from her lap to the ground.

"Thank you all," she said, looking round the room with her keen hawk's eyes, her thin beautiful mouth trembling a little. "Thank you all with all my heart and darling Martin for being so brave. I wish Henry were here to speak for me, but he is away somewhere, isn't he, Merry?" she asked, with a quick anxious look at Miss Merriman.

"Yes, Lady Emily," said Miss Merriman in her usual matter-of-fact way.

"So I shall have to make the speech myself," said Lady Emily, with her old brilliant mischievous smile. "I tried to write a poem about today, but I hadn't got any red or blue chalk, so I didn't. Thank you all, from my heart, and may Rushwater have new children and new love and new life from generation to generation. God bless you all. And," said her ladyship to Miss Merriman,"I know that I left my spectacles, I don't mean the other ones but the *other* ones, in the flap of that old leather writing-case on my table at Holdings. Do you think Conque will find them?"

Miss Merriman answered her employer that Conque would most certainly find them. Clarissa and Miss Merriman then retrieved most of her belongings from the floor and persuaded her to go back to the morning-room and rest, which she did without protest.

The party then dispersed to the garden to rest or to amuse themselves as they wished till teatime. Agnes and Miss Merriman went into the great drawing-room to see that all was prepared.

"Do you think mamma remembered that papa was dead when she asked if he was away somewhere?" said Agnes. "One doesn't quite know what she remembers, Merry."

"I know," said Miss Merriman. "The dividing line is very thin with some people. When old Lady Pomfret was ill she thought Lord Mellings was away with his regiment and would be back soon, so we agreed with her. I think he had been dead for thirty years."

There was a silence while Agnes reflected and Miss Merriman thought of the late countess, for the Lady Pomfret of whom she was speaking had died before the war and Miss Merriman had been her quiet, wholly reliable secretary and knew her better than many of her friends. She had been very happy at Pomfret Towers and at the Casa Strelsa in Florence and in the big London house, quietly reliably keeping everyone in order. For reasons of her own she had not remained there after the countess's death, though old Lord Pomfret would have paid her handsomely and given her a free hand, and since then she had been with Lady Emily and was the only human being who could control that wind-blown rainbow fountain; though of late the winds had been stilled, the sparkling waters no longer tossed their rainbow spray so high.

"Well," said Agnes with a sigh, "I must go and look after everyone and see what Sylvia's plans are. Are you coming out, Merry?"

But Miss Merriman said she would sit in the library so that she could hear if Lady Emily wanted anything, for Siddon would be fully occupied with the servants' hall and the food. So Agnes went away to the garden and Miss Merriman sat in the large leather chair where Lady Emily's husband used to sit and thought about the past and about the present and a little about the future, for even the best and most skilful service is not always an inheritance and when Lady Emily no longer needed her she would have to make up her mind to take another post or to go and live with her invalid sister. It would be pleasant in some ways to be one's own mistress and she and her sister were on very good terms, but the habit of caring for others cannot be lightly shed, and when Miss Merriman thought of a future in which she had no one to protect, to serve, and in her own quiet way to guide, she hoped she would die in harness.

These thoughts, which weren't leading her anywhere, were interrupted by a slight noise at the door and Lady Pomfret came in.

"I didn't know you were here, Merry," she said, sitting down in another of the leather chairs. "What a dear thoughtful boy Martin is. He asked Macpherson to show Gillie the new plantation and they can talk about larches and things and be perfectly happy, and Gillie won't be so tired. I wish he were as strong as Aunt Emily."

Miss Merriman asked if Lord Pomfret had had a trying summer.

"I suppose so," said the countess, "but everyone is having a trying time. Only Gillie is so good and works so hard and is so unselfish and everyone takes advantage of it. I am trying to take over more of his county work myself, but I can't neglect the children. Mellings doesn't go to his prep school till next year. It isn't easy."

"I expect Mr. Wicklow is a great help," said Miss Merriman.

"Good old Roddy," said Lady Pomfret, for her brother Roddy Wicklow had been in the Pomfret agent's office in old Pomfret's time and had taken over the whole work of the estate at about the same time that the present Lord Pomfret succeeded to the title, and as both men were silent and hard workers and loved the Pomfret lands deeply, they were on very good terms and kept going as well as the times would allow. "Gillie likes going round the place with him more than anything. It is so good for him to get away from the Towers. When I see all the work on his table I could burn it sometimes," said Lady Pomfret wearily.

"I remember when I was with old Lady Pomfret that Mr. Foster, as he was then, used to let me help him in the office sometimes," said Miss Merriman, looking back into the past.

"What a winter that was when Roddy's father died," said Lady Pomfret. "Gillie said you were marvellous at everything and Aunt Edith didn't know what she would do without you. Oh dear, I wish you were at the Towers, Merry."

Lady Pomfret was lying back in the big chair, but not at rest. Miss Merriman could see that she was like a fine steel spring ready for action at the slightest touch, just as her husband was, only with this difference, that Lady Pomfret had perfect health and Lord Pomfret rarely knew what it was to be quite well.

"I was very happy at the Towers with Lady Pomfret," said Miss Merriman, thinking of the days before the war and her countess moving with her own kindly dignity from one great Pomfret house to another untroubled by the details that Miss

Merriman dealt with so well. "Very happy," she repeated almost to herself.

"I want to ask you something, Merry," said Lady Pomfret, "but you needn't answer if you don't want to."

Miss Merriman stiffened all through her body. She knew that Lady Pomfret would ask her a question and that the answer to that question would need all her intelligence, all her knowledge of the world, all her self-command.

"If I can help you of course I will answer," she said.

"It's Aunt Emily," said Lady Pomfret looking troubled. "I hadn't seen her lately. Merry, when she asked if Uncle Henry was away somewhere, did she remember he was dead?"

"I don't know," said Miss Merriman, in a way disappointed, in a way relieved that the question was not what she had expected. "As people get older they often forget on the surface the things they really know underneath."

"Poor Aunt Emily," said Lady Pomfret, forgetting her own pressing troubles in her compassion for Lady Emily. "Gillie and I are so thankful you are with her, Merry, and how Agnes would manage without you, I can't think. Poor darling Aunt Emily."

"No one really knows," said Miss Merriman. "But I think she is not unhappy. A little bewildered sometimes, and then it passes. She was naturally excited today and Martin's speech was so right and so good."

Lady Pomfret stood up, looking still to Miss Merriman very like the Sally Wicklow with the best hands in the county who had won the heir to the Pomfret earldom and been a perfect wife to him.

"Gillie and I both want you at the Towers, Merry," said Lady Pomfret, looking ahead as she used to look when taking a fence, "if ever you want to come. That's all."

She went out of the room and as she passed Miss Merriman she brushed her shoulder with the tips of her fingers, lightly and affectionately. Miss Merriman saw no reason to move, or to do anything but consider the understanding that Lord and Lady

Pomfret, Gillie and Sally, had of other people's needs. What Miss Merriman had felt years ago at Pomfret Towers was hardly known even to herself, for she had resolutely shut her mind to what had never happened. Now for a short space she allowed herself to remember the day when young Mr. Foster had announced his engagement to Miss Wicklow, sister of Roddy Wicklow, who was under Mr. Hoare, the old agent, and had on the same day heard of his father's death, which made him immediate heir to the earldom, with all its heavy responsibilities. "Oh, Merry," he had said, "I do wish you were going to help me," but he had no idea with what difficulty Miss Merriman said she was indeed sorry but she would be with Lady Pomfret. And how she had passed that night was, like the rest of her private life, only her own affair. Then her countess had died and she had presently gone to Lady Emily and had so taken the measure of her entrancing, wilful and maddening employer that she was able to circumvent her in many of her meddlesome and impractical schemes and was much liked and valued by Lady Graham, Sir Robert Graham, and the whole family.

Time had passed. Service was no inheritance nor did it make an abiding-place. It might be that Holdings would need her no longer, that the wind-blown fountain would sink back to the springs whence it rose. When that day came Miss Merriman would grieve, but she now knew there would be fresh duties for her and that she would still be able to tend, protect, and help the people she loved in a place that she knew. She sat quietly for a long time. Then she heard Lady Emily moving and went to the morning-room to help her employer to collect herself and her belongings for tea.

Not for many years had Rushwater seen so many young people and heard so many young voices. The hub as it were of the party was an encampment under the tulip tree where Miss Eleanor Leslie and Rose's two babies slept in perambulators, or kicked on a rug, silently worshipped by Robert, while the two nurses were more than gracious to each other and agreed that Robert was quite an old-fashioned child. Agnes, with Mrs. Belton and Mrs. Marling and Rose, sat at a little distance and talked families while Mr. Belton and Mr. Marling visited the farm and discussed the Barsetshire Pig-Breeders' Association and deplored the degeneracy of pigs. Lord Pomfret and Mr. Macpherson were safely away in the woods, looking at the new plantation in a companionable silence.

In the kitchen garden the three Leslie boys with James and John Graham were engaged in the wholly delightful task of cleaning out the pond and luckily had all brought bathing-suits with them in hopeful anticipation of water sports of some kind. Leslie minimus was given a kitchen dipper and baled gold and crimson fish into a large pail. The water was then allowed to run out of the pond, revealing the most delightful, or revolting, according to taste, masses of very smelly slimy green weed, which all the boys threw at each other, or slipped on, so that the grown ups withdrew to a safe distance. Leslie minimus was then dispatched to get brooms from the gardener's shed, and the floor of the pond was thoroughly swept.

"I know what," said Leslie minor, "we ought to scrub it with soap."

"Soap's rationed, you idiot," said John Graham. "Didn't you know that?"

"Of course I do," said Leslie minor. "That's why the back of your neck's so dirty," upon which the cousins fell into mortal combat, in which the other boys enthusiastically joined.

Agnes Graham with Charles in attendance, Mary Leslie, Captain Belton, Oliver and Lucy Marling, and Clarissa were attending the cleaning ceremony and had wisely chosen a large semicircular seat at a little distance from the green slime and the mess when even louder shrieks reached their ears, and John Graham came rushing towards them, closely followed by Leslie major.

"Mercy! Mercy!" shouted John Graham, who was carrying something in his hands which hampered his running.

"Justice! Justice!" shouted Leslie major, chasing his cousin round the box-edged walks.

John Graham, cutting straight across a newly dug bed, came like an express train between two rows of peas and threw himself on one knee before the company, holding out his hands, in which was sitting a large, surprised, indignant frog.

"Mother! It's my frog," said John.

"It isn't, Aunt Agnes," said Leslie major, who was now brandishing a tall globe artichoke as an offensive weapon. "I saw it first."

"Anyway I got it first, Aunt Mary," said John, appealing to his rival's mother. "And it particularly said it wanted to talk to me."

"It only wanted to tell you what a fool you looked," said Leslie major. "Put it on the ground and see who it hops to."

John Graham, suddenly full of Prevention of Cruelty to Animals, said the frog was quite happy and didn't want to hop, to which Leslie major replied that if one held frogs too long one got skin disease.

"I'll tell you what," said Lucy, unable to resist arranging people's plans for them. "Put some weeds in a pail and the frog can sit there till the pond is full again."

The plan was agreed to and the quarrel composed. Leslie major got a pail, Leslie minimus obligingly provided some slime, and John Graham put the frog in it. Most of the party then walked over to the pond. Leslie minimus dragged up the garden hose, the water was turned on and the pond refilled. The frog was decanted onto a large stone, the water-lily pads floated up to the surface, and all was clean and peaceful.

"When Emmy was quite little," said Lady Graham to Charles, "she fell into the pond. There was a charming French boy whose name I have quite forgotten and he went into the water and pulled her out, so I said: 'Oh you must change your trousers or you will catch cold,' so one of the footmen got him a pair of Martin's flannel trousers and he played tennis after tea."

Seldom have so many emotions raged simultaneously in the human breast as in Charles Belton's while Lady Graham unfolded this stirring drama. Sympathy for Lady Graham seeing a child in its watery grave, envy of the French boy, a certain pleasure that Lady Graham had forgotten his name, reverence for Lady Graham's beautiful compassion to the wet Frenchman, and deep contempt for anyone who could play tennis while Lady Graham was about.

"Do you suppose," said Clarissa to Captain Belton, "that he is the frog prince?"

She looked towards the frog, who had sunk into a kind of trance, broken from time to time by a lightning flash of his tongue as a mutton chop or a roast quail sailed past him disguised as an insect.

Lucy Marling, remembering her Grimm, drew nearer.

Captain Belton's mind went back to the day at Holdings when Clarissa found the remains of the gilded ball in the little pool.

"King's daughter, fairest," he said to Clarissa, "let me eat from your golden plate and drink from your golden cup," and Clarissa, a little intoxicated by the sun, the excitement, her sense of importance because she was helping Merry take care of Gran, the heroine of the day, and perhaps a little to show off before Charles and Oliver and the Leslie boys, gave Captain Belton a glance that would have done credit to a finished coquette.

"You'll have to kiss the frog if he is to turn into a prince," said Leslie minimus. "Let's try. I'll get him," and he waded into the water, while Captain Belton looked on amused by the pretty, spoilt child's posturing. One could not be angry with her.

"Here he is," said Leslie minimus, who by a masterly flank movement had captured the frog and bore him dripping to land. "Quick, Clarissa."

Clarissa shrieked in a ladylike way and clung to Captain

Belton's arm. The frog, remembering his grandmother's warn-
ing against allowing human girls to kiss one, as they were apt to
turn one into a prince and one could never get back to the green
slime of the pond, hit out with his hind legs, described a
parabola in the air and dived deep under the lily pads. This, it
seemed to Captain Belton, was a suitable moment for Clarissa
to stop clinging, but to his annoyance she continued to cling in
a rather exhausting way, prattling to him about Mr. Adams's
works, a subject in which he felt no interest at all. The party
strolled back towards the house, and Lucy Marling fell into step
with Leslie major, who confided to her that he was going to
learn forestry and get a job at Rushwater when Mr. Macpherson
retired. At any other time Lucy, who was interested in anything
to do with estates and liked the human boy, would not only have
listened but also have imparted her own views, telling Leslie
major what in no uncertain terms. But her heart was heavy
because a pretty spoilt child was clinging to Captain Belton's
arm. In vain did she remind herself that Captain Belton could
walk arm-in-arm with all the pretty girls in the world if he
wished. No reasoning could prevent her feeling low-spirited and
wishing the day were over and herself safely back at Marling,
where she could be alone.

"Clarissa darling," said Lady Graham, "do look for Merry and
ask her if Gran is getting ready for tea. We mustn't be late or
Gran will be so tired."

In spite of all Clarissa's grown-upness it had never yet occurred to her to disobey her mother, for gentle and loving and
silly as Agnes was, she had an unexpectedly firm streak in her,
which was probably why she always kept her servants, who still
secretly felt proud of a mistress who could keep a tight hand on
them. So she unhooked herself from Captain Belton, and went
into the house by the back way.

"It is such a pity," said Lady Graham to Captain Belton, "that
Clarissa has not had a good finishing governess. I hoped we
might get dear Miss Bunting, who was the only person that

David was frightened of, but she died," and her ladyship uttered
a gentle sigh which almost implied that Miss Bunting could
have stopped herself dying if she had given her mind to it.

"Girls do need discipline," said Captain Belton, thinking of
his sister Elsa. And then the words "discipline" made him think
of another girl who through duty well and selflessly done had as
it were been through her furnace and come out purest gold. But
alas for human constancy: it was not of a bomb-shattered house
on the cold east coast that he thought, but of the Cathedral
cloisters with grass and clover falling before old Tomkins's
scythe and a pair of steady eyes lifted to his. If she did not care
for him she was none the less gold. But, which shows how very
foolish men can be when they love, so far it had not occurred to
him that the way to find out why Susan Dean avoided him was
to ask her. And above these thoughts he talked quite easily and
lightly to Lady Graham and Mrs. John Leslie, till they got back
to the tulip tree.

The nursery encampment was now breaking up for tea. Miss
Eleanor Leslie had suddenly waked up in a very benignant mood
and was talking in her own liquid, cooing jargon to Robert, who
appeared to understand her perfectly.

"Oh, Nurse," he said pleadingly, "do you think I could have
tea in the nursery? Eleanor wants me to come. She said so, didn't
you, baby darling?"

Miss Leslie smiled a wide toothless smile and kicked violently.

"You ask Robert nicely, you little roguey-poguey," said Nurse,
not displeased by Robert's preference for the nursery, "and
perhaps he will come and have tea with us. Now what do you
say?"

"Oo," said Miss Leslie, beaming upon a world from which she
had never had anything but love.

"There's a good girl," said Nurse complacently. "You understand every word, don't you? A little poppet. Are you ready,
Nannie?"

"That'll be nice to have a little gentleman to tea," said Nannie. "When we were at Hartletop little Lord Dumbello used to come to nursery tea every day. Dorothy said she loved him, didn't you, Dodo? But Henry was a naughty boy and said he didn't like his lordship a bit," which may have been true in spirit, but owing to the tender age of Rose's babies was literally impossible; nor did Nurse wish to hear about a lord having tea with Nannie's children, so she said standing there wouldn't make the kettle boil and Robert could carry the rug indoors, which he happily did and so the nursery party vanished on its milky way.

CHAPTER 10

From the woods, the farm, the kitchen garden, the lawn, the morning-room, the library, the relations were now converging upon the drawing-room. The floor had been polished by old Bertha, the housemaid, the windows had been polished by one of the outside men. Each tall window, its long faded brocade curtains hanging from a gilded rod tipped with gilded pineapples, framed a view of the lawn, the great tulip tree, and the gentle rise of the ground to woodland beyond, for Rushwater had inherited the site from a much older house built according to English custom in what David Leslie called a froghole, so that the cellars gently grew mushrooms and the stone floors of the servants' quarters sweated through at least eleven months of the year. But no one had been carried off by galloping consumption, no Leslie was more rheumatic in the damp than people who lived on a hill or on gravel, for rheumatics are simply English usage and rather pride themselves on cropping up whatever the conditions. Trestle tables had been arranged as for a public dinner, an E without its short leg, and in the middle of the long side Lady Emily was to sit. Behind her chair of faded gilding and faded stamped velvet Clarissa with elegant clever fingers had arranged a great Chinese vase from which branches of beech and the tallest flowers of the garden sprang, so that the birthday seat was almost canopied, and other great vases were

placed against the white panelling with its faded golden decorations. Above Lady Emily's chair a large round gilded mirror
with every proper apanage of gilded balls and carved branches
dripping with lustres, the whole surmounted by an eagle from
whose beak golden festoons draped the tarnished convex glass,
gave a Shalott mirage of the green world outside. Old Bertha
had taken the curtains of India muslin from the chest where they
were stored, and through them the light was filtered so that the
glare of the early afternoon, for it was only half past two by the
real time, should not weary the eyes of the feasters.

Agnes and her sister-in-law Rose, who had been helping
Siddon to arrange the tables, were taking a last look to see that
nothing was wanting to the comfort of Lady Emily or the
guests, while Sylvia and Emmy made themselves responsible for
herding any stray revellers back from farm and field to the feast.

"Where is David? said Agnes. "I haven't seen him since
lunch."

Rose said he had started with Lord Pomfret and Mr. Macpherson and was going on to the vicarage.

"How very peculiar," said Agnes. "Darling David used to go
to the vicarage to be coached in Latin when Mr. Banister was
here, but I really do not know why he has gone today. He was
confirmed at school."

Rose, in her careless husky voice, said it wasn't confirmation,
it was christening.

Agnes said you simply could not be christened twice. Not
even the Bishop, she said, would think of such a thing.

"Oh, not himself," said Rose, casting a swift glance of extremely affectionate toleration at her sister-in-law. "He wants to
have Henry christened here. Dodo was christened in London,
though somehow one never feels that a London christening is
quite legal."

Agnes, considering the question as deeply as her nature
allowed, said she quite felt what Rose meant, and though she

always went to church at Holdings, she never quite felt that churches in London were the same, except of course the Abbey, only you couldn't quite call that a *church*.

"I know," said Rose sympathetically. "But a wedding seems all right. I mean wherever you are married it seems like a church. I suppose christening depends more on who christens you. If the Bishop," said Rose, who though born and bred in the Shires had adopted Barsetshire with passionate loyalty, "dared to christen one's baby, one would feel quite sure that something would go wrong."

"Like a wicked fairy at a princess's christening," said Agnes, with a rare flight of imagination.

"On the other hand," said Rose, "Hermione had her third baby christened somewhere on the south side of the Thames, most peculiar, but it was a Wren church and the vicar gets on well with babies. Hermione's girl talked at the top of her voice all through the service and the vicar seemed to understand what she was saying. But she is going to have the new one done at Tadcaster, because Tadpole's cousin has got a living near there."

Agnes, who was not much interested in Rose's sister, Lady Tadpole, and even less in her extraordinarily worthy husband, Lord Tadpole, returned with the persistence of a gentle nature to the question of Henry's christening.

"I think darling David is *quite* right," she said, "because Henry is called after papa, and none of the other grandchildren are. I cannot think why none of our boys were called after papa. James was called after my father-in-law of course and John after darling John and Robert of course after Robert. And the girls being girls one couldn't call them Henry."

As this mild thought seemed to distress her, if her mild dejection can be given so positive a name, Rose forbore to suggest that Henrietta would have done and put her arm affectionately round Agnes as they stepped out of one of the great sash windows, opened to allow guests to go in and out, and they stood together on the little flight of stone steps watching the company gather. David came round the corner of the house with the vicar and joined them.

"This is indeed a sight," said the vicar to Agnes, whom he adored in a highly respectable and clerical way.

"Like the animals coming into the ark," said David.

The vicar looked pained. Not that he objected for himself, for he kept, or always said he did, an open mind in all things that were Cæsar's, though neither he nor anybody else quite knew what this included, nor who Cæsar was. But he had an instinctive feeling that one so exquisite as Lady Graham should be protected against the rough world and careless talk.

Agnes, who combined her great sweetness and understanding with a healthy insensitiveness to some of the finer shades, said how that would amuse mamma and went off to see if that lady was ready for tea.

"It's all right, Rose," said David. "Bostock is going to take Henry on. We saved him up specially for you, Bostock."

The vicar, whose eyes and thoughts had followed Lady Graham, started nervously and said it was a privilege. He had never, he said, had the privilege of knowing Mr. Leslie, but he felt that to receive a grandson of Mr. Leslie's, and he added a son of David and Mrs. David Leslie, would be a privilege which would be indeed a—and such is the addling effect of love in its higher forms as exemplified in the vicar's feelings for Lady Graham that he nearly said privilege for the fourth time and hastily substituted the word "gratification."

"One doesn't often hear that word," said David. "It sounds a bit like a tip. In Scotland a mortification doesn't mean your sore toe going bad like Tom Sawyer but giving something to the church. How delightful words are!"

The vicar said indeed they were.

Clarissa then appeared, carrying a number of daisy-chains and not only necklets of daisies but of whatever flowers she could find with stems splittable by the human thumbnail.

"Soft you now, the fair Ophelia," said David.

"I've really not seen you properly yet," said Clarissa, giving her uncle a perfunctory but not unaffectionate embrace. "Nor Rose," whom she kissed with loving elegance. "First you were late and then I was looking after Gran and then I was watching the boys clean the pond. Where have you been?"

"Rose has been listening to Agnes cooing," said David, "and I have been in the vestry with Bostock. We are going to have Henry christened in Rushwater Church. Will you be godmother, Clarissa?"

"We would love it," said Rose in her low charming voice.

Clarissa, the sophisticated woman of the world, the holder of a mathematical scholarship, the future employee of Mr. Adams, was for a moment so overcome that she could only gape like a school-girl. Then she collected herself, laid her flower-chains on a chair, kissed her uncle and her aunt by marriage very lovingly, and expressed her delight.

"And I am *hideously* sorry I was rude to you, Uncle David, the summer you and Rose were engaged," she added.

Rose laughed.

"You were very good for David," she said. "He needed setting down."

"But I didn't need a chit like Clarissa drawing attention to the bald place on the top of my head," said David. "The result is that it has spread."

"Let me see," said Clarissa, and lightly perched on the stone balustrade.

"Yes, you have to brush your hairs across carefully now," she said rather sadly, and as she said these words Emmy came up.

"Hullo, is Uncle David getting bald? Cadet Roussel a trois cheveux, Deux sur la face, un sur la queue," said Emmy, who from long conversations with her grandmother's maid Conque was well up in literature. "Where's Gran? Everyone's coming in now."

And all the family and the less close relations came in from the garden or through the house and Sylvia and Emmy ushered them to their places, which had all been planned beforehand. There was a good deal of well-bred noise, discussion, and laughter. Clarissa, deliberately self-conscious but none the less elegant, walked round the tables, slightly embarrassing various guests by throwing her flower-chains about their necks. When she came to Captain Belton she hesitated. He was for the moment the subject of such of her maidenly reveries as were not concerned with an engineering career or, within the last quarter of an hour, the grown-upness of being a godmother. That he was more than twice her age did not occur to her, nor would it have troubled her, for fiction holds precedents for such attachments. Even Marianne Dashwood, for all her sensibility, settled down happily with Colonel Brandon, who was by the way no connection at all of the Barsetshire Brandons. He had been sympathetic about her wish to meet Mr. Adams, and if he had not exactly effected the introduction himself, his mother had done so, which was the next best thing. Clarissa liked his manner, his sailor's distant blue eyes, his face, the comfortable feeling of his coat sleeve as she hung on his arm, and as she had not as yet the faintest idea of what being in love meant, she found this kind of affection highly satisfactory. So as she passed behind his chair she put a wreath of clover flowers round his neck.

Captain Belton looked up, startled and conscious of looking an ass.

"What on earth are you doing, Clarissa?" he said. "This isn't Hawaii."

At these words Clarissa's heart broke. Or to put it more truthfully she suddenly realized that Freddy was not the companion she had thought but, awful discovery, a grown-up. A gulf was suddenly between them and Clarissa had no intention of leaping into it.

"Oh, don't you like it?" she said. "It was just for Gran's

birthday. Too too childish of course, but simply for fun. Uncle David adores wreaths, don't you, darling?"

David looked round at his niece. He remembered and she remembered, and each knew the other remembered the day two summers ago when he had teased Clarissa and Anne Fielding from sheer idleness and Clarissa, dropping a daisy-chain over his head, had deliberately commented on his thinning hair.

"Spitfire!" he said. "Yes, I'll have a wreath. Anything you like, but *not* yellow crown imperials because they smell of foxes."

"So they do," said Mr. Marling, who had overheard these words. "Extraordinary thing it is. I remember Amabel had some in her herbaceous border, and I said to the gardener: 'There's been a fox through here,' but it was those what-do-you-call-'ems. Queer these things are."

"What about me?" said Charles Belton, who being far away from Lady Graham was philosophically eating a large tea and quite ready for amusement.

"It's the last I've got," said Clarissa. "Forget-me-nots," and she put the wreath round Charles's neck and the feel of her cool, elegant fingers as they brushed his ears was far from disagreeable. Then Clarissa, having finished her garland-bearing, squashed a stool in between Charles and Mrs. John Leslie and ate her tea with a very hearty appetite and discussed with Charles the possibility of having a drag with crown imperials, which made them both laugh. And from this they fell into talk about horses and such hunting as the war and the peace had afforded in England or, in Charles's case, in other parts of the world.

Tea, as is well known, is a messier, a crumbier meal than lunch, and of this fact Lady Emily was taking full advantage.

"Siddon," she called to her housekeeper, who was dispensing tea from a table near the door. "Is there a slop-basin?"

"Yes, my lady," said Siddon, and set before her old mistress a delicate china basin with the Pomfret crest in raised gilding upon it. "It's the last of the service his late lordship gave us when your ladyship's father died."

"So it is," said Lady Emily fingering the crest. "Sally darling, you ought to have this. It was made for my great-grandfather by Wedgwood himself. And my great-grandfather was Gillie's great-grandfather, or was it great-great-uncle? Merry, you can tell me when we get back to Holdings. And I *know*," said her ladyship, emptying the dregs of her teacup into the slop-basin and steeping half a scone in it, "that no one has thought of the canaries. Nurse told Ivy, but she always forgets. There always used to be some groundsel in the kitchen garden, which I suppose is a weed and had no business to be there, but they do like it. We will get some after tea. James knows where it is."

Agnes's eldest boy looked up at this mention of his name with his mouth much too full of cake, puzzled but ready to do anything his adored grandmother wished. Before he could bolt what was in his mouth and answer, Lady Pomfret, who had caught a glance from Miss Merriman, thanked Lady Emily for the slop-basin and said she and Gillie would love to have it and so led Lady Emily to talk of the Pomfret Towers of her youth and her sister Agnes, who had died young, and the hunting.

"What canaries does mother mean?" said David Leslie to Miss Merriman in a low voice.

"I think it is the birds they had in the old nurseries the summer Lady Graham and the children were here while Sir Robert was in the Argentine—of course it was Colonel and Mrs. Graham then. There was a very stupid nursery maid called Ivy."

"Good Lord! How the wheel does come full circle!" said David. "Agnes's nurse practically forced Ivy on Rose the moment we were engaged. Anyone would have thought I was marrying Rose to make an honest woman of her. And Ivy is our nannie, but Rose stands for no nonsense."

Miss Merriman, for perhaps the first time in her capable, devoted life, was absolutely taken aback. It is true that she had only seen Rose's nannie in the distance, but that she should have failed to recognize in her the Ivy who had been spoken to, awful words, by Mrs. Siddon for skylarking in the pantry with Walter, the second footman, the Ivy who had cried her face into a kind of swollen red sponge when the cock canary's new wife turned out to be another husband and pecked him to death, this was a severe blow to her quiet self-confidence.

"Do you think mamma will want to go to the nursery and see the canaries?" said David anxiously, but Miss Merriman, resuming her usual poise, said she would manage to head her ladyship off.

"It would be too too Kilmeny, as Clarissa would say," said David, feeling a faint chill at his heart. "I went up to look at the rocking-horse, and everything was dust-sheeted and squeaked and gibbered in the Roman street."

"Mrs. Siddon and Sylvia had to shut the old nurseries," said Miss Merriman. "One can't keep all those rooms on the top floor in use now. Don't worry, David. In any case I think Lady Emily will forget about it," and then Lord Pomfret on the other side claimed her attention and said in his diffident, quiet, tired, kindly way that he believed Sally had been talking with her and that he entirely agreed with Sally and would trust Miss Merriman to let them know if she would like at any future date to come to the Towers.

"Come as an old friend, Merry," said Lord Pomfret. "I have often wished you were there to help me. Rather selfish, for a lot of it is dull grind," he added apologetically.

Miss Merriman, with her usual composure, thanked Lord Pomfret and said that if at any time she was free to help him and Lady Pomfret she would very gladly do so, and then the subject was dropped, not to be mentioned again, only to be remembered in the stilly night.

As always happened in any gathering where Lady Emily was present, a great deal of arranging took place between the powers who were responsible for controlling, so far as anyone could control or even guide, her ladyship's career. Lady Emily had earlier in the day expressed a wish to visit Mr. Macpherson in his own house after tea and to call on every old friend in the cottages of the little village, with such additional interfering and meddling as occurred to her fertile mind. But this would undoubtedly fatigue her extremely and there was the little service to be considered, so with great cunning Sylvia and Agnes had arranged for Mrs. Siddon to ask her ladyship to visit the housekeeper's room, where Mrs. Siddon would get out all her photograph albums and keep Lady Emily's attention till it was time for church.

The Graham and Leslie boys then went off in a band towards the estate sawmill, where Martin said they couldn't come to much harm as he had taken the precaution to lock the cupboard where the switchboard lived that controlled the circular saw, and if they liked to cut up tree-trunks with the big two-handed saw it would be quite useful. The elder relations preferred to stroll or sit in the garden as the heat was so great, so the younger people thought they would walk up to the Temple and look at the view.

To those who knew Rushwater the Temple needs no description. For the benefit of those who have not been there we will describe it briefly. Built of yellowish stone by old Mr. Leslie's grandfather, it stood in a slight depression like a dew pond on the top of a beech-clothed hill, and partook in nature of the pyramid, the pagoda, and the mausoleum. Its lower story was lighted by four enormous heavy sash windows. From the ground floor a wooden ladder staircase led through a trapdoor to the upper chamber whose windows, of semicircular shape, were on the level of the floor, having been designed more with a view to exterior proportion than to any possible convenience for people using it. The walls of this uncomfortable abode sloped inwards and it was crowned by what can only be described as a serrated peak. On the plastered walls of the stifling uncomfortable upper room were the scribblings of may young Leslies, including John Leslie's famous distich on Fräulein Hagenstolz.

"Let's go in and see the murals," said David to his sister-in-law Mrs. John Leslie. "Lord! How beautiful I thought my own picture was! Do you remember it, most romantic?"

Mrs. Leslie said she didn't remember it and would like to see it. Oliver and Lucy Marling accompanied them and greatly admired David's spirited drawing in nursery chalks of a tower with a long-haired princess leaning out of it and a prince riding past. Mrs. John Leslie said it was exactly like an old master.

"And worse you couldn't say, my love," said David. "It all shows how the child is father of the man, or really great-great-great-grandson of course. I drew the picture just as a possible Lorenzo Lorenzi detto Il Lorenzaccio or the Master of the Flower-Pot would have painted it in—well, whenever people with names like that did paint pictures like that. They had just discovered perspective and couldn't think of anything else. Look at the tower and the stones. I believe my vanishing-point is still there," and he pointed to a small cross on the wall which represented the height of the young David's eye and the point at which all parallel lines would theoretically meet.

Oliver Marling said there was something to be said for the Chinese, who always painted cubes getting larger at the far end if David saw what he meant.

"I'll tell you what," said Lucy, who had been bringing her intellect to bear on the subject. "It isn't an old master, it's an illuminated manuscript. I mean the way six people's faces all rather crooked look out of the window when even one of them couldn't possibly have got into the room in psalters and things."

She looked round for approval.

"You are perfectly right," said David. "The princess's head is at the window, or rather it fills up the whole window, but she obviously can't have a body at all as there wouldn't be room for it in the tower."

Oliver Marling said if not taking the trouble to see what things were really like and then painting them all wrong was a mark of an illuminator or an old master, the world was quite full of them at the present moment, but no one heard what he said because David and Mrs. John Leslie were admiring the very poor chalk drawing of Clarissa in her perambulator done by James at a tender age.

As so often happened when Leslies got together, the family circle seemed to close. Nothing was further from David and Mary's mind than to exclude the Marlings, but their sense of family and of the past had got the better of them. Mary was not a born Leslie, but she had married a Leslie, was the mother of three Leslie children and a niece of Agnes's husband, and her short happy romance with John Leslie had been born and come to flower at Rushwater, in a summer as warm and as golden as this, but long before the days of desolation. So she and David went from picture to picture, exclaiming, remembering, making plans for Leslies still in their perambulators to add their handiwork; and the Marlings felt that they were excluded. Not by an angel with a flaming sword, or by any discourtesy, but simply because they were not of the family and had not the past in common. So they went down the ladder staircase and out into the sunshine, perhaps also relieved to be out of the upper room, to which fresh air had never penetrated except by the trapdoor since it was built, and what air there was so full of dust and plaster that one could hardly breathe, though Leslies were apparently immune to its effects.

"Let's look at the back," said Lucy, so they walked round into the shade on the far side of the Temple where on the ground were a ladder and some pieces of rope, probably left by workmen, for Martin had had the Temple carefully repaired since the war and all cracks in the masonry made good. A slight scuffling noise from among the rhododendrons that edged the dell or cup in which the Temple stood attracted their attention, and Leslie minimus came cautiously out of the bushes.

"Oh, sir," he said, recognizing in Oliver someone in authority and managing to convey a kind of courteous non-recognition of Lucy as not being really there, "could you be awfully kind and go away? It's something rather important we're doing and it's a secret."

Oliver, amused by the youngest Leslie's mixture of deference and firmness, said he and his sister were only walking round the Temple to see what it was like and were at that moment going away.

"Oh, thanks *awfully*, sir," said Leslie minimus, who had exchanged a hurried whisper with unseen allies lurking in the rhododendrons. "And if you see Uncle Martin or Aunt Sylvia, please could you explain that we are doing something in the wood," and he waved his hand towards the beeches which crowded upon the rhododendrons and covered the top of the rising ground. "And we'll be back in time for Mr. Bostock's service, sir, word of a Leslie."

"All right," said Oliver, rather wishing he were young enough to be a conspirator, or a Red Indian, or a commando, or whatever it was the boys were being at the moment. Strange creatures, boys. Queer agreeable animals hiding their enthusiasms under an air of ancient wisdom, critically kind, agreeably aloof, living private lives in the public eye, indifferent to dirt on the neck or hands, much concerned with a tie or a scarf. He and Lucy finished their circuit of the Temple and emerged into the hot sunshine in front where the Belton brothers were talking to Sylvia and Emmy, while Clarissa talked to Rose, for the two in spite of the difference in their ages had been great friends as well as affectionate cousins since the summer when David had deliberately tried to provoke Clarissa, and Clarissa had been extremely impolite to her Uncle David, and Rose after admonishing them both had married David out of hand and so kept him out of mischief for ever.

On seeing Lucy, Emmy hastened to secure her as a potential ally in an argument she was having with Captain Belton about the use of artificial fertilizers.

"Freddy says his father uses Holman's Phospho-Manuro," said Emmy, who though, as we have before mentioned, in a silk dress and wearing stockings appeared to her audience's mind's eye to be in breeches and leggings, wearing a smock and chewing a straw, so strong was her personal atmosphere or aura. "But Martin and Macpherson like Corbett's Bono-Vitasang."

"I'll tell you what," said Lucy, also by field-magic giving the impression that she was in full land-girl's outfit, "have you much chalk on your place? We're one mass of it being so near the downs, and father's tried everything. We did get some really good dung, all rich and full of straw, when the Barsetshires were in camp in Nutfield," said Lucy, her eyes gleaming at the thought of real horse-manure, "but the peace spoilt all that. Father thinks Washington's Vimphos or Phosvim—I can't ever remember the name—is best."

"We've some chalk on the hills, but the sheep manage that for us," said Emmy. "It's the arable we were wondering about. I say, we haven't time now, but when Mr. Bostock has finished his service come and have a look at the seven-acre field. You want to *feel* soil," and Emmy to illustrate her words picked up some loose earth and crumbled it in a knowing way between her forefinger and her thumb, having done which she wiped her hand on the side of her frock.

"Oh, Emmy," said Rose and Clarissa with one breath.

"What's the matter?" said Emmy. "Oh, bother this frock. I knew something would happen if I put it on."

And then she and Lucy resumed their fascinating, useful, practical talk about soils and artificial fertilizers, and from time to time Lucy looked in Captain Belton's direction, rather hoping he would be impressed, not, alas, realizing that his interest in fertilizers was slight and indeed mostly assumed to please his father, and that if he succeeded to Harefield and could afford to farm some of it, he would certainly take advice from the bailiff. For however long you may have ploughed the wine-dark ocean, the experience does not really help you to speed the plough on dry land.

Then David with Mary Leslie came out of the Temple.

"Hail, calm acclivity, salubrious spot!" said David. "What I mean to say is that this is like a cool hand on a fevered brow after an hour in the Temple. I now know exactly what Casanova felt like under the Leads."

"I thought he was on the tiles," said Charles and felt he had perhaps been too coarse, but as Rose and Clarissa both seemed amused, he was reassured and thought it was clever of little Clarissa to take his meaning.

"The extraordinary noises in there," said Mary Leslie. "I think there must be a jackdaw's nest in the pyramid part. Scratchings and bits of mortar or something falling."

Oliver and Lucy did not look at each other, but each knew that the other was full of suspicion. The sudden appearance of Leslie minimus from the undergrowth, the certainty that his elder brother and his Leslie cousins were also in hiding, the ladder, the pieces of rope; the puzzle jumped together complete in his mind. Of course those boys were going to climb the pyramid roof of the Temple and the young devils had sworn him to secrecy with their host and hostess. Luckily Martin was not there, but Sylvia was, and Oliver had to make up his mind quickly whether death for the Leslie boys or dishonour for himself came first. Not that they were likely to kill themselves, because boys rarely did, but if they were climbing and one of them did break a leg or sprain a wrist, it would certainly be discovered that he had known what they were going to do and Sylvia and Martin would not be grateful to him for holding his tongue.

Most of us would have split on the conspirators at once, but

Oliver, reserved and diffident by nature, was paralysed, hoping
as we all do when in mental or moral difficulties that things will
be all right on the night. Those very words did indeed come into
Oliver's head and further confused the issues for him by making
him think of Jessica Dean and how he had supped with her
more than once in her flat and would sup with her again. And
even as this celestial vision floated into his mind, an arm and a
leg became distinctly visible near the peak of the pyramid, and it
was too late.

"Damn those boys of John's, I'm sorry, Mary," said David.
"Did anyone say they could do that?"

"No. John told them not to and so did Martin," said Mary
Leslie, growing pale. "I'm sure they're all right, David,"
she added, her natural gentle politeness making her wish
to spare David any anxiety, "but I do wish to *goodness* they
wouldn't."

The grown-ups, not knowing whether to shout at the climber
would make him lose his balance and fall into a crevasse so that
they would have to wait a hundred years or so at the foot of a
glacier till he emerged, a horrid example of the preservative
qualities of ice, or on the contrary would dissuade him from
going any farther, stood irresolute.

> Yet I,
> A dull and muddy-mettled rascal, peak
> Like John-a-dreams, unpregnant of my cause,
> And can say nothing,"

said Oliver half-aloud to himself, which being overheard by
Clarissa caused her to say also half-aloud but with every intention of being heard: "Too, too helpful, my dear."

Leslie minor, for the arm and leg were now identifiable as his,
now appeared in full view, working his way via the stone
crockets, if that is the correct term, on the angles of the pyramid
to the peak, so all remonstrances were useless.

"Don't say anything," said Captain Belton quietly. "The boy seems to have a good head."

"He has," said his mother gratefully, though not without anxiety in her voice. "He climbed all round the roof of the school chapel and up the spire. But it was an iron spire, and this stone is rather crumbly."

Leslie minor, comfortably established with his legs twisted round the peak, bowed slightly to the audience and announced that this was the Rushwater Home Service speaking and he had got to the top of the pyramid and taken possession of it in the name of His Majesty King George the Sixth. He then produced a small Union Jack, tied it to the highest crocket, bowed to the onlookers, and prepared to descend. Suddenly his face changed.

"Get down, you young fool!" he shouted. "Hi! James! Get hold of his blasted legs."

Mary Leslie and Captain Belton ran round to the back of the Temple. Leslie minimus, against his elder brother's orders, was evidently trying to follow him, but to be a good runner and boxer and cricketer does not imply a mountaineer's head, and half-way up his nerve had failed and he was on the verge of tears and obviously ready to fall off at any moment. Captain Belton pushed the other boys unceremoniously aside, went up the ladder by which they had scaled the lower stories of the Temple, tested the stone-work, mounted a few feet, and seized the gibbering Leslie minimus by the top of his grey flannel knickerbockers.

"Now let go with your hands and come down quietly," said Captain Belton, thinking with some amusement that he sounded more like a policeman arresting Larry the Cosher than a naval gentleman getting an idiot schoolboy out of a scrape.

With the reassuring feel of a strong steady hand in the small of his back, Leslie minimus reached the top of the ladder and came down it under the convoy. His mother, distracted between anger and relief, was ready to box his ears or embrace him, preferably both as a vent for her feelings, but Captain Belton took command with the authority of the quarter-deck.

"Did your father and your uncle forbid you to climb that thing?" he said to Leslie minor.

The natural attitude for a schoolboy in such circumstances would be to assume an air of injured innocence which could deceive nobody and by saying: "*Forbid* me, sir?" or "Did you mean the *Temple*, sir?" do his best to confuse the issue. But before Captain Belton's blue, far-seeing eyes Leslie minor felt that subterfuge would be useless and with diabolical simplicity said: "Yes, sir," thus forcing his opponent to make the next move.

"Well, why the dickens did you disobey them?" said Captain Belton. "You have frightened your mother. Your younger brother might have broken his leg or his neck."

"I don't know, sir," said Leslie minor. "At least it was really because I wanted to boast about it. Uncle Martin said he had tried when he was young and he fell off and sprained his wrist, so I thought if I could get up, it would be one better than Uncle Martin. And I did claim it for King George," he added, suddenly standing to attention with so military an air that the onlookers half expected to see a life-size Union Jack broken on the top of the pyramid and hear a brass band play *God Save the King*.

"Martin will be very angry," said Mary Leslie.

"Now," said Captain Belton to Leslie minor, "I am going to give the sentence. Not one of you boys is to speak about this today. But before you go back to school next term you are to tell your uncle and apologize. And now," he added to a rather chastened Leslie minor, "go up and take that flag down. It's perfectly all right," he said to Mary Leslie, who wished the Temple five hundred feet under the ground. "That boy of yours has a good head. He ought to have sailed with Nelson as a midshipman," which tribute to what is really only an accident of nature made Mary so proud that she battened down her fears while Leslie minor climbed the pyramid, took down the flag, and returned safely to earth.

"And now," said Captain Belton to the boys, "put the ladder and the ropes back where they came from, the carpenter's shop I suppose. And no one here," he added, looking round at the company, "will mention what has happened. It might spoil Lady Emily's birthday. Off you go."

The conspirators took their scaling ladder and rope and went away down the hill. Clarissa put her arm through Captain Belton's as she had done on the return from the kitchen garden.

"You managed marvellously," she said. "Too, too Nelson. Those boys are such babies. Martin will be *livid*. What fun!"

But this time Clarissa had gone too far. Captain Belton disengaged his arm without ceremony from her embrace, saying curtly that if no one told Martin, he need not know, while Sylvia, always watchful for anything that might make Martin's leg begin to ache, said, quite angrily for her, that if Martin came to hear of Leslie minor's escapade she would know who had told him and shake her, while even Rose, Clarissa's firm ally in the past against MEN, said in her attractive husky voice, quite dispassionately, that what Clarissa needed was to go back to school and learn to behave.

"Let us go down," said Captain Belton to Mary Leslie, who gratefully accompanied him. David followed with Sylvia and Emmy, planning to make sure as far as possible that Martin should not hear of the escapade till later, nor Lady Emily's birthday be marred in any way. Oliver and Lucy, who not being quite family were rather out of it, went down the winding paths among the beech trees together. It occurred to Oliver that he had often been alone with Lucy even when other people were there, friendly people. Was it a sign that they were to make up to each other in some way for a part of life that neither of them had explored? Perhaps they would be in the end like old Mr. Thorne of Ullathorne and his spinster sister Monica, who had lived together in amity for all their lives and whose names were still mentioned by old people near Ullathorne, though most of their land was now red-brick villas and corporation dumps. He thought how hard Lucy had worked during the war, how uncomplainingly, how her whole life had been devoted to Marling. He had worked too, but in Barchester at the Regional Commissioner's office, where one met people and heard news. Then when the war ended he had escaped to London and taken up his old work, while Lucy remained a serf as it were, adscripta glebæ, a phrase echoing through his mind. What would the end be? And then, as we are all naturally selfish, the thought of London sent his mind flying to Jessica Dean. And Jessica Dean was to have a holiday at Winter Overcotes before her autumn season began, and perhaps there, away from the distraction of London, the ceaseless coming and going and telephoning, she might hear what his fond heart would say. So they accomplished their descent in silence, but Lucy did not mind nor indeed notice, for she had had a beautiful thought. She would get the bailiff to send some of her father's favourite artificial fertilizer to Captain Belton at Harefield, who would then try it on the estate, after which they would have a really good talk about it. And it must be said in justice to Lucy that though a dialogue on manure with Captain Belton seemed to her very desirable, it was as much from a scientific farming point of view as anything, for of arts to catch men she knew little and thought less, having no opinion at all of people who went mooning about when there were potatoes to be lifted or swedes to be stacked. Oliver knew this side of his sister and sometimes wished it were otherwise, for he could have said, as Noel Merton had said years ago of Miss Lydia Keith, that she was so unacquainted with men that her tameness was occasionally quite shocking to him. Then his thoughts returned to Jessica and they came out of the beechen shade into the sunlight.

But who can describe Clarissa's feelings when that pretty, precocious spoilt child suddenly found herself in disgrace, neglected by the grown-ups, almost sent to Coventry even by Rose, who had supported her against David through thick and thin two summers ago. Tears leapt to her eyes, stinging her with their salt. Angrily she brushed them away with her hand and then sniffed loudly.

"What on earth's the matter?" said Charles Belton. "I say, hadn't we better shut the Temple? Tramps or somebody might get in and burn it down."

"I wish they would," said Clarissa. "I hate the Temple and I hate everybody and I wish they were dead."

"Well, let's shut the Temple first," said Charles, whom his army experience had inured to different manifestations of shellshock. He went across the grass, Clarissa following him, entered the Temple, and pulled down the heavy sash windows and bolted them.

"There," he said. "Now we can shut up."

But Clarissa, seating herself on a dusty box with a dusty set of quoits in it, relic of some bygone age, set herself to cry with a perseverance worthy of a better cause.

"I say, don't," said Charles. "After all, it s your own fault, you know."

Clarissa, at once adoring the hand that struck her, stopped crying.

"Now look here," said Charles, just as he might have said it to young Dean, or Pickering, or Addison, "you aren't playing the game. You know it's your grandmother's birthday and your uncle has a gammy leg and then that young idiot cousin of yours had to show off on the roof, and all you did was to say it would be fun when Martin heard about it. If he hears today his leg will ache frightfully and your grandmother will probably have a stroke. Just think that over."

"Was I really as awful as that?" said Clarissa, beginning to fancy herself in the role of home-wrecker.

"You were," said Charles. "Here, have my handkerchief. That's better. Now, give me your word of honour, and we'll forget it. Sylvia will tell Martin when the party is over I expect."

"Word of honour," said Clarissa meekly.

"And one thing more," said Charles, "don't be rude to Freddy. He's worth ten of you and me. Now that's all. Come on."

They went out of the Temple and Charles locked the door and put the key in his pocket.

"Rum you girls are," said Charles looking at Clarissa. "One minute you're howling, another you look as if nothing had happened. Now come on. We mustn't be late for the service," for the bell of Rushwater Church was sounding, like an older and wiser sheep-bell, through the gardens and fields and woods.

So they also went down the shady winding paths under the beech trees and though Clarissa hung heavily and affectionately on Charles's arm, as earlier in the day she had hung on his elder brother's, Charles seemed to find it quite agreeable.

Meanwhile the company had been filtering into the church, where Charles and Clarissa joined them. At the back was Mrs. Siddon with Bertha, the old housemaid, the rest of the little staff, and a few old farm-hands. The cottagers were also there, from Davida and Davidette, the twins at Hacker's End, to old Cruncher at Hacker's Corner who had never been to church in his disgraceful life since he was married there some sixty-five years previously.

"A very good show," said Sylvia in a low voice to David. "The cowman isn't here though. He wanted to lead Rushwater Churchill into the churchyard as a tribute to Aunt Emily, but Martin thought it might frighten him, the bull I mean, so the cowman is sulking. I think everyone else is here," and her practised eye, the eye of the squire's wife who came herself from a long line of squires and knew everybody and exercised firm impartial benevolence and stood no nonsense, looked on the congregation and approved.

"I often wished I could sulk in the cowshed myself on Sunday morning when I was little," said David. "Still, church was fun once one got there. Lord! how my darling mamma used to fuss and meddle!" he added irreverently. "When I was confirmed she got the Bishop, I mean Uncle Archie, not that old Puss-in-gaiters at the Palace, to do it here and afterwards she had a kind of reception in the chancel and she sent for a book about Lord Palmerston that she thought Uncle Archie would like to see and Conque wouldn't bring it into the church because she said 'L'église de miladi n'est rien moins qu'un temple et le révérend père Ossquince m'en dira des nouvelles si j'y mets le pied.' Father Hodgkins was the R.C. padre where she went and a jolly good sort and of course Conque made it all up about not putting foot inside the church. So Walter, who was the second footman then, had to take it from Conque at the church door. Here she is, bless her."

The little congregation fell silent and rose to their feet as Lady Emily on Martin's arm and leaning on her ebony stick entered the church, followed by Agnes and Miss Merriman, who were in a state of lively apprehension as to what her ladyship might be up to. But for once Lady Emily's eager spirit was in repose and she allowed herself to be shepherded with loving care into the front pew, where she had worshipped by her husband for so many years and from which, we may add, she had so often sorely distracted the worshippers. Here John and David were waiting for her. Agnes followed, and Martin, only child of her first-born and now the head of the Leslie family, took the seat next to the aisle. Mr. Bostock, having seen from the vestry that her ladyship was at last established with all her impedimenta disposed according to her wishes, Agnes at hand and Miss Merriman in the pew behind to aid or check Lady Emily in any further disarrangements she proposed to make, now entered the church.

When the idea of a family service to give thanks for Lady Emily's birthday had first been put forward, her ladyship had expressed a strong desire to compose its order herself and her son David said he would not be in the least surprised if his respected mamma insisted on turning up in a gown and Geneva bands, whatever they were, and preaching from the pulpit. Mr. Bostock had been very willing to co-operate, but as the form of service adumbrated by Lady Emily was made up largely of extracts from a commonplace book kept by her over a number of years in her beautiful flowing writing and in a state of hopeless muddle with letters, pressed flowers, pieces of ribbon, and water-coloured drawings all put between the leaves and falling out of them, and was gradually extending its scope to include the whole of Wordsworth's "Ode on Intimations of Immortality," Lady Graham had taken counsel with Mr. Bostock, who had agreed to all Lady Emily's plans and then quietly put together a short service of praise and thanksgiving most suitable to the occasion. In earlier days Lady Emily might have insisted on her own irresponsible wilful way, but within the last year she had given up many of her activities and was coming to accept the life of old age. And though Agnes and Miss Merriman sometimes felt a pang at her acceptance, they were thankful that she was at last sparing herself and allowing them to do what they could for her.

The tablet to the memory of her husband was upon the wall of the chancel arch, opposite the family pew, and upon it Lady Emily's eyes were fixed while Mr. Bostock led the little congregation in prayer and thanksgiving. A hymn was now to be sung.

"David," said Lady Emily, who had so far given in to her family as not to try to kneel during the prayers.

David looked down at his mother, thinking even as he said: "Yes, mamma darling," how strangely small one's elders can become, how their bones seem to become less. For many years he could only remember his father as a tall, fresh-faced, heavy-built man, active in all he did, a Samson of strength in the eyes of a little boy and a growing boy. But after the war had begun and Agnes had insisted on her father and mother being under her wing at Holdings, what a frail old man his father had seemed! He remembered laying his hand once on his father's shoulder, and the bones beneath felt like the bones of a bird, so thin and brittle. Now these bones were dust. And his mother in her turn had diminished. Partly the arthritis which had cruelly crippled her, also the flight of time. But there hung about her a mother-of-pearl sheen of past beauty and her dark eyes still gleamed like a falcon's, though the arm that one took under one's own to help her up or down a step felt so thin, so hollow.

"Yes, mamma darling?" he said.

"Your father," said Lady Emily with a loving gesture towards the tablet as if Mr. Leslie were in residence behind it, "could *never* find the lessons. Holden always marked them for him and I remember one Sunday after you had had whooping-cough Holden was away for a week and your father was very much put out. Mr. Banister was the vicar then and went everywhere on his bicycle and he had to come and find the lessons for your father."

David nearly said: "On his bicycle?" but pulled himself up in time.

"No one knows how to find the lessons," he said. "One is supposed to find out at the beginning of the Prayer Book with Golden Numbers, such a lovely name, but it is really logarithms in disguise."

Mr. Bostock, who thought her ladyship had had enough rope, now brought the short service to an end, blessing the little assembly and those whose spirits were, he reverently hoped and believed, somewhere about at the moment, though he was unequal to deciding where. There was a silence so deep, so peaceful that even Lady Emily was stilled. Then her ebony stick fell with a clatter on the stone floor, her bag slipped from her lap, and her scarves began almost to writhe in confusion like the Lady of Shalott's web.

"Now," said Lady Emily, rising with David's help while Agnes and John collected her belongings, "we must go into the vestry and kiss John and Gay."

Luckily only David and Agnes heard, so no one else knew that her mind had gone back to John's wedding so many years ago and not in this church. Gay, John's childhood friend, his young love, his adored wife, had melted from his thoughts, a blissful gentle shade, long, long ago and his life with Mary had been quiet complete happiness. If he had heard his mother's mistake it would not have hurt him, except for a fear that she might notice it herself.

"I think not, mamma darling," said Agnes with great presence of mind. "John and Mary have got to get home and take the boys with them. Shall we go and see papa's grave, mamma?"

His sister Agnes, David reflected, might be an angelic idiot, but to idiots there are sometimes vouchsafed moments of unusual sense, and Agnes had struck exactly the right chord. Lady Emily at once embraced the suggestion, and a general move was made into the open air and sunshine. On its south side the little churchyard was embanked above the Rushmere Brook, now if the truth must be told rather smelly owing to the prolonged drought, but even more attractive than usual to the young of the village owing to the flotsam and jetsam of old tins, broken boots, bottles, and even an occasional cat, left high and dry upon the little pebble ridges among which the trickle of water meandered towards the Rising. Here was the Leslie burying plot, surrounded by a sweetbrier hedge in which the original hideous railings were quite buried and lost, and here Lady Emily stood, and pinched a brier leaf and rubbed it between her thumb and forefinger and smelt the fragrance. Sylvia, watchful always of Martin's leg, had quietly asked John to take his place and give his arm to his mother, and Martin was glad to sit on the low churchyard wall that overlooked the lane and rest.

"Dear Aunt Emily, we must go," said Lady Pomfret. "What a lovely birthday, and thank you so much for it," and then Lord Pomfret made his farewells and said he hoped Lady Emily would be able to visit the Towers before the end of the fine weather.

Lady Emily shook her head, and the old mischievous smile flashed out.

"I don't think I shall see the Towers again in this life, Gillie" she said, "and certainly not in the next, except that there is always a hope, because when we don't know what a place is going to be like it is no good thinking about it beforehand, for it is always *quite* different. But I *would* like to see papa again."

Her ladyship spoke these last words a little wistfully, and as no one was quite sure whether she wished to see the sixth Earl of Pomfret at the Towers or in another world, Lady Pomfret thought it best to kiss her and take Lord Pomfret away.

"Thank you for a delightful day," she said to Sylvia. "Does Martin ever feel quite fit?"

"Never," said Sylvia. "I suppose Gillie doesn't either?"

"Never," said Lady Pomfret. "Thank goodness you and I can bear some of their burdens," to which Sylvia answered gracefully and truly that Martin's burdens were as nothing compared with Lord Pomfret's, who had to go to London to the House of Lords as well as everything else. Then Lady Pomfret said she was sure Sylvia's nurse was sick of Mellings and Emily and Giles and took her tired, good, conscientious husband away.

"And now, Mr. Bostock," said Lady Emily with one of her most brilliant smiles, "you must be absolutely worn out. And I cannot tell you how beautiful the service was and how we all loved it. When David and Agnes were small I used to take them to Mr. Banister's afternoon service for children and David had a pencil and some paper to keep him quiet but he drew so *loudly* that Mr. Banister had to ask him to stop. You are at the vicarage too, aren't you? I am sure you and Mr. Banister get on excellently, for he was always kind about coaching the boys in the summer holidays." David, who had heard what his mother said, was standing by to rescue Mr. Bostock if need be, but the vicar had sympathetically realized the confusion of time in Lady Emily's mind and said he liked Mr. Banister very much and believed he was a canon now.

"Then he will have to live in the close," said Lady Emily. "Wasn't old Canon Robarts's house vacant, David? It would be rather large for you, Mr. Banister, but you could shut up the top floor. Canon Robarts had six maids and they all slept in one room, and the others were full of books. Did someone tell me that, David, or do I remember it?"

David had most luckily been with his mother on her last visit to the close and was able to remind his mother that the house belonged to the Fieldings now and that Lady Fielding had taken her over the house.

"Of *course*," said Lady Emily, unpinning a long lace scarf and getting its ends well entangled in the sweetbrier hedge. "And there was that pretty, quiet Anne Fielding and she is married to Robin Dale now. I remember Robin's mother. She died quite young. A lovely creature. Well, Mr. Bostock," said Lady Emily, giving the vicar his own name this time and speaking in a very business-like way, "I am *sure* Dr. Crawley will find something for you. And thank you again with all my heart."

Mr. Bostock, who had earned the eternal gratitude and respect of Lady Emily's children for taking her in his stride as it were with such simplicity and kindness, bowed over her thin jewelled hand and respectfully paid his farewell, asking for her to be blessed.

"I do wish," said Agnes to Miss Merriman, "that mamma would be a little tired. She is so well this afternoon, but if we don't get her home to rest I am sure she will feel it tomorrow. Perhaps David can make her come back to the house."

So happy was Lady Emily at her husband's grave, the sweet-brier perfuming the warm air, all her family about her, that it seemed to Miss Merriman that nothing short of physical force would move her ladyship, when suddenly a terrific bellow rent the air.

"Oh, DAMN old Herdman," said Martin from the low wall above the lane. "He's brought Rushwater Churchill."

All eyes were now turned towards the lane outside the church where the old cowman was holding at the end of a stick what looked like five or six hundred cubic tons of bull with a ring in his nose. Lady Emily with unflagging interest began to limp on her ebony stick towards the low churchyard wall and John came to her side and gave her his arm.

"I thought you'd come, your ladyship," said old Herdman, looking malignly at Martin and Sylvia. "Mr. Leslie he'd have liked him, my lady. Just look at him. He's the best we've had at Rushwater since Master Henry's grandfather had Rushwater Ramper. There's a bull for you."

Lady Emily, to whom it seemed perfectly natural that Herdman should speak of her late husband as Mr. Leslie and Master Henry in one breath, expressed deep admiration of the bull and asked if he had been shown.

"Not yet, my lady. If them meddling old devils up in London, begging your ladyship's pardon," said Herdman, alluding to His Majesty's present Government, "let us have the Bath and West Show going again, then old Churchill he'll beat the lot."

"Well, I am very glad to see you, Herdman," said Lady Emily, "and I must tell Mr. Leslie all about the bull," and she stretched her thin jewelled hand across the wall. After a moment's hesitation Herdman rubbed his right hand on his trouser leg and shyly shook hands. Then with a last defiant look at his employer he led Rushwater Churchill away and the whole company began to move towards the house, whence they could disperse to their homes. The Beltons and the Marlings were the next to go, feeling that the field should be left clear for the immediate family. It was now too late for Lucy to make a tour of the estate, but she made a plan with Emmy for visit and counter-visit and a really good talk about artificial fertilizers and so went away not ill-content with her day. As she talked about fertilizers the whole way, Oliver was able to think of seeing Jessica at Winter Overcotes before long and how she was quite different from all other actresses; in which he was perhaps right, though not as he meant it. And if Lucy talked a little louder and little longer than usual to drown the memory of Clarissa's arm linked in Captain Belton's, no one was the wiser.

Lady Emily's family were now assembled in the drawing-room. The trestle tables had been removed and the big armchair with its faded velvet and tarnished gilding placed near the window, and here Lady Emily sat enthroned to receive the farewell homage of her descendants, looking extremely well and ready to interfere to any extent in any plans made for her benefit. David, who was her favourite child so far as her generous overflowing love could have a favourite, was telling her how he and Rose were going to the United States to see old friends, among them Martin's mother and her American husband and Martin's half-brother and sister.

"Then your babies must come here," said Lady Emily triumphantly. "The nurseries can be ready for them whenever you like. I must let Siddon know at once."

"My dear mamma," said David, "bless your heart but we are taking them. Rose is quite besotted about them and they go everywhere with us," on hearing which Lady Emily fell into a frenzy of arrangements about baby-food, milk supplies, and fruit pulp, evidently looking upon America as practically virgin forest where bears' paws and hemlock shoots would be staple diet. "Besides," she said, laying her hand earnestly on David's arm, "the journey will be too much for them. I remember when I took you and Agnes to Boulogne when you were little how *dreadfully* sick you were."

David threw a despairing glance in the direction of his wife. Rose, who had never failed him yet, caught the glance and came over to him.

"Dear Rose," said Lady Emily, "you mustn't let David take the babies to America. They will be dreadfully sick and I expect the food there is quite different and will upset them. They must come to Rushwater."

Rose thanked her mother-in-law very sweetly and affectionately and said they were flying and the babies would hardly notice it at all.

"But the atmosphere is rarefied," said Lady Emily, rather proud of having made this point, "and one has forced landings. And how can you heat their food? Much better to leave them here."

Rose, always showing an affectionate deference to her husband's adorable but highly exasperating mother, said Nannie would manage beautifully, and called to Nannie, who was at the end of the room with her young charges.

"Nannie, Lady Emily is rather worried about the babies flying," said Rose. "Tell her how much they enjoyed it when we flew to Portugal and back."

"Oh yes, my lady," said Nannie. "Quite air-minded as they say Dorothy and Henry are. Quite little travellers. And over in America they say the baby-food's lovely and I dare say the Americans will make quite a fuss of them."

Lady Emily, happier but not altogether convinced, asked if the perambulator could go in the aeroplane.

"Oh dear no, my lady," said Nannie. "They say there are some quite nice prams in America and the babies always travel in their Karry Kots," and she looked towards the end of the room where both babies lay fathoms deep in slumber in hooded baskets covered in blue washable plastic, each basket with handles for transportation. "Excuse me, my lady," she added, "but I remember so well the summer Lady Graham and Master James and

Miss Emmy and Miss Clarissa were here. You wouldn't know me, my lady. I was only second in the nursery then."

"Now, wait," said Lady Emily, rummaging in her bag for her spectacles. The bag opened its mouth, turned over, and ejected most of its contents on the floor. "Wait," said her ladyship, looking searchingly at Ivy and paying no attention at all to her property, which Miss Merriman and Clarissa were rescuing. "I know. Canaries! Agnes, I did ask at lunchtime if Ivy had remembered the canaries, didn't I? They like groundsel and I meant to get some in the kitchen garden, but perhaps Ivy has remembered it."

"Yes, indeed, my lady," said Rose's Nannie, the ci-devant Ivy, puzzled, but realizing that Lady Emily had got her name right and anxious to oblige. "There was a lot of lovely groundsel in the corner of the cucumber frames."

"Then that is all right," said Lady Emily, much relieved. "Thank you, Ivy," and then Rose sent her Nannie back to the babies, where she boasted dreadfully to Mrs. Siddon, who was busy finding likeness in Mr. David's children to every member of the family whether blood-relation or merely connection, about how her ladyship remembered all about her.

"I dare say," said Mrs. Siddon. "And so do others, Ivy, and skylarking in the pantry with Walter it was then, and leaving Bessie to take the fruit up to the nursery. Well, things are different now, children going in aeroplanes and everything."

"Dodo loves flying, Mrs. Siddon, and so does Henry," said Ivy. "I'd love to be an air hostess."

"That's quite enough, Ivy," said Mrs. Siddon. "Air hostesses need their heads screwed on the right way. And as for Miss Dorothy and Master Henry," said Mrs. Siddon, enouncing their proper names and titles with awful clarity, "no one knows what they do or don't like at that age. Well, good-bye, Ivy. I'll never forget how you cried the day the nursery canary died. A perfect fright you looked," to which Mrs. David Leslie's Nannie, the competent, hardened traveller, authority on baby-culture, found no answer.

"Bless you, darling Rose and darling David," said Lady Emily as they bent to kiss her. "Come again soon to Rushwater. The door is always open."

She watched them as they went out, followed by Ivy and some willing helpers carrying the babies in their baskets. At the door they turned and smiled and then they were gone.

"Good-bye, mamma dear," said John Leslie, who had collected his wife and three sons.

"Thank you for such a happy day, dearest Lady Emily," said Mary, and then the three young Leslies made their farewells.

"I say, Gran," said Leslie minor, getting very close to his grandmother and speaking confidentially, "it's been a marvellous day and thank you for having such a lovely birthday. Gran, I want to tell you something; privately."

Lady Emily, her bright dark eyes alight with interest, turned towards her grandson.

"Gran," said Leslie minor, impelled by heaven knew what mixture of feelings to relieve his mind of a burden and at the same time to boast of his exploit, "I climbed to the top of the Temple this afternoon."

"I wish I had seen you," said his grandmother with great spirit. "Martin nearly got up once, but he sprained his wrist. Does he know?"

"No, Gran," said Leslie minor. "He told me not to and so did father, but I simply couldn't help it. And I did want you to know," he added, doubtful as to how his grandmother would take the news. But there was much of the wild proud Pomfret blood in Lady Emily's veins, though all in her was turned to favour and prettiness, and her eyes sparkled at this rebellious news.

"Well done," she said with her most brilliant mischievous smile. "How pleased papa would have been. But we mustn't tell

Martin. He might worry, poor boy," and she looked compassionately towards her eldest grandson.

"None of us will split; word of a Leslie," said Leslie minor, and much solaced by this unburdening he followed his family and was gone.

"And now, mamma," said Agnes, "are you ready to go?"

She said this in a matter-of-fact voice, but her serenity was for once a little disturbed, for her mother, as she had feared, was for the time being convinced that she was staying at Rushwater. However, Agnes by her mild persistence managed to persuade her mother that Holdings was waiting for her, and Conque with her shawls and books. Sylvia, Martin, and Emmy were there to say good-bye, James, Clarissa, and John were waiting.

"Where is Robert?" Agnes asked.

No one knew. His brothers and sisters called from the steps. Their voices echoed from the hill below the Temple, but no Robert came. Martin, always anxious for the well-being of his guests, began to wonder if anything had happened. The bull, the sawmill, the pond, the roof; all of these things might be danger for Robert. He was increasingly conscious of the drag on his leg and Sylvia saw his face. Robert had been quietly in evidence all day, exchanging views on the sun and the leaves and the flowers with the nursery contingent. Since teatime he had not been seen. He was not in the church. And then Sylvia remembered that the nurses and babies had not been in the church. "I know, Agnes," she said, "I'll run up to the nursery."

Not to the old Rushwater nursery where the rocking-horse and the Polyphone mechanical organ were dust-sheeted, the pictures wrapped in newspapers on the nursery table, the carpet rolled like a giant's sausage along the wall. Miss Eleanor Leslie had a less romantic but warmer and sunnier nursery in one of the second-best bedrooms looking south, with large windows and a faded Chinese wallpaper of crooked bamboo stems and huge sprawling peonies. Sylvia went in. Nurse was sitting in a low chair with a large basin on a chair before her and a muslin-lined basket at hand. The soft smell of baby and baby-powder greeted her like airs from heaven. On Nurse's lap was Miss Eleanor Leslie, who had lately been washed and put into her charming and unfashionably long nightgown, tied like an Empire gown just below her irresistible arms, and was having a refreshing supper of warm milk from a bottle, her blue eyes nearly bursting out of her head in her enjoyment. Robert was sitting on a hassock, his little finger imprisoned in her tiny fist, looking with great approval at her greed.

"Mother is waiting for you, Robert," said Sylvia. "Gran is rather tired and she wants to take her home. Say good-bye and come along."

"Oh, Aunt Sylvia, must I?" said Robert. "Eleanor did ask me to see her have her supper, didn't you, baby darling?"

Nurse said he was quite old-fashioned, but obviously thought well of his devotion to his small cousin.

"Tell Aunt Sylvia I can't come yet," said Robert. "She's your mother, my darling."

Miss Eleanor Leslie, roused from her debauch by this appeal to her finer feelings, suddenly jerked her head away from her bottle and burst in a rippling cascade of melodious madness and rich chuckles, ending with her favourite remark, an echoing "Oo" like a bell sounding fathoms deep in a well. Nurse's face became one simper of pride in what she called except when Sylvia was there My Baby, and Sylvia felt that if there were a heaven on earth, it was this, it was this.

"Well, just till Eleanor has finished her bottle, Robert," she said, "and then she can kiss you good night."

"My darling baby," said Robert, "eat your bottle very slowly and then Robert will stay with you and you can hold his finger. You like holding my finger, don't you, darling?"

Miss Eleanor Leslie opened her mouth in a toothless all-embracing smile. Nurse seized her opportunity of putting the

bottle back into it and Miss Leslie again applied herself with
fury to the meal, loosing Robert's finger the better to do so.

"She said good night herself, Aunt Sylvia," said Robert. "My
darling baby, good night, my rosebud-hearted baby."

He then shook hands with Nurse, took Sylvia's hand, and
dragged her out of the room.

"I am not crying, Aunt Sylvia," he said as they went downstairs. "I only think it is rather sad not to stay with Eleanor. She
is my special friend."

Sylvia, who felt uncomfortably close to emotion herself, said
Robert must come and stay at Rushwater for a few days and take
baby to see the cows, which prospect so cheered him that he let
go of Sylvia's hand and went down the rest of the staircase by
hops. Lady Emily was already in the car with Agnes and Miss
Merriman. The Graham children bundled into the other car,
waving and shouting good-byes. Martin stood by the window of
the first car and took Lady Emily's hand.

"I hope you aren't tired, Gran," he said. "It has been a perfect
day for us and we all loved having you here."

"Tired, but happily tired," said Lady Emily, winding a scarf
turban-wise about her head in a most becoming way. "Martin,
you know John's second boy climbed to the top of the Temple.
It was very disobedient of him when you and father told him not
to, but it is my birthday and we won't say anything. He reminds
me so much of papa. And now good-bye and God bless you all."

She kissed Martin through the window, flashed her loving,
all-embracing smile upon Sylvia and Emmy, upon beloved
Rushwater, no longer her home, and the car drove away, leaving
Martin and Sylvia and Emmy upon the steps. The great birthday party was over. Everything had gone perfectly and now there
would be the reaction, the empty rooms lately so full of relations
and friends, the deserted lawns, the echoing voices stilled.

Emmy, who disapproved on principle of softer feelings as
waste of time on a farm, sniffed in a very unladylike way and

stated that she was going to put on some sensible clothes and go down to the cowsheds, where she later took occasion to confide to the best Jersey heifer that parties were all right but you felt beastly afterwards, and found considerable solace in the Jersey's attitude of kindly attention combined with entire lack of real interest.

"Let's sit down for a bit," said Martin to Sylvia, and they went out to the great tulip tree, whose shadows were lengthening.

"You know what Gran is like," said Martin thoughtfully. "She doesn't seem quite to know where she is always, nor where anyone else is for that matter. She said John's second boy climbed the pinnacle of the Temple. I suppose she invented it. I forbade the boys to do anything of the sort and so did John. Gran said: 'It was disobedient of him when you and your father told him not to,' and whether she meant my father or if she was thinking of grandfather and thought he was my father, I don't know. Anyway she invented it all, bless her. What energy she has! I feel as if I'd been twenty-four hours in a tank in North Africa. So does my leg."

Sylvia's heart ached at this news, but it was no good talking about Martin's leg, and Dr. Ford had hopes of some new electric heat treatment at the Barchester General, so she thought that to change the subject she might as well tell him what had happened at the Temple.

"Young devils!" said Martin angrily. "And pretty well young liars."

Not liars, Sylvia said, because she and Freddy Belton, who had got the youngest Leslie boy down, had forbidden any allusion to the Temple that day for fear of alarming their grandmother. And spoiling your day too, she added to herself.

"But Gran didn't say John's youngest," said Martin, even more puzzled. So then Sylvia had to tell him the whole story and how Leslie minimus had lost his head and how well Freddy Belton had handled the situation. Martin was silent and his golden Sylvia wondered if she had done wrong in speaking and whether Martin was going to fall into one of his very rare moods of rage, but presently to her relief he began to laugh.

"I suppose the fact is," he said, "that I'm jealous. I tried to climb the Temple myself when I was a boy and only sprained my wrist. Let's forget it. How is Eleanor?" and then their talk passed to the unusual gifts and merit of their daughter. Martin said his leg was easing off again. After supper they read the newspapers in the morning-room in peace, Emmy being down at the Women's Institute giving a talk on The Cottager's Pig. Presently the telephone rang. Sylvia, who did all she could to spare Martin unnecessary walking when he was tired, answered it.

"It's Agnes," she said. "Something about Gran. She wants to speak to you."

The same cold thought sprang in them both, but neither gave any sign of it. Martin limped over to the telephone and took the receiver.

"Martin darling," said his Aunt Agnes's soft voice, "something so sad."

Sylvia saw the lines of worry on Martin's forehead and came over to him. Two people cannot listen to one receiver, but it was the old-fashioned standard kind and with goodwill something can be done. "Darling mamma stood today wonderfully," Agnes's voice went on, "and when we got back she went straight to bed and Conque took her dinner up on a tray, and then a quite dreadful thing happened. What is it, Merry?" her voice said and for a moment there was silence.

"Has anything happened to Gran?" said Sylvia. "Oh, Martin."

Martin said: "No, of course not," but he felt a kind of paralysed fear, and Agnes was still silent and they knew nothing.

"I am so sorry, darling Martin," said Agnes. "It was Merry. Gran thought she had left her black lace scarf in the church, but Merry says she has just remembered that she got it entangled in the sweetbrier on papa's grave and thinks it may be in the churchyard—just a moment, Martin. Oh, it is all right, Martin darling. Conque had taken it away to mend because the sweetbrier had torn it. I shall try to keep darling mamma in bed tomorrow for a good rest. We all loved our happy day and seeing you and Sylvia and your darling Eleanor. Robert says he is going to live with her in a cottage when he is grown up. Good night, darling. All our love to you and Sylvia and your precious Eleanor."

Martin hung up the receiver.

"And after that, my precious Sylvia," he said, in faint mockery of his Aunt Agnes, but also because he adored his wife, "bed seems the best place for us," to which Sylvia agreed. Lady Emily was well. Reunion at Rushwater had been a great success and there was nothing they wanted more than a good night's rest. As for Miss Eleanor Leslie, whom they visited on tiptoe on their way to bed, she was industriously doing her duty be lying in deep abandoned slumber, her fists lightly clenched, her cheeks like warm rose-petals.

"I think Baby is the nicest smell in the world," said Sylvia.

At Harefield the Beltons were quietly having their evening meal, Captain Belton and his parents slightly the worse for their outing, for Lady Emily and the combined Leslies and Grahams were enough to exhaust the strongest.

"Clarissa is a most attractive child," said Mrs. Belton, throwing this remark into space as an abstract idea, but of course secretly thinking how nice it would be if Freddy married a really nice girl and had a family.

"A plaguey little nuisance," said Captain Belton most unromantically. "She needs slapping. She would have told Martin about that idiot Leslie boys' escapade for twopence, just to see how much he minded."

"You can't handle women, Freddy," said his younger brother, bolting a large mouthful of raspberry pie the better to express his feelings. "I ticked her off good and proper and she ate out of my hand."

Mrs. Belton made no comment. Charles's army language rather frightened her and she did not always understand it, but if it meant that he and Clarissa were on good terms she could begin to do her secret match-making again. Secret it would have to be, for though her heart's wish was to see both her sons happily married, she knew that she could not influence either of them in their choice of a bride; so she very wisely determined to like and love any bride they chose, even if she were an outsider, by which Mrs. Belton meant, with no snobbishness but simply as part of her upbringing and her creed, someone whose family had not been established in Barsetshire for at least three generations.

"Emily looks shaky," said Mr. Belton, who in common with most elderly people took considerable pleasure in seeing his coevals decay. "Doesn't always know what she's saying. My old mother was like that. Used to call me Charles. Thought I was old Uncle Charlie. He had a wig and drank a bottle of port every night till he died."

"Good old Uncle Charlie," said Charles Belton. "He left me a hundred pounds. I wouldn't mind wearing a wig if I had port every night. But I'd rather have whisky," at which artless barbarism his father fell into a quite eighteenth-century rage till his sons laughed him out of it.

After supper, for the Sunday evening meal supplied by courtesy of the old family nurse, Wheeler, now parlour-maid, owing to Cook's Sunday off, cannot be described as dinner, Mr. and Mrs. Carton came in by arrangement to have coffee. The evening was warm and still, and a large yellowish moon invited the party to sit under the cedar tree and be gently eaten by mosquitoes.

"Well, Carton," said Mr. Belton, "how are things in Oxford?" for Mr. Carton was a Fellow of Paul's College and a classical scholar of some note.

"Much the same," said Mr. Carton with gloomy relish. "We have some good men up, but most of the tutors are barbarians. Ours are civilized on the whole, because the dean has the master under his thumb. You know our dean I think, Mrs. Belton. He married one of the Deans from Winter Overcotes."

Mrs. Belton said she didn't think she had met him and it was hard enough to have the Dean of Barchester and the Deans at Winter Overcotes without the Dean of Paul's.

"I know him," said Charles Belton. "His name is Fanshawe and he married Helen Dean. She's marvellous with cars. She took me and Jessica over to Steynes Agnes at about eighty miles an hour, all winding lanes with hedges."

Mr. Carton, brushing this interruption aside as irrelevant, said that if colleges would choose tutors because they were supposed to be authorities on certain subjects rather than because they could teach, they were digging a pit for their own destruction. The history tutor at Lazarus, he said, was no more than a journalist and thought far more of getting his very shallow and ephemeral books on Slavo-Lydia published and talking pretentious and tendentious nonsense on the wireless than of getting his men through their schools. And as for his wife, said Mr. Carton, her only merit was that she proved, if proof were needed, that colleges were not founded for the benefit of young married couples. Spoilt children all over the place and a lot of ignorant talk about our debt to Russia. Bah! said Mr. Carton, which impressed his hearers considerably.

"Sidney always forgets that he is a married fellow himself," said Mrs. Carton, who until her marriage a few years previously had been the headmistress of the Hosiers' Girls' Foundation School. "By the way, Mr. Belton, we had lunch with Mr. Adams and Heather the other day in Barchester, before Miss Fielding's wedding. Heather had improved enormously since she went to college. And I liked young Mr. Pilward, who was there."

Mrs. Belton said Heather owed a great deal to the Hosiers' Girls' School and to Mrs. Carton.

"But more to you," said Mrs. Carton. "I couldn't have given her what you have given. She has a real sense of what is worth while and what isn't. I gather that she has made friends with one of the Dean girls at Winter Overcotes, the one who works for the Red Cross, I think."

"Susan?" said Freddy Belton, wondering how so unexpected a friendship had risen, for though he liked Heather well enough, the gulf between her and Susan Dean seemed to him very great.

"I think so," said Mrs. Carton. "And talking of the Red Cross, do you know that Mrs. Updike has been taking a first-aid course? She said she really ought to know how to bandage herself because she was always getting cut or bruised by things."

Mrs. Belton asked if she had passed the examination.

"Not really," said Mrs. Carton, "because she pulled up a stake that was marking a wasp's nest and was too swollen to do the exam, but she can try again before Christmas," and then talk meandered into local gossip and the prospects of the weather for the Conservative Rally and whether the Pomfrets would really be able to bring an extremely distinguished guest who would be spending the previous night with them. Charles, rather bored and missing the common-room talk at the Priory School, had slipped away. Presently he came back, apparently much re-freshed.

"I've been telephoning to Holdings," he said. "Clarissa says Cousin Emily had supper in bed and has begun to write her life and wants Miss Merriman to type it. Clarissa's coming to the Conservative Rally, mother, but Cousin Agnes isn't sure if she can come. I said Clarissa had better hook on to us. If she came to lunch here first we could all go together. I said I knew you'd like her to, mother."

Whether Mrs. Belton had liked it or not she would probably have agreed, as her chief pleasure was to forward her sons' wishes in every way. Charles's wishes were easy to satisfy. If only Freddy would have a wish she would do her utmost to gratify it, but though he was so good, so reliable, so affectionate, she did

not know what he wanted. He had spoken in highly inapprecia-
tive terms of Clarissa, and unless this was a feint to divert
attention, his mother must give up the hope she had nourished.
She longed to hope again, but could see no girl on whom to
place her hopes. The moon hung behind the flat branches of the
cedar tree against the night sky, and the talk went gently on till
the Cartons went away.

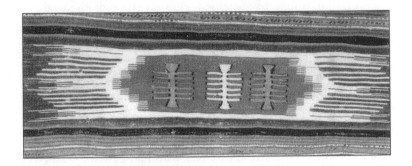

Curiously enough it was at Winter Overcotes, in a family with no particular claims to birth, with few roots in the county, that the old life of the county families still survived in something of the shape it had before the second World War (or War to End War for the Second Time). One cannot explain these things. One aristocracy, one landed caste, gradually perishes. Another gradually takes its place and in its own time will decay in the eternal cycle of change. Mrs. Dean was a much younger sister of Mr. Palmer, the squire at Worsted, but the Palmers had no pretensions to be more than country gentleman-farmers. Mr. Dean was of good middle-class stock from somewhere in the north of England and had made his name and his fortune by his unusual gifts for business and engineering combined. He and his wife had lived a great deal abroad, where his various engineering contracts took him, and it was not till about four years before the last war that they settled for good in Barsetshire with their large family, first in the Dower House at Worsted and then at Winter Overcotes, since which time the Dean family had quite unconsciously been taking root in the county. It may have been partly Mr. Dean's abilities and wealth that earned him consideration: it may also have been his wife's rich beauty and her amicable laziness, which made other women feel that though she might attract men she would neither exert herself to attract them nor mind in the least if they were not attracted and moved on elsewhere. Nine or ten good-looking clever children may have helped, though through the years of war the boys were all abroad in one or other of the services, one married daughter was in America, one was driving for the army, one was in the Red Cross, and the youngest under the conscripted age, so that they were not in evidence except on leave. But as the horrors of war were succeeded by the tyrannies of peace, it became evident to the county that the Deans must have brevet rank and that one step more would assure them of the permanent position. Laurence, who had married Margaret Tebben, was a partner in his father's firm; the twins were rising rapidly and equally in the senior service. Gerald had remained in the army, Robin was learning to farm. Of the girls the two elder were outside Barsetshire, Helen Fanshawe in Oxford and Betty Van Dryven in New York. Susan, who had worked for the Prisoners of War Educational Books Department, had transferred to the Red Cross Hospital Libraries and as we know was Depot Librarian in Barchester, second only to Lady Pomfret and liked and respected by everyone worth considering.

This was a not unremarkable contribution from one family, and though the Deans went on doing their various duties conscientiously and with great efficiency, there were so many of them and so united a family that they did not consider whether they were of the county or merely in it; a subtle distinction that Mrs. Mounstuart Jenkinson would doubtless have appreciated. And then, just as peace was breaking out, there was the sudden rise of the brilliant young actress Miss Jessica Dean, who was almost as important in the making and acting of Aubrey Clover's plays as the gifted author-actor-manager was himself. This outburst took the county slightly aback, for so far no one from their ranks had burst onto the stage in a really professional way and the matter needed consideration. Though Barsetshire still remained very local in its interests and had been about very little during the war, by now a good many people had seen Jessica at the Cockspur Theatre, and it was well known that

Aubrey Clover often came to Winter Overcotes as a friend. There was a moment when opinion had wavered about Aubrey Clover's association with the Deans, but when the archdeacon reported that the Bishop's wife had been very rude to him at a charity matinée for the Perpetual Curates' Benefit Fund and that Aubrey Clover had after the pattern of Theodore Cook at once sat down to the piano and sung a venomous little impromptu with the refrain: "I took my husband's gaiters off and put them on myself," the whole mass of well-thinking people in the close and county became ardent supporters of the young actress and her brilliant partner. Old Lady Norton, better known to her friends as the Dreadful Dowager, who not content with being the widow of a respectable baron had taken to dropping her g's, the better to mark her position, had been heard to say: "One good marriage and the county will be takin' those Deans up," and though the Dowager Lady Norton was a snob and a quite dreadful bore, her social sense spoke truly. But all this was unknown to the Deans, nor we may say would it have interested or moved them in the least.

The Cockspur Theatre had closed for a month. Three of Aubrey Clover's plays were out in the provinces, not to speak of the tremendous success of his latest play in New York. Mr. Aubrey Clover had come down to Winter Overcotes to finish his new play, and his leading lady, Miss Jessica Dean, was much enjoying a lazy life with her family and doing nothing, while Aubrey Clover wrote and swore and smoked and rewrote and swore again in the room that had come to be known as Mr. Aubrey's Room. Partly by luck, partly by the kind connivance of Lady Pomfret, Miss Susan Dean, the Red Cross Depot Librarian, was given a week's holiday the better to enjoy her sister's company, her place being taken by the efficient secretary, Miss Grantly from over Chaldicotes way, who knew who people were. The large house was filled with Deans by birth and by marriage. Mr. Fanshawe of Paul's with his wife Helen, Mr. Woolcot Van Dryven of New York and his wife Betty, Laurence

Dean and his wife Margaret, all with their children; and a coming and going of twins, Gerald and Robin on leave or on holiday filled the house and garden with noise and talk, but all so friendly, and companionable that even the irritable Aubrey Clover admitted the unusual quality of Deans.

"Unfortunately," said Jessica, who was amusing herself on the lawn by painting her exquisite legs with sun-tan and making elaborate clocks on the simulated stockings, "there are far too many of us for you to put into a play, darling. You know perfectly well you can't write for more than three people; or five with a butler and a maid."

Mr. Fanshawe, who had a liking for Aubrey Clover and had gone so far as to compare him with Terence, chiefly it must be admitted on the ground of his expressed contempt for the play-going public, said A Day with the Deans would make a very good play.

"And that, Charles," said his young sister-in-law, "is where your toes turn in. A Day with the Deans would do nicely for matinées with lots of women eating tea off trays, but absolutely no use, my dear, for my and Aubrey's sophisticated public. Not so very sophisticated either," added Jessica, who though she gave her entire body and mind to her audiences remained keenly critical of them. "Aubrey and I are getting like Gilbert and Sullivan."

Mr. Fanshawe said that such a comparison appeared to him complimentary in the highest degree.

"What I mean," said Jessica, industriously pursuing a new scheme, which was to make a pretence ladder in a pretence stocking that the trompe l' œil effect might be enhanced, "is that We are Perfect, but our blasted audiences laugh before the jokes and clap before we have made our exits now."

Mr. Fanshawe said this was an interesting point and that for himself, in spite of his deep admiration of Gilbert and Sullivan, their audiences were so ill-trained, barbarian, and herd-minded that he had issued a Self-Denying Ordinance to himself and would never go to one again.

"Someone or other had a good idea," said Jessica, "that when the copyright of Gilbert and Sullivan runs out those people at Glyndebourne might do them. Properly, with a really good band and no interrupting or encores. Are you coming to Aubrey's first night, Charles?"

Mr. Fanshawe said that unless it coincided with Paul's Gaudy he would like to come very much and sit incognito in a box, and then Laurence Dean's wife, who had been Margaret Tebben, came out of the house full of excitement.

"It was mother ringing up," said Margaret. "Richard's engaged. Isn't it heavenly? You *are* pleased, Jessica?" she added anxiously.

"Bless your heart, my love," said Jessica, who was sitting on the grass with her exquisite legs straight out in front of her admiring her handiwork, "did you think that because Richard saved my life when I was a horrible little girl I shall pine and die? Who is it? No, wait, it's the Swedish girl. Not Dogstooth; not Cracknel. Krogsbrog, that's it. The Valkyrie who runs day nurseries for the cretinous poor of Stockholm."

"Petrea says there aren't any poor in Sweden and all the children are very healthy," said Margaret, who with all her gentleness could be roused to the defence of anyone connected with her dear brother Richard.

"Then Petrea must be a Christian Scientist," said Jessica, but seeing Margaret look puzzled and a little dashed, she got up and kissed her and said Richard must bring Petrea over to see them and she would give him a whacking wedding present. Various other Deans who were present then did their best to please Margaret by assuming an interest and enthusiasm that none of them felt, and Margaret took it all for Bible truth and was delighted to find that her dear Richard's engagement gave such satisfaction.

"Oh, Jessica," she exclaimed suddenly, "a ladder in your nylons!"

"So it is," said Jessica, pleased at the success of the trompe l'œil. "Well, they'll do to polish the furniture."

Such extravagance horrified Margaret, who said there was a nice little shop in Barchester where one could have ladders mended. This, said Mr. Fanshawe, was according to modern theory highly unsocial, as the chief end of man was considered by Them to be consumption; beside which production or repair work were as nought. Margaret again looked unhappy, but remembering that Mr. Fanshawe like her father and other Oxford men she knew was given to sarcasm, or what in her innocence she considered such, she smiled at him and went away again to ask Richard and his Petrea to tea.

"Well, that's that," said Jessica, carefully repairing the ladder with a brush and her bottle of sun-tan. "Come along, Charles. Lunch. Aubrey's in a filthy temper today. The end of the second act has died on him," but when they sat down to lunch no one would have known how bad Mr. Clover's temper was, for he was reserving it till he got back to his work, determined that the second act should come to a satisfactory end if it cost his last drop of blood. To the Dean family, except the few Deans who knew him well, he appeared like a quiet literary guest who was enjoying the country air and the good country food, so much so that Robin, who for the moment breathed, slept, ate, drank, and talked farming, found him a most appreciative audience for his views on farm drainage. There was a good deal of noise with so large a family united in good health and good spirits, while the grandchildren at a separate table ate quietly and persistently, rather despising their elders for behaving as no well-conducted nursery party would behave. Mrs. Dean in her usual half-awake condition looked benignly upon her descendants and said to Aubrey Clover that he ought to write a play about a large family.

"My dear lady," said Aubrey Clover, rapidly becoming an Edwardian playwright who had been summoned by telegram and come in a hansom to lunch with a fashionable hostess, "we are not wholesale. Deans, and nothing more delightful exists, are sent out in dozens, but my line is individuals. Now you, Rachel—may I call you Rachel?" he added.

"But you usually do," said Mrs. Dean mildly.

"I know," said Aubrey Clover, "but it seemed the right line. You, Rachel, would make a perfect play."

"Would I?" said Mrs. Dean, almost waking up. "Why?"

"I can't tell you," said Aubrey Clover. "We musicians know—that's a line from Browning—what I mean was people who write good plays know what will make a good play; sometimes," he added thoughtfully.

"Would you call yours good, then?" said Mrs. Dean, flattered by so intellectual a discussion.

"Yes," said Aubrey Clover. "And the curse of it is that when I am dead and Jessica has gone into Shakespeare and plays Volumnia as a star part with her lines pinned up all over the stage and on other people's backs and her own fan, or whatever Roman matrons had—"

Mrs. Dean suggested tablets. Aubrey Clover said that was Denmark; Hamlet had tablets and always seemed to have a good deal of difficulty in finding them.

"If my father were a ghost," said Mrs. Dean, suddenly waking up and speaking with authority, "and came and frightened me with a beard and a helmet on, I would *not* take down what he said. I would listen attentively and say: 'Yes, father,' and not do it. I should very much dislike it if any of the children made notes of what I was saying to them. Luckily none of them know shorthand, except Susan, and she has a secretary so she needn't."

She then relapsed into what her unchivalrous guest had once called her ruminant mood, and indeed the comparison between Mrs. Dean and a very lovely placid cow with huge dark eyes, slowly munching its way through life, was one that had occurred very lovingly to more than one of her friends. The mention of Susan had made Aubrey Clover look at her across the table, and he thought, not for the first time, that something had happened to her since his last visit. Love was the cause of pretty well everything in Aubrey Clover's experience, but he had never associated Susan with love. Yet when he looked at her, his back to the window, she facing the light, his observant eye caught a little shadow below the cheekbone, the faintest touch of dark below her eyes, and he knew, on no grounds at all, that something was up. He was fond of Susan in an unemotional way and respected her powers of hard work and concentration. Susan must be helped if he, Aubrey Clover, could help her; but who was troubling her eyes and shadowing her face? In his mind he ran through the various men he had met at Winter Overcotes since he knew the Deans. The only man he could think likely to give Susan a heartache was Francis Brandon, but Francis was now an old married man and Susan was on excellent terms with his wife. Perhaps someone he hadn't met, some friend who was not a frequent visitor. Or what about Oliver Marling? He had noticed Oliver's assiduity towards Jessica, but he was not and never could be the man for her. It would be just like a man, thought Aubrey Clover, dispassionately considering himself as a strolling player set apart by his vocation never to compete in the fields of domestic affection, to make a fool of himself over one woman because he was attracted by her sister. Little Jessica liked Oliver very well; but even if the stage were not parent, child, and husband to her, she would never care for him deeply. Of that he was certain without knowing why. And his industrious brain began to weave these three characters into a stage design, which occupation while it lasted gave him a delightful feeling of being like God, holding no form of creed, but contemplating all; a quotation that Mrs. Robin Dale would at once have recognized. But when you weave real people into your own design it is at your own risk and you may find yourself the more deceived.

After lunch they all sat in the garden, not huddled into an angle of the house and wrapped in coats as during the preceding summer, but glad to be under the trees and watch the air quivering with heat over the garden. Tennis was to be played, but there was a general feeling that after tea would be the time.

There was a coming and going as friends of one or another Dean came to talk and exchange news, for the threat that petrol would be stopped in the autumn made everyone use his car as much as possible and seldom had the A.A. had a busier month. Nor had there ever been so many road accidents, some of which as always were attributable to driving with one arm round a young woman, or never being quite sure which of those handle-things were which, my dear, and I don't know how I got through my driving test except that the policeman was *too* sweet. But a very large proportion of the accidents were due to strain and fatigue borne over a number of years and accentuated since the outbreak of peace by deliberate undernourishment of the people of England to make them too listless to resist petty tyranny. To the same cause may be attributed a number of very bad railway and mine accidents besides the increasing tendency to go out without one's shopping list, lose one's purse, put one's ration book down on the counter and forget to pick it up, go to a room to get something and stand in a daze completely unable to remember what one wanted and have to go back to the place where one was when the thought first came into one's head and wait for it to return, to be perpetually flurried or anxious about things that really did not matter, and in the case of the majority of house-wives who were giving their own weekly rasher of bacon and their one monthly egg to a husband or growing children not to speak of their ration of so-called meat, a growing wish to sit down and die except that one's death would mean a weekly rasher of bacon the less and a monthly egg the less.

Still, for the moment the sun shone and cars came grinding and jerking because they were wearing out and spare parts were not for the English to the Dean's house, and the garden was full of talk and laughter as the afternoon wore on. Tea was laid on a large garden table outside the house, and people helped them-selves and stood or sat or strolled as they wished.

"Did I tell you, Rachel," said Mr. Dean to his wife, "that I had asked Adams and his daughter to tea?" to which his wife replied that he hadn't and she supposed the reason was that he meant to do what he had intended to do; but there was no malice in her words, for she adored her husband and would have received any guest whom he thought it agreeable or politic to ask and flowed in her even course gently round and over any guest like a peculiarly amiable stream of lava or a tin of golden syrup.

"Adams is doing a lot of work for me," said Mr. Dean, "and his girl is at college, quite a handsome young woman. I believe Mrs. Belton took her up. Young Tebben is one of his men now. Margaret tells me that her brother is engaged to a Swedish girl. Do you remember, Rachel, that we thought years ago that he and Susan were attached to each other? Just as well it went no further. Richard is a good man at his job, and I like his father; but it would never have done."

"Nonsense," said Mrs. Dean, lifting her eyes to her husband's face. "You knew Richard was in love with *me*. He wrote that poem that I can't remember about me. *So* dull," and then her thoughts were distracted by the arrival of the Marlings.

"How nice," said Mrs. Dean, at once annexing Oliver though without any unkindness to Lucy. "The young people are all on the tennis courts now, and we can talk," after which friendly greeting she picked up her tapestry work, did a few stitches, and gently relapsed into afternoon coma. Oliver and Lucy did not quite know what to do, as a sleepy hostess is a problem not often encountered in polite society. They looked at each other and then Oliver laughed ruefully.

"You see, we aren't young people," he said, to which his sister Lucy said stoutly that people were whatever age they were and if one hadn't come with tennis things one couldn't play tennis and what she wanted was to talk to Mr. Dean about artificial fertilizers because he was farming a bit as a hobby and might give her a few tips. People who had a lot of money to spend on their land usually got a return for it, said Lucy, and then she sighed, for there was so little money going into Marling now and so little money coming out of it, and the shadow of the

County Council or a Government department hung over them. For it cannot be denied that when a good landowner has seen his capital diminish year by year and has to face some kind of nationalization, even National Trust, though They will doubtless nationalize that soon, with no redress for anyone, his feelings are much the same as those of the cottager who in old age had to go to the workhouse. It may not be one's fault, but the sense of guilt and a bitter degradation is there. And on Lucy the chief burden fell and would fall, for her elder brother's heart was in the army and Oliver had his work in town. If gentlemen groaned at afternoon parties Oliver would have groaned, so he had to pretend it was a kind of cough.

"Adams; Sam Adams," said a voice near him. He started and looked up to see a powerfully built man with a tall well-dressed girl, of whom the best description is that she was not unhandsome. "There didn't seem to be anyone about, so we came through the house."

"My name is Marling," said Oliver, "and this is my sister Lucy."

"Pleased to meet you," said Mr. Adams, gripping Lucy's hand firmly and receiving as good as he gave, for Miss Marling's strength of handshake, of whose ferocity she was quite unaware, was famous among her friends and acquaintances.

"And this is my daughter," said Mr. Adams. "Do you know where our host and hostess are? Mr. Dean asked me and Heth, that's my daughter, Heather her name is, but she's Daddy's little Heth, to come out to tea and I haven't had the pleasure of meeting his wife."

"Here she is," said Oliver, "but she has gone to sleep. She always does. I expect she will wake up in a minute."

"Well, that's queer," said Mr. Adams letting himself down into a chair. "There was a mate of mine when I was at Hogglestock, Sam Hoggett his name was, same as mine, the Sam I mean. And that boy used to sleep standing. I've seen him asleep on his feet, supposed to be minding a machine he was, but if you'll credit me, the minute anything went wrong that boy was awake again."

"I think," said Oliver, who had often heard of the wealthy ironmaster M.P. for Barchester and now found something about him that he liked, "that Mrs. Dean is much the same. She wakes up when new guests come."

And even as he spoke, Mrs. Dean opened her eyes, resumed complete consciousness as far as she was ever really conscious of anything, and greeted Mr. Adams warmly, evidently thinking that he was an old friend who had been mislaid.

"Adams, that's my name, Sam Adams," said her guest, who after what Oliver had said and by his natural shrewdness realized that Mrs. Dean had not the slightest idea who he was. "And this is my daughter."

"Now I know all about you," said Mrs. Dean. "You do a lot of business with my husband, or he does with you. He told me he had asked you. And where are you living?"

"At the works," said Mr. Adams. "Hogglestock that is. But my Heth and me we've got a flat in London, seeing how Parliament takes up a goodish bit of time. And if the petrol's going to be cut, we'll have a suite at the White Hart next winter, for Sam Adams isn't the man to get petrol when the Government stops it. It wouldn't look well for a man in my position, see?"

"I say," said Lucy, who had been studying Heather Adams with detached interest, as she might have studied a valuable new heifer, or even, to compare large things with small, the effects of a new fertilizer, "you know the Belton's, don't you?"

Heather said Mrs. Belton had been very kind to her and so had Mr. Belton, adding that daddy thought the world of Mrs. Belton.

"Freddy and Charles are awfully good sorts," said Lucy. "Charles is somewhere about, playing tennis. Do you play tennis?"

Heather said she did, but not very well.

"Same here," said Lucy. "Average county family, and that's not saying very much nowadays," she added in a burst of confidence.

"I suppose I'm average third-year college and that's not saying very much either," said Heather. "Golf's my game."

"It must be awfully interesting to run a works," said Lucy, establishing herself with knees well apart and toes turned in for a good talk on really interesting subjects. "My cousin Clarissa Graham wants to go into your father's works. Do you know her?"

Heather said she did.

"We met at Miss Fielding's wedding," she said. "Dad and I think she is a very clever girl, but she won't stay the course. You know, Miss Marling, her class marry," and with such scientific detachment, with such complete absence of any class feeling was the remark made that Lucy accepted it as it came and thought for a moment.

"I expect you're right," she said. "Clarissa will go to college and then she'll marry somebody. They all do now," and if there was a tinge of melancholy in the last words, there was no envy. "I say, do you know anything about artificial fertilizers?"

Heather Adams, who if complete readiness to accept any situation is the mark of a lady was rapidly qualifying for her degree, said she didn't herself but her father did. At least, she added, he was interested in the business side and was practically the owner of Holman's Phospho-Manuro.

"I'll tell you what," said Lucy, "I must talk to him when he's finished talking to Mr. Dean. Hullo, here's Charles. Did you win? Here's Heather Adams."

"I lost like anything," said Charles. "Your brother Robin can serve double faults more times running than anyone I've ever met. How are mathematics?"

This question was addressed to Heather, who said with composure that they were doing very well and she hoped to get a good class next year and her wedding was to be at the end of July when she had got her degree.

"Sooner you than I," said Charles, alluding we imagine more to the mathematical studies than to the wedding. "Did you know I was a schoolmaster now?"

Heather said Freddy had told her and, having asked Charles a few questions about his work, dismissed him and resumed her conversation with Lucy, for though she had long ago decided to forgive Charles for slighting her when she was a hideous school-girl and wished him no ill, she took very little interest in him. Nor did she now take very much interest in Captain Belton, for though he had picked her out of the lake and told her about his buried romance, her real affection was for his parents, in whom she had found staunch friends and through whom she had vastly improved in her manners and general outlook. Presently Mr. Dean came up with apologies for his absence and tried to get Mr. Adams to himself. But Mr. Adams refused to be abstracted from Mrs. Dean until that lady had relapsed into a somnolent condition and left him free.

"Now, Adams," said Mr. Dean, who was getting impatient, for he was an important man and a successful man and used to getting what he wanted, "I want to have a few words with you. Would you like to come to the library?"

"No, thank you," said Mr. Adams. "Fack is, I'm here on a social call, as you might say, and I don't mix business and pleasure. But any day in the week you'll find Sam Adams at the office when Parliament isn't sitting and pleased to talk things over. And if it's the Mngangaland hydroelectric concession, you needn't worry."

"Oh, Mr. Adams," said Lucy Marling, who had been strain-ing at the leash ever since the name Holman had been men-tioned, "you know Holman, the fertilizer man, don't you?"

"That's right, young lady, I've forgotten your name, thank you, Miss Marling, and I won't forget it again. Not quite a lady's subject."

"But it *is*, said Lucy earnestly. "You've no idea how chalky all father's land is and he's been using Washington's Vimphos, and

Martin Leslie uses Corbett's Bono-Vitasang and Mr. Belton uses Holman's Phospho-Manuro, and it's most *frightfully* important for us to do the best we can for the land and I thought you might know something about it, and Mr. Dean too because he's farming. I'm most awfully sorry to butt in, but you've had no idea how important it is about the land. It's like children. You've just got to give the right food."

"I get you," said Mr. Adams. "Put it this way. I've got a new combined helical-gear point-one-two-five compressed grablock turner, *with* compensation gear. Now if some damned fool goes and puts a cheap machine oil near that machine, next thing is it seizes and the gear's stripped, and a matter of two thousand pounds or so down the drain. Now, I'm not a hard man," said Mr. Adams, "but anyone that did that I'd fire him and tell his union to go to hell. What you want to give that machine is the finest lubricating oil you can get, and if you'll credit me that's why I've put a matter of ten thousand pounds into Mongolian Oil Products Limited. Mind you," said Mr. Adams, "I'm expecting to see my money back, but I'll see it back through good stuff and stuff that my engines will run sweetly on. And I take it that's what you feel about your father's property, Miss Marling."

"I'll tell you what," said Lucy, a glorious hope beginning to shine within her. "You said not mix business and pleasure. Can I come and talk to you in your office?"

"Well, Heth?" said Mr. Adams to his daughter. "She's my little partner, Heth is," said Mr. Adams to the company in general. "And we talk everything over, don't we, Heth?"

"That's right, dad," said Heather seriously. "As I see it, dad, Miss Marling wants your advice. She wants to help her father, just as I want to help you. I'd like you to go into it, daddy."

"Well, that's that," said Mr. Adams. "I'll tell my sekertary to phone you up—no, I'll say write," said Mr. Adams thoughtfully, "because you don't want your father to hear what you're up to, eh? And she'll tell you when I'm free and you can come along and I'll tell you all I can—and that's not much," he added, "for land hasn't been in my line; not as yet. But you never know what's coming at you round the corner," said Mr. Adams, "and as often as not it comes round at you sideways."

Lucy expressed her gratitude. Oliver was afraid that she might, as she so often did, flog a willing horse and make Mr. Adams regret his generous offer, but she remained quiet and the talk was almost at once interrupted by the arrival of Richard Tebben and Miss Krogsbrog.

Richard Tebben, though graceless in many ways, was well set-up and not ill-looking and enjoyed looking down at most of the women he met. But Miss Krogsbrog, as we have already observed, was cast in a heroic mould, and if she had suddenly grown a helmet and a kind of tin brassière and outsung a full-sized orchestra no one would have been surprised, so that when she appeared beside Richard any woman present was apt to think that at the wedding it would be advisable for the bride to wear flat shoes and the bridegroom the cothurnus neatly disguised, or even a small pair of stilts. Mr. Fanshawe, joining the party at that moment with his wife, was forcibly reminded of the tag Vera incessu patuit dea, adding in a kind of aside to himself: "But only a Scandinavian one."

"Richard!" said Mrs. Dean, who after a nap was apt to greet any newcomer with deceptive warmth just to show that she had been awake the whole time.

"How do you do, Mrs. Dean?" said Richard. "This is Petrea Krogsbrog that I'm engaged to."

"Come and sit by me," said Mrs. Dean, pushing a bundle of silks and embroidery off a chair. "We have known Richard for years. You know he saved Jessica's life. She is looking at the tennis, but she will be here quite soon. How beautiful you are, my dear!" For like most beautiful women, though men in their ignorance prefer to think otherwise, Mrs. Dean loved beauty in her own sex. And we think it will be found that this holds good in nearly every case: that beauty admires beauty and that beauty is set off by beauty, and only an exceptional fool would surround herself with plain friends to set off her own good looks.

"We are all beautiful in Sweden," said Miss Krogsbrog, gratified but not surprised by her hostess's praise. "It is because we are very health-minded. I have always done gymnastics and sunbathing and respected my body. Also we do not neglect our minds. Richard and I have many intellectual interests in common, and I shall teach him sociology."

"Well, that will be *very* nice," said Mrs. Dean vaguely. "I suppose everyone is a socialist in Sweden. Richard was terribly in love with me when he was a young man and wrote me such a nice poem. I always forget the words, but the children can recite it. Jessica," she called to her youngest daughter, who exquisitely yet rurally smart, her naked nylons now showing no trace of a ladder, had joined the group, "do tell Miss Krogsbrog about Richard's poem."

"You have a wonderful body," said Miss Krogsbrog, eying the actress with admiration.

"One has to," said Jessica, "in my profession. Selma Lundquist spends *hours* keeping fit. Would you like to hear the poem?"

"I shall be honoured if you will recite it," said Miss Krogsbrog, deliberately disregarding her affianced's signs of distress.

Jessica drew up one exquisite leg so that the sole of her right foot rested against the inside of her left heel, an attitude considered restful by some tribe in darkest Africa and one not easy for an outsider to cultivate, and in a low beautifully modulated voice recited Richard's one and only love lyric. She then let down her leg and in the same movement made a charming curtsy.

"Very good," said Miss Krogsbrog to Richard. "You shall join the Poets' Circle in Stockholm. Is it true, Miss Jessica, that Richard saved you from a bull?"

Jessica as we know had very little use for Richard, but she did owe him a debt. She had deliberately stood on one leg while reciting the poem to annoy him, and could see from his speaking countenance how successful she had been. Having shown him in this hieratic language of gesture exactly where he got off, she would now be the good well-behaved little youngest Dean girl. So she said it was quite true, and Richard had shown great coolness and courage, and she would never forget it.

"And now," said Mr. Adams, "as Richard is one of my young men, I'd like to meet his fiancée. My name's Adams, Miss Krogsbrog, Sam Adams, and I may say that Richard is well thought of in the office and we'll wish you both all the best when the happy event comes off. And this is my daughter Heather. We're partners, aren't we, Heth? And you'd never think to look at her that she doesn't hardly remember what a mother is," said Mr. Adams, as if to have lost a mother in early childhood made one bear a permanent and visible stigma.

The young women shook hands and said a few words, but it was evident that neither had much opinion of the other, Miss Krogsbrog's contempt for people who studied pure mathematics being only surpassed by Heather's poor view of people who talked about sociology as if it were an exact science.

"Well, Heth and I must be going," said Mr. Adams. "Timon tide waits for no man as they say, and I've got plenty to do. I expect we'll all meet at the Conservative Rally."

"But aren't you Labour, Mr. Adams?" said Lucy Marling.

"That's the ticket I got in on," said Mr. Adams, "and when Sam Adams has given his word he keeps it. But it doesn't prevent me thinking a bit. And I may add," said Mr. Adams, dropping rather to the terror of his hearers into what sounded like the beginning of a political oration, "that when the Labour Committee in Barchester did me the honour to ask me to stand, I said I was a plain man and believed in plain speaking and if they thought I was always going into the lobby the way they told me they'd have some surprises. And if everyone treated their employees fair, the way I do, I said, there wouldn't be any need for all this labour unrest. And, I said, if only Mr. Churchill would take the leadership of the Labour Party, England would get on all right. And that's why Sam Adams is going to the Conservative Rally."

He looked round to see how his imaginary constituents were taking it.

"I find your précis of your views most interesting," said Mr. Fanshawe in his don's dry voice, "though your first statement appears to me to be in the nature of a non sequitur."

"Oh, Mr. Adams," said Mrs. Dean, suddenly waking to her duties as a hostess, "this is my son-in-law, Charles Fanshawe, who married our eldest daughter, Helen. This is Helen."

"Not the Mrs. Fanshawe who won the two hundred kilometre trophy in a Crowline 50 just before the war?" said Mr. Adams. "I'm proud to meet you. I did some of the parts of the Crowline engine and a prettier one I've never seen. And to return to what your husband was saying, I take his meaning though the words are a bit beyond me, but Sam Adams has been knocking about long enough to have a pretty fair idea of what a man means, and what he meant was, there was a link missing in my chain of reasoning so to speak. Well, yes, it *was* a missing link, and the missing link may turn up at the rally if what they say about Pomfret Towers is true. Give me a man that *is* a man," said Mr. Adams thoughtfully. "Well, Mrs. Dean, good-bye. I'll be seeing you at the office before long I hope, Dean, and you too, Richard. And there'll be a wedding present coming along from me and Heth and not a stingy one neither. And, Miss Marling, I won't forget. You'll hear from my sekertary and I'll see what I can do."

Heather also said her good-byes and asked Jessica where Susan was because she had met her at Anne Fielding's wedding and would like to meet her again. Jessica said Susan was still playing tennis and she would give her the message.

Though everyone present liked Mr. Adams, there was a distinct feeling of relaxation when he and his daughter had gone. The rest of the Dean family came to find tea and exerted themselves to be nice to Richard, though mostly, it must be said, for the sake of his gentle sister Margaret, whom they loved. Presently Margaret had to go to the nursery about some matter and Mrs. Dean kindly asked Richard if he and Miss Krogsbrog would stay to supper.

"Everyone's staying," she said. "It is only a kind of scratch meal."

"It's most kind of you," said Miss Krogsbrog, "but Mother Tebben is preparing a special dish for us and I do not think we should disappoint her."

"Oh, mother won't mind," said Richard, "and you know how ghastly her suppers are. We'd love to stay, Mrs. Dean. Thanks most awfully. I'll ring mother up if I may and tell her we are having supper with you. Come on, Petrea."

At these words, words which were so like Richard that none of his friends would have paid much attention to them, Miss Krogsbrog got up and stood towering over the company, apparently ready to let loose the Valkyrie's war-cry. But instead of Heia-ho, which Richard would have infinitely preferred, she said in a commanding voice: "Richard! Not!"

"What's the matter, Petrea?" said her betrothed.

"The matter is discourteousness to Mother Tebben," said Miss Krogsbrog, who appeared rather glad than otherwise to rebuke Richard before a large party of his friends. "You say in England a boy's best friend is his mother, and so it is. We shall go back and have our evening meal with Mother Tebben and Father Tebben, and when we are married Mother Tebben will come to us for long visits while Father Tebben shall stay with my father and they shall discuss philosophy and philology. Goodbye, Mrs. Dean, and many thanks for our happy visit."

"Where are you going to be married?" said Mrs. Dean, who took a proprietary interest in marriages owing to her large family.

"Mother Tebben wished it to be at Worsted," said Miss Krogsbrog, "but my father says rather shall it be by our pastor. Father and Mother Tebben will come for the wedding, as my father's guests. Now, Richard," and she spoke to Richard in what was evidently Swedish and of a rather overbearing nature.

"All right, Petrea," said Richard. "I only thought you'd like it," and so they vanish from these pages.

"Well, the limping Avenger has overtaken him," said Mr. Fanshawe as the couple departed, Miss Krogsbrog appreciably a little taller than Richard, "and I may say that his antecedent crimes, or misdemeanours, deserve all they are getting," but though several of his hearers were thinking to the same effect they did not pay much attention to him, being on the whole illiterate.

After this there was more tennis and then a rather rowdy competition for the three bathrooms, where Mr. Dean, by an elaborate system of electric, gas, oil, and coke heating was able to ring the changes throughout the year and was never without boiling water, and then a cold supper enlivened by food from America, Australia, Canada, Denmark, and other places where the Deans had business friends and personal friends. The noise was terrific and Jessica flirted so outrageously with Charles Belton that they both laughed till they choked. Oliver Marling, watching them, felt that he was of another generation. Oliver could not be jealous of Charles, who was so young, but he wished he could be as gay as Charles, for he was beginning to realize that Jessica did not think of life as going to bed early with a book. Her life had its own hours. But whenever he looked at her and saw her eager mobile face and felt her immense yet controlled vitality, the more he adored and the more he feared.

The so-called scratch meal was so good and lasted so long that when at last they rose from the table the dusk was beginning to spread its wings over the world and in the west there was one star shinning. In twos and threes the company drifted onto the lawn and soon from farther afield came the sounds of strayed revellers, especially of Charles and the younger Deans who were having a kind of all-in wrestling match on the edge of the lily-pond with the laudable ambition of pushing each other in.

"England," said Woolcot Van Dryven, Betty Dean's husband, "is a very, very great country."

We shall not transliterate this repeated adverb as vurry, for that is not what Mr. Van Dryven said, but it had a pleasantly exotic tang. His remark also killed conversation, so to put his father and mother-in-law and his wife's relations and his wife's young friends at their ease, he proceeded, with the facility born of many generations of speech-makers on every occasion, to enlarge upon what he had said. And his enlarging was so kind, so flattering to the down-trodden English, so full of confidence that the Old Country would make good, that his older hearers could have wept, hoping that he was right, gnawed by a fear that he might be wrong.

"I'll tell you what," said Lucy Marling, whose talk with Mr. Adams had put her into very good spirits, "we'd be all right if we got enough to eat."

Mr. Van Dryven gave figures of calories and other unintelligibilia.

"Calories are rot," said Lucy, squaring up for a good fight. "No one knows what they are. What father's men on the place want is good beer and fat bacon and plenty of bread and cheese. That's what Barchester has lived on and what *everyone* wants."

"And when I say Europe I shall be desirous now and then to read England," said Mr. Fanshawe aloud to himself, but as no one else present had ever heard of Canning except vaguely as a name, no one took any notice, but probably Mr. Fanshawe was right, and when we say Barsetshire we may be understood also now and then to read England.

Mr. Van Dryven said the caloric value of liquor was very doubtful.

"Well, beer isn't liquor," said Lucy. "Gin's liquor and whisky, only you can't get any, and rum. Rum's a bit easier to get."

That Charles Belton said was because the lower orders hadn't taken to it and he jolly well hoped they never would.

"Well anyway," said Lucy belligerently, "that's what the agricultural workers want and soon they'll all be too tired to work at all and I don't blame them. I can't do as much as I used myself."

Mr. Van Dryven, appalled by the thought of an English gentlewoman (for he had been properly brought up in New England) suffering privations, said he and his wife would think it a very great privilege to send food parcels to Miss Marling.

"It's most awfully kind of you," said Lucy, "and I can't tell you how grateful we all are to the people who send us food from America, but it's the cottages I'm thinking of. They don't get parcels, and if we gave every parcel we get to them there wouldn't be more than a mouthful each. It's like those *beasts* who say the royal family get too much money," said Lucy, going bright red in the face with loyalty. "I worked it out from *Whitaker's Almanac* and if the civil list was divided among the whole of England they'd have about a halfpenny each. I do HATE people," she added vaguely.

Mr. Van Dryven, impressed by a factual appeal (his way of speaking, not ours), became serious and said Miss Marling had given him something to think about, and proceeded to think about it aloud and at great length. His mother-in-law went to sleep on the chaise-longue where she was gracefully reclining. Oliver looked at Jessica. With a common impulse they rose and walked across the lawns to where the ground fell away towards the Woolram. Here a seat was placed suitable for people who, strolling about the garden at dusk, wished to contemplate the quiet English landscape at their ease.

> "Let contemplation with extensive viewgia
> Survey mankind from China to Perugia,"

said Oliver thoughtfully.

"I expect that is a misquotation," said Jessica, "but I can't be bothered to ask you. Charles made me laugh so much that I am quite weak," in proof of which she laid her head affectionately on Oliver's shoulder.

"Did you notice," she said, "that Aubrey wasn't at dinner?"

"Now you mention it, I didn't," said Oliver. "How thoughtless of me. He isn't ill, I hope."

"Oh, no, not at all," said Jessica. "He promised himself that he wouldn't leave his room till he had conquered the second act. He often does that. Once he spent three weeks in a *revolting* hotel at Nice because he didn't like to break his word to himself."

"It's rum," said Oliver, very gently putting aside a lock of hair which had fallen in admired disorder over Jessica's cheek and thinking as he did so how incredibly soft that cheek was, "how often one doesn't notice Aubrey. That sounds rude but I didn't mean it to be."

"Not a bit rude," said Jessica. "You see he is always the right person in the right place. Protective colouring."

Oliver considered this statement and found it enlightening.

"I think I see what you mean," he said. "He is always acting the person he ought to be."

"That's it," said Jessica. "When he's here he looks like any guest in any country house. Father thinks he is interested in engineering, mother thinks he is that nice Mr. Clover; when I took him to the Deanery Dr. Crawley thought he was a clergyman without a dog collar. If he goes to a funeral it's like the Importance of Being Earnest only not overdone. He's a kind of Happy Hypocrite only with a hundred masks instead of one."

While she was speaking, Oliver's disengaged arm had unconsciously, or so it said, found its way round Jessica's waist. Without pausing in her analysis of Aubrey Clover she gently unwound the arm, which pretended not to know that it was being unwound, and Oliver suddenly thought of Miss Skiffins and laughed.

"Are you laughing at me?" said Jessica in her black velvet voice.

"No, darling," said Oliver. "At Mr. Dickens. Jessica, what is Aubrey really like? Behind all the masks."

"I don't quite know," said Jessica. "But I shall in the end. I think he is the Theatre," on which word her beautiful speaking voice dropped a tone and made the word sound like a muffled bell. Oliver could have listened to the sound dying away in the dusk hour for ever, but he was a little afraid.

"And talking of theatre," he said, "look, how the floor of heaven is thick inlaid, or at any rate it will be in another half-hour, with patines of bright gold."

Jessica said, very sweetly, that they all said that to her, even if it was the ceiling of the Wigwam, which was painted in neophallic designs by Maboul, who was a pupil of Braque.

"If they do, they probably mean it," said Oliver. "I mean it. It's fun to talk Shakespeare to you, because you do know him. I didn't mean to tell you, but I can't help it."

"Oh, do help it. You must," said Jessica urgently, but not moving.

"I can't help it," said Oliver. "I am nearly twice your age. I earn my living and have no prospects, the younger son of an impoverished country gentleman. I don't particularly care for the theatre except you. I have incidentally never been really in love in my life. Charles Belton would be much more suitable, but I am not Charles. I don't know how to say what I want to say."

"My poor lamb," said Jessica, gently moving from his arm. "Is it so bad?"

"Well, I shan't blow my brains out or go to Australia if you won't marry me," said Oliver, "not that the blasted Government would let me go to Australia if I wanted to. We have spent so many hours together this summer, Jessica, and I know you haven't so many hours to spare in your life, so I thought you might care for me," and in his agitation he got up and stood before Jessica imploring help.

"No," said Jessica. "No to everything, my dear, except going on as we were before."

"If you think that is enough you are very insensitive," said Oliver. "Will you marry me?"

"I won't," said Jessica, standing up.

"Is there—" said Oliver and paused. "No, damn it, I will say it even if it's bad theatre. Is there another man? If so I will shoot him."

"Of course there isn't the other man," said Jessica scornfully. "You don't seem to understand that I am a servant of the public. I haven't time for men or other men, except my real friends like you. There's only one person I could possibly marry."

"I suppose you want me to ask who he is," said Oliver, feeling that as an actor he had missed every cue and fluffed every line and would be sacked on Friday; also as a gentleman uncomfortably conscious that he was behaving in an uncivilized way.

"You needn't," said Jessica. "I'll tell you. Aubrey. Because he is the Theatre," at which Oliver almost sat down flat upon the garden path like Miss Betsy Trotwood and remained silent from sheer inability to speak.

"You would ask," said Jessica, "and now you know."

"Does Aubrey know?" Oliver asked, though quite conscious that it was someone else speaking.

"I don't know," said Jessica. "It is all quite unimportant. It's what goes on at the Cockspur between seven and half past ten every evening except Monday, matinées on Wednesday and Saturday, that matters and rehearsing twenty-five hours a day. And one has to get a little sleep. But between the acts, darling, one does truly love one's real friends."

The voice of the strayed revellers came unmelodiously across the dusk air with loud splashes and yells.

"Thank you," said Oliver. "Well, your real friend truly loves you, only quite differently, and there's an end. Good-bye."

"Don't be theatrical, my lamb," said Jessica. "Will you take me out to supper next Wednesday? I'm always dead after the matinée."

"And except nothing?" said Oliver.

"If you call it nothing," said Jessica, making a face of mock sulks, "to have my company and never to have the door shut against you."

"Well, half a loaf is better than no bread to anyone as broken-spirited as I am," said Oliver and went down on his knees on the grass and kissed both Jessica's hands. Part of him hoped the moment would last for ever, another part hoped he would die at her feet, and they remained motionless for time enough to take a curtain, at which moment Aubrey Clover suddenly burst upon them. Oliver wondered if he would have to fight a duel.

"My God! I've done it," said Aubrey Clover, who appeared to take their attitude as a matter of course. "I locked my door and I told that second act the door was staying locked till one of us was dead. Well, it's dead, Jessica. I've knocked every nail into its coffin."

"Oh, my *lamb*!" Jessica cried. "What happens to Mrs. Parafine? Quick, Aubrey. I must see. Oliver wants to marry me."

"Oh, all right," said Aubrey Clover. "But mind. No family till the new play has finished the London run, and the New York run too. And we might be doing South America wherever that is. Come on and I'll read it."

"I'm coming," said Jessica, and she quickened her pace to keep up with him while Oliver, not quite knowing what part he was cast for or whether he was wanted, strode beside them, "but I'm not going to marry him."

"Marry whom?" said Aubrey Clover. "Oh, Oliver. Of course not. Come to Jessica's flat on Monday night, Oliver, and we'll read you the second act. God! I'm tired."

"I expect you haven't had anything to eat," said Oliver. "You weren't at supper."

"And that's the first sensible word anyone has said for the last hour," said Jessica. "Oliver, be an angel and tell Susan Aubrey needs some supper. She's the only one with any sense. Good night, darling."

She stood on tiptoe, flung her arms round Oliver's neck and kissed him warmly, and then hurried into the house after Aubrey Clover. Oliver found Susan and gave her Jessica's message.

"All right," said Susan. "I'll see about it. You do look tired, Oliver. You ought to go home. I expect it's the heat. Lucy was looking for you."

So Oliver went through the house and found his sister Lucy yawning ferociously while Mr. Woolcot Van Dryven told her how libraries should be run. She was glad to be rescued, and as they drove home so full was she of Mr. Adams and her forth-coming interview that for once she did not notice that her dear brother had his headache look, and Oliver was just as glad that she didn't.

Susan found the cook still up and collected food and drink on a tray, which she took to Aubrey Clover's room, where he and Jessica were arguing so fiercely over a line that they did not notice her till she had put the tray on a table.

"Don't forget to have some supper, Aubrey," she said, and turned to go.

"Thank you a thousand times, darling," said Jessica, kissing her elder sister with for once a total disregard of her make-up. "Oh, and I forgot to give you a message from Heather Adams. She says she met you at the Fielding wedding and wants to meet you again."

Susan thanked Jessica and went away, trying very hard not to remember how Heather, not meaning any harm, had killed her heart as surely as frost in a spring night kills the young buds; and then she had to try even harder not to remember that the white clover and the green grass had fallen before old Tomkins's scythe in the cloisters. In the hall Charles Belton was waiting to say good-bye.

"It's been a marvellous evening," he said. "I think I'm the only one who didn't get pushed into the pond. I expect it's a spot of commando stuff I did. Even your tough naval brothers couldn't do it, but they broke my wrist-watch. I say, Susan, you look a bit washed out. I hope we haven't been a nuisance. Oh, Freddy sent you his love."

Cruel, cruel to send such a mockery of affection. But she

thanked Charles and sent her love to his mother. Luckily there was plenty for her to do before all the children and grandchildren were in bed, for everyone took it affectionately for granted that Susan, or Aunt Susan, would look after everyone. From her bedroom she looked across the angle of the house to Aubrey's room, where a light shone, and across the warm still night air she could hear their voices alternately and then sudden spasms of both talking at once. Stageland. The most sincere falsehood, the falsest sincerity in the world. Then she went to bed and of course lay awake through most of the short summer night, thinking of all the things she must not think of. Being a very honest girl, she bore no rancour against Heather, for Heather had meant no ill, but she hoped she would not see Heather again till she had lost the feel of pain.

CHAPTER 12

This summer, as those of us who are not too tired to think will remember, was one of the rare English summers when plans could be made for weeks ahead without fear of rain. Indeed, the only fear in Lord Bond's mind as he surveyed the brown grass and cracked earth in the home-field at Staple Park was that the Conservative Ralliers would tread even the roots of the grass out of existence and leave him with the English equivalent of a Dust Bowl. These fears he confided to his cowman, who thought but poorly of his employer though admitting that his lordship knew enough to let well alone; by which he meant that he knew Lord Bond was terrified of him and intended to keep his lordship in that state of bondage.

"Ar," said the cowman. "So they do say. Great gormed fools I call them," which remark being obviously directed towards Lord Bond made him even more terrified than before. "No. That old grass she's all right. My old father he trusted in the Lord he did, even when it was a calf with two heads. And *he* never worritted about the droughts. Let them worrit as the ground belongs to, he said, and I say the same. And what's more the Pig-Breeders they'll leave some good pig-dung, and early in the year I'll fork that dung on the two-acre. And don't let anyone come a-asking me for any of the dung because he won't get none, not if it was Lord Stoke himself. Now, he's a gentleman as understands dung; and grass too," added the cowman malevolently, and having thus abased his employer he went off in very good spirits to meet the secretary of the Barsetshire Pig-Breeders' Association, listen to his requirements for ground-space, and give him exactly what he thought fit.

For the next ten days or so Staple Park was a very fair representation of the Normandy beaches superimposed upon any tract of English country taken over by the War Office. The Conservative Rally was having a large platform and, as a propitiatory offering to Jupiter Pluvius, an outsize marquee though everyone hoped it would not be needed. The Pig-Breeders were creating a magnificent city of prefabricated temporary sites where the competitors could spend their leisure hours. Electricians were trailing wires all over the place for loud-speakers and despising the men who were digging temporary drains, while the caterers were erecting tents of their own and despising the electricians. Conservative stewards and pig stewards were doing what they called getting the hang of things, heartily despised by all the workmen, or technicians as we are now expected to say. Lord Stoke drove over from Rising Castle in his dog-cart nearly every day to keep an eye on the pig-park and drove his brother-in-law, Lord Bond, nearly distracted by taking the drain-diggers off their work to open a trench in a small hillock at one end of the field in the hope of finding some Viking's bones and so unearthing a badger, who bit the foreman's thumb and escaped into the tangled thicket behind the fields. Never had the Fleece at Skeynes had so many customers nor so little to give them, and though by the courtesy of Messrs. Scatcherd and Sons, the Barsetshire caterers, some extra supplies were obtained, the Fleece said it would have to close at two o'clock for the next fortnight. This dire news percolated through Lord Bond to Mr. Palmer at Skeynes on a Monday when they sat together on the Bench. Mr. Palmer mentioned it to his sister Mrs. Dean, who in one of her lucid intervals mentioned it to Jessica, who told it as a joke to Charles Belton. Charles, realizing that this was no laughing matter, told Lucy Marling, whom he met in Barchester on market day, having great confidence in her knowledge of things in general and her capability in every department.

"Oh, I say, they *must* have enough beer for the Pig-Breeders," said Lucy. "I wish I knew Pilward's Entire. Oh, I say, Charles, I'll tell you what, I'm just going to see Mr. Adams at Hogglestock. Heather's engaged to young Pilward, so we might work something. I say, father's Ford van has broken down and we're wondering how on earth we'll get the pig over," to which Charles, so lightly do the young dispose of their parents' property without making any inquiries, replied that he was sure his father would lend his van if Mr. Marling's wasn't mended, and then Lucy hurled herself into a Hogglestock bus and went away, leaving Charles to reflect on what he had said and wonder if his father would cut up rough, which he occasionally did.

Those who knew Hogglestock in the days of Dr. Crawley's grandfather would not have recognized it now. Where a tiny remote village with a church, a shabby parsonage, and a few labourers' cottages had been, there was now a large and hideous suburb. The Hogglestock Rolling Mills, established in the nineties, had been the beginning. Land had risen in value, the farmers had sold and moved back into country as yet purely agricultural, the church had been rebuilt by a pupil of Waterhouse in angry red stone, which when floodlit for King George V's jubilee produced a truly terrifying effect, inspiring the Reverend (by courtesy) Enoch Arden, who had come over from the Hallbury Ebenezer to preach at the Hogglestock Beulah, to a trenchant parallel between the Church of England and the Gates of Hell. The shabby old parsonage had long since been secularized and turned into a shop, and the new vicarage was indistinguishable from several hundred other red brick villas with bow windows.

It was at about the time of the jubilee that Mr. Adams had acquired a controlling interest in the Rolling Mills and so laid the foundations of a works now employing several thousand people, from which beginnings he had, as we know, gone very far and was a man of considerable weight in the world of business and finance. The little four-room house where he and his wife first lived had been exchanged for the red-brick villa with front and back garden and side entrance where his wife had died and Heather's lonely childhood had been spent. Though Mr. Adams never forgot his wife, or Mother as he usually called her, he had no sentiment for bricks and mortar and had at the beginning of the war bought an old stone house, stranded with its garden and coach-house among the villas of the new suburb, and there he and Heather had lived ever since. It had been at first a lonely house, for Mr. Adams had few friends and Heather had not the gift of making them, but since she had been at the Hosiers' Girls' Foundation School and had been befriended by Mrs. Belton things had changed. Mr. Adams, however busy he was, found it not unpleasant to meet young people of Heather's age and when she went to college he told her to ask anyone she liked for the vacation. Many of his wealthy business friends also had boys and girls growing up and his house had the attraction of garden, tennis court, and billiard table, at which last game Heather was particularly competent owing to the coaching of Miss Holly, the present headmistress of the Hosiers' Girls' Foundation School, who was a first-class amateur player.

But of this house Lucy did not know, nor had any of the Beltons seen it, for Mr. Adams, though he made incursions into many kinds of society, had preferred to keep his home for what he called his own sort. Exactly what he meant by this we cannot say, but we think that in his real though unsentimental feeling for his late wife he wished the house to be frequented by people that Mother would have felt at home with. Even Mrs. Belton had not been asked to visit it, and though she liked Mr. Adams and was quite fond of Heather, she would not have wished to be asked and in any case the journey to Hogglestock was a tiring one, involving as it did a change of motor-buses and the chance of not getting a seat, though the actual distance was not great.

Lucy, however, was going towards Hogglestock at a good

moment when the human tide was seething towards Barchester and arrived punctually at Mr. Adams's office, which was in a large ugly red-brick house next to the works gates. The porter on duty knew her name and telephoned to Mr. Adams's secretary, who came down to meet her and took her upstairs through an office where inferior orders of secretaries were working and into an inner room where there was a large desk with a kind of battery of house-telephones and electric buzzers on it which interested Lucy very much, and as Mr. Adams was still engaged she begged the secretary to explain everything to her, which the secretary obligingly did.

"I'll tell you what," said Lucy, "it's like the Regional Commissioner's Office at Barchester used to be in the war. My brother was working there and he showed me everything. I mean everything that wasn't secret."

The secretary said Well now that was very interesting because she had worked there herself, on the teleprinter, and it came back to her now that Mr. Oliver Marling had brought some friends to see the room and wasn't Mr. David Leslie one of them and on learning that he was and that he was now married and had two babies she shed her professional manner and became quite human.

"Mr. Adams won't keep you long, Miss Marling," she said. "He's in conference with Mr. Pilward. We do a lot of business with the brewery." And as she said this the inner door opened and Mr. Adams came out with the owner and managing director of Pilward's Entire.

"Good morning, Miss Marling," said Mr. Adams. "Punctuality is a virtue and I'm sorry I kept you waiting. Three minutes," he added, looking at his wrist-watch. "Well, Bert, that's all right. Your order will be through by the 30th. Thanks for the visit."

"Oh," said Lucy, who was not easily abashed and stopped at nothing when it was a question of helping her friends, "is that Mr. Pilward? I'm Lucy Marling. Are you going to the Conservative Rally, Mr. Pilward?"

Mr. Pilward said cautiously that politics weren't much in his line.

"Pilward's the third member of the Liberal Party and no one knows who the other two are," said Mr. Adams, but this was evidently an old joke as both men laughed and Mr. Pilward said he hoped to be there because he was showing a pig.

"Then I'll tell you what," said Lucy. "Do you know the Fleece at Skeynes?"

Mr. Pilward said it was a free house, but he had supplied them regularly for a long time.

"Well, they're out of beer," said Lucy. "I only heard it this morning. And if the Pig-Breeders can't get beer the show will be absolutely ruined."

"Pigs are thirsty work," said Mr. Pilward thoughtfully. "You know, Sam," he continued turning to Mr. Adams and speaking as if Lucy were not there, though without any rudeness, "we've been trying to get the Fleece for a long time. It's an idea. And the Pig-Breeders' Association has a lot of good men in it. I wouldn't like them to go short. I'm going back to the brewery and I'll keep it in mind. Thanks, Miss Marling. Is it your father that owns Harefield? There's some nice land round there, on the Barchester side. I dare say I'll see you at the show," and after shaking hands he went away and Mr. Adams took Lucy into his office.

"Well, now, young lady," he said, "it's eleven fifty; should have been eleven forty-five, but I hadn't reckoned on old Pilward. Now, Sam Adams is a plain man and likes plain speaking. You tell me exactly what's on your mind. My little Heth and I we've had a talk about what you said the other day and Heth says I ought to do what I can for you. And," added Mr. Adams, looking with approval at Lucy's handsome weather-beaten face and her capable hands, "I should like to do what I can for you."

Thus encouraged, Lucy put her case as clearly and shortly as possible.

"Father's just got to sell some of the land," she said. "The Town Council bought a bit on the Nutfield side for a school, but he still has more than he can farm. He'll have to sell some more and then I think I can keep the rest going, but we're going to need a lot of fertilizer and I thought you could give me some advice. Everyone says something different and I'm ready to try anything, but I don't think I'll ever get that piece of land on the Barchester side into good condition. It needs draining and we can't afford it, so the best I can do is to cultivate it as well as I can. Poor father, it's ghastly for him," and Lucy felt very near to tears, a form of weakness that she particularly loathed and despised.

Mr. Adams made no answer and her heart fell. She had come so full of hope, though her hopes were very vague, and now Mr. Adams, who had seemed so safe and encouraging, hadn't even listened to what she said.

"Well, I expect I've been talking rot," said Lucy. "I'm sorry and it was most awfully good of you to see me."

"Now, sit down and take your time," said Mr. Adams. "Business is a funny game, Miss Marling, and there's more to it than pounds, shillings, and pence. You've thrown a spanner into the machinery, but it's going to turn out all right. Now, I don't know about land, but I know what land is needed for. And when Bert Pilward began to talk about the land on the Barchester side something told me he needed it for the brewery. Now I've been thinking about my works. We've got a fine recreation ground this side of Barchester, but what I want is a bit of ground where I can get all my own vegetables for the canteens. We feed a matter of five thousand or so one way and another. Now I've got an idea, Miss Marling, at least it's my Heth's idea and mine, so half of it's good. We were talking about what you said and Heth said to me, dad, she said, you buy some ground and put some money into it and grow vegetables and so forth and it'll pay you hand over fist. Well, to cut a long story short, for Sam Adams isn't one to waste his breath, I'd like to talk to your father about buying some land. Would that bit Pilward wants grow vegetables?"

Lucy, speaking seriously on a serious subject though her heart was pounding furiously, said if it was drained and properly treated it would. "And I know," she added. Not boastfully, but as one who had had experience.

"Right," said Mr. Adams. "Say—mind you it isn't in writing yet, but once Sam Adams has taken a job on, his word is as good as his bond—say your father will sell, say I'll drain and give the land all it wants. It'll be up to old Holman to do his best for me as it will be a thundering good advertisement. And say you run a market garden for me. A proper salary, say what machines you need and the kind of labour you want. I've pals at the Labour Exchange, don't worry about that. You'll be the boss, and once it's going you won't want to be there every day. You'll have time for your father's place too. Now, don't hurry, think it over."

He finished speaking and sat back. Lucy to her horror and shame found that tears were running down her cheeks unchecked. With a kind of bellow she tried to apologize.

"Now that's all right," said Mr. Adams kindly. "Overwrought. That's what you are, the way my Heth was when she was studying to go to college. But she got what she wanted all right, and so will you. You think it over, Miss Marling, and let me know. And if you agree, then leave it to me and I'll have a word with your father some time. Don't you worry. I'll let the old gentleman roar at me and think he's doing me a favour," which words showed so keen an insight into Mr. Marling's mind that Lucy stopped crying and began to laugh, but in a comfortable way, not a hysterical way.

"Well, it's nearly half past twelve," said Mr. Adams. "The best thing for you, Miss Marling, would be some dinner. We have our dinner in the canteen from twelve o'clock to half past two. Come and see what you think of the lay-out. You might give me a hint or two."

This suggestion was very favourably received by Lucy, so they went downstairs, across a stone-paved yard, and into the canteen, a large light room with long tables and a constant coming and going of men and women with trays, full and empty.

"Cafeteria system," said Mr. Adams. "Self-help. That's the idea. Here's a tray."

Following her guide, Lucy helped herself to tray, knife, spoon, fork, pepper and salt, and then collected a meal from the large choice of cold and hot dishes.

"We'll sit here," said Mr. Adams, leading the way to a kind of high table. "When things are a bit easier we'll have cardboard glasses and fill them at a drinking-water fountain. This is Mr. Evans, our production manager, Miss Cowshay of the casting department, Miss Pickthorn, my sekertary, you've met. I want a word with you, Evans, about those castings," and he held his production manager in talk while Lucy ate her lunch and chatted, as the newspapers say when they mean talked, to the secretary and to Miss Cowshay, who turned out to be none other than the Miss Cowshay whom Lucy had seen in the Regional Commissioner's Office and who used to be in the cashier's office at Pilchard's Stores at the desk marked G to M. When the meal was over Lucy thanked Mr. Adams and said she must go.

"Now, wait a minute," said Mr. Adams. "I've got to go home. Would you very much mind walking with me? It's not far and I want to know your opinion of the canteen. The bus stops almost outside my house, or if you're in a hurry I'll send you back in one of the works cars. It's only seven or eight minutes," and without waiting for Lucy to say yes or no he took her across the yard, out of the gates, along several drab streets of small red-brick houses, asking questions and listening attentively to her answers. Lucy had thought highly of the canteen, and with what was for her considerable diffidence she put forward one or two suggestions which Mr. Adams said he would like to consider. By this time they had come to a long stone wall with a green wooden door in it before which Mr. Adams paused.

"Side entrance," he said, opening the door. "Come in."

Inside the wall was a long old-fashioned garden with fruit trees and a long border and a lawn. To their right was a dull but not ugly stone house of three stories with well-proportioned windows and flowers outside each.

"My mother liked window-boxes," said Mr. Adams. "She never had a garden. We'd only a yard. But she always had flowers outside the window. Let's go and find Heth."

He led the way into the house. Lucy was not particularly sensitive to houses, but she had always lived among good furniture, and though the house was dull she found nothing jarring about it. In a small room overlooking the garden Heather Adams was sitting at a table reading and making notes.

"Well, girlie," said Mr. Adams, kissing his daughter, "here's Miss Marling. I've told her about our plans, Heth, and she's going to consider it. Now you two have a talk, because I've a board at two thirty and I want a word with Evans first. You'll be hearing from me, Miss Marling, and I dare say we'll meet at the Conservative Rally."

"I hope you are going to go in with dad," said Heather, and Lucy was interested to find Heather, who was a good half-generation her junior, treating her as an equal whom she respected, and came to the conclusion that her attitude to Heather was much the same. "He's keen on land and I think he ought to go ahead. That's where our food is. Ted and I are going to farm a bit. Of course he will stick to the brewery, but farming is important. You mayn't make money but you're doing something real."

Lucy said everyone she knew was losing money and she hoped Mr. Adams wouldn't lose his.

"If dad buys land, that land is going to pay or dad will know why," said Heather quite seriously. "But it's too late for dad to go to an agricultural college and he wants a partner that knows the job. Do say yes, Miss Marling."

"I say, I'm Lucy," said that lady. "I'd simply love it, so long as my father doesn't mind. He'll probably be furious at first, but he'll get used to the idea. After all, I'm not a child," she added, remembering her age, a thing that she rarely did.

"Dad can handle that," said Heather confidently. "Thank you very much, Lucy. You know dad is going to miss me when I'm married. I shall be pretty busy. Ted travels a good deal and I mean to go with him and then there'll be babies and all that. Dad needs someone to talk to, someone that isn't the works or business, and likes you, Lucy. Do help him if you can."

"Well," said Lucy thoughtfully, "I'll tell you what. I've been awfully down because of father having to sell land and getting poorer and poorer, but if your father is going to buy that bit of land and let me work it I'll swear I'll make it pay. You can't think what it would be to be able to get the tractors and things one needs. Like having food given you for your children if they are hungry. I expect I'll make a lot of mistakes, but I'll do my best. I say, when does the bus go?"

The next bus went in ten minutes, and Heather came out and stood with Lucy at the bus stop. Some girls might have begun kissing and darling-ing after a talk so intimate, though short; but in Heather Lucy recognized a girl who, while not of her class, was of her own way of thinking; downright, of single purpose, and highly unsentimental. The bus scooped Lucy up and took her away. Heather went back and shut the green wooden door. "Poor old dad," she said aloud and then fell into some dream of her own. But dreams do not get one a first-class, so she walked once round the garden to clear her mind, returned to her study, and applied herself to the Friction of Constant Relations.

When Lucy got back to Marling, there were a hundred small things to do and she did them with her usual efficiency, but her mind was on a large piece of ground over on the Barchester side of Harefield, and visions of cabbages, cauliflowers, potatoes, onions, lettuces, and every kind of green stuff, with such additions as a watercress bed where that little stream ran and a good irrigation system for dry seasons. Of this she said nothing to her parents, but when Oliver came down on Friday night she poured out to him all that had passed between herself and Mr. Adams.

"Did you have a good week?" she said, suddenly remembering that one must occasionally think of other people.

Oliver said quite good. On Monday he had been to Jessica's flat and heard her and Aubrey Clover read the second act of his play. On Wednesday he had taken Jessica out to supper and they had danced.

"I'll tell you what," said Lucy, "why don't you marry Jessica? She's awfully nice and you both like living in London and then you'd only need one flat instead of two. Lots of actresses are married."

Oliver said it was a good idea, but he didn't feel like it, and then the conversation went back to Mr. Adams and his schemes and Oliver was sincerely happy to see his dear Lucy so alive and full of interest and enthusiasm, and hoped all would go well for her in this new venture and that his father would also be relieved from various pressing difficulties. But when his family had gone to bed he walked up and down the long grass walk in the hot moonless dusk thinking of a night not so long ago, a night of scented gardens and the distant shouts of strayed revellers, when his hopes had fallen to the ground. His love was unchanged and with that love he must pass his nights: but not with Jessica; not with Jessica.

Mr. Pilward was as good as his word. He had a short but fruitful talk on the telephone with the Fleece and came to an amicable arrangement with it. Whether tied houses are a good or a bad thing it is not for us to say. It depends largely on the value one sets upon freedom. The Fleece, an honest, hard-working inn, had been a free house for many years. Now circumstances, or to put it more precisely the beer shortage, were forcing it into bondage. Mr. Pilward did not govern with whips and scorpions, and the Fleece was probably going to get slightly better supplies than it did under the old arrangement, but one more individual liberty had fallen. In Mr. Pilward's opinion a nation that walked in darkness had seen a great light and he took genuine pleasure in ordering a fine new signboard with the beautiful words Pilwards Entire and a portrait of one of the enormous grey horses that still delivered beer rather ostentatiously in the neighbourhood of Barchester. So Mr. Pilward scored on beer, but in the matter of Mr. Marling's land he lost, for Mr. Adams as we know had got in first and we think Mr. Marling will do better out of him than out of Mr. Pilward.

Cheered by the supplies of beer that had begun to flow into the Fleece, the work of preparing the ground for the Conservatives and pigs went on apace, and though the quarrels between the various workers were just as frequent they were distinctly less bitter. On Friday the competitors for the B.P.B.A.'s cups and medals began to arrive in lorries, Ford vans, and, in the case of Lord Bond's Cropbacked Cruncher and Mr. Middleton's six-month-old Norfolk Nobbler, under their own power, to the joy of all the little boys in the neighbourhood and the great indignation of the local dogs, who saw no sense in letting pigs walk down a sloping board from a lorry into a sty when there were plenty of unemployed dogs ready to bark and snap them into the ways they should go. By opening-time all the competitors were safely housed and the Fleece was doing very nicely.

Next day the sun rose on what was afterwards found to have been the hottest day of the year. Lord Bond, looking down from his dressing-room window in the servants' wing, felt that short of being Lord Lieutenant of the County he had reached the height of worldly ambition. In his park was to take place the double event, the like of which had never before been in the annals of Barsetshire politics or pigs. The Conservative Party were to have their yearly outing, known for no particular reason as a rally, and the Barsetshire Pig-Breeders' Association their annual meeting and a show. And which of these two events was the more important is a matter of opinion, but we may safely say that great as would have been the disappointment if the Conservative Rally had had to be postponed, it would have been far greater if swine fever had broken out, and if human sacrifice could have placated the gods of swine fever Lord Bond would probably have offered himself.

As soon as he had finished his breakfast, Lord Bond, carefully eluding his wife, who wished him to rest and not get excited, slipped away to the pig settlement to admire his own entry and mildly criticize his friends' entries, in which entrancing occupation he was joined by other pig-fanciers till such a galaxy of pig-breeders and owners was collected as had never been seen before, even at the Barsetshire Agricultural before the war. Among these the preeminence must be given to Lord Stoke, Lord Bond's brother-in-law, who, besides knowing a great deal about pigs and having a first-rate pigman, had the additional advantages of a loud voice, a complete belief in his own judgment, and increasing deafness, which quality was particularly marked when his lordship expected to hear anything he disapproved. Wherever Lord Stoke's hat, a most respectable affair rather like a grey bowler with a flat top, was seen, to it did the pig-fanciers rally even as the Huguenots rallied to the white plumes at Ivry.

"Mornin', Goble," said Lord Stoke, raising a finger to his hat as he addressed Sir Robert Graham's bailiff. "What have you got up your sleeve?"

"Only a little one, my lord," said Goble, standing aside so that Lord Stoke could see the White Porkminster, Holdings Goliath, who looked at them malevolently out of one small evil eye.

"I've seen worse, I've seen worse," said Lord Stoke, reaching over with his stick and scratching the pig's back in a most feeling manner. "Who's the runner-up?"

"Well, my lord, it's not for me to say," said Goble. "There's your Pompey, my lord, and there's Mr. Marling's Magnum and there's Lord Pomfret's Blockhouse and there's Lord Bond's Staple the Second. Mr. Belton has some nice young ones, my lord, but not in our class."

"Well, let's see them," said Lord Stoke, and accompanied by an ecstatic crowd of pig-lovers and small boys, he moved on to where Marling Magnum was standing, apparently on nothing, for except by bending double one could not see anything of his feet, so immense was his bulk.

"A bit low in the undercarriage, my lord," said Goble, "but a nice bit of bacon. We've got our money on Holdings, but it's going to be a near thing. That Magnum's over fifty score, my lord. There's only one thing I don't like, my lord. Sir Robert can't get down this weekend. I said to the General, I said, Holdings Goliath will do well, Sir Robert, but he'll do better if you are there. It'll hearten him up like. They say the farmer's boots are the best muck, I said, and it's the same with your eye, Sir Robert. If the General had an eye on Holdings Goliath he'd put on another two pounds before he's weighed, my lord."

"Please, sir, is that true?" said a voice at about the level of Lord Stoke's elbow.

He looked down and saw three small boys.

"What's that?" said Lord Stoke. "Speak up. Whose boy are you, eh?"

"I'm Dean," said the spokesman in a loud voice, "and this is Addison and this is Pickering. My grandfather's got some little pigs here, sir. Would you like to see them? I'll show you where they are."

"Dean, eh?" said Lord Stoke, who appeared to have no difficulty in hearing the speaker's words. "You're from Winter Overcotes, aren't you?"

"Yes, sir," said young Dean. "Aunt Susan brought me and I've got Addison and Pickering with me and we're going to have lunch in the tent. I've got some peppermints and some cakes in case we're hungry. Would the pig like some, sir?"

He pulled from his trouser pocket a dirty paper bag from which he extracted an unpleasant mass of squashed cake and a few peppermint bull's-eyes embedded in it.

"No, my boy. Mustn't feed show animals," said Lord Stoke. Young Dean's face fell.

"I know," he exclaimed, brightening. "I might be a competitor trying to dope the prize pig. I wish someone would try to dope it and I'd knock him out. The school sergeant says I've got a good uppercut. Would you like to feel my biceps, sir?"

He pulled up his shirt sleeve and exhibited an undoubted swelling in the upper part of his right arm.

"Pickering's still got a bad knee where he fell off his bicycle," said young Dean, taking Lord Stoke's hand in a confiding way the better to pull him down to little-boy level. "It's because he will keep on pulling off the scab, sir. Show him your knee, Pick."

Master Pickering unknotted a very dirty handkerchief and exhibited with modest pride a very unpleasant half-raw knee.

"He lost his bandage, sir, so I gave him my handkerchief," said young Dean as Sir Philip Sidney might have said: His need is greater than mine.

"Here you, boy, what's your name?" said Lord Stoke. "You'll be getting blood-poisoning. Come along to the first-aid tent. See you later, Goble," and taking Master Pickering's hand in his disengaged hand, he led the two little boys away, while Addison jumped round them to express general goodwill. In the first-aid tent a Red Cross nurse and a St. John Ambulance attendant were discussing Soviet Russia on a solid foundation of knowing nothing whatever about it and were rather annoyed by the interruption.

"Now, I know your face," said Lord Stoke to the St. John attendant. "Never forget a face. I'd know any cow of mine if I met her in New York. My old father was the same. I know where I saw you. You were carrying the stretcher on one of those damn-fool Victory Days. Fellow climbed up the War Memorial, or was it the South Africa War Memorial, and fell off. Now, tie this boy up for me."

The Red Cross nurse bandaged the knee. Lord Stoke thanked her gallantly, saying he wished he was a boy with a skinned knee, and removed his charges.

"And now show me your grandfather's little pigs," he said to young Dean and they made a kind of consular progress through the show grounds with the three little boys as clients, eager to please and almost exhaustingly eager to impart information, usually of an erroneous nature, which Lord Stoke did not profit by as much as he might owing to his deafness. At the enclosure reserved for young pigs they found Mr. Dean wondering which were his.

"Morning, Dean," said Lord Stoke, touching his hat with one finger, a gesture much admired by his clients and one that was going to bore their masters a good deal for the first few weeks of next term. "Nice little lot of yours. Is that the whole litter?"

"I really don't know," said Mr. Dean. "You see," he added apologetically, "I'm not often at home and my bailiff sees to it all," which frank but injudicious remark caused Lord Stoke to give Mr. Dean a lecture on the duties of a landowner, for Mr. Dean's engineering fame did not interest the county and it probably did not occur to Lord Stoke that he had other and more pressing interests.

"You mustn't tease papa," said a voice from behind Lord Stoke. "He is frightfully hard-working. I've just seen your pig and he's too, too divine."

"My daughter Jessica, Lord Stoke," said Mr. Dean resignedly and glad on the whole to have his lordship's criticism diverted.

"So you are the actress, eh?" said Lord Stoke, raising his hat and almost winking. "My sister Lucasta, Bond's wife, you know, took me to your show last Christmas. Lucasta didn't like it. Too modern for her, she said. Modern, I said, there's nothing modern about Jessica Dean's legs. If I were a younger man, I said to Lucasta, I'd drink her health in champagne out of her shoe, only champagne gives me rheumatism at once. Queer idea, drinking out of a shoe, bad for the shoe too. Now, if you've got a pair of boots that squeak, you soak them in castor-oil and it does wonders. But not champagne."

"You are so, so right," said Jessica. "And this is Aubrey Clover. He's frightfully keen on pigs," upon which Aubrey Clover became in face and manner a man pig-minded from birth and entered into a grave discussion with Lord Stoke about the difficulties of pig-food in these days.

"Well now," said Lord Stoke looking at his old-fashioned watch, "the earlier we lunch the better. You'd better come up to the house, it's less crowded than the tent," and overriding any protests, he took Mr. Dean, Jessica, and Aubrey Clover in tow, and attended by his three clients, who were after the fashion of small boys getting dirtier every moment without any visible cause, he continued his consular progress to the house, where a good many county friends were already assembled.

"I think," said Jessica to Lord Stoke as they went in, "that we won't tell Lady Bond I am on the stage," and so clear was her beautiful voice that the words though softly spoken penetrated Lord Stoke's deafness with ease. His lordship, delighted to enter into a conspiracy with so charming a young woman, again almost winked as he said to his sister: "You know Miss Dean, Lucasta, and this is Mr. Clover, who knows all about pig-foods. Miss Dean's father is showing a nice little litter of Crunch-backs." Lady Bond received the newcomers graciously and passed them on. Aubrey Clover, who had had enough of pigs, melted imperceptibly to an ex-butler brought in for the occasion and handed refreshments so well that no one took the slightest notice of him.

"Protective colouring again," said Jessica to Oliver Marling, who had decided that it would be better to avoid her for the present and found his legs deliberately carrying him in her direction.

Oliver followed her eyes, saw Aubrey Clover, and couldn't help laughing.

"That's better," said Jessica. "How is Lucy and where?"

Oliver said he thought she was somewhere about with Emmy Graham and that she had made friends with Mr. Adams and was full of plans and much more cheerful than she had been for a long time. He then asked Jessica if the lunch was pigs or politics.

"Oh, politics now, quite definitely," said Jessica. "From now onwards we are Conservatives. When the speeches are over we become pigs. Watch Aubrey. As soon as we go outside for the rally he will be a Tory squire. You were asking the other night what the real Aubrey was like. You saw him when he had finished his second act. It's only on the stage that he's real. I'm only second-class; I can't do that."

Oliver had dreaded this moment of remeeting, but Jessica was making it extraordinarily easy, and though her look, her voice, her gestures pierced his heart, he was not going to lose one moment of that sweet bitterness. He did not expect, nor perhaps wish to have her to himself, and when Denis Stonor, detaching himself from Mr. Middleton, came up, he stood a little aside.

"My sweet Jessica," said Denis, holding her hand in both of his. "I made Uncle Jack and Catherine bring me entirely to meet you. Have you seen my play?"

"My sweet Denis," said Jessica, "have you seen *my* play?"

"I couldn't," said Denis. "My dear, I couldn't. I have to be in that theatre every night. I simply *long* to see you, but it looks as if we are going to run till Christmas."

"Well, we are going to run till Kingdom Come," said Jessica. "So neither of us will see each other, which is too, too sad. And what is even sadder is that they aren't our plays. You only write the music of yours and I'm only an actor in Aubrey's. Second-class personages, my lamb."

For a moment the talented and famous composer of light music looked almost sulky, and then he was suddenly natural and his sad and rather monkey-like face was lit by a very attractive smile. Mrs. Middleton saw the smile and wondered if it could ever tear her heart again. But though she half wished and half feared that it might, she was a truthful woman even with herself and knew that it could not. It was rather bitter to confess it; not because she wished to suffer again, but because if a woman does not suffer through old or new loves, she knows she is old. Still, it is something to be safe, to have reached firm ground at last, and some old loves can turn to new friendships.

Word had by now gone round that Mr. Middleton's nephew by marriage who had written that enchanting music for *Sweetest Sorrow* was that tall man over there, the one with the high forehead, my dear, and don't you feel as if his eyes were looking *straight* through you? They say he has no love life at all, but you can't tell about that sort of thing. I call it a *melancholy* kind of face if you know what I mean, but of course you can't judge anyone by their face and what mine is looking like I daren't *think*. Denis received his admirers with the long practice of first nights and made the proper grateful and whimsically self-deprecating remarks, but his eyes were far away from his words till at last he saw Lord Bond, and excusing himself with a charm that was none the less attractive for its obvious falseness, he clove his way through the press till he reached his host.

"Denis?" said Lord Bond. "My *dear* boy. I am delighted to see you. And how is your music?" for Lord Bond, some years before the war, had taken a liking for that invalid nephew of Mr. Middleton's, and because Denis had played Gilbert and Sullivan for him and all the charming simple tunes that had delighted Lord Bond's musical-comedy-going youth, he had offered to back Denis in his ballet music and had put up a sum that to Denis had seemed fantastic, asking for details of how it was spent, but no repayment. Denis had justified his backing and Lord Bond felt a peculiar pride in having spotted a genius who wasn't in his line of country; rather as if his wife had backed a Derby winner, or the Bishop had decided to adopt what had turned out to be a champion crooner.

"Thank you, sir, my music is going nicely," said Denis. "May I come over and play some of it to you one evening? I'm staying with C.W. and Daphne for another week. There's a song called 'I loved you at sight and I love you tonight' that I think you'd like. And I've brought you a present from New York, sir, if you will accept it," said Denis, taking a small parcel from his pocket and handing it to Lord Bond with his attractive melancholy smile.

"For me, my dear boy?" said Lord Bond. "I must open it at once," and he undid the parcel, which was an extremely expensive platinum lighter with a special wind-screen that came up automatically and shielded the flame.

"*Exactly* what I wanted," said Lord Bond, with a boy's delight in a new toy. "Splendid when I'm out on a windy day. I can't tell you how touched and gratified I am. And an inscription."

"It's the words of the first song hit I made in New York," said Denis. "'You did for me what no one else could do.'"

Lord Bond, genuinely touched by Denis's present and the quotation, confounded himself in thanks and nearly cried with pleasure.

"Showing off. We all do," said the voice of Aubrey Clover beside Denis.

"It is expected of one," said Denis. "And curiously enough they like it."

"There speaks the amateur," said Aubrey Clover. "Art is to conceal art. When you can go about the world and no one notices you, then you are the artist. Like me."

To which Denis retorted that if Aubrey were about six feet high and had a face like a suffering monkey and enormous hands and feet he wouldn't find it so easy to be inconspicuous, and then they began to argue about what the Lost Chord was really like while the rest of the party straggled across the garden to the field where the Conservative Rally was to take place. Below the platform there were a few rows of chairs for distinguished visitors and here Lord Bond found Lady Pomfret.

"I am sorry we couldn't get here earlier," said Lady Pomfret, "but he was a little difficult, so Gillie and I came straight to the field. He will drive past on the way to the station in a few minutes, but he can't wait."

Lord Bond appeared to understand these words and nodded. Along one side of the big field where the meeting was to be held ran the back drive that led to the servants' wing of Staple Park and continued across the park in the direction of the station. It was not much used now except by tradesmen or the coals, and the sight of Pilward and Son's Entire in majestic progress, drawn by two grey monster horses, raised a loud cheer from the spectators, led by the Mertons' agent, Mr. Wickham, who had come over to inspect pigs and was talking to one of the electricians.

> "And damn his eyes, whoever tries
>   To rob a poor man of his beer,"

said Mr. Wickham, who happened to be near a microphone at the moment so that these beautiful words resounded from every side of the field and caused a good deal of laughter and cheering. By this time the notabilities, including Mr. Gresham, the member for East Barsetshire, were on the platform, and Lord Pomfret, who was chairman, rose to introduce the speakers. At the same moment a car came along the back drive going towards the station. Lord Pomfret paused. What Mrs. Tebben afterwards reverently described as a Something made the audience turn their eyes towards the car in which unmistakably was sitting ONE, recognizable even by the meanest reader of the daily press, foursquare as a White Porkminster, commanding as a Cropbacked Cruncher, but unlike these intelligent quadrupeds smoking a large cigar. A shout that reminded all the clergymen present of a Cup Final rent the summer air. The foursquare figure lifted its hat, waved its cigar in recognition towards its friends, and the car disappeared round the bend. For a second the crowd was silent.

> "Why we are downhearted I'll tell you exactly,
>   We chucked good old Winnie and now we've got Attlee,"

said Mr. Wickham, who may or may not have remembered that

he was next to a microphone, adding as he turned from the instrument: "Good Lord, I'm a poet. Never knew I had it in me," but his remark to himself was drowned by the hurricane of laughter and cheers evoked by his extempore distich and it was quite five minutes before Lord Pomfret could begin to speak. The meeting then behaved like any meeting where nearly all the hearers are of the same opinion. The speakers lamented the present state of England but no one had any particularly constructive ideas to offer beyond the magic words General Election.

"Well, Adams," said Mr. Belton to the Labour M.P. for Barchester, "I didn't think I'd see you here. What do you think of it all?"

"I'll tell you," said Mr. Adams, "as near as I can. My father was a working man and I've been a working man all my life. If you took me out of the shafts I'd fall down dead. I like work. Work made me and I made my Works. Most of my men are good decent fellows, but they don't *want* to work, and though I'm a Labour man I say raising wages and shortening hours isn't everything. There's hardly a tradesman now that's proud of doing his job well. You'll not credit it, Belton, but when I was a boy there were little master craftsmen all about Barchester and Hogglestock, and today for example there's one old locksmith in Barley Street and he hasn't got a single prentice. The boys are all right but no one encourages them to learn. Ten years from now if your lock is broken you'll have to take it off and buy a new one, and it will be the same with everything. Don't mend anything: throw it away and buy a new one, it's good for trade. That's what turns my stomach. When we went into this war Mr. Churchill offered us blood, tears, and sweat. We trusted him and he kept his word. If there was a party that offered us hard work, no spoon-feeding, and to keep England's name high, I'd join that party. But there isn't. I got into Parliament on the Labour ticket. If I resigned today and stood again as a Conservative I'd get in all right," said Mr. Adams with a kind of grim humour, "because

Hogglestock knows and Barchester knows that Sam Adams's word is as good as his bond. But the Conservatives haven't anything to say, any more than our people have, and what both of them say at present doesn't make sense."

Mr. Belton was silent, for there was really nothing to say. He thought of Disraeli and Young England in a confused way, but saw no Young England before him.

"I dare say you are right, Adams," he said. "I stick to my side and you stick to yours, but we both want something better. How is Heather?"

"She's a good girl," said Mr. Adams, "and a worker. And I'll tell you another worker, that's Miss Marling. She and my Heth have seen quite a bit of each other and Miss Marling is in on a big scheme with me. I'd like to tell you about it some time. Is Mrs. Belton here? I'd like to see her."

Mr. Belton said his wife and the boys were somewhere about, and then the real business of the day began. The mere politicians had tea or went away, but the pig-fanciers now congregated round the piggeries, where perhaps part of the true England lives. Round these stately animals was the best blood of Barsetshire, not Omniums and Hartletops, who are of mushroom growth, but Pomfrets, Thornes, Greshams, Hallidays, Leslies, the yeoman farmers, to whom Mr. Wickham belonged, and the Puckens, Polletts, Margetts, Powletts, Gobles, Hubbacks, Scatcherds, who had been in Barsetshire long before their betters and remained purely native under a veneer of films and wireless.

During the earlier part of the day a number of what the *Barchester Chronicle* called the porcine competitors had been eliminated and the judges were making a final inspection of the entries from Holdings, Rising Castle, Marling Hall, Pomfret Towers, and Staple Park. Mr. Belton was in a very good humour as his young pigs had a first-class and he had beaten Mr. Dean.

"The county class tell in the long run," he said to his wife and the Philip Winters, who were standing near. "Dean's a very good fellow, very public-spirited, and I enjoy a talk with him at the club," said Mr. Belton, who would have enjoyed a talk with anyone whose pigs he had beaten, "but there's just that something wanting in his pigs that you only get if you live by your land."

"I'm sorry to hear that," said Philip Winter. "I was thinking it might be a good thing to have a pig club at the Priory and make the boys pig-minded. But I'm only an outsider, so perhaps it wouldn't work."

His wife told him not to be silly and Mr. Belton didn't mean that, upon which Mr. Belton confounded himself in apologies and said they always thought of Philip as one of themselves, but somehow he had never quite got used to the Deans.

"You will have to, my dear," said his wife. "That nice Susan Dean who used to send books to Freddy's ship is a delightful girl and Sally tells me she is an excellent worker. And her sister Jessica is quite famous," upon which Mr. Belton said that was just what he meant and neither of *his* sisters had ever gone on the stage.

"I should think not, father," said Charles Belton. "I don't see Aunt Elsa or Aunt Mary on the stage unless they did the Widow Twankey. That's a splendid idea of yours, sir, about the pig club," he continued, speaking to his headmaster. "We could have a couple of father's prize piglings to begin with."

"And a couple of Mr. Dean's," said Philip. Then catching sight of some of his own boys, he called out: "Hi! Dean! do you think your father would let us have one or two of his little pigs for the school? We might have a pig club."

"Oh, *sir*," said young Dean and began to jiggle up and down in a kind of static war dance, ably seconded by Addison and Pickering, whose bandage so far had not come off. "Do you mean us to take care of them? I'm awfully good at feeding pigs, sir. Grandfather's pigs have perfectly scrumptious swill and I go round with the bailiff in the hols. And can we have rings in their noses, sir?"

"Sir," said Pickering, who was obviously bursting to impart information, "my father has a pig and we're going to have it killed in the Christmas hols. He wanted to kill it before Christmas, but the butcher says no good comes if you kill a pig when the moon's past the full. He killed a pig once when the moon was nearly over and two of his hens ate their eggs that very same night. Sir, will we kill our pigs?"

"Shut up, Pick," said Addison. "*You* couldn't kill a pig. Sir, I've seen a human killer. Can we have one, sir?"

"Humane, he means, sir," said young Dean scornfully. "Grandfather!" he shrieked. "Mr. Winter's going to have a pig club at school and we're going to kill two of your pigs. Oh, *please,* grandfather, can we?" to which Mr. Dean, who was talking with his daughter Susan, said he would like to hear what Mr. Winter had to say before answering. Philip explained that his plan was only born that afternoon, but if Mr. Belton and Mr. Dean would let him buy a young pig or two he thought it would be a very good occupation for the boys and they would have a certain amount of swill from the school, and the housekeeper's husband, ex-Sergeant Hopkins, understood pigs.

"And you will be a benefactor, won't you, father?" said Charles Belton, who believed in asking for what he wanted. "There's Freddy, we'll see what he thinks," and in three strides he penetrated the crowd, cut Captain Belton out in a masterly way, and brought him back to the family. Captain Belton said how do you do to Mr. Dean, also to his daughter Susan, and strongly recommended his father to do as he was asked. "But mind you stick out for a good price, father," he said. "These private schools make money hand over fist."

"Don't teach your father to suck eggs," said Mr. Belton, who was enjoying this form of chaffering immensely. "Now this is my last word. I'll give the school two pigs if Dean will give two. I'm not selling."

"Done," said Mr. Dean, holding out his hand. "I believe that at this point somebody ought to give someone a silver sixpence, but I'm not certain of my facts."

"It's Winter, here," said Mr. Belton. "Caveat emptor."

"You'll have to shell out, sir," said Charles, and while the pig-talk went on, Mrs. Belton talked to Susan and liked her as much as ever, even going as far as to wish her own beloved Elsa had something of Susan Dean's quiet friendly serenity. Susan talked very nicely to Mrs. Belton and wished she were a thousand miles away, or that Captain Belton would wave his sword, crying: Now my lads, let's board, and that what Heather had told her was only a bad dream. But life went on as usual, and though she once or twice looked at Captain Belton just when he looked at her, she quickly pretended that it was a mistake and wished she could go away and cry. As for Captain Belton, he knew that one did not die from a broken heart or he would have died long ago, but he was puzzled and almost angry and would have been glad for an excuse to kill someone just to relieve his feelings. Luckily none of the party noticed anything unusual, and then Emmy Graham came up with her mother and Clarissa. Mrs. Belton inquired after Lady Emily.

"Oh, mamma is really very well," said Lady Graham. "She was a little tired after her birthday, but Dr. Ford was *most* helpful when he came to see her. He said that when people get older they seem to lose some of their recuperative powers," and having repeated this remarkable statement she looked round mildly for applause. There was a second of silence and then Mr. Belton gallantly plunged into the fray.

"My old mother lived to be ninety-three," he said, eying everyone with a challenging look as if defying them to believe it. "Wonderfully energetic woman she was. She practically killed three companions."

"I wonder what's the longest a cow ever lived," said Emmy. "One doesn't think of cows as grandmothers, but I don't see why not. I say, you're Susan Dean, aren't you?"

Susan, who knew Emmy by sight but had never met her, said she was.

"Well, you know your brother Robin," said Emmy, "I mean Robin Dean is your brother, isn't he?"

Susan said he was and he was learning to farm at an agricultural college.

"That's the one," said Emmy. "The people there wrote to me to know if I'd take someone called Robin Dean for six months. He wants to do cows. It's really awfully easy," said Emmy, who had from her early years been so cow-minded that she had practically nothing to learn, "and he'll get plenty of practice at Rushwater. We've bought a lot more cows, and Sylvia and Martin and I are going in for dairy farming in quite a big way. I thought you must be his sister, because he said he had a sister called Susan when he came to see me, and as you were Susan I thought you must be the one."

Susan, relieved on the whole by this breath of fresh air from the cowsheds, said Robin hadn't told them he was going to Rushwater and she was so glad.

"He didn't know till yesterday," said Emmy. "Martin has written to him. There's only one drawback. We haven't had a case of contagious abortion yet. If he wants that he'd better go into West Barsetshire," said Emmy with a fine if narrow local pride. "They've had it at Gatherum and at Hartletop Priory."

Susan said she was sure Robin would be much happier at Rushwater.

"Well, when he comes you must come over for a night and see him," said Emmy. "Sylvia and Martin would love it. You're Red Cross, aren't you? Martin got one of his legs hurt in Italy, so you'll have something to talk about," said Emmy, who evidently thought that without some form of fracture or disease conversation would be impossible, and Susan felt quite apologetic when she had to explain that she was only Depot Librarian.

"Well, Martin likes reading," said Emmy, ready to make the best of everything. "I say, you don't want any books for your library, do you? Martin wants to get rid of a lot of old books. Ghastly books of sermons and things with the binding all cracked because no one had the sense to keep them fed. Lanolin's the thing for calf," by which time Susan was so addled, partly by her own private emotions, partly by Emmy's mixture of cows and books, that she wasn't quite sure whether Emmy was recommending lanolin for books or the young of cows. "I'd bring them in the Ford van if you don't mind them smelling a bit of manure or creosote," Emmy continued. "Things always seem to smell of something in the van."

Susan thanked Emmy warmly for her invitation and said that she would like to look at the books when she came and then she could tell her which would be suitable, and as they talked she saw Captain Belton walking away with Clarissa towards the pig-judges, so she said to Emmy how very interesting a librarian's work was and how she hoped Emmy would come and see them at work some time, which Emmy promised to do, for though that young woman was no reader she had a respect for people that were; like her father and Martin and quite a lot of people she knew. Then they all followed Clarissa and Captain Belton.

The pig-judges were not known to the county in general, though highly thought of in the pig world, so we shall not say anything about them except that they were old and wise and knew that the chief end of man was to breed the best pigs, to scratch their backs with a stick on Sundays, and in due time to eat the varied and delicate products of pig. The transit of the Great Man, foursquare as a White Porkminster, commanding as a Cropbacked Cruncher, had vastly heartened them and each one of them had said during the afternoon, as an entirely original thought, that if only He were running things pigs would go ahead like anything and a working man would be allowed to have his own pig and kill it and eat it too, and it stood to reason that people who didn't understand pigs weren't fit to be in Parliament. Now, Mr. Gresham, that was a man that knew a pig when he saw one, and if there was more like him and Mr. Gresham and fewer of those—but here we will stop, for pig language is full of fine words quite unsuitable for the printed page.

Mr. Gresham, who was permanent honorary chairman, now made a short speech extolling the virtues of pigs and their breeders and called upon the Government to reconsider their attitude to pig-keeping; but this was merely a matter of form, for everyone present knew that the Government believed the things you bought nowadays were sausages, and pitied their ignorance and despised them. He then put on his other pair of spectacles and said he was going to read the awards, at which a kind of anticipatory shudder ran through the assembly.

The first prize and Challenge Cup, he said, had been awarded without one dissentient voice to and then he turned over two pages at once and cursed the Pig-Breeders' secretary in round terms, partly because he was annoyed with himself for his own clumsiness, partly because he affected an eighteenth-century manner of speech and liked to keep in practice.

"Allow me, Mr. Gresham," said the secretary, who secretly liked being sworn at because it showed that he and Mr. Gresham were on good terms, for Mr. Gresham would have scorned to swear at an outsider who would not appreciate his language. "Page two, I think."

"All right, all right," said Mr. Gresham. "Thanks. The first prize and Challenge Cup, Mr. Marling's Marling Magnum. Second prize—"

But the name of the runner-up (who was Holdings Goliath) was completely drowned by the applause, for Mr. Marling, though not a very social man, especially of late years when farming had become increasingly difficult and expensive, was known to be just and a hard worker and was much respected in that part of the world. It was common knowledge that he was hard put to it for money but would not raise the rents of his cottages and still gave milk and vegetables to his people on the estate, and the clapping and cheering that followed Mr. Gresham's announcement were in the nature of a demonstration to show that whatever the Government might do in raising the wages that he paid and the taxes that he paid and encouraging his men to work less and less and probably making him die so poor that the Marlings would have to leave Marling Hall, the county was solidly behind him.

It speaks worlds for Mr. Marling's self-control that he did not have an apoplectic fit on the spot, which would have been extremely inconvenient on a Saturday. Politeness to the other exhibitors and the other exhibitors' wish to hear whether their pigs were placed prevented an immediate general rejoicing, but when the lists had been read and Sir Edmund Pridham had made an excellent and very short speech of congratulation to the Barsetshire Pig-Breeders' Association, Mr. Marling's friends of all ranks and ages surrounded him and his wife, who could have cried with joy to see her husband so happy. Lucy, whose spirits had as we know been much improved by her new friendship with Mr. Adams and his daughter, was able to rejoice wholeheartedly in her father's success and hoped that its mellowing influence would make him more likely to listen to Mr. Adams's plans. Oliver too was more moved than he would have cared to say, for the decline of Marling had saddened his heart and wounded his pride. Now not only was there a chance of things looking up if only his father would listen with patience to Mr. Adams's proposals, but there was public recognition for the man who had bred the best White Porkminster in the county, turning the scale at over fifty score, a very Churchill of a beast.

"My lamb," said a beautiful low voice at his side," "how too too perfect your father is! I adore him. May I be introduced?"

"I would do more than that for you," said Oliver, full of the incredible joy that her presence gave him and trying not to remember that she had said Aubrey Clover was the only man she would think of marrying. "Stick close to me, there's such a crowd." Jessica slipped her arm through his, and as he forced a passage through the crowd for her he wondered if she would feel how tumultuously his heart was beating, when he realized that Jessica was on the wrong side for heartbeats, which made him laugh aloud at himself.

"What is it?" said Jessica. "I like the way you laugh sur la qualité de la voix. That's what Monsieur Houby used to say when he coached me for French parts."

"Do you know," said Oliver, while his other self thought how interesting it was that he could be so happy and so normal with a woman who had broken his heart and knew it, "do you know that I loved you for your laugh the night I first dined at Winter Overcotes? You were talking with Charles Belton and both being silly, and I thought it was the most enchanting sound I had ever heard. I do still. Your voice when you wish the snow-drops back, though it stay in my soul for ever," he added half to himself. "One more push and we'll be through."

"What was that?" said Jessica. "It wasn't you speaking. I like it."

"Clever child," said Oliver. "It was an old man with a beard called Mr. Browning, who knew a thing or two about love."

"Oh, I almost love you for it," said Jessica, "but not quite."

She sighed in pity for Oliver and let go of his arm as they emerged safe though battered before Mr. Marling.

"Papa dear," said Oliver, "this is Jessica Dean."

The quiet little youngest daughter of the Deans almost dropped a curtsy as she begged to be allowed to congratulate Mr. Marling on his success and said she did not think any pig could be so big as Marling Magnum.

"My father is going in for pigs," she said, "but he is only a beginner."

"Goin' in for pigs, eh?" said Mr. Marling, who was having a violent attack of his Old English Squire manner owing to his success. "Who's your father, young lady?"

"Dean, papa," said Oliver, "Mr. Dean of Winter Overcotes."

"Dean," said Mr. Marling. "Don't know the feller, but I'm always glad to hear of anyone goin' in for pigs."

"You *do* know him, papa dear," said Oliver, slightly ashamed of his father but heartened by Mrs. Carvel's famous wink which Jessica bestowed on him to show her appreciation of his father's reading of his part. "You meet him at the club. And you know Jessica's name. She acts at the Cockspur."

"Oh, is *that* the young lady?" said Mr. Marling, looking with great interest towards her exquisite legs. "Very nice of you to come and speak to me, my dear. You're a friend of Oliver's, aren't you? He keeps all the pretty girls for himself," said Mr. Marling, thus increasing Jessica's admiration for him.

"Yes, Oliver is a very great friend of mine," said Jessica, making what Oliver afterwards called sheep's eyes at both the gentlemen. "Of course he wants to marry me. They all do. But I'm far too busy with my work. And may I tell you a secret? I really like much older men, especially men who win prizes for pigs."

She then cast her lovely eyes down and gave every appearance of blushing.

"Devil!" said Oliver.

"Quite right, my dear," said Mr. Marling, cutting his son out completely in his triumphal day. "Let's have a kiss. Amabel, my dear, this is Dean's daughter, the one who acts."

Jessica shook hands with Mrs. Marling with nicely calculated respect and a wish to please and then to Mr. Marling's intense delight flung her arms round his neck and kissed him.

"That's enough," said Oliver. "Baggage. Come along."

"I'm so sorry," said the Fair Penitent, again taking Oliver's arm, though this time on the side nearest his heart. "I am a rogue and a vagabond. I can't help it."

"You can," said Oliver. "You do it on purpose."

"Bless your heart, you are the nicest man I know," said Jessica, at once licking the hand that beat her. "No, Oliver. I don't love you and even if I did I wouldn't marry you. Let us go and find

Aubrey. We ought to be getting home. There are people to dinner and mother *will* go to sleep."

So Oliver accompanied her to the house to tear Aubrey Clover away from Denis Stonor, and though his heart ached for Jessica he accepted his half-loaf like a gentleman and the real friend she wished to have.

Mr. Adams, who with his daughter Heather had been the round of the pigs under Lucy Marling's guidance and had shown a really intelligent understanding of the difference between Porkminster and Crunchers and properly despised Mr. Middleton's Norfolk Nobblers (which we are glad to say were not placed), now approached Mr. Marling to offer his congratulations. The crowd had mostly dispersed and only the Beltons and some Leslies and Grahams lingered.

"Father," said Lucy.

"All right, all right, no need to shout. I'm not gettin' deaf yet," said Mr. Marling

"Yes you are," said Lucy in a voice just inaudible to her respected father, and then added in her usual voice: "Mr. Adams wants to congratulate you."

"I'm not a pig-fancier myself," said Mr. Adams, "and the only pigs I've ever had to deal with are the pigs we run out of the furnace, but I'd like to say your Porkminster deserved all he got and more. I've had a look at the other exhibits. They're a fine lot, a very fine lot. But Marling Magnum has just that extra bit of bacon where it's wanted that makes you think. I'd be proud to turn out a machine as good as that pig of yours."

"That's very good of you, Adams," said Mr. Marling. "I'm lucky, you know Pucken here," and he jerked his hand towards the old pigman, who was grinning broadly and twisting his Sunday hat into a pancake, "knows the job. Father, and son, they've handled pigs since the Saxon days, and before that. And I've got some good land too."

"So I hear," said Mr. Adams, "though I've everything to learn about land. My mother always wanted a little garden to grow vegetables and all she had was an asphalt back yard, poor soul. But she grew chives and herbs in a window-box in among the flowers. I've often thought I'd like to grow some vegetables."

"Well, you'd better ask my daughter Lucy," said Mr. Marling. "She's the vegetable expert. She was talking the other day about trying to grow vegetables on a poor piece of land over Barchester way. It's no good, I told her. Land wants drainin' and I can't afford to drain it, though it drains me," he added, trying to make a joke of it and not bringing it off very well.

"Funny things, drains," said Mr. Adams, as one indulging in abstract speculation. "I've had to do quite a bit in my time on my work sites. I'll tell you what, Marling," said Mr. Adams, using perhaps unconsciously Lucy's favourite expression, "lunch with me at the club next week. I'd like to hear your views on drains and put one or two difficulties of my own up to you. Make it Wednesday if that suits you."

It is possible that on any other occasion Mr. Marling would have become restive or even in his own phrase given the wealthy ironmaster M.P. a setting down, though Sam Adams—we must be pardoned for using that gentleman's own name for himself— had become successful in more ways than one and there were few houses where he could not have been a guest had he wished it, though he was not, in his own words, one to put himself forward. But on this glorious day of victory Mr. Marling could afford to scatter largesse and he said Wednesday would suit him very well.

"Right," said Mr. Adams. "I know the sekertary pretty well and he has a bottle of real Montrachet put away for me. Say one o'clock. I must go and find my daughter now. She's always running away with some young man or other. I think I see her with Captain Belton."

"Montrachet?" said Mr. Marling. "I didn't know Pritchard had any left. You young fellers get everything now. I say, Adams, we'll drink it between us, eh?"

"I get you," said Mr. Adams. "Knee to knee as the saying is. And no third parties," and he went off in search of his daughter, well content with his day's work and pleased to think of Lucy's approval.

Heather Adams, after talking to Lady Fielding and getting news of the lately married Anne Dale, had as she often did gravitated to the Beltons. Mrs. Belton was talking to Lady Graham and did not notice Heather, so she turned to Captain Belton, saying: "Hullo, Freddy."

Captain Belton seemed pleased to see her. Clarissa, who was beside him looking unaccountably unhappy and unlike her usual elegant poised self, looked defiantly at Heather and turned her back.

"It's nothing," said Captain Belton in answer to Heather's look of inquiry. "Only Clarissa in a tantrum. I'm sorry for girls. They are half grown-up and half not grown-up and the wrong bit is always coming up on top. Well, Heather, how is everything? I've not seen you since Anne Fielding's wedding. You were pitching into the champagne like anything."

"I wasn't," said Heather indignantly. "Only two glasses, and the first one was by mistake."

"Well, I saw you with the second one," said Captain Belton. "You were in the window with Susan Dean."

It was better to get used to saying her name. One would be bound to meet her and one must behave normally. Even if she had for no reason turned from sun to darkest night one must pretend one did not know.

"I like her," said Heather. "We were talking about you."

Captain Belton lifted his eyebrows.

"I told her how you were my hero when I was a dreadful fat schoolgirl," said Heather with no trace of embarrassment, "and how I used to make up stories about how I'd marry you. Of course I didn't know Ted then," she added, anxious to show her maidenly preference for young Mr. Pilward.

"You've done much better with Pilward than you would with

me," said Captain Belton smiling. "I have to be at sea. Also I'm old enough to be your father."

"And I thought you wouldn't mind," said Heather, impelled by the deep instinct in us all to tell what is better untold, "if I told her about your friend that was killed. After all, it's a long time ago and I think it's rather wonderful to always go on loving a person even if they're dead."

Then Captain Belton at last understood. He could not knock Heather down, nor could he call her a damned gossiping fool.

"Oh, Diamond, Diamond," he said and Heather stared, for excellent though the teaching at the Hosiers' Girls' Foundation School had been, it had not included the life story of Sir Isaac Newton's dog.

"Freddy," said Clarissa suddenly and taking no notice of Heather, which was most unlike her usual good manners.

"Well," said Captain Belton, not very sympathetically.

"Oh, all right, if you don't want to listen you needn't," said Clarissa. "Everything's too, too, ghastly and you don't care a bit. Everyone's horrible and I hate them."

Even in her sudden rage she could not look anything but pretty as she literally stamped with rage and tears sprang to her eyes, followed by a loud sniff.

"You're all *beasts*," said Clarissa, and walked away as fast as she could with her head in the air, owing to which she stumbled over one of the ropes of the tea tent and nearly fell.

"Hullo," said Charles Belton, neatly fielding her. "You must look where you are going. Do you want some tea? I've made friends with the lady at the urn and she will do anything for me. I say, is anything really the matter? If it is, you'd better tell me."

"It's the pigs," said Clarissa. "I *did* so want father's Goliath to win and so did he and so did Goble. Goliath is *much* nicer than Mr. Marling's horrible pig. I was making a poem for father about Goliath and now it's no use and father can hardly ever get away from London and I'm *glad* he couldn't today because it would have been so beastly for him. Do you think the judges cheated?"

"Of course not," said Charles. "Somebody's pig has to be first. Better luck next time," on hearing which philosophic and comforting words Clarissa gave a muffled wail and began to cry like a child.

"Well, sit down if you've got to make that noise," said Charles, seeing a wooden form outside the tent. "That's better."

"It isn't," said Clarissa. "It's worse. And Freddy was talking to Heather Adams and didn't care a bit nor did she. All right. I won't go into her father's works. I'll go to college and then I'll come back to Holdings and help Goble with the pigs and get first-class everywhere," at which beautiful thought she cried afresh.

"Now don't," said Charles and put a comforting arm round her.

"Good old Charles," said Clarissa, leaning her head on his shoulder and gradually abating her fury.

"That's all right," said Charles, secretly flattered that Clarissa found him a present help. "Look here. The headmaster's going to start a pig club at the Priory—that is, if this blasted Government lets him. I'm all for it. We might do some pig study together. If you go to college you'll get longer holidays than we do, so you can come over and give a hand. I'm sure Hopkins won't mind. He's Selina's husband at the school. Is it a bargain?"

During that speech, which for Charles was a very long one, Clarissa had stopped crying, and though her eyes and nose were still rather pink she looked much happier.

"Thank you very much indeed," said the precocious second Graham girl, just like a child who wants to forget that it has been naughty, "I'd love to come to the Priory and see you," and then Mrs. Belton and Lady Graham, who were rounding up their families, came round the end of the tent and were both struck at the same moment by the same thought. Each mother felt, nay knew, that her child was far too good for the other's child, but such is the contrariness of women that simultaneously with this feeling came a conviction that it would be a very good thing. And what that thing was is the business of the two ladies concerned, who made no comment aloud but understood each other quite well and had no intention of communicating their thoughts to their husbands. Lady Graham then resumed possession of her daughter and said good-bye. Mrs. Belton and Charles collected Mr. Belton, but could not see Freddy anywhere. Charles with the easy optimism of a brother said that Freddy was all right and had probably gone back with somebody else and the navy always came out on top. So his parents agreed not to worry and went back to Harefield, where Charles made an excellent supper and talked cheerfully about the Priory School and how it was on the whole a good thing for a schoolmaster to be married, especially if he wanted to start a school himself some day. Mr. Belton, comfortably tired by the day and pleased with the class his young pigs had taken, went gently to sleep, while Mrs. Belton listened to Charles's prattle and wondered if Freddy would ever forget the Admiral's daughter who was killed so long ago. The evening wore on. Mr. Belton suddenly jerked himself awake and went off to bed. Charles walked down to Plassey House to see the Perrys, and Mrs. Belton sat alone in the warm dusk thinking of her children. Charles and Clarissa might make a match of it. Clarissa was young, but so was Charles. They had their life before them and most of their generation were marrying early. But what about Freddy? The old wound, she believed, had healed. It was time he married and had an heir to what would be left of the Belton lands. She had thought that very nice Dean girl might be her future daughter-in-law, but evidently she was mistaken. The Deans had not lived long in the county, but everyone liked them. They were good citizens, and a daughter of Mr. Dean's would probably not come empty-handed. One cannot blame Mrs. Belton for this thought, for land had always demanded money and Mrs. Belton came of a long line of landowning Thornes. Susan Dean would have done very well indeed, she thought, but Freddy must choose for himself and she prayed that he might choose soon.

The great day was over. The Conservative Rally had taken place and left the Conservatives and everyone else exactly where they were. Lord Pomfret had driven back to the Towers with his wife, almost too tired to speak, or to be disappointed that his Pomfret Blockhouse had not been placed, but glad that their guest had shown himself to his supporters. There would be the usual pile of business letters for him to read and answer, the usual appeals for his presence or his money. Sally would help him as she always had, from the day when she unrolled the estate map in the office and showed him where Hamaker's Spinney was, but it pained him to see her life of ceaseless toil; nursery, house, estate, county, Red Cross, those were only the beginning.

"It would be nice if Merry were here," he said, thinking of her quiet helpful presence when he was only young Mr. Foster and not even the next heir to the earldom. His wife agreed, but she knew the only terms on which Miss Merriman would come to them, and could not wish for the day to be hastened.

Denis Stonor had gone back with Jessica and Aubrey Clover to talk theatre shop till far into the summer night, while Mrs. Middleton dined quietly with her husband and wondered whether she and Denis had really walked in the lane on that summer day before the war, speechless with the pain of parting. Now it was all as if it had never been and she was neither glad nor sorry. One had to take life as it came, and things which had seemed like life and death were now small and indistinguishable.

"Pigs," said Mr. Middleton pregnantly.

"Yes, Jack?" said Mrs. Middleton.

"No," said her husband. "The subject is too large. I cannot adequately deal with it. Not even I. Denis is getting very bald."

"He is," said Mrs. Middleton, and with this mortifying admission she knew that whenever they met again there would be no jot of former love to trouble them. Another step in growing old; also a step towards peace.

General Sir Robert Graham, K.C.B., was quite satisfied by Holdings Goliath's second prize and when he came down the following weekend accompanied Goble round the sites and gave him a handsome tip. Lord Stoke had the great pleasure of telling his pigman that if he hadn't been so damnably pigheaded, no, that was too good a name for him, mutton-headed he would say, about the winter feeding, Pompey would certainly have been second, and then became deliberately deafer than usual to anticipate the pigman's self-justification. As for Lord Bond, his disappointment about Staple the Second was almost forgotten in Denis Stonor's beautiful lighter with its inscription.

The great unwieldly monsters were being loaded into the trucks, Ford vans, lorries that were to take them home, while Lord Bond's Staple the Second, who lived less than a quarter of a mile away, jeered loudly at his friends and said it all came of not staggering their holidays same as what the Government told them, for he was a common-minded illiterate pig in spite of his size and believed everything he heard on the wireless.

Mr. Belton's young pigs and Mr. Dean's young pigs were also being put squealing into their farm trucks. Mr. Dean had wanted to get home early, so Susan had lent him her car and said she would come back with the pigs. Captain Belton, after looking for Susan in vain, had told himself that having waited in silence for so long he could well wait another day, which reasoning gave him no satisfaction at all. His family had gone home, so he went back to the pig-enclosure to see if he could get a lift, and then he saw Susan by her father's farm truck watching the piglets as they were unceremoniously bundled in. One of them got between the driver's legs and ran squealing into the wide world. The driver put the back of the truck up and ran after the truant, and Mr. Belton's man followed him. So Susan was standing by herself when Captain Belton came up.

"I have looked everywhere for you," said Captain Belton. "We can't go on like this."

"Like what?" said Susan, looking with great interest into the middle distance where the piglet was defying the driver to catch it.

"Not understanding each other," said Captain Belton. "Heather Adams, whom I would like to have keelhauled and hung at the yard-arm," said Captain Belton, "told me what she said to you at the Fieldings'. She had no business to tell you."

His voice was so harsh, he looked so stern, that Susan was afraid, but she stood her ground.

"I'm glad she did," said Susan, "because I wouldn't like to interfere. I couldn't bear not to know the truth and it isn't your fault if you go on loving someone who is dead. But I thought perhaps I had better not see you very much," she said with an unconscious pleading in her voice.

"I'll wring Heather's neck presently," said Captain Belton with sad want of chivalry. "Listen, my darling. The beginning of the story is true. There was a girl in the Wrens and we were engaged. And almost the next day there was a raid on the east coast and she was killed. I did love her, very much. One does, you know, when one asks a girl to marry one. But that is past and done with. When we talked in the cloister you asked me not to press for an answer. I didn't. And then Heather, apparently owing to two glasses of champagne, told you I could never love anyone again I suppose, silly little idiot."

"Oh, Freddy, you have been unhappy," said Susan.

"And you?" said Captain Belton.

Susan looked at him and looked away. From the far end of the field a final despairing squeal told them that the piglet had been captured at last.

"You asked me not to tell you what I meant," said Captain

Belton. "I shall now tell you whether you like it or not. Will you marry me and be a sailor's wife and help me to farm when I am retired on half-pay with a wooden leg?"

"I'll do anything in the world if you love me," said the very competent Depot Librarian of the Barsetshire Red Cross Hospital Libraries. "I love you so dreadfully."

"We've got him, Miss Susan," said Mr. Dean's man, who had the piglet tucked under his arm, "and a nice dance he gave us, didn't you, Spotty? Are you ready, miss?"

He bundled the piglet over the tailboard among his brothers and sisters and got into the driving-seat.

"Good Lord!" said Captain Belton. "My people have gone. Can you take me as far as the crossroads? I might get a lift there. My darling," he added in the same tone, so that the driver might not suspect anything; which was pure waste of time.

"Could you perhaps come back to Winter Overcotes?" said Susan. "There will be a lot of people at dinner and no one would notice us much. And we could tell mother and father after dinner; oh, and Jessica and Aubrey. Unless you'd rather not."

"The only thing I'd rather not do is to leave you for one moment," said Captain Belton.

"There's plenty of room, Miss Susan," said the driver, who had been taking the liveliest interest in the scene. "Let the gentleman come next me and you sit the other side of him, and then he can put his arm round you like," he added, but only to himself. So Captain Belton, followed by Susan, got onto the hard, shiny, unsympathetic seat of the farm truck and Captain Belton put his arm round Susan in case she fell off, and discussed the pig show with the driver while the Depot Librarian rubbed her face against his shoulder from time to time, partly to show him that she was there, partly to assure herself that it was not all a dream.

In the hospitable noisy atmosphere of Winter Overcotes anyone could have been newly engaged without attracting no-

tice, which was just as well, for Captain Belton did not quite
hear what anyone was saying and Susan found herself unable to
answer anyone sensibly. Only Jessica and Aubrey Clover, attuned to voices and shades of behaviour, noticed that anything
unusual was happening and they were not going to give away so
delightful a stage secret. The dinner came to an end and the
party, as on so many other nights of that summer, went into the
garden. The newly affianced couple would have liked to walk to
the Paradise Garden among the roses and the night-scented
stock, but they were diffident and wished to keep their newly
discovered happiness as their own secret for an hour.

From the house the shrill insistent voice of the telephone was
heard. Susan got to her feet by force of habit.

"If it's the Cockspur, say I'm sick, I'm dead," said Jessica.

"And if it's my secretary tell him I'm dead too," said Aubrey
Clover.

Mr. Woolcott Van Dryven said if it was New York he would
be right along.

Susan went into the house and a few minutes later came out.
Jessica, who had been sitting by Captain Belton, said she simply
must sit on the grass, and Susan could have her seat.

"Anything amusing?" said Jessica, settling herself gracefully
at Oliver Marling's feet.

"Only Colin Keith," said Susan.

"It makes me yawn to think of him," said Jessica, out of the
dusk. "I used to think he was fond of you, Susan."

"So did he," said Susan, emboldened by the growing darkness
under the trees. "That's what he rang up about."

"My lamb! Did that half-warmed fish propose?" said Jessica.

"I think so," said Susan cautiously. "It's difficult to know with
Colin because he talks so much about what he means that you
can't understand it. But I said I was engaged."

Some of the family laughed. Her mother opened her lovely
eyes and said what were they all laughing at and went to sleep
again.

"Have you followed your secret heart, my lamb?" said Jessica, putting out a hand and pulling Susan down towards her.

"Yes," said Susan in a low voice.

Jessica looked towards Captain Belton and raised her perfect eyebrows.

"Yes. Tomorrow I'll tell you," said Susan. "It is a secret tonight. It is heaven."

Oliver, so near Jessica, heard what she said. So did Aubrey Clover, but neither wished to betray her and Aubrey Clover was as usual improving the scene in his own mind and giving one or two of Susan's lines to Mrs. Parafine for his third act.

"But what to me, my love, but what to me?" said Oliver Marling in a low voice, leaning forward so that his face almost touched Jessica's hair.

"Love's Labour's Lost," said Aubrey Clover out of the dark. "Shakespeare always has the last word."

COLOPHON

This book is being reissued as part of Moyer
Bell's Angela Thirkell Series. Readers may join
the Thirkell Circle for free to receive notices
of new titles in the series as well as a newsletter,
bookmarks, posters, and more. Simply send in
the enclosed card or write to the address below.

The text of this book was set in Caslon, a typeface
designed by William Caslon I (1692-1766). This
face designed in 1725 has gone through many
incarnations. It was the mainstay of British
printers for over one hundred years and
remains very popular today. The version used
here is Adobe Caslon. The display faces are
Adobe Caslon Outline, Calligraphic 421,
and Adobe Caslon.

Composed by Alabama Book Composition,
Deatsville, Alabama.

Love Among the Ruins was printed by Wickersham
Printing Company, Inc., Lancaster, Pennsylvania,
on acid free paper.

Moyer Bell
Kymbolde Way
Wakefield, RI 02879